TAINTED BLOOD

D0030124

MARY ANN MITCHELL

LEISURE
BOOKS

$6.99 US
$8.99 CAN
$14.95 AUS

50699

9 780843 950915

0-8439-5091-9

RAVE REVIEWS FOR MARY ANN MITCHELL!

"Mary Ann Mitchell writes expressionistic hallucinations in which fascination, Eros and dread play out elaborate masques."

—Michael Marano, author of *Dawn Song*

"Mary Ann Mitchell is definitely somebody to watch."

—Ed Gorman, author of *The Dark Fantastic*

SIPS OF BLOOD

"Mitchell casts a spell with her prose to make it all come out unique. A compelling read."

—*Hellnotes*

"Mitchell is able to write without the stuffiness that puffs out the majority of modern vampire novels and given the chance she can turn on the gruesome as good as anyone."

—*Masters of Terror*

"Gut-churning good. I haven't read a vampire novel this 3-D in quite some time."

—*The Midwest Book Review*

"Rich in imagery and sympathetic characters, *Sips of Blood* is a fast-paced and intriguing tale that vampire fans are sure to enjoy."

—*Painted Rock Reviews*

DRAWN TO THE GRAVE

"Mitchell knows how to set a mood, and how to sustain this eerie novel."

—*Mystery Scene*

DEADLY BAIT

"Taste me, *Maîtresse la Présidente*." The girl raised herself in offering to Marie.

"Your blood is rotten, child. Poison. Why would I want to take any?"

"Because I need you to. I need to bleed and ease the pain inside me. My veins are scarred from carrying this boiling blood within me. Please."

"How did you get that blood?"

"Once long ago . . ." The girl broke out into hysterical laughter.

"She is crazy, Marie. Let's leave her," Anthony urged.

"You've destroyed other vampires with your blood, haven't you?" Marie asked the girl.

The girl slowed into a giggle and nodded her head.

"You are a vampire hunter," Marie said.

"Not by choice. I need to."

"Mmmm."

"Marie, what the hell are you thinking?" Anthony asked.

"That it would be so nice if she could tempt Louis. . . ."

TAINTED BLOOD

MARY ANN MITCHELL

LEISURE BOOKS **NEW YORK CITY**

A LEISURE BOOK®

July 2003

Published by

Dorchester Publishing Co., Inc.
276 Fifth Avenue
New York, NY 10001

ISBN 0-8439-5091-9

Visit us on the web at www.dorchesterpub.com.

TAINTED BLOOD

Chapter One

The Hugheses were dead and resided in a contemporary four-bedroom house with hardwood floors and granite-top kitchen counters. The yard overflowed with wisteria, which covered the wooden gazebo and made it unusable. They had no pets, unless one counted the large number of spiders that decorated the ceilings and walls throughout most of the house.

Mother and Father Hughes were attractive centenarians who looked not more than thirty-five. Father worked as a traveling salesman, selling Relaxa Vibrators. Mother hungered for the eighteenth century and whenever possible wore clothes from that time. She did not wear them as often as she would have liked, since Roger, their eldest child, was very modern, even though he had been born in 1900.

Eight-year-old Vanessa was four years younger than her brother and hated having to remain a child. Chuckie, the toddler, cooed and smiled in public but used the harshest of language within the family.

Given his family situation, Mr. Hughes was happy to travel frequently. He volunteered for assignments in the most obscure parts of the world. Drifters and prostitutes frequently slaked his thirst. His family, on the other hand, were careful where they fed. Mostly they drank animal blood. Pets never lasted more than a day in their house. Roger complained about this and tried to hide his dogs in his room, under his bed. But, of course, the dogs would whimper and bark, attracting first Chuckie, then the rest of the family.

The children were intelligent and street smart enough to live on their own, except there was no place for them in society. Social workers, policemen, medical personnel, and do-gooders believed the children needed protection. So this tightly knit family was stuck together.

"Christ sake, what the hell happened to the remote control?" Chuckie complained.

"Third bookshelf in the living room," answered his mother from the kitchen.

"And how the hell am I supposed to reach up there?"

"Use the footstool."

"I can tell you what to do with that footstool." Chuckie's plump little legs marched across the room to retrieve the footstool. He hadn't gotten far

2

when he heard the loud thunk the lid of his sister's coffin had made.

"Someone woke in a good mood," he yelled.

"I hate waking every day to dimples and curls." Vanessa stepped into the living room wearing her footed pajamas. "Look what I had to wear. Mom hasn't even come close to washing my Victoria's Secret lingerie."

"The stuff hangs on you anyway." Chuckie dragged the footstool to the bookcase.

"My dear, you know where the dirty laundry is, why don't you walk it down to the laundromat?"

Hearing her mother's words, Vanessa made a goofy face at Chuckie. He giggled and stepped up on the stool.

Vanessa squatted down on the floor and pushed the power button on the television. The screen lit up in a rainbow of colors that flowed into a rushing train. Since the sound had been turned down, she couldn't tell what was being advertised. All of a sudden, an engine whistle screamed out from the speakers. Chuckie didn't turn it down until his sister jumped up and tore out of the room. An angelic smile turned up his baby lips.

"Oh, God, no!" Mother rushed into the living room carrying a pink, perfumed envelope and stationery. "She's coming to visit."

"Aunt Marie?" Chuckie asked.

"Yes."

"Uncle Louis isn't coming with her, I hope."

"From the sound of this letter, I think she's on the run from Louis."

3

"Figures." Chuckie surfed the stations.

"Your father's not going to like this."

"He'll find some excuse to get out of the house."

"Not this time." Mrs. Hughes was tired of entertaining her husband's relatives every time they came through town. She was determined to have him by her side every day Marie resided in their house.

Roger lumbered into the room carrying his roller blades.

"Your Aunt Marie is coming for a visit."

"That's cool, Mom."

"What?"

"Isn't she the old bag with all the sex paraphernalia?"

"She's your father's cousin. Second or third."

"Doesn't matter. The lady knows how to get down and dirty."

"Mom already knows that. That's why Mom's so upset. The last time Marie was here Dad—"

"Chuckie, that's enough. She may be more reserved now."

"Yeah, like maybe she's doing church work now."

"The Church of the Spread-leg Evangelists." Chuckie completed his brother's remark.

Mrs. Hughes listened to Chuckie's babyish giggle, and her stomach churned. He'd never grow in size, but he certainly gained in knowledge every day. It just didn't seem right. Sometimes she wished she could diaper him and protect him from all the lurid things of the world.

TAINTED BLOOD

"Get your ass out of the way of the TV screen. You're not invisible, Roger."

Sometimes Mrs. Hughes wished she could move and not tell her family where she'd gone.

5

Chapter Two

Marie rubbed his back muscles slowly, sometimes allowing her nails to drag on his flesh and cause scratches. At first his body had stiffened when he felt the fire her nails made on his skin, but overall he bore the pain well. He was a first-time customer, and Marie wanted to err on the side of caution rather than have a wild man running out of her condo onto the fancy Paris boulevard on which she lived. However, he seemed to be growing too comfortable with her ministrations. She caught him almost dozing once or twice.

This damn worry over whether Louis would come for her stood in the way of her carrying on with her work as a dominatrix. How could she tighten leather thongs just enough to make her customer feel trapped without leaving telltale bruises?

Even the silk scarves she had used on yesterday's customer had left deep bites in his skin. Today she was sure he had dark bruises that might make him cancel his next appointment. Even with a whip in her hand she felt unsure of herself. Her mind was always preoccupied with thoughts of Louis.

Why had he allowed her to escape? She hadn't been crafty enough to fool him; he had allowed her to escape. Were his plans for her so devious that he could wait for the fruition of his vengeance?

Marie now kept her coffin locked. The locksmith had fastened a lock both on the outside and the inside. He had certainly thought it strange and had had the audacity to ask why one would need a lock on the inside. She had told him the truth, and he had sneered at her for telling what he believed to be lies. Truth always worked in her world. Either the innocent would think she was sarcastic, or the worldly would scoff at her eccentricity. Very few thought her mad, since she presented such a self-contained image.

When she snapped the lock shut from the inside, she feared only fire. But he could have set her on fire the last time he caught her sleeping, and he hadn't. Louis had admitted that watching her suffer over a period of time was his main goal. No quick demise for her, he had promised.

A snore interrupted her thoughts.

She pressed down and dragged her sharp fingernails across her customer's back. Blood flowed profusely and he woke.

7

"What the hell are you doing, mademoiselle?" he asked.

"I am a dominatrix, not a wet nurse, monsieur. I expect your attention at all times."

"What the . . . ? I'm bleeding," he cried, feeling the wet drops dribble down his sides.

"Nothing major. I will have it lapped up in no time."

Marie stooped and touched her tongue to his freckled flesh, catching the rivulets of fresh blood. The customer made to rise, but when he realized what she was doing, he sank back down on the leather-covered table.

After a few minutes he asked, "Are you going to put some antiseptic on the wounds when you are done?"

She gave him a passionate nibble and scolded him for not trusting in her completely.

"The man who sent me here was right. He said you were super-kinky."

"Please, monsieur, no names. I never speak of customers with anyone."

"Oh, he isn't a customer. He said he heard about you. Only know his first name anyway. It was Louis. There are tons of Louises out there."

Marie's stomach revolted, and she almost splattered the customer's back, except that she stood tall, allowing her bile to return to her stomach.

Quickly she began to sponge his back, and to add a touch of pain she poured on the iodine.

"Our time is up, monsieur."

"What? I thought I paid for an hour. It's been barely thirty minutes."

She slapped the burning skin on his back. "Don't ever contradict me. In this apartment I rule, and you must do whatever I say."

"But this is a cheat. I didn't even get off. You didn't get naked. I could have gone to my health club for a massage."

"This kind, monsieur?"

"Jon just keeps his nails trimmer than you do."

He sat up and stared at Marie. She noted that his privates were deflated, unlike they had been when they had begun.

"I expect at least half my money back."

He stood before her, his chest bald, his small muscles flexed with rage, and his paunch sagging grotesquely.

"Monsieur, go back and complain to your friend Louis. He may even do a better job than I."

"I'll see to it that you lose customers."

"What will you do? Picket my apartment? And will you be doing that in disguise? Are you sure no one will recognize those slouching shoulders and that little tic that vibrates the tip of your nose?"

He stood as tall as he could. "My clothes, mademoiselle."

Marie went to the front closet and pulled his clothes from the hangers. Her hand searched the pockets for additional money she could take. If she was going to America to visit the Hugheses, she

would need every cent she could put her hands on.
Her fingers fumbled among small change and credit
cards were too much trouble.

Damn the cheap bastard!

Chapter Three

"Marie? Are you sure about that?" Mr. Hughes tilted his head in a fashion his wife hated.

"I've shown you the letter, Stephen."

"But it doesn't quite look like her hand to me."

Mrs. Hughes reached into the garbage pail and pulled out the pink stationery her husband had just discarded.

"There's the odious flourish Marie always makes on her *m*'s." She held it to the bridge of Stephen's nose.

"Darling, I can't see that up close." He took the paper from her fingers. "Chuckie," he called.

The toddler crawled over to where his father sat on the Barcalounger.

"Does this look like Auntie Marie's handwriting to you?"

"Hey, Dad, do I look like a handwriting specialist to you?"

"No, with that pained expression, you look like a child who is about to crap his pants."

"Mom, he's doing it again. He's picking on me because of my size."

"That letter is from Marie." Mrs. Hughes put her hands on her hips. "She sent no return address, so we can't even tell her we'll be away on holiday."

"Even better. We'll lock up the place for a couple of months and act like we never received the letter."

"She will track us down, you know that. When she finds us she'll be as rude as she can to punish us."

Chuckie laughed. "Rude like in setting Dad on fire with a blowtorch when she ran into us in Houston ten years ago?"

His father shivered with the memory.

"It took several weeks for you to heal," Mrs. Hughes reminded her husband.

"Can't you and the children entertain her for a while? I mean, she probably feels bad about what happened the last time and won't know what to say to me."

Chuckie snorted and Stephen swatted Chuckie's retreating behind with his newspaper.

"No," Mother answered. "She is your cousin."

"Cousin? What the hell are you talking about?"

"Well, however the hell you two are related, you're family."

"We do not share mutual genes, Gillian. Blood, yes. Genes, no!"

"She's often said you two are related."

"Marie turned me into a vampire. Her hellish hunger is what got us into this mess."

"One second: I always thought you had gone off to visit a relative. Isn't that why you were staying with her in Nice?"

Stephen sighed. He should have left well enough alone and let his wife continue to believe that there were close family ties binding he and Marie. Marie had been smart to use that lie.

"Stephen, why did you stay with Marie in Nice?"

"She was a customer." *Or I was a customer,* he thought. After all these years, he couldn't remember if she had been doing the purchasing, or he had.

"She's made her living as a dominatrix," said Gillian.

"Yes, and I've sheltered my family by selling pleasure enhancers. Used to be whips and paddles, but after I spoke to Freud, I realized vibrators were the way to go."

"It took you a month in Nice to sell her pleasure enhancers?"

"We got along well and she suggested . . ."

Gillian had spent many years with her philandering husband. Most times she turned her head, refusing to acknowledge his frequent peccadilloes. As long as the children were kept in the dark, she didn't see any harm in his straying. However, to be confronted with the identity of the vampire who turned Stephen, thereby giving him an impossible hunger for his own family's blood, was beyond her capacity to forgive.

13

Keeping in mind that Chuckie still remained in the room, Gillian lifted the trash can filled with stale pipe tobacco, orange peels, a rotted peach, and ink-stained paper wetted down with Vanessa's garish nail polish and flipped it over Stephen's head. A minor punishment for all the family had endured, but still a statement.

Gillian walked stiffly out of the room, picking up the bits of clothing that her family had discarded at various times of the day.

"Why did she do that?" Chuckie asked.

Stephen answered, sending an echo from within the trash can.

"Huh?"

Slowly Stephen removed the can from his head, bits of ash and rotted fruit spilling onto his shoulders. An advertisement for a divorce lawyer remained glued to his face with ghastly mauve nail polish.

"Dad, you looked better with the can on your head."

Stephen looked at his son's serious face and knew Chuckie was laughing on the inside.

"Would you like to try it on for size?" he asked his son.

"Don't you dare," yelled Gillian from another room.

Chuckie wrinkled his face and stuck out his tongue.

The trash can crashed against the end of the television stand, falling onto the floor inches away from Chuckie's feet.

Wisely, the child retreated to watch his cartoons.

Chapter Four

Marie stopped at a newsstand to pick up *Pariscope* and *L'Officiel*. She had every intention of browsing the weeklies for an English-speaking movie. Going back to the United States meant brushing up on her use of the English language.

Thank you, Cecelia, for at least placing my skull in the coffin of an attractive female. What a dreadful experience it would be, she thought, finding her way back to this world as, say, an old man or woman. Oh, and she could have been forced to steal an ugly body; but no, her skull or her powers had managed to penetrate into a fetching body. Unfortunately, Louis now knew of her improved appearance and could easily recognize her.

How could her poor daughter have had the bad taste to marry Louis? Ah, but she herself had been

15

fooled by his sincere, educated manner. Marie had encouraged the idea of marriage between her daughter and the Marquis de Sade. Why not? Her daughter would gain a title, even if he had very little money. If only she had known he had no morals. But she wouldn't exist in this stolen body right now if she hadn't met him and demanded he make her a vampire like himself. Instead, she would long ago have crumbled into dust, weighed down by her beloved French soil.

Perhaps a movie was not the cure for her sour mood today. She walked along the Seine, watching the tour boats carry tourists through the city's lights. The miniature Statue of Liberty was always a favorite with the American tourists. *We should have kept the big statue and sent them the miniature,* she thought, although the statue sent to the States might have been too large for the Seine.

A man sat on a bench under a streetlight reading PARIS LA NUIT SEXY. He looked every bit the tourist, with his Yankee baseball cap, his polo shirt with a Ralph Lauren logo, and his Nike running shoes, and she guessed his jeans would say something like Calvin Klein on the back tag. She knew that most of what he read in the book would be about restaurants. But Marie could take his hand and lead him to the best places for sex, the Théâtre des 2 Boules and the Théâtre Saint-Denis. Prostitution had been made illegal in 1946, but it didn't stop the customers and purveyors from flocking to certain Paris locations.

Marie leaned against a tree trunk and watched

the man intently thumbing his way through the many pages. Heavens! Throw down that book, she thought, and get a move on. Sometimes he flipped back several pages to refresh his mind.

"The train stations of Montparnasse," she shouted. "The Place Pigalle. Or the Boulevard Clichy."

The middle-aged man looked up. He had the beginnings of a gray stubble on his chin and his eyes were wide, a measure of his guilt at being found out.

She pushed away from the tree and walked toward him. Her long silk skirt hugged her thighs and her laced-up boots peeked out demurely.

"That book is a waste of time. Gare du Nord, Gare de l'Est, or Les Halles are where you should be participating in the fun, monsieur. You need a woman's arms wrapped around your shoulders." Marie reached out her hands and clasped them behind his neck. Her legs she spread on either side of his. Immediately she could feel him pull away from her.

"I don't have much money, and I haven't had a chance to convert it as yet."

"Do you have a credit card?"

He flipped the book shut and felt his inside pocket.

"Money isn't what I want, monsieur. I should be offended, but what can you think of my brazen introduction? I'm Marie. *Et tu?*"

"And me . . . I'm . . ."

"Think of a good name. One that will reflect the passion and bulk you have to offer."

Marie's hips tilted slightly in his direction.

"I . . . have a room, but . . ."

"A room! We do not want to lock ourselves away, monsieur. *Mais non.* We shall seek companions for our ribald games."

"I hadn't really considered a group orgy." He looked down at his book as if he were sorry he had ever stopped reading.

"Don't consider, monsieur, act."

A short time later Marie and Casanova, the name she had dubbed him, since his imagination couldn't come up with anything at all, were walking in the Bois de Boulogne. At first they passed mothers wheeling baby carriages and fathers chasing their sons in jest across the fields. She never let go of Casanova's hand, even though his perspiration made his flesh sticky.

Quickly she reached out and plucked his book from under his arm and tossed it into a wastebasket. When he hesitated, she pulled him along. From the corner of her eye she watched him looking back forlornly at the filthy wastebasket.

"What, monsieur?"

"I'll have to buy another copy."

"*Non,* after tonight you will not need a guidebook." She winked at him, and he gave her a faint smile.

"And what is under your hat?" She removed the baseball cap and placed it atop her own dark curls.

A fringe of gray hair, flattened and damp with sweat, was not what she had expected, but he'd do.

The path had turned lonely. No small children and parents out for a stroll. The number of trees increased as they walked toward the center of the park.

"Is it safe?" he asked.

"You're with me. No one else can have you."

He smiled. "I'm sure you can stamp your feet and cry as well as any woman, but someone with a weapon . . ."

"Useless."

"Oh, miss, I would certainly attempt to protect us. But it is difficult fighting someone with a gun."

She stopped and touched his cheek with her hand.

"You misunderstand. You are useful, monsieur. A gun, a knife in mortal hands is totally useless against me."

"You're not mortal?"

"Haven't been for centuries." She kissed him hard on the mouth; her tongue darted in to challenge his.

One of his hands clutched one of her breasts, and his other hand forced her hips against his body. She pulled back her head and traced his lips with her tongue.

"I was thinking we could go back to my hotel . . ."

Marie pushed away from him.

"We are here in the midst of this beautiful park, with a moon that is almost full and the smell of nectar dripping . . . from the flowers and trees wishing to pollinate and reproduce."

"I have no desire to reproduce, honey." He took several steps away from her.

"And you never will."

"Maybe someday, when I feel ready." He appeared to be miffed by her pronouncement.

"Come, there are many people for us to meet." She took his hand and led him off the path onto the dewy grass and toward a grouping of trees.

Chapter Five

Louis's leather coat flapped in the breeze. He had his arms folded across his chest. It was not difficult to keep to the shadows and follow his prey. She looked delightful this evening, slightly jumpy, but she had been this way since running from his estate.

The couple walked deeper into the forest of trees and he followed. Her scent was strong, American, and so was her companion.

Marie stopped several times to caress the man. Furtive, the man would attempt to pull her down onto the grass, but she would teasingly pull away. How long would she torment him with her kisses and promises?

Lay her on the ground on which you stand, Louis silently suggested. *Or lean her against the closest trunk of a tree and take what you want. Before day*

*comes she will steal from you. At least die a happy
and satisfied man.*

He heard a yell and realized that Marie and her
companion had disturbed a nighttime rendevous
between two fairly husky gentlemen. Each had
matching tattoos on very private parts of his anat-
omy.

Marie laughed, but her companion made as if to
run. Swiftly, she intercepted him and threw him to
the ground.

"Pounce now, my flower. Tear his throat and lux-
uriate in the taste of blood." Sade's voice was soft
and carried only a short distance, too short for the
couple to hear.

Marie did not spring; instead she knelt next to
the man, baring her breasts for him, offering him
compensation for foiling his escape.

A near-naked girl, high on drugs, wandered
through the scene. The girl's beautiful charms were
not missed by Marie's companion. The man
watched her walk toward the path. Marie called to
the girl. Several times she called to her, but got no
response. Finally, in frustration, Marie rose and
pulled the girl back to join her companion.

"A feast, my dear. You are preparing a banquet
for yourself. Young blood mixed with old will certainly help you to sleep soundly when the sun
comes up."

Again Sade's voice was soft and barely carried in
the quiet night. Oddly, the girl seemed to hear him.
She turned in his direction, and he pulled deeper

into the shadows. She reached out a hand and pointed directly at Sade.

The man had gotten to his feet. Fear and maybe a little lust held him to one spot. He could have run. Marie would have chosen the girl over the aged blood of her companion.

Chapter Six

"Child, stay with us. There is nothing over there in the shadows. We have just come from that way. If there had been any life, we would have joined in. Isn't that right, Casanova?"

The young woman turned and faced Marie's companion.

"Are you really Casanova? Have you survived all these years?"

"And still quite the lover," Marie whispered in the girl's ear.

"Show me," the girl said simply. "Show me what it is like to burn in your arms."

Casanova looked from one woman to the other. Marie spread her arms wide in invitation. "Needn't choose just one, monsieur. I did promise you an orgy, small as this one is."

24

"Holy shit!"

"Pull down your pants and give it to them both," yelled a voice off to the right. "If you won't, I will. I always believe in satisfying the ladies."

A dark-haired man appeared, as if in a puff of smoke.

"Where the hell did you come from?" Casanova looked around, waiting to see what crowd was about to reveal itself.

"Marie I can vouch for. The young one seems eager to learn."

"We don't need you here, Anthony." Marie iced her voice.

"You want to feast alone?"

"I'm sure you've already been here a while and don't need to poach." Marie drew herself to full height.

"He's watching us and laughing," the girl warned.

"Who?" Marie asked.

"The Marquis de Sade." The girl's cold eyes met Marie's.

Marie spun around to face the shadows to which the girl had been pointing. Nothing moved there. She listened and heard nothing. He would call her. He would want to terrorize her with his presence. He wouldn't remain silent, she told herself. Louis would torture her with his voice, with his eyes, with a smile.

"I don't know any of you," Casanova said.

Anthony offered his assistance. "You are Casanova." A small chuckle escaped his lips. "I am Anthony. And the ladies are Marie and—could it be Ophelia?" He cocked his head in puzzlement.

"I am Casanova's lover," the girl said.

"Marie, don't leave me. Where are you going?" asked Casanova.

Marie felt the grass crumple under her feet. Her legs ached with weakness. She could see nothing hidden. Her eyes deceived her, she knew. Sade's awful stink was in the air. How could she have missed it?

"I know you are there, Louis."

Casanova appeared at her side. "Are we leaving?"

"No matter where I go, you'll be there. What do you wish to steal from me?"

Sade stepped out of the shadows and whispered, "Your prey."

He pounced on Casanova and bled the tired man dry.

Chapter Seven

"Who is he, Marie? Who frightens you so much that you stand and watch him steal your prey?"

Anthony and Marie stood over Casanova's dry husk. Sade's force had been so great that Casanova's neck was broken, and his own teeth had bitten into his bottom lip.

"We still have the girl," Anthony said.

"You have her."

"Are we experiencing a loss of appetite? That has never happened to you before, Marie. This vampire is your maker, isn't he?"

"He means to see me slowly starve. He would force me to swallow blood that I would normally reject."

"Why?"

"Because I would destroy him if I had the chance."

"Stay away from him, then."

Marie laughed. "I've run from Louis. Only not often enough."

"I sense that centuries have passed for you, Marie. This means he must be even older."

"I have been on earth longer than he. However, he was turned first."

"You knew him in your mortal life?"

"He is my son-in-law. The Marquis de Sade."

"But you look . . ."

"This is a stolen body. He destroyed my real body years ago. He burned the flesh and ground the bones but retained my skull. A girl stole my skull and placed it in a coffin with a staked vampire. And several young men freed me from limbo. I never found my skull. Do you think I have two skulls? One wrapped around the other, repressing the real owner of this body?"

"I wouldn't dare to speculate. There are too many unbelievable things that have proved to be real." Anthony touched Marie's arm. "Let's share Ophelia. I'm sure it will make you feel better."

Marie turned to the girl. The girl who had recognized Sade's presence long before Marie.

"Who is she, Anthony?"

"Some young chit taking a tumble on drugs, I'd say."

"No. She knew about Sade. How?"

She looked at Anthony and he shrugged his shoulders.

"Ophelia doesn't have the smell of a vampire," he said.

"There are those who are half-human and half-vampire, you know."

"Never met one."

"I have. But she doesn't have the same look. Her eyes are a pale gray. Have you seen them change color at all?"

"No; why?"

"Because the last half-breed I knew . . ." She placed a hand on Anthony's shoulder and pulled closer to him. "His eyes would change from a muddy earth color to jade green."

"Hard to keep that secret."

"He was fond of dark glasses."

Anthony nodded.

"Call her," Marie demanded.

"Ophelia." The girl did not respond. "Perhaps that is not her name. I don't feel like going through a dictionary of first names. Why don't we join her?"

"Why has she stayed?"

"Marie, I wish you would stop asking me all these questions I can't answer. On the other hand, Ophelia looks so wasted that she might not know any of the answers either."

"Child," called Marie. Slowly she walked toward the girl. "Child, I would like to speak to you."

The girl swayed back and forth.

"Is Casanova truly dead now? He looks so quiet, and Sade showed no mercy."

"Sade never shows mercy. But you know that, don't you?"

The girl nodded her head.

"Did he take you?" Marie asked.

"Where?"

Marie heard Anthony guffaw behind her.

"Are you a child of a mortal and an undead?"

"I am dead in spirit only," the girl replied.

"I'd attest to that just by looking at her," Anthony said. "She probably doesn't even know what you're talking about. Marie, let's have her and move on with our night. She awaits us like a lamb, innocent and naive."

"She is neither, Anthony. Not if she can sense Louis. Her blood could be rancid. I want to know what she is before I take her. Unless you would like to take the first sip, Anthony?"

"If I take the first sip, I'll take the last. I'll not share what you fear to attack. Go, and leave her for me."

"Are you that much of a fool? You don't know her strength."

"Earlier you pulled her back easily. There's no fight in that wilted body. She's right, her spirit is dead and the body is only waiting to die. And I, Marie, will grant her wish."

Anthony strode past Marie. When he reached the girl, he took her in his arms and kissed her lips. She did not respond, but that did not put off Anthony's lust. They lowered themselves to the ground slowly. He stroked her cheek in a hypnotic manner. She seemed totally under his control.

The few rags that covered her body were removed quickly. Her long legs wrapped around Anthony's waist.

"You are hot, mademoiselle. In way too much of a hurry. Slow down and let Marie rue the fact that she hesitated. And give me some time, mademoiselle, to bare my rapier."

The girl held him fast between her legs. She brought her head up and kissed him on the mouth.

Marie watched his ass rise and his heels try to catch in solid earth. The girl spread her fingers through Anthony's dark, curly hair that normally hung to his shoulders. She rested her head back down on the grass and sighed while bucking her hips.

"Mademoiselle, you do not quite understand the complete action of fucking. We are only playing as children. I must unzip myself if we are to achieve our goal."

Anthony tried to pull her legs from around his waist but could not.

"Marie, are you still here?"

"Yes, Anthony, I am."

"Perhaps we could call a truce and you could give me some assistance with this young one?"

"I warned you, Anthony."

"And I bow to your wisdom. Now release me from her hold."

Marie kneeled down on the ground next to Anthony.

"I felt her strength earlier when I pulled her back, but she gave in to my grip. I did not have to force her. I wonder just how strong she is."

31

"Marie! Stop dealing with this as a scientific experiment and get her the hell away from me."

"So many men think they want to be in control, Anthony. I find in my business that what they really want is a woman to rape them. Relax and see where she goes with this."

"Damn. I will kill her right here if necessary and stop with the foreplay if you don't help me."

"Maybe I can reach your zipper. Try lifting your hips a bit," Marie suggested.

Paying no attention to Marie, he brought down his head and ripped a tear in the girl's throat. For a second he seemed to be feeding and then changed to purging. The blood he had taken in during his night's escapade flowed out of his mouth, soaking the grass and the girl. His body went limp with the force of the regurgitation. All his power lay in the act of emptying himself of blood. Marie pulled away from the pair, fearing that she would be contaminated by whatever poison had caused Anthony's illness. The girl's body still humped against his jeans until finally she climaxed wildly, uttering a soft sigh. Her legs relaxed, and Marie immediately pulled Anthony off the girl. She laid Anthony on his back and watched as he choked on the clotted blood.

"Don't be a fool, Anthony. You must keep blood in your body or this could be your end."

Anthony coughed and gained control.

"Her blood is venom," he whispered. "She is a black widow ready to feed off her lover."

"Your tongue, Anthony; it looks seared."

"She has no blood, Marie. Lye flows through the girl's veins."

Marie turned to look at the girl, who was bathing in the afterglow of her orgasm.

"How do you know the Marquis de Sade, child? Tell me."

"I know all of you. I see you in dreams, and I hear your voices on the wind, Marie." The girl smiled at Marie and reached out a hand, as if she wanted to touch the older woman.

"What is she, Marie?"

"You told her my name earlier."

"You are Maîtresse la Présidente, grandmother to the Marquis de Sade's children," the girl said.

"I thought you said you had changed bodies."

"I look nothing like the grandmother I was, Anthony. I don't know how she understands all of this."

"Taste me, Maîtresse la Présidente." The girl raised herself in offering.

"Your blood is rotten, child. Why would I want to take any?"

"Because I need you to. I need to bleed and ease the pain inside me. My veins are scarred from carrying this boiling blood within me. Please."

"How did you get that blood?"

"Once, long ago . . ." The girl broke out into hysterical laughter.

"She is crazy, Marie. Let's leave her."

"What, not kill her?"

"I won't touch her," Anthony said.

"You've destroyed other vampires with your

blood, haven't you?" Marie addressed the girl.

The girl slowed into a giggle and nodded her head.

"You are a vampire hunter," Marie said.

"Not by choice. I need to bleed and climax at the same time."

"Then go home and cut your finger while playing with a dildo," Anthony said.

"I could feel how much you wanted me, Anthony. The passion drove me on, and I could not stop when you asked. If you unzip now . . ."

"The girl is nuts. She has no connection to your maker. She is a vampire groupie. Let's get out of here, Marie, and leave her to catch some other blood sucking idiot."

"I never thought you would admit that about yourself, Anthony." Marie looked at him with a stunned expression.

"It's not the first time my peter got me in trouble." Anthony sat up. "Hell, I feel weak. How the hell am I going to catch myself a new meal? I have to eat before sleeping or it will take me weeks to heal."

"Mmmm."

"Marie, what the hell are you thinking?"

"That it would be so nice if she could tempt Louis."

"Leave her to find him on her own and go wherever the hell you were headed. If you help her, then you will also find Sade, and he may not allow you to survive next time."

"You are right, of course. But tell me, child, can

you locate the Marquis de Sade on your own?"

The girl shook her head. "I know a vampire when it is near, but I'm not a bloodhound, madam. You can't put a leash around my neck and make me lead or follow you." The girl got to her feet.

"Wait, child. What is your name?"

"Ophelia. Rapunzel." She ran her fingers through her long red hair. "Snow White, or maybe her wicked stepmother." Her eyes glinted with humor, and she directed her last words at Anthony. She bent to pick up the few scraps of clothing that were still wearable. "I start the night with lovely dresses that are specially made for me. But I always go home in tattered, unrecognizable pieces of cloth." She shrugged and walked away.

Chapter Eight

Having had his fill of blood, Sade turned to sating his sexual hunger. The pretty child Marie had possession of would have been an ideal partner, but his sense of melodrama had forced him to give her up. Instead he would take advantage of the selection to be found at Pigalle. It might cost him a few Euros, but he had lots to fritter away after investing so well over the centuries.

"Do you have any spare money you can give me?" asked a girl of not more than eighteen.

Perhaps his lust would not cost very much this evening, he thought.

"How much do you need, mademoiselle?"

"I only want to buy some food."

"Beluga or pheasant?"

"Don't make fun of me, monsieur. I honestly am

36

hungry. I have been raiding the trash cans for the past few days."

"You need a bath."

"I need food."

"A good bath might enable you to get money for food."

"I am not selling myself, monsieur." Indignantly, she turned away from Sade.

"No? Then you are killing yourself."

She stopped.

"A charming woman like you could easily win the heart and pocketbook of a man, and for a few hours of . . . love, you could eat for a week."

She turned around and said, "There is no love in what you are talking about, monsieur. You only want to flex your power to abuse me."

"I have something far better to flex than power. This is not charity, mademoiselle. This is mutual gratification. We each have a hunger and can barter our way to fulfillment."

"You are old." She scrunched up her face.

"And experienced. And gentle, at times. And wealthy."

"Then why not just give me some money? I *am* begging for charity, monsieur."

"I will not permit you to demean yourself."

"No, you would make me a whore instead."

"Merely a working girl. We don't have to get specific about titles. Ah, is that your stomach rumbling? I will make you a generous offer: Come home with me and I will feed you, and depending on how grateful you feel, you may choose to repay me."

"A simple café crème and croissant is all I need, monsieur." The girl cautiously stepped across the threshold into a softly lit foyer. She felt the cold marble floor through the thin soles of her shoes and saw her rumpled hair and dirty face in the ornate gold mirror she faced. "I look dreadful," she said, surprise making her voice quiver.

"Mademoiselle, I did not lie. You definitely need a bath. Come."

Sade grabbed her arm and pulled her farther into the apartment.

"It is too dark, monsieur."

Sade sighed and turned on a Tiffany lamp. The multitudinous colors of the glass reflected onto a cracked and peeling wall. Stubby white candles were lined up next to the lamp on a dark, curvaceous console.

"Come, come. I refuse to feed you until you have bathed. I could never allow the filth you carry into my kitchen. Come. Stop the sightseeing. You will have time later to inventory my furniture."

"I don't want to intrude . . ."

"Yes, you do. You interrupted my plotting thoughts in the park. For that you will pay."

The girl became frightened and pulled away from him.

"With a bath, *mon ange*. All I ask is that you scrub the filth from your skin. I will even do your back . . ."

The girl turned her back to him and headed for the door. He grabbed her arm and forced her to face him.

"You are hungry. You will not get a better offer than this tonight. Not the way you look. How many people give you a wide berth? How many ignore your cries? *Non,* mademoiselle, you will not be a fool and spend another night hungry. Besides, here you are safe from rapists who would take advantage of your plight."

"You are not one of those?" she asked.

Sade smiled. "I know that you will not find such a gentleman as I in that horrid park. Not in the depths in which you choose to wallow. Please, you do not expect me to believe you are an innocent. How many times have men taken you and offered nothing in return? Too many for you to count, *oui?*"

Tears made her eyes glow in the dim light. Her bottom lip quivered, and she kept her hands gripped together in front of her.

"You will be clean and have new clothes when you leave here," he said. He leaned forward and whispered in her ear. "Best of all, you'll have a full stomach."

"And your fingerprints all over my flesh."

"Ah, mademoiselle, you are too much of a bore. Go!" He pointed toward the front door. "I tire of this game. You are not a delicate bud, mademoiselle, you are a wilting rose that can still add some beauty to the world. But the time is growing short and your petals are ready to fall." Sade reached out

MARY ANN MITCHELL

and plucked a scarf from her shoulders.

She grabbed at the rayon material, and Sade reeled her into his arms.

"Will you be gentle? So many of the others were coarse and clumsy."

"I am never clumsy, mademoiselle. My lovemaking is precise and fulfilling for everyone involved."

"Will there be others?"

"Not tonight. Tonight will be quiet and I am . . . Let's say I've had my fill tonight and will gladly allow you to leave when it is over."

"You promise?"

"*Oui!* I am a nobleman."

"And will you give me some money to make my struggle easier?"

"At the end of this evening you may state an amount, and I will give it to you."

"You have that much in this apartment?" Her acquisitiveness sparked an ember of courage.

"More than your small mind can ever imagine asking for."

She walked past him and down the shadowed hall, peeking into each room, reaching inside for a ceiling light. Not finding what she wanted, she continued until she came to the end room that, when lit, glittered with gold and marble.

"You'll find clean towels already in the cabinet." He came up close behind her and began to disrobe her body. Mesmerized by the wealth before her, she did not stop him. He found her breasts to be high, her waist narrow, and her hips sloping into gradual curves. He did not allow the clothes to touch the

40

floor; instead he immediately took them out to the landing, where he dropped them into the garbage chute.

When he came back, he heard the bathwater running. He needed to fill her stomach before taking his fill of her.

Chapter Nine

"Mom, do you think Uncle Louis might show up anyway? I mean, yeah, she's trying to avoid him, but if he wants, he'll track her down."

"Chuckie, I can't answer that."

"I don't like Uncle Louis."

"None of us does."

"Then maybe Dad's right: We should run."

"How often has your father ever been right, Chuckie?"

The toddler shrugged his shoulders.

"Maybe you could send me away to day-care or something."

"Some innocent child would bring his pet rabbit to show and tell, and you'd suck it dry."

"The kid or the rabbit?"

"We've discussed this topic already. Never touch a human."

"Dad doesn't have any restrictions."

"He's a fool, Chuckie." Gillian was repairing one of her antique gowns. The hem had come undone the last time she had worn the dress. As she recalled, that had been fifty or sixty years ago.

"If not day-care, then a foster home or an orphanage."

"You don't need either. Your father and I are very happy to take care of you." The needle slipped and punctured her finger. Chuckie's eyes came to attention. "This is why I couldn't trust you away from home. You have no self-control."

"People would think I was a weird kid who likes to see gory things."

"And you wouldn't touch?"

Chuckie's shoulders slumped.

"You can barely contain yourself around me, and I'm your mother."

"I feel liberated around you because you know what you made me."

Gillian knew this was her son's way of getting even. He reminded her as often as possible that she had changed the innocent toddler into a nonaging vampire.

"We could take a trip down to the pet store today," she said.

She liked seeing his eyes light up and hearing his small lips make smacking sounds.

"We could even go to the zoo at midnight."

Chuckie was so happy that he clapped his hands. This was her little boy. Glowing with youth and eagerness. He always loved the trips to the zoo. The bigger, undomesticated animals were more of a challenge, and their blood had a randy taste that appealed to Chuckie. Yes, they would stop at the pet store for an appetizer. Later they would slip into the locked zoo and make their choice.

Chapter Ten

Sade became so enmeshed in preparing the quail and truffles that he almost forgot his guest. The smell of lavender-perfumed soap intruded distastefully on the splendid odors already filling the kitchen.

"Into the dining room, mademoiselle. There is champagne already chilling, and the glasses you will find in the freezer."

She stood staring at the food. His paisley silk robe was loosely fastened around her body.

"Quick, quick. Let us not allow our food to grow cold by dawdling."

As he heard the freezer door open, he asked her name.

"Camille, after the artist Camille Claudel," she said.

"Ah, the woman who went insane. For a while she was Rodin's favorite." He shook his head. "How fickle we men are." He looked at her and smiled.

"I don't need to learn that lesson anew." Her voice sounded colder than the frosted glasses she carried to the dining room.

Sade chuckled and completed his gourmet efforts.

The meal did not take long to complete. Camille gobbled her food, and Sade merely picked at the quail and truffles. The champagne bottle had to be replaced by the middle of the meal, and dessert was a simple confection of strawberries with fresh cream.

"And now?" she said.

"Now you may clear the table and wash the dishes." Sade rose from his chair and wandered into the bedroom. After lighting several black candles, he removed his ascot and undid the sleeves of his Egyptian cotton shirt.

"You brought me here to be your maid," Camille shouted from the doorway.

Slowly Sade unbuttoned his shirt.

"What can you do for me, mademoiselle?"

Her long fingers touched the sash tying the robe together. He saw cuts and bruises on the backs of her hands; from digging in the smelly trash cans, he surmised. Sade took off his shirt and carefully laid it on the back of a black satin chair.

"What are they?" she asked, pointing to the far wall.

46

"My collection of whips, paddles, and various leather bonds."

"Do you mean to use them?"

"Are you intrigued, Camille? Have you never felt the sting of a braided whip or felt the freedom that bonds give you?" He reached out a hand to her. She refused to touch him, but she did come deeper into the room.

"Would you like to touch the leather of one of the whips? You may."

Camille undid the sash on her robe and walked over to the far wall to remove a whip with a short handle and many leather strips. She weighed the whip in her hand, then snapped it into the air.

"*Non,* mademoiselle, your grip is too limp." He placed his arms around her body and covered her hand with his own. "Do you feel the tension and strength that I use?"

Camille nodded her head. Sade took his hand from hers and brushed the robe from her shoulders, letting it fall to the rug. After freeing the whip from the material, she held her arm out straight and attempted to duplicate his hold. The whip snapped with a crackle in the cool air of the bedroom. The sound of Sade unzipping his fly immediately followed.

"Am I doing it correctly, monsieur?"

"Not enough power behind the strike, Camille. But don't worry, before day dawns you will be an expert in the uses of the whip."

Chapter Eleven

Marie and Anthony dined at Cléopâtre.

"I don't believe this huge bloody steak is going to last me through the morning, never mind getting me through the entire day."

"It's merely a snack, Anthony. Enjoy the meal. I must say that one civilized thing about Louis is that he never lost his taste for well-prepared food." She popped another morsel of food into her mouth.

"I'm not Sade, Marie, and you should be glad of that instead of complaining. Why the hell did you want to come here? We could have rounded up some real sustenance in the park. Mating and drugs tend to distract the prey's attention, making the pickings easy."

"Sluts, lowlives, drug fiends. Don't we deserve better than that, Anthony? We can practice *échangisme* with doctors, lawyers, or even respectable parents from the suburbs. Hervé Béhal, the owner, knew that the straitlaced needed a place to swing. A lovely dinner with one's mate, and then off to the upper chambers for a night of debauchery with two like-minded strangers. Far better than meeting up with the likes of Ophelia, Rapunzel, Snow White, or whatever the hell that vicious girl's name was.

"There are two hundred and fifty of these *échangiste* clubs in Paris. All you have to do is pick up a journal such as *Purple Sexe* or *Couples* to find the location of the one nearest you. There is even an English-language journal called *Deliciae Vitae*."

"And all we had to pay was a fifty-dollar cover charge." Anthony shoved a block of beef into his mouth. "It's free in the park."

Marie watched the meat roll around inside Anthony's mouth as he spoke. Coming alone might have been a better idea, except that she couldn't leave a droopy, weak vampire like Anthony on his own. In the park she had gifted him with a taste of her own blood to save him. Why couldn't he have paid attention to her warnings? she wondered. But she herself regretted past mistakes she had made and had mercy on Anthony.

"Save some room, Anthony, for the major event." Marie laid a hand on Anthony's lower arm, preventing him from putting another bite into his mouth.

"Can we go now?" Anthony threw his knife and fork into his oval plate.

The couple slowly rose, and as they walked toward the staircase they smiled their thank yous at the help.

"Behind me, Anthony."

He fell into step behind Marie and climbed the plushly covered stairs. On the landing there were rows of curtained rooms.

"Our playmates are supposed to be behind the rose-colored curtain."

Anthony pointed to the first set of curtains.

"No, that's more fire-engine red."

"Marie, what if a customer is color blind?"

"I'm sure one could call for assistance. Ah, down here, Anthony."

She led him to rose-colored curtains that had been drawn back with velvet ties.

"Pull those ties open as we walk into the room, Anthony."

He followed her instructions.

Marie became ecstatic. A male, six feet, four inches tall, stood as she entered. His dark wavy hair fell onto his forehead and shoulders. His pale blue eyes twinkled with his smile, and his chiseled face warmed with the glow of a tan. A little weather-beaten about the eyes, and perhaps some gray touched his sideburns, but otherwise he was perfect. The short sleeves on his muscle shirt revealed the firmness of his physique, and the swollen veins told her that he had recently worked out.

"Marie, I think we have the wrong room," said Anthony.

"Wrong room?" and as she turned, she caught

sight of the wife. Acne scars pitted the woman's bulbous nose, and her chubby face quickly announced what the rest of her would look like.

"She's not my style," Anthony whispered.

"You want the husband?"

"Marie, that is not my bent. The wife is too plump; besides, she reminds me of a relative."

"A close relative?"

"A second cousin."

"Then you don't have to worry about incest."

"I'm famished, Marie. Let's take them quickly and move on."

"To the next curtain? I'm sorry, but we only paid for one."

"Hi, my name is Louis." The male extended his hand toward Anthony.

Marie heard Anthony chuckle under his breath. He was so overcome with mirth, he didn't bother to take the extended hand.

Embarrassed, the man pulled his hand back and introduced his wife, Celeste.

"We've been here . . . for what?" He turned to his wife.

"At least forty-five minutes. This is our first time, and we are very excited." When she smiled she looked pretty. Her teeth were perfect. The orthodontia work must have cost her parents a fortune, Marie thought.

"Can we order anything for you? Brandy? Champagne? It's your call."

"Thank you, Louis, but we've just come from

dinner, and I don't believe either of us could manage anything else."

"Speak for yourself, Marie." Anthony cleared his throat.

"Besides, we should set some guidelines first. I love role playing; do you?"

The man and woman looked at each other and then nodded to Marie.

"Wonderful! I don't want to use our real names tonight. Louis, why don't we call you Hercules?"

Anthony groaned loudly behind her.

"And Anthony will be Brutus. The name suits him so well."

"Oh, I'll be an Amazon warrior," the wife said.

"Madam, they cut off one of their breasts better to shoot their bow and arrow." Marie couldn't quite see this woman as a tall, lithe warrior.

"Dear, how about Madame de Pompadour?" the husband asked. "My wife adores reading about Madame de Pompadour," he said as an aside to Marie and Anthony.

"An overrated actress," Marie stated.

"But she was so generous to the arts."

"So that she could play at being a true artist. She had no talent, and Louis the Fifteenth spoiled her. The slut wanted to be his mistress for years. Everyone knew even her family called her "reinette." But then, they were both shams. Each night there was a public ceremony when Louis the Fifteenth went to bed. Off he would go to the state bedroom to sleep. Someone would drag the boots off his big feet and someone else would hand him his nightshirt. After everyone had gone, he got dressed and went out to party in the town of Versailles or even Paris. Most times he ended up in the bed of a mistress."

Anthony nudged Marie.

"What?"

"As you can see, Marie is a history buff. Right?"

"Oh . . . Yes, of course," Marie said.

"You must have been quite a gossip back then," Anthony whispered into Marie's ear. "Let's stop with our game of choosing names. I, for one, want to remain Anthony. My companion is Marie, and you, sir, are Louis, if I heard right. And your charming wife is . . ."

"Celeste." Louis spoke his wife's name softly.

"Things aren't going well, are they?" Celeste asked.

"Nonsense. We've just taken a while to get to know each other." Marie reached behind herself and undid the zipper of her dress.

Louis and Celeste suddenly looked panicked.

Marie immediately slipped out of her dress and stood proudly in her red lace teddy. The lace barely covered her nipples, and a brief piece of lace covered her pubis. Her legs were bare. The only other article of clothing she wore were her stiletto sandals, with straps that wrapped around her ankles.

"I guess we should all take the hint," said Anthony, smiling and unbuttoning his cotton shirt.

Celeste's pale face stared at Anthony's slow striptease. His act must have been good, since she, too, began removing her jacket, then hurried to get naked. Her husband couldn't decide whether he wanted to cover her up or join her.

Celeste's body bloomed from the sustenance of rich food. The folds of flesh were damp with perspiration.

"Ah, Hercules, you are dawdling when the rest of us are growing impatient."

"Louis," Anthony reminded Marie.

"Why did I bring you?" she asked Anthony. In return he shrugged.

Celeste walked past Marie and fell to her knees in front of Anthony, taking his penis deep into her mouth. A surprised cry came from his lips before he placed both his hands behind her head.

Marie attempted to make eye contact with Anthony, but he stoutly kept his eyelids closed.

"Celeste," called Louis. "Celeste, I thought we were going to . . ."

"Throw your plans to the wind, my Hercules, and unbind that luscious flesh of yours." Marie reached out and ripped open his shirt. Her fingers ran through the rough hair on his chest and tweaked his sensitive nipples. She pushed the shirt down off his shoulders and brushed her sharp fingernails across his back. Her lips parted and her teeth showed blazing white. "Your wife has begun without you," she whispered.

Louis awakened from a stupor and began undoing his jeans when a sharp yell drew his attention back to his wife.

Celeste was bleeding. The drops slipped down her neck, folding into the crevices of her fat.

"He bit me," Celeste yelled.

"Love play, madam. My companion is over-zealous." Marie glared at Anthony. The red smear on his lips marked him with guilt. "He is eager to bury his senses in all your beauty."

"No one mentioned blood play," said Celeste.

Anthony wiped the back of his hand across his mouth. "There is nothing else." His voice came out like the warning hiss of a snake.

Louis pulled his wife into his arms and licked her neck clean.

"Marie is right. You have overstepped, monsieur. My wife is delicate and needs to be drawn into our games slowly. Shall I say she needs to be tempted by soft touches, not brutalized by your passion?"

"Damn it, Marie. This is torture. How long do you expect me to go hungry?"

"Some champagne and appetizers! I can have the waiter bring them immediately," said Louis.

Anthony reached out and pressed his fingertips into Louis's neck.

"He's mine!" shouted Marie as she pushed Anthony backward onto the floor. She felt her breasts heave with such force that the tips forced their way beyond the lace.

Celeste scrambled to retrieve her clothes from the floor. Marie swung out and backhanded the woman before she could run.

Louis watched Anthony crawl catlike toward his unconscious wife. Louis did nothing until Anthony's hand rested on Celeste's upper thigh.

"She is not my wife," he said. "I hired her to

accompany me for the evening. I don't care what you do to her, if only you'd show me how to use the violence you obviously thrive on."

Marie ran her hand over the hardness of Louis's penis, and he shoved the denim jeans over his hips, allowing them to pool at his ankles.

"Bring her to the bed, Anthony," Marie said. "Lay her across the sheets and fill your need. Monsieur and I will join you."

Louis slipped the straps of Marie's teddy from her shoulders. He bent over and suckled at her breast before nipping her flesh with increasing fervor. One of his bites drew blood. He began to draw backward until her hands urged him to stay the course.

The smell of blood perfumed the air, making Marie sway in ecstasy. She heard the ripping of her teddy, the lapping sounds of Anthony, and the whimpers of the semiconscious Celeste. Louis's callused hands buffed her body into the sweetness of desire. His hot breath on her flesh almost made her feel human again. She remembered passion without the need for blood. He lifted her easily into his arms and carried her to the bed. She felt the cool silk sheets welcome her and felt him thrust into her without requesting permission. He took her as no man had in centuries. She, the prey, lay beneath him, submitting to his demands, allowing him to own her body until the niggling hunger for blood overcame her.

Chapter Twelve

The fur of the monkey tickled Chuckie's nose. The wirelike hairs reached up into his nostrils, forcing him to wiggle his nose. Mother softly patted down the fur and wiped Chuckie's chin clean with a finger that she washed off in her mouth.

"Don't make a pig of yourself, darling. Frequently, these undomesticated beasts give you tummy cramps if you overdo."

Chuckie tightened his grip and shook his head violently at his mother.

"This is your second monkey, and you're such a small boy; please don't make yourself sick."

He wanted to complain that she took him to the zoo too infrequently, that was why he felt he had to pig out, but he feared that she would grab the animal from him if he lifted his mouth to speak.

"The guard will be making his rounds again," she reminded her son.

He began to move away from the cages, but his short, stubby legs got caught in the monkey's appendages. Mother swept both up into her arms and carried them to the safety of the dark shadows.

Chuckie began to suck air.

"That's enough, darling. There isn't any more left. Here, give me the monkey now."

There was a minor bout of push and pull for the dried carcass, and then Chuckie finally conceded. Mother flung the waste into a nearby lake.

"Are you all right, darling?" She patted his back.

"Mom, I'm not an infant. I know how to burp on my own without your help. Matter of fact, I won the burping contest over both Roger and Vanessa. Believe me, they made it as difficult as they could by tickling me through the whole contest."

"I'm worried, Chuckie."

"About Aunt Marie?"

"Yes. What influence will she have over you children? Hers is a violent and dangerous existence. I don't know why your Uncle Louis hasn't done away with her yet."

"Maybe he likes her."

Mother looked askance at Chuckie.

"Okay, maybe she helps him find victims. Given the kind of work she does and the number of clients she has, Uncle Louis may take the leftovers."

"Your uncle never settles for seconds."

"I would," Chuckie muttered. "Do humans taste better than animals, Mom?"

"They're different."

"From what?"

"Monkeys, rats, pigs . . . There is always a slight variation between species."

"Is the blood thicker or sweeter?"

"Chuckie, you are not missing anything by restricting your feedings to animals."

"I don't believe you, Mom. Dad always looks forward to his business trips, and we know he does humans when he is away from home."

"Who told you that?"

"Dad." Chuckie felt tired and reached up his arms to his mother to be carried.

Stooping down, she swept her son into her arms.

"It's a macho thing with your father. He's out on the road, meets another vampire, and they set off together for a taste of the forbidden. He probably wouldn't notice the difference if he was handed the blood in a glass. It's like the snobbery of imbibing expensive wines. Whether expensive or cheap, the final outcome of drinking too much wine is the same."

"But my question is, does one guy have a better time getting drunk then the other? I know I can survive on rats, but they can be stinky and dirty."

"I haven't tasted a human in decades," she said.

"Decades?"

"Oh, okay, in a century. See, I can't even pinpoint the exact date."

"Mom, would Roger and Vanessa taste the same as regular humans?"

"Their blood is a bit tainted, darling. You did

taste my blood when I brought you into the vampire world."

"I can't remember the taste, Mom. I feel like I'm missing something important. Damn it, you're going to force me to run away from home. I know— I'll ingratiate myself with Aunt Marie and go off with her. I could be handy in her business by . . ."

"Chuckie, don't speak of those things in front of your mother. I created you from my own flesh."

"And blood, but hell if I can tell you what you tasted like."

"Rest your head on my shoulder, darling, and try to think happy thoughts."

"I'd be happy if I got to try some human blood."

Mother sighed and thought, *so would we all.*

Chapter Thirteen

She smelled them in the sewers. She felt their cold touch on the Metro when all seemed mundane. She heard the chittering of their voices above the night sounds. Vampires enveloped her in their world.

Her blood excited them. Her blood poisoned them. Vampires saw none of the danger inherent in her blood. Their hunger overcame the possibility of their truly knowing her.

Babette leaned out her bedroom window and watched the rush of crowds on her Paris backstreet. Fresh food markets dotted the block. She loved passing the stands filled with ripened fruit. Their sweetness sometimes blinded her to the vermin stink of the vampires.

Casanova hadn't smelled of earth, but all the others had. Sade smelled of earth, blood, and sex. She wished she had been able to seduce him instead of that imbecile who thought she was Ophelia. The imbecile would have been destroyed that night, had it not been for the bitch who intruded. Maîtresse la Présidente, the beast from Sade's nightmares.

An old woman with a small dog looked up at Babette's bedroom window. The dog snarled, distorting his muzzle into canine ugliness. Babette expected the woman to shake a fist at her, to curse her, or even shriek at her in a witchlike voice. The old woman's rheumy eyes held Babette's gaze for too long. Babette became fidgety. Someday one of them would come for her and that vampire would not drink of her poison. Would not succumb. Instead that vampire would take her life.

The dog yelped, and the old lady lifted her dog into her arms and pointed at Babette.

"Remember her," Babette imagined the woman saying. "Remember the beautiful face, the curves of her body, the rhythm of her breath."

I should invite her up, thought Babette. She could call the butler and have him fetch the old woman and her dog. They would feast on madeleines and herbal tea. The dog would chase the serving girl around the drawing room, snapping at her heels and scratching at her nylons.

The old woman will fall under the spell of my home and wish to stay, wish to share the blood flowing through my veins.

Babette looked down and noticed that the old woman had placed the small dog on the sidewalk. She petted the dog's head and took a final look up at Babette's window. Babette almost raised her hand to beckon the woman, but a knock sounded at her door.

She crossed the room and opened the door. There stood the landlady, her hand extended, waiting for her monthly payment.

"It's not yet the last day of the month," Babette complained.

"You want me to come back at midnight?"

"Of course not, but you could have waited until tomorrow. I was going to invite a guest, and now I'm afraid she's gone."

"You can barely fit yourself into this room. Why would you want to bring in someone else?" The landlady withdrew her hand to the pocket of her housedress.

"I was going to serve madeleines and herbal tea. Freshly baked madeleines with some chamomile, or perhaps I have some dandelions left."

"Count me out. I just want the rent."

"We must accommodate her dog, of course."

"No pets, Babette. You know that. No live-in pets or visiting pets. I keep a clean boardinghouse. The money, girl, or I'll be calling the loony bin to take you away."

Babette fingered the torn lace around her neck and turned back to her room. The window was open. Oh, yes, she wanted to invite the old woman for madeleines and herbal tea. But first the help was being obstreperous, wanting their money way before it was due. She crossed the small room to her bureau and opened the top drawer. She counted out the sum she'd need. Way too generous, she thought to herself.

"If my friend comes later, you will inform me immediately, won't you?" She handed the money to the landlady, who nodded her head while counting out the money.

"But no dogs," the lady reminded. "Not even a fish."

"That's silly. People don't carry around their pet fish."

"Yeah, yeah, I know."

Babette put her hand on the landlady's forearm. "Don't let her get too close to you."

"Who?"

"My guest. She may be very hungry by the time she gets here."

"Hey, I don't want any criminals roaming these halls."

"She isn't a criminal. At least, not according to our civil laws. However, in the eyes of God she is condemned."

"At least she's not condemned to keep this house going."

Babette leaned closer to the landlady and said softly, "She is condemned to hell."

"Aren't we all," said the landlady as she walked down the dimly lit hall.

Chapter Fourteen

Vanessa screamed.

"He bit me. Chuckie bit me."

"What have I told you? Your brother's and sister's blood is tainted with the same disease we all have. They will never taste human again." Gillian rapped her son on the side of the head.

"She tastes awful anyway. She tastes like incense."

"That's my perfume, you idiot. Mom, we'll have to destroy him if we can't trust him."

"Destroy? All I did was give you a little bite on the neck. Hell, I hardly drew any blood."

"Yes, you did. Yes, you did." Vanessa drew a white embroidered handkerchief across her neck. "See." She held out the handkerchief so Mother and Chuckie could see it.

"That's nothing but an embroidered rose on your filthy hankie." Chuckie made as if to snatch the handkerchief, but Vanessa quickly pulled it away.

"We have to destroy him, Mother. We obviously can't trust him anymore. What if he comes after us while we sleep in our coffins?"

"I can't even reach the lid of your stupid coffin."

"Remember when there used to be a bedtime?" Mr. Hughes said.

"Dad, you are so reactionary," Chuckie said.

"Ah, they are some of my fondest memories. Seeing all the children tucked away in their beds. Roger slept with his fanny in the air for years. Vanessa curled herself around a porcelain doll. And you, Chuckie, spitting up all over your pillowcase."

"How come you don't have any cute memories of me?"

"Because you're not cute, Chuckie," said Vanessa.

"Leave my baby alone," said Mrs. Hughes. "He doesn't need to be cute. He has a strong personality. A character that no one can forget."

"Tell me again, Gillian, why didn't we leave him on the church steps? Was it really necessary for you to appease your appetite before we reached the church?"

"She didn't want to give me up, Dad, unlike you."

"All of you would have been better off in the clergy's hands. We should never have kept any of them with us, Stephen. It was cruel."

66

"But Chuckie's been getting even ever since, Gillian."

"Listen, we have to pull together. Aunt Marie could show up any day. What will she find?"

"Dad trying to sneak out the back door," guessed Chuckie.

"Your father has committed himself to staying with us. He knows Aunt Marie better than any of us. And if Louis should show up . . ."

"Then we all try to sneak out the back door," said Chuckie.

"Mom, aren't we going to destroy Chuckie?" Vanessa asked.

"He's your brother. You wouldn't really consider staking him?"

"Mom, he's dangerous. He tried to bite me."

"See, see. I didn't draw any blood. She admits that I *tried* to bite her but didn't."

"And he admits that he wanted to."

"Aunt Marie can't see us like this, right, Stephen?"

"Maybe she won't stay long if we keep Chuckie around," said Mr. Hughes.

"I'm going to barf." Roger entered the room with his skateboard under his arm. "Gross! Gross!" He didn't stop to explain; instead, he immediately went to his room.

"It's time for a father/son talk, Stephen."

Mr. Hughes looked at his wife. "You had to have kids, Gillian. You weren't happy when there was only the two of us."

"Maybe if you had spent more time at home and

less time visiting relatives in Nice I would have felt differently."

"Perish the thought, Ma," said Chuckie.

"I don't know, Chuckie. If we didn't have this set of parents, maybe we'd be normal now," said Vanessa.

"You'd be dead," Mr. Hughes reminded Vanessa.

"She wouldn't know the difference," said Chuckie.

"You wouldn't have stayed two feet high, idiot. I would have grown into a glamourous woman. And Roger probably would have been some sort of gigolo."

"What are we going to do when Marie gets here, Stephen? We can't let her hear the constant bickering. What will she think?"

"Are we any worse than her relationship with her son-in-law? Gillian, the woman doesn't care about our family. My guess is that she's hiding out. I think her own family problems will blind her to ours.

Chuckie screamed.

"Vanessa bit me!"

Chapter Fifteen

Marie walked down the winding street filled with fresh food markets. Should she send the Hughes family a basket of fruit, or maybe some flowers? Chrysanthemums were meant for funerals. Hmmm . . . those might be appropriate in this case. She spotted a beautiful bouquet of carnations. No, they represented bad luck, and she didn't need any more bad luck tied to her life. Red roses were reserved for lovers and very close friends. Maybe she should send Stephen Hughes a bunch to remind him of the past. But then, she didn't want to flaunt this in his wife's face.

Chocolate, she thought. Candy would even win over those horrid children. Repulsive, she thought, and shivered. How anyone could make small children into vampires was something she couldn't understand. Especially those children. Poor Stephen had such bad luck.

Obviously unhappy with the selection, a young woman with severe acne squeezed melons. The owner of the market finally spotted her and attempted to chase her away with a wave of his hands. Evidently the woman had missed one or two and attempted to reach for a small melon. The owner would have none of it and began letting go with a whirlwind of French expressions that would never appear in a child's grammar book.

Marie laughed to herself. She would miss this sort of everyday event. She bumped shoulders with an old woman.

"Sorry, madam, I wasn't looking . . ."

The woman immediately reached for her small dog and began an exhortation about a witch who lived up the block. Her gnarled fingers pointed to a simple boardinghouse on the opposite side of the street. As best as Marie could tell, the open window to which the old woman pointed had a yellowed white lace curtain.

The old woman grabbed Marie's arm, and the dog took the opportunity to drool on Marie's new silk blouse. Marie flicked her fingers against the dog's nose, causing him to yelp.

Silly old woman, wasting my time with her trivial fantasies. Just then, Marie looked up at the window and saw a familiar face. The wicked girl from the park sat on the windowsill and stared blankly down at the street. Ophelia wore a thin nylon blouse that offered a perfect outline of her breasts; the shadows of the nipples darkened the material into sharp peaks.

Marie looked back at the old woman, who was now hysterical and indignant over her dog's stung nose.

"Madam," Marie began, "forgive me. The little . . ." *Rat* came to mind, but she refrained. "The little fellow is adorable. I only meant to lightly tweak his nose." She reached out to pet the animal, who snapped at her fingers.

The old woman moved away from Marie to protect her dog and knocked over a bushel of onions.

The chaos gave Marie one of her familiar headaches. The tightness across her forehead and pulsing at her sinuses caused her outrageous pain. Luckily, the young boy tending the market approached with a worn broom, attempting to sweep the old woman and Marie away. Marie willingly moved to the curb and crossed the street. She never turned to see what the dog was yapping about; instead, she moved forward to the entrance of the boardinghouse. The dreary vestibule needed to be painted, and the hallway had one small twenty-watt bulb.

She knocked on the landlady's door. A chubby middle-aged woman opened the door and eyed Marie from head to toe.

"Excuse me. I'm looking for a young girl. She has a front window."

"You must be the woman Babette is waiting for. I'm glad to see you didn't bring your dog. We never allow pets into the building. Dogs and cats smell up the halls with their filth. We maintain a clean house."

"I'll never bring a pet, madam, do not fear. But could you tell me what room number she has?"

"Two flights up. Number seven."

"Thank you."

As she walked to the stairs, she could feel the landlady's eyes taking in her expensive shoes and her silk stockings. Marie turned for a moment and smiled at the woman before climbing the steps.

The door to number seven was painted the same dark brown as every other door. A few nicks in the paint allowed the prior blue to show through. She rapped on the door and waited a few moments. An elderly woman down the hall opened her door wide enough so that she could peek at her neighbor's visitor.

Marie smiled and waved, and the door instantly slammed shut.

Again Marie rapped at the door, more loudly and with more authority.

"I can smell you. Go away," shouted the occupant.

"I don't think your landlady tolerates scenes. Do you have the money to seek a new place to live?"

The door opened.

"How did you find me?"

"I caught your scent with the help of an old woman and her mongrel. May I come in?"

"Why?"

"Because your neighbor is eavesdropping on our conversation."

72

The young girl stood out of the way, and Marie entered the single room.

"The landlady indicated that your name is Babette, not Ophelia."

"You knew that was not my name, merely a tag your friend decided to attach to me."

Marie nodded and looked for a clean place to sit.

"Mind if I sit on the windowsill and get some air?" Marie didn't wait for an answer.

"You saw me at the window."

"An angelic sight, with wisps of hair surrounding your face and your charming attributes advertising you're for sale."

"I am not."

"Sorry, but you should put more clothing on when staring at people, since they'll be staring back at you."

"I am proud of my body. Why have you come here? Have you changed your mind about feeding from me?" Babette unbuttoned the top buttons of her blouse.

"You're so pathetic and obvious."

"I have trapped others."

"But not as many as you could have, had you been trained to be more sophisticated."

"Are you offering a crash course, Maîtresse la Présidente?"

"I have a serious problem, Babette. The Marquis de Sade holds grudges. As a matter of fact, several against me. He haunts my existence. I've allowed him to take up most of my mental energy."

"And you can't afford that."

Marie allowed the sting of those words to wash over her. No, she would not become angry with this child. At least not until she had served a good purpose.

"None of us can afford to be obsessed with any one person. There is too much to learn in the world, and too many people willing to educate."

"He hates you."

"Actually, I believe there's an element of love there also."

Babette laughed.

"No, it is true. There has to be a kind of love. Not to say that it is a healthy love. Yet I believe he would miss me. I am connected to all that he loved in the past."

"The bad as well as the good."

"Yes, you understand. To rid himself of me he would have to give up the past completely. And he did have some . . . what he considered good times."

"When you allowed him his freedom."

"I protected the name of our family and protected my grandchildren from his scandals. Any woman of noble birth would have done as I did."

"Such a woman would not have wanted to become a vampire herself."

"When your hair is white and your flesh sags and the lines on your face cast a new image, you will understand the fear of dying. Youth is immortal, but youth fades and the body wilts."

"Why do you look so young?"

"You can sense who I am, but no details of how I got here?"

Babette shook her head.

"Ah. This is a stolen body. My own was destroyed by Louis."

"Then he is capable of doing away with you."

"No. He saved my skull, and in doing so gave me a second chance. And recently he granted me a third."

"Because he cannot completely sever ties with you?"

"Because his past is too important to him. Louis loved once. His niece was beautiful, intelligent, and naive. He made her a vampire. He allows her to wind her way aimlessly through the world, brushing against the living only fleetingly. She could break his heart."

Marie looked over her shoulder toward the street rather than allow Babette to see her own pain in her eyes.

"On the other hand, I do not rate teardrops. My guess is that I comfort him when he lays in his coffin, abandoned by everyone he has known. Except for me. He knows I can remember the touch of my daughter's hand, the giggles of my grandchildren, the comfort of the many estates we owned, the dark lectures of our church fathers, and the coldness of his prisons."

"I doubt he wants to remember all that."

"He does. Because they are all interconnected. One does not exist without the other. His happiness and his pain share equal nobility in his life. Therefore it all comes down to me."

"Grim," said Babette. "And would you miss Sade for the same reasons?"

Marie turned back to look at the girl.

"Definitely not. If he were destroyed, I would be free to move on with my life. I have a new body. Why not make new memories?"

"And forget your family?"

"I was good to them while they were with me, but now I must seek solace in the new."

"Why are you here?" asked Babette.

"I want your help."

"You want me to poison Sade for you."

"Yes."

"I told you before: I will not be your hunting hound."

"Oh, you don't have to. If you stay with me, he will find us." Marie smiled and let the hatred she felt flush her face.

"You are far more cruel than Sade."

"No, far wiser."

"You would bring Sade to me?"

"I think it would be best if we allowed him to find us. I am going to the United States to stay with family, and I want you to come with me."

"What would I do there?"

"Oh, there are vampires there, certainly. But wait; I have a better idea. There are children in this family who have not been very well educated. They can read and write but lack social skills. The parents have been too doting. They care for the children as if they were babes instead of nearly a century old."

"They are vampires?"

"Their father and I had a fling."

"And he infected his family. Do you feel any remorse?"

"Have you heard anything I've said? These children are not my concern. But they do have a use. I will bring you to the States to teach them French and social skills."

"While my real job is to seduce Sade when he runs you down."

"The eldest child was born in nineteen hundred. The others came a few years later. There are three in all, two boys and one girl. Each has his or her own idiosyncrasies, as you can imagine a child vampire would."

"I could poison them."

"No! At least not until you have finished with Sade. Then you can have the entire family." Marie shrugged her shoulders and sighed.

"Why should I go with you?"

"Because you are unhappy in these cramped quarters and would be unhappier to be homeless."

"You'd see to it that I was tossed from this boardinghouse?"

"I want my son-in-law destroyed, and I've just explained the intertwining of our lives. You are nothing to me except a blunder I tripped over in the park."

Chapter Sixteen

"I can't wait around forever for that woman to show up."

"It's only been a couple of days since we received the letter, Stephen."

Gillian wasn't sure she could stand any more of her husband's pacing. Their lovemaking seemed just a way for him to pass the time. The passion was missing from his touch, from his words.

"We should set up a time limit. Say, if she's not here by Friday, then I can begin setting up my sales calls."

"Friday is tomorrow."

"Yes. So . . ."

"Stephen, I will not put up with that woman alone. She is someone with whom you became involved when you should have been home with your family. You will wait until I feel comfortable that she has changed her mind about staying with us. I doubt she will, though. Her letter sounded desperate."

"Melodramatic." He sat on the corduroy sofa and put his bare feet on the glass coffee table.

"If I had Sade tracking me down, I'd feel desperate. The man is a monster."

"Then they're suited for each other."

Gillian looked out the window and saw Chuckie beating the overgrowth. He had announced that if he couldn't get human blood directly, he would capture mosquitoes and drain them dry of human blood. All these years and he couldn't fully rebel, but it is difficult to rebel when you're two feet high.

"What the hell is that kid doing now? Is he purposely making a spectacle of himself?"

"Children do silly things like that, Stephen."

"Excuse me, Gillian, but the boy is not really a toddler."

"The neighbors don't know that."

"We've had this toddler here for the last five years. I thought we agreed to keep him hidden."

Gillian sighed. She hated to call her son back into the house. At least his new project kept him out of the way. His whining had started to become a nuisance. She had even considered offering her own blood to him.

She tapped on the windowpane to get Chuckie's attention. Eventually he noticed her, and she beckoned for him to come in. He snubbed her with a gesture no toddler would use.

"We should really destroy him."

Gillian turned and saw Vanessa standing next to her.

"He'll give us away someday, Mother."

"He's frustrated."

"We're all frustrated, Mother. However, he's the only stupid one."

"Vanessa has a point, Gillian. That boy is too wild, too high-strung."

"That's because he has your genes, Stephen."

"Do you see me going out and whacking bushes? What the hell does he gain by that?"

"He's looking for mosquitoes."

"Mother, your son is deranged and puts the rest of us in grave danger."

"He's your brother, Vanessa. You should have sympathy for him. Instead, both of you drive him crazy with your superior attitudes. He's a toddler, and he has the hardest time adjusting to the vampire life."

"We should pity him?" Vanessa folded her arms and continued to stare at her brother.

"No. Protect him and support him. He is part of our family. There are only five of us, and what would happen if we lost one? Think, Vanessa. With Chuckie gone, you would be the bottom of the food chain."

Vanessa unfolded her arms and her hands tightened into fists as she turned and glared at her mother.

"Sometimes there are problems being daddy's little girl," said Gillian.

"In defense, let me say that I believed Vanessa and Roger would acclimate to being vampires. It was you who refused to give up your baby boy," said Stephen.

Gillian closed her eyes.

"Why are we fighting each other? We have nothing to gain and no one can win." She opened her eyes, hoping the world would have changed. Chuckie still whipped the shrubbery. Vanessa seethed, with her face in a sour pout. And Stephen had gone back to pacing.

Chapter Seventeen

Sade had been wrong. His appetite for blood had been greater than he had thought. Ridding himself of Camille's body had not been easy—a good reason why he tried to feed away from home.

He noted the small crowd up ahead and almost decided to turn back, but something drove him forward. The narrow sidewalk was made worse by the markets that thrust their wares under the pedestrians' noses. A teenage boy who should have been in school stood on the sidewalk, arguing with a woman his grandmother's age. Onions rolled along the sidewalk and spilled out onto the cobblestone street. A tiny dog nipped at the boy's pant leg.

"No, no, madam, you are the one who is in the wrong. You toppled our basket, and now you blame me for losing your friend?"

"That woman isn't my friend. I merely bumped into her here on the sidewalk. This is her fault. I told her about the witch. The one who lives just over there." The old woman pointed at the nondescript boardinghouse.

"There are no witches living on this block, madam. The local tenants group forbids it. Calm down, please." A man who must have been the market's owner and the boy's father had joined the lively trio. "Believe me, madam, we've driven out the witches, and they'll not return. What is here for them? Only owners of simple markets trying to make a living. Demons have given up on trying to steal our souls. We're not worthy of God's mercy, nor of Satan's wrath."

"One is truly here. She sits at her window and chooses her victims. Your son could be her next lover, or you yourself," the old woman said.

The owner heaved a sigh and sent his son back inside. The dog attempted to follow, except he was shocked to a halt by his collar.

"Madam, I'm a somewhat happily married man. I do not seek out more trouble than I can handle. A witch would definitely be a no-no."

"She slowly takes your soul while you sleep."

"My wife?"

"No, you fool, the witch."

"Sounds like my wife." The crowd that had gathered across the street laughed and cheered the owner.

"She uses her body to insinuate herself. She uses few words, monsieur."

83

"Then you are definitely not talking about my wife." The owner grinned.

"The demon is boiling in her blood, heating her with charms to capture innocents."

"Excuse me, monsieur. May I make restitution for whatever this woman has unknowingly destroyed?" Sade reached inside his jacket for his wallet.

"Monsieur, I want nothing from this woman except for her to move on. Would you perhaps know her?"

"Yes. We try not to let her out too often." Sade spoke in a low voice to the owner. "If I can manage, I will take her with me."

"Much appreciated, monsieur."

"Come along, Mother." Sade reached out and touched the woman's bare hand.

Her eyes opened wide and she dropped her dog's leash and muttered the word "Death."

The dog took off for the open doorway to the shop, the owner chasing after, lunging forward occasionally in an attempt to step on the leash.

"Mother, it is time for you to come with me," said Sade.

"But I haven't been to church yet."

"I think there's one two or three blocks ahead." He attempted to pull her along, but she refused to move.

"I'll not pass the witch's house again. Not on my way to the grave."

"And which house would that be, madam?" He smiled, thinking the woman reminded him of many

84

he knew at Charenton, the insane asylum.

With her free hand she pointed to a window. Sade looked up, and his smile became exhausted, falling into a weak grin that did not suit his face.

Marie sat on the windowsill and yammered endlessly to someone inside the apartment. He wondered what she would be doing in this part of Paris. The boardinghouse was typical of those used by pensioners and students. A clean place, but no sign of luxury anywhere. Not Marie's style.

"Madam, is that the witch up there at the window now?"

"No. I warned her, though. I told her about the witch, and the foolish thing didn't listen. She'll lose her soul while up there."

"Or steal someone else's," he murmured.

Marie now made elaborate hand motions toward the street but didn't bother to look down.

"Her dog, monsieur." The owner of the market was again by their side. "He has ruined our fresh chanterelles."

"What?" Distractedly, Sade questioned the owner but never turned to look at him.

"He peed on the chanterelles, and we had just opened the crate. Fresh this morning. I've many customers that expect fresh chanterelles. I have them every Wednesday."

"I'll pay for them."

"What about my customers? What can I tell them?"

Sade looked at the owner. "I'll pay for them, and you'll take the chanterelles out back of the store and hose them down. *Oui?*" Sade handed the owner more than enough money to pay for the chanterelles.

"Not me, monsieur. I could never do that."

"Then have your son do it."

Sade let go of the old woman's hand and crossed the street, mesmerized by the innocence of the building. He could have walked by without knowing who the building harbored. Ah, but something had directed him here. The old woman was a charm that had attracted him here.

"Death will take her this day." The old woman's voice sounded in the distance. She had served her purpose and now could fade into the mundane shadows of the market streets.

"May I help you, monsieur?"

The landlady had become aware of his loitering.

"I'm looking for my wife. She came here to visit a friend."

"Do you have the dog with you, monsieur?" She searched and peered around him.

"No, I'm alone."

"As I told your wife, I don't allow pets. Never have. They like to mark their territory, and . . ."

"To which apartment did my wife go?"

"Number seven."

Chapter Eighteen

Sade sat on the top step just in front of the door that led to the roof. After about thirty minutes of waiting, he heard a door open below and feminine voices agreeing upon a meeting place. He stood and leaned over the rail just far enough to make out Marie's profile.

"Death will not come to her today," he softly said, recalling the old woman's words.

After Marie had left, he waited several minutes before descending the stairs and knocking on the door of number seven.

A young woman, a child but not an innocent, opened the door and curtsied deeply before him. Clothed in a nylon blouse with a tattered lace collar and a skirt that barely touched the floor, she could have been a student. But she wasn't. Neither was she a streetwalker or a grandchild keeping Granny company on lonely afternoons. She stank of . . . He couldn't quite place the smell. It was old, but new to him. The smell was an undomesticated animal's smell, an animal hiding in the bushes, slinking along to the rhythm of its prey.

When she raised her head he knew her immediately. The girl in the park. The one who had sensed his presence.

"I didn't expect you so soon," she said.

The girl was worse than a witch. Fear ran through his body, almost forcing him to run down the stairs and flee.

"Come in, Monsieur Sade."

The room behind her appeared to be furnished with simple taste. None of the objects were decorative. The room was done in earth tones, the only spot of color being the girl herself. Her long red hair touched her waist. Her lips were not painted and yet glowed a deep, perfect red. Her eyes were diamond blue and her flesh whiter than a first snow.

Crossing the threshold seemed too frightening. He would have tried talking to her from the hall, but he heard the click of a peephole being opened down the hall. Stepping into the room, he caught the stale smell of cheese and wine.

She closed the door softly; he only heard a hint of the lock slipping into place.

"Is that the true color of your hair, mademoiselle?"

"No."

He laughed at her ingenuousness.

"Is anything real about you?"

"No."

"Then I am safe, because you are only a figment of my imagination."

"No."

"Are you a memory from my past that I cannot banish?" He touched her hair and felt the softness. This was unadulterated hair.

"I'm sometimes real and sometimes not."

"But always a liar."

Her face grew troubled, and she snatched her hair from his fingers.

"Do you want my blood?" she asked.

"No. I want you to tell me a story." He sat on a rolled-arm chair that had once been overstuffed but now was covered with a gray-green slipcover. Much of the stuffing had been lost over the many years it had served.

"You followed your mother-in-law here?"

"That is the story I want you to tell me."

"She hates you and wants you destroyed."

"And she's given the assignment to you, since she has failed in the past."

He watched her cross the room to the window and pull down the fringed shade.

"What we do here is secret," she said.

Her breasts did not sag, her skin was unblemished, her fingers were long and the nails unpainted. The thin material of her skirt showed off the shapeliness and length of her legs. Her feet were bare, and she wore a single ring on her right big toe.

"You've been told to seduce me, *oui?*"

"I don't have to. You already are, Monsieur Sade."

Sade licked the tips of the fingers of his left hand and offered the hand to her. She pulled up her skirt so that he could see the lush white of her thighs, and then she knelt before him and took his hand in her mouth. Her tongue played between each of his fingers and rolled across the knuckles slowly, catching the full taste of his flesh. Her blue eyes stared into his blue eyes and invited him into her. The blue was the color of the deep ocean and as fresh as a spring day. He leaned forward to have a closer look, and to seek the smell of her blood. Her blue eyes turned into a blood-red that dripped red drops down her white cheeks. Quickly he pulled back, and the eyes were blue again and the cheeks a bare white. His hand glowed under her wet saliva.

"Where is she taking you?" he asked.

"You mean where is she going? You do not care where I go, Monsieur Sade."

"Where?"

"To the States. I'm to tutor three ancient children."

"The Hugheses." He rested his hands on his thighs. His erection pulsed between his legs.

"You are to follow us. Will you, Monsieur Sade?"

"Mademoiselle . . ."

"Babette," she corrected.

"Babette, I would follow you into a poison ivy patch for one lustful round of fucking. And as a boy, I learned the awful pain of that mistake."

"My bed has frayed and stained sheets but no ivy to punish you for your pleasures." She smiled. She had a small space between her two front teeth, but otherwise her teeth were perfect, white and straight and strong.

"When I bed you, Babette, I will be armed with charms and amulets to drive away your curses."

Sade stood and walked to the door.

"My curses will follow you, Monsieur Sade. They'll bring you back to me, and you'll be helpless and willing."

Chapter Nineteen

Roger sulked in his room. The stereo system didn't drown out the noises made by the rest of the family. They managed to clobber around and screech in high piercing levels. He could run away from home. How weird that sounded. He was old enough to be a skeleton; why should he hesitate to be on his own? There were street children far younger than he surviving. And he could survive off them. The hell with what his mother had drilled into him.

A pounding on his door forced him to turn off the stereo and answer the rude summons.

"What the hell do you have in here? An actual band?"

"Dad, it's my stereo system."

"Please, leave it off for a while. Give my eardrums a chance to recuperate."

"Dad, did you ever think about running away from home?"

"What? You're thinking about leaving us?"

"Running away."

"Roger, you don't have to run. I'll hold the front door open for you while you stroll out."

"But you and Mom would try to stop me."

"Why?"

"Because . . . How would I take care of myself?"

"You could catch stray dogs and cats like you do now." Dad shrugged his shoulders.

"What if I was caught?"

"By the ASPCA?"

"Well, what if they learned that I was a vampire?"

"People don't believe in us, Roger. You could go out in the middle of the street and yell 'I'm a vampire' to the world, and no one would believe you. Might think you're a nut job, but a harmless one."

"I'm not harmless, Dad. I have the capacity to murder. The thirst to drain the entire town. An appetite for cruelty and a need for revenge."

"Have you been watching some of those stupid movies? If this keeps up, I'm going to take away your Blockbuster card."

"Dad, you kill people."

"Keep it down, Roger. Your mother doesn't like me talking about that at home."

"Why not, if we're truly demons from hell?"

"I'm from Chicago. Mother was a nurse and Dad was a fireman. I've never met Satan and have no desire to."

"But, Dad, we're damned."

"*Cursed* is a better word. I'm cursed with a family of eccentrics, and you're cursed with wild pretensions."

"What are you two doing?" Gillian asked on her way down the hall.

"We're having a father-and-son talk."

"That's wonderful, Stephen. See, we got something out of your staying home for more than a week at a time. You and Roger are finally bonding." She grabbed her husband and gave him a kiss, after which she turned to tousle her son's unkempt hair.

The front doorbell chimed to this family tableaux.

Chapter Twenty

Feeling elated, Gillian hurried down the stairs to answer the door. Her hand lightly touched the bleached-oak banister. A few more weeks of Stephen at home, and he'd be taking the kids out on hiking or bicycle trips. There was an upside to Marie's visit after all. Gillian didn't bother to check who was at the door. She grabbed the glass doorknob and swung open the front door.

A pair who appeared to be mother and daughter stood on the top step of the porch. The older woman smiled warmly while the younger sulked.

"Gillian! It's wonderful to see you again," said the older woman.

Again? Quickly, Gillian attempted to go back over her long existence and place at least one of the people standing before her, but she couldn't.

"Stephen," Gillian hurriedly called, hoping he could rescue her from this embarrassment.

"Oh, I should explain who I am. I've had this body for so long that I forget that old friends can't recognize me."

"What's the matter, Gillian?" Stephen stumbled over his own feet when he caught a glimpse of the women at the door. "Marie," he whispered.

Gillian watched the older woman laugh and lunge at Stephen, giving him a generous kiss and rubbing his derriere as if it were Aladdin's lamp.

"Stephen, is this one of your clients?" she asked.

He unfastened the arms that cinched him in a preternatural grip and turned to his wife.

"This is Marie, Gillian. Although I must say, she looks incredibly good. But I know the look in her eyes, even if they don't appear to be the correct color. Have you taken to wearing contacts, Marie?"

Marie lightly slapped his cheek, and this time Stephen threw his arms around her.

"She doesn't look like herself," said Gillian, puzzled.

"Of course I don't. This is a completely new body." Marie peered at Gillian over Stephen's shoulder.

"How did you . . ."

"Don't worry, sweetheart, I'll explain it all after I've had a chance to freshen up."

"You're fresh enough for me, Marie. Couldn't imagine anyone fresher," said Stephen.

"It's my naughtiness you like most, Stephen, admit it." Marie drove her right fist into his stomach, knocking the wind out of him.

Without thinking, Gillian closed the door behind her so that they all stood on the porch.

"What did you do that for, honey?" Stephen asked. "We were just about to go into the house. Marie here wants to freshen up and . . . Should I know your friend, Marie? Please tell me it's not Louis with a new body."

Gillian grabbed hold of the door frame.

"No, no. Didn't you get my letter? I'm trying to avoid that man; running away from him, actually. No, this is Babette. She is French and is a tutor."

"What does she tutor?" Gillian asked.

"Children. I brought her for your darlings. There is much she can teach them. French. Social graces."

Stephen laughed. "Are you saying our children don't have the proper social skills?"

"Do they, Stephen? An honest answer will welcome Babette into your home."

"There's nothing wrong with our children. They do the best they can, given what they are." Gillian had no idea whether the tutor understood that they were vampires. She certainly was not one.

"Don't worry, Gillian. Our secret is safe with Babette. She already knows that we're . . ."

"Don't say the word. We never say the word in public," Gillian warned.

"Are your neighbors wiretapping your home, Gillian? Because I don't see anyone around to hear our conversation. It's such a quiet neighborhood.

Babette and I noticed that before I rang the door-bell. A bit boring, Stephen."

"You'll change that, I'm sure," said Stephen. He felt his wife's glare begin to melt his polyester shirt.

"He'll be here, you know," said Babette. "He'll follow Marie for an eternity."

"A name we shouldn't mention," said Marie, glaring at Babette.

Babette drew closer to Marie. "That won't keep him away. That's why I'm here." She turned and directed her last remark at Gillian. "But you would have guessed that. I'm the sacrificial offering."

"No, you're not," said Marie. "You are the tutor. And if we can go inside, you'll get to meet their lovely children." Marie looked expectantly at Gillian, and Stephen didn't dare move.

"She's here to seduce Louis within our house. My children should not be exposed to your form of revenge, Marie. I will not permit this woman inside my home. You and she can go elsewhere."

"But we have nowhere else to go, Gillian. We came all this distance to visit with you and Stephen and the children."

"You came here to hide, Marie. And if you can't hide, you'll at least distract him with this young girl."

Marie walked over to Gillian and touched her hair. "You don't want to send us away. You're such a tight-ass about vampirism; you wouldn't want any rumors to start about you and your family. Think of the witch hunt. I know, I've been there. Being afraid to open the door. Not knowing where to go when you do decide to flee. And the financial hassle of all this. I would hate for that to happen to you. At least I didn't have children to worry about, especially very vulnerable children, like Chuckie. How is he? I imagine he's becoming more worldly wise by the day, while you can still hear the patter of his little feet."

Stephen reached an arm around Gillian's waist. "Let's go inside. I certainly want to hear how you lost all those years, Marie. You look thirty years younger and shapely," he said, taking a step back to look at her figure.

Marie giggled and released strands of Gillian's hair before reaching for the doorknob.

Chapter Twenty-one

"If Aunt Marie can make herself younger, then I should be able to make myself older, right, Mom?"

"Chuckie, she had to be destroyed before she was able to come back in a new body."

"Well, go ahead and chop off my head, then. But be careful about whose coffin you put me in. I don't want to come back a girl or an old fart. Thirty-five sounds like a reasonable age. Worldly wise, but still having the spunk to live it up. Don't tell the others what you're doing, and don't tell them what I'll look like. I could surprise them; better still, I could avoid them and be right in their faces."

"Your father recognized your Aunt Marie immediately. You're his son; he most certainly would know you. And what about your brother and sister? You'd break their hearts if you disappeared."

"That's life, Mom. Besides, they'd only miss kicking me around."

"I'm afraid the only heart that would truly be broken is yours, Gillian." Marie stood in the doorway of the kitchen. "I doubt the little scamp could survive without you. You've ensured that, haven't you?" Marie walked into the kitchen and knelt down in front of the standing Chuckie. "I could chop off his little head and store it away in a nice cozy coffin. Would you prefer above or below ground? But then, we'd need a staked vampire. Where would we find one? There's your father, but I doubt he would volunteer."

"I wouldn't trust you, Aunt Marie. You'd bring me back as Frankenstein if you could, and think it a wonderful joke."

"And it would be. You'd go from being a cumbersome small fry to being a big klutz. Let me ask you, Chuckie, how do you like Babette?"

"I don't want to come back as a girl."

"No, no, Chuckie. She's not even a vampire. I'm not sure what would happen if we put you in a dead person's coffin. Would you be able to give the body new life? Interesting experiment," Marie said, turning to Gillian.

"Stop threatening my son."

"But he's so cute and easy to tease." Marie grabbed hold of Chuckie's right cheek and squeezed hard.

"Mom," Chuckie cried out.

Gillian rose to her feet and demanded that Marie leave the kitchen.

After she left, Gillian and her son sat in silence for a while. He sat on the kitchen chair, kicking the leg of the table. Gillian swept her fingers repeatedly through his hair.

"Mom?"

"Yes, baby?"

"She's right. We'd need a staked vampire."

"I know."

"Would you miss Dad very much?"

"Please, Chuckie, he's your father."

"But he's hardly ever here, and when he is, all he does is make fun of me. I don't think Dad likes me."

"He loves you but doesn't know how to show it. He's overwhelmed with guilt for what he did to this family. He doesn't know how to say he's sorry, and when you think about it, there are no words that could make us completely forgive him."

"I'd forgive him."

"Oh, my baby, you have such a generous heart."

"If he let me stake him. That could make up for all he's done."

"Shush. Never let him hear you say that. He might . . ."

"Run away forever; then I'd never get the chance to grow up. He is my one true salvation. We don't know too many other vampires, and Roger is too young. I want to be an adult. Someday we have to really consider the matter. You know that, Mom."

"I've never . . ."

"Thought about it before. Of course not, because we didn't know it was possible. We know now, Mom. What are we going to do about it?"

Chapter Twenty-two

"I know you are not far away, Monsieur Sade. I can sense you close. As close, perhaps, as the toolshed in the backyard. Or maybe you've already invaded the house, and you are making yourself comfortable in the basement with the rats and other vermin.

"Babette is here waiting for you. Waiting for our duel to begin. I will willingly give you Marie, but in return I want your existence at an end."

Babette heard a noise in the attic. A scuttle of feet ran across the ceiling.

"The attic. Is that where you've taken up residence? I'm bathing in your scent. Your body pressed against mine freezes my flesh into goose bumps. But I keep my blood warm for you."

Babette lifted scissors from a bureau and brought

the sharp edge to her right index finger and slashed. The blood slipped down the finger and onto the rough carpeting on the floor.

"Smell it."

She ran her tongue across the wet red drink.

"And it tastes wonderful. It tastes better than any that you've had before. My blood is worth giving up this world. Die, finally, with the taste of my blood on your lips and my flesh in your hands. Die the way you should have. Die while inside me, jerking to your climax, bucking to the sounds of my pants and screams. Know that I am the last. You will desire or need no other woman. I am the woman you've wanted throughout the centuries."

Her voice rose into a near shout within the small guest bedroom. Marie opened the door and entered.

"What are you doing?"

"I'm calling to him. He's near."

"He's found me already? How could that be? He wouldn't have instantly suspected my coming back to the States. You have to be wrong, Babette."

Babette shook her head.

"We've just gotten here."

"And so has he."

"How close is he?"

"He is either near or in the house."

"Locate him!"

"No, he will come for the both of us. Give him time."

"Hell with giving him anything. I want you to get rid of him."

104

"Rid of who?" asked Stephen.

"I'm sorry. Were we making too much noise? I was trying to give her some lovelorn advice. Not that she'll follow it. Much too young to understand all that we know, isn't she, Stephen?"

Babette stood in her flimsy, transparent night-gown.

"I suppose I, too, could take the time to talk to her, Marie. If it would help."

"Why would she believe you any more than me, Stephen? Gillian is already cross with me. I certainly don't want to encourage you to do anything that would make her angrier."

"You're scum," Babette said to Stephen.

Marie swiftly turned and slapped Babette, knocking her back onto the bed.

"Stephen, I'm sorry. Sometimes she says things she doesn't mean."

"She meant that, Marie. Where did you pick up the little bitch?"

"We met in a park. We were both out for a stroll."

"Marie, I'm familiar with the parks you stroll in. I wouldn't dare take my family to any of them."

"Strolling. Cruising. Whatever you want to call it, Stephen. You know me. I have difficulty connecting with quality people."

"And what is she supposed to be teaching my children? Certainly not respect for their elders."

"French. Yes, French. Mainly French."

"I'm not sure she belongs here, Marie. Of course

you are welcome to stay, but the bitch doesn't seem to really serve any purpose."

"Because I won't lick your cock and spread my legs?" Babette rose up onto her knees.

"She stays, Stephen. I have need of her. She'll stay in her room most of the time. I'd advise you to avoid this part of the house. Babette and I like our privacy. No, we absolutely need our privacy."

Stephen turned and walked out of the room. Immediately Marie ran to close the door. When she returned to the bed, she reached out and wound Babette's red hair around her fingers.

"Idiot! Your cockiness will ruin our plan. And, by the way, don't try any of that lip with Louis. It will drive him away. You want to seduce men, Babette, not belittle them."

"They do that themselves."

"Even if they do, you can't. Dominate them, spit on them, but never let them know that you don't treasure their cocks. Make them work for their pleasure, but never make them crawl farther than they want to go."

"And what about Monsieur Sade? How far will he crawl? How much of my blood must he drink before he's truly dead?"

"He will drink you dry, child, and savor every moment of his own pain."

Chapter Twenty-three

The doorbell rang, and the contents of Gillian's stomach rose up into her mouth. Slowly, she crossed the living room, hoping that the person would go away. But if it was who she thought it was, he wouldn't leave. She opened the door only a crack.

"Gillian, you look lovely. At least your left eye does."

"Louis, why are you here?"

"To pay a visit." He nudged the door all the way open and took her free hand in his to kiss the palm. "Ah, a new scent. Very different from the one you wore the last time we were in bed together."

"Quiet! That was only once."

"And not enough."

"Are you here to take Marie away?"

"Oh, Marie and I have been on the outs lately. I don't think she would go anywhere with me."

"Then why are you here?"

"To snatch some time in bed with you again." His blue eyes twinkled. "Stop being so uptight, Gillian. Certainly Stephen isn't uptight when he's traveling." He walked past her and into the house.

"Uncle Louis."

"Is that disappointment I hear in your voice, Chuckie? No hug and kiss?"

"You don't want me to do that."

"So tiny and yet so perceptive."

"Aunt Marie is upstairs. She brought some lady with her."

"And you and your mother seem to be delighted about that. Gillian, I'm not going to be fighting any battles in this house."

"Then leave," she said.

"And where's your little Lolita, Vanessa? Ah, Roger is the third one, isn't he?"

"Roger's at school," answered Chuckie.

"How many years has he been in school?"

"He likes school," said Chuckie.

"Vanessa. Is she still trying to get her tits to grow and her rear end to take shape?"

The toddler chuckled until his mother swiped him across the back of his head.

"Does Stephen still keep Pinch around the house? It would be in the living room, wouldn't it?" He walked to his left and peeked into the room. "And no doubt this is Stephen in the Barcalounger.

Don't get up, just tell me where the Pinch and a glass can be found."

Gillian put her arm around her son's shoulders. "Maybe we will have a vampire body for you."

"But he's an old man. What about sowing my oats in my youth, Mom?"

"Little man, did I hear you speak of sowing oats?" Sade turned toward Chuckie. "And of course Marie has told you, Gillian, about her transformation. You've actually seen proof of it." Sade looked over at Chuckie's mother and gave her a wink.

Stephen looked as flummoxed as he usually felt when at home.

"Where did he come from?" Stephen asked his wife.

"Paris," Sade replied. "Don't get up to shake hands, Stephen. We're such old friends, it isn't necessary."

Sade found the whiskey and poured himself three full fingers. He raised the glass to his audience and downed the liquid in one swallow.

"Gee, Louis, I'm sorry I won't be staying, but I have a sales trip planned . . ."

"You canceled that trip. Don't you remember, dear?" Gillian's voice cracked the air like a whip.

"Ah, that's a bit of a disappointment, Stephen. I had hopes of luring Gillian into bed. If you insist on staying home, it will make it inconvenient, but still doable."

"Marie is upstairs on the third floor. The farthest bedroom down the hall," Stephen said.

"Hmm. I guess I should take the basement, then. As I recall, it was pleasantly furnished. The moose head and Scandinavian furniture are such a change from my usual surroundings. It will really feel like I'm away from home. But that is sort of your retreat, isn't it, Stephen? The well-worn carpet shows the tread marks of a contained wild animal."

"You may stay in the basement," said Gillian. "The children have their rooms on this floor, but they can be moved to our floor, dear."

"What for?" Stephen asked.

"They'll be less bothersome to Louis that way."

"What is that American term? Circling the wagons. Is that what you are doing, Gillian?" asked Sade, turning his back to pour himself another glass of whiskey.

"Mom, I think he's starting to bald in the back. I'd prefer a full head of hair."

"Your father certainly has a thick mane, Chuckie. Just the kind of hair you'd like. Girls could run their fingers through the grease. Ah, but maybe your sanitary habits would improve if you were older and could reach the faucets." Sade turned his head and gave Chuckie a small smile.

"Let me show you to the basement, Louis."

"Gillian, I didn't suspect you were in such a rush. Please ignore any of the noises that come from the basement, Stephen. Oh, and you may not see Gillian for a day or two."

Chapter Twenty-four

"Cripes, are you gonna let Mom go down to the basement alone with him?"

"Chuckie, your mother has always been capable of putting a man in his place. I know from experience."

"Yeah, but this is the Marquis de Sade."

"And not your limp old man; is that what you're saying, Chuckie?"

"Kinda."

"He's here. I can smell him." Marie walked gingerly into the room.

"He's down in the basement with Mom."

"Did you allow her to go down there alone, Stephen?"

"Since when has my wife become a delicate blossom?"

"It has nothing to do with flower buds. Louis might turn her against you, against all of us." Marie made elaborate hand movements that caused dust particles to rise and spread.

"He's here for you, Marie. Louis doesn't give a fig about us. He never would have visited if you weren't here. Do we ever hear from Uncle Louis, Chuckie?" His son shook his head. "Do we ever invite Uncle Louis to visit?" Chuckie shook his head with more energy. "We don't invite you either, Marie, but that doesn't matter. You feel free to walk into our house any time you're running away from trouble. Thus our quiet home becomes a stadium for your battles."

Marie knelt next to Stephen's ear.

"I might not come back if Louis were not able to chase after me. What I need is a cohort." Chuckie attempted to snuggle close to Marie. "Someone more than two feet tall," she said, waving the toddler away with her hand.

"What if you and your cohort fail?" asked Stephen.

"Fail?"

"You have many times. How many of your cohorts are no longer material flesh?"

"Babette's up in her bedroom pouting."

"Give it time. She'll be dead before she ever gets to go back home. And you don't care."

"But I care about you, Stephen." Marie reached out and drew her long, glossy nails through Stephen's hair. "Haven't I proven that many times?"

"Before you arrived, Chuckie reminded me of

112

how you treated me the last time we were in Florida."

"The blowtorch. An accident. I only wanted to frighten you with a big flash. I didn't know you were so flammable. Must have been all the alcohol you had. You must have breathed out at the wrong moment."

Chuckie giggled and was rewarded with stern glares.

"Stephen, why didn't you come with . . ." Gillian noticed the intimate tableaux of Stephen and Marie. "Am I intruding, Marie? Did you need more time alone with my husband?"

Marie stood.

"I've had plenty of time with Stephen, and it's all been wasted."

Marie walked over and patted Chuckie on the head, whispering, "Come see me later."

She turned to Gillian. "Should I go visit Louis now, or is he not in the mood for company after you rejected him?"

"I can't imagine why you'd want to see him. However, it might speed things up if you went down now."

"We could rip each other to pieces in your basement. Messy, Gillian, very messy. Out of respect for my hosts, I shall return to my bedroom and fit the door with a new lock."

"Don't you dare mar the paint," shouted Gillian.

Marie turned to Stephen. "How can you stand it?"

Stephen shrugged.

After Marie had left the room, Gillian suggested that Chuckie go to his room to play.

"What the hell for? I'm part of this stupid family. I have a right to know what kind of plotting is taking place. Hell, maybe you could even use me as a spy. I could swoop into Aunt Marie's room, curl myself into a ball, hide under the bed, and eavesdrop."

"The things you'd learn under her bed your father already knows."

Stephen moaned and rose from the Barcalounger.

"I need some air."

Chapter Twenty-five

The moon was so bright that daylight seemed to have refused to quit. The sprinkler system had just bathed the soil, causing Stephen's shoeless feet to get wet instantly. He knew that Sade, like Marie, would unobtrusively sneak his coffin into the house. Coffins were almost like dirty laundry. Shifting them from one place to another was a necessity, but no vampire wanted to advertise his or her vulnerability. In the hush of night, a vampire would sneak into his new abode with a coffin weighing down his or her back.

Stephen had gotten used to traveling without his coffin. A suitcase partially filled with soil was all he needed. Lord knew what the chambermaids thought of the filth he left behind in his sheets.

Stephen took a step and heard the crack and

squish of a snail underfoot. He cleaned his foot against the wet grass, cursing country life as he did.

He heard a high-pitched whistling come from the side of the house. He didn't recognize the tune, but he guessed it sounded French. He was about to turn back when he reminded himself that Marie was going to her room, and the pitch was too high and sweet for Sade. He decided to take a chance and turned the corner of the house.

Babette was clipping the rosebushes with a pair of rusted shears from the toolshed. She wore a peasant-style dress that was almost as white as her flesh.

"I know what you are."

Babette twisted away from the rosebush she had been pruning and faced Stephen.

"I know exactly what you are," he repeated.

"What am I?"

"I have been acquainted with Marie for many years and know her lifestyle."

"What am I?" Babette repeated.

"You're her lover." Stephen gave her a broad, confident smile.

"Am I?"

"Admit it. You're not here solely to distract Louis. You and Marie have separate rooms, but I hear the doors click closed and the floors squeak."

"You think I climb into Marie's coffin to comfort her during her daylight sleep."

"Comfort?" he laughed. "More than that. You satisfy her."

"With my mouth? With my fingers? With one of your vibrating dildos?"

"All of the above. Before I go to my deep sleep, I imagine the two of you entwined, licking, poking, kissing. Even now it makes me hard thinking of it. All you need do is feel me to know I'm telling the truth."

Babette weighed the shears in her right hand. She allowed the shears to slip from her fingers and heard the muffled sound they made on the lush bed of grass.

Stephen waited expectantly for her to step forward.

"Do you want my blood?" she asked.

"A taste. Just a taste to enhance my orgasm. You have to be missing the real thing by now."

"Are you real?" she asked.

"My cock is."

"Let's see."

Stephen laughed. "How about we find a private place where the neighbors . . ."

"And your wife . . ."

"And Gillian and the children can't see."

"I'm not going anywhere unless I know it's worthwhile."

Stephen looked around nervously. The neighbors were probably in bed, watching a late-night show. Gillian and the children . . . What the hell, he could say he was taking a piss when Babette happened upon him. He unzipped his pants, and his erection proudly advertised itself.

"How about we go to the base . . ." Stephen remembered his unwanted guest. "The toolshed."

"Isn't that what little boys say to girls?"

"I'm not a *little* boy," Stephen answered. "I'm a cautious man."

"Then you should put your dick away and zip up your fly," said Sade, standing behind Stephen.

"I came out here to get away from everyone."

"Now, Stephen, that's not quite true. Babette seems to have captured your attention to the point that you're begging," said Sade.

Stephen closed his eyes. His penis had already folded back inside his pants, and he simply zipped his fly. He stooped and picked up the shears that Babette had dropped.

"I'll return these for you."

"Ah, Stephen, you are a gentleman after all." Sade patted Stephen's back.

Stephen twirled around to face Sade with the shears upraised in both his hands.

"Shame that these are so rusty, Louis. Otherwise I'd snip your head off. So many of us would be relieved." Stephen lowered the shears and walked toward the toolshed.

"Why did you protect him?" Babette asked.

"Maybe I thirst for all your blood, Babette, and don't want to share a drop with anyone else." Sade reached out and touched her red hair. "Are you a witch, Babette, or are you an innocent being misled by the demon?"

"Marie is no greater a demon than you, Monsieur Sade."

Sade rubbed the strands of her hair between his

right index finger and thumb. Quickly, he tugged, carrying away several strands. Instinctively, Babette stepped away from him.

"I'll sleep with these wrapped around . . . *Mais attente,* I'll let your imagination soar." He smiled and was about to walk away when Babette grabbed at his left arm.

"I'm not a witch that you can counter with poppy dolls. Attaching those few hairs to a crude imitation of me won't save you."

"Voodoo, *ma chére,* is a petty sport to play. My powers exceed what simple articles can do." He put his right hand around her throat. "The power is inside me, Babette." His hand tightened. "With one hand you are no more." He shoved her against a tree. His mouth met hers, and he bit her lips until they opened. His tongue stretched deep into her mouth as his hand tightened even more. He felt her attempting to gasp for air, but she didn't fight him off. He let her go. "You're deader than I am, Babette."

Chapter Twenty-six

Chuckie's small fist rapped upon Marie's bedroom door. He kept checking over his shoulder to make sure that none of his family caught him. The sound he made was soft, almost silent, compared to the creaks made by the house itself. He knocked rapidly once more before Marie opened the door.

"Chuckie! My favorite little man. Come in."

He rushed into her room and willed her to immediately close the door. But she stood at the door and peeked out into the hall.

"You haven't seen Babette, have you?"

"No, Aunt Marie." Chuckie rolled backward and forward on the balls of his feet.

"Makes me nervous when I don't know where she is or what she's doing."

Eventually she closed the door, too loudly for Chuckie.

"Now, little man." She lifted Chuckie off the ground and stood him on top of her coffin. "Why are you here?"

"You invited me." Anxiety made him jittery, and he lost his balance.

"Oooops! Be careful," she said, reaching out and capturing him by his shirt collar. His feet skidded on the coffin's shiny surface. "Do I make you nervous, Chuckie?"

His head shook too fast for it to be a well-thought-out response.

"Maybe we should put little suction cups on the soles of your shoes. You'd be like a car ornament, except you'd be on my coffin."

"I don't want to decorate anything, Aunt Marie."

"What do you want?"

"You know. You had a similar problem, except instead of being a toddler, you were an old lady." Chuckie's eyes were soft and honest.

"I was a more mature woman than what I appear to be now. *Old lady* is way too harsh. You should really learn to be more tactful."

"You're not."

"I don't have to be. It's you, Chuckie, who must learn to deal with the dullards of the world. You can't even kick someone in the shins."

Chuckie attempted a kick and almost made contact with her chin. Instead he landed on his ass.

"You're quite a gymnast. If I help you up, would you like to try it again?"

"Aunt Marie, why did you want to see me?" His rear smarted so bad he didn't want to move.

"Like a fairy godmother, I want to grant you a wish."

"Any wish?"

Marie reached out and grabbed a long slender vibrator that had been sitting on the dresser.

"Think of this as a magic wand. Many people do."

"I want to be tall enough to get respect and old enough that I don't have to yammer like a baby anymore."

"You want a new body." Marie flicked on the vibrator, which whirred until she switched it off. "My wand would be happy to grant your wish."

"But I don't want Uncle Louis's body. He's too old. I want Dad's."

"This sounds Oedipal, Chuckie. Perhaps your mother wouldn't approve of the switch."

"Mom wouldn't have to know. I'd look and sound like Dad, only I'd be a nicer person."

"More compassionate, you mean." She put the vibrator down on the coffin.

"And I wouldn't have to drink stinky animal blood."

"Yes, human blood is far superior." She cocked one of her eyebrows.

"What's it taste like?"

"Mother never let you have any?"

"No, but she doesn't stop Dad from glutting himself on it."

"Wouldn't Gillian miss her little boy?"

"Maybe we could blame my demise on Vanessa."

"But she's such a charming girl. Who would believe that?"

"Mom, if it was presented just right."

"And you'll leave that in my hands?"

"Don't have to. When I come back as Dad, I can break it to Mom."

"Don't mind breaking her heart, do you?"

"Only temporarily. I'll be so nice to her that she'll forget about everyone else." Chuckie inched his legs over the side of the coffin.

"Need help getting down?" Marie asked.

Chuckie checked the height of the jump he'd have to make and scratched his head. He hated to ask for help, especially from Aunt Marie, but wasn't that what he was doing anyway?

"Yes." Chuckie reached out his arms toward Marie and waited for thirty seconds before dropping his arms back by his side. "You don't really want to help me, do you?"

"I want to make a trade. I'll stake your father and chop your little head off if you assist me in ridding the world of Louis. And if you do a very good job, I'll even put your head in Stephen's coffin."

"That's the important part," whispered Chuckie.

"Oh, make no mistake, each is equally important. You'd never be able to overcome your father's spirit if he weren't staked. And I believe your spirit has to be looking for a home in order to take over another body. This is all conjecture, of course. I obtained a new body by pure luck."

The frown on Chuckie's face bordered on a cry. He would have to put his existence in the hands of an immoral woman in order to steal a bastard's body. Life seemed so dirty and almost hopeless. Almost. There was still the possibility that Aunt Marie would live up to the deal.

"I can't destroy Sade." He verbalized the fact that had suddenly popped into his mind.

"I want your assistance. I don't expect you to destroy your uncle. Wouldn't be very nice to ask a young child to do that. No, I just want to know that you'll give whatever help I ask for. It may be as minor as distracting your uncle's attention or as great as holding the weapon for me. My plans are not fully formed as yet."

"I'm not fully formed yet either; that's why I'll go along with you."

"Never tell anyone about this conversation. Not only would I be in trouble, but I don't need to tell you how badly Stephen would take being condemned by his own flesh and blood. He's not a very forgiving father, is he?"

"He doesn't like me."

"Well, certainly our plan wouldn't help endear you to him."

Chuckie rubbed his nose hard and sighed.

"Second thoughts?" Marie folded her arms and looked at Chuckie. She had to unfold her arms and reach out to grab each of his legs in order to stop him from kicking the coffin with the heels of his shoes.

"I want to grow up," Chuckie said sadly.

Marie lifted him off the coffin and, right before releasing him, gave him a hug. A hug that lasted so short a time that he almost missed it.

Chapter Twenty-seven

"I'm going to run away from home."

Vanessa had broken the handle of a broom in two and was now shaving down a point on one end, so intent on her mission that she didn't bother to question her brother.

"Did you hear me, Vanessa? I'm running away from home."

"When?"

"Probably by the end of the week. I have a date tomorrow night."

"Good luck."

"Doesn't anyone care about seeing me go?"

"Roger, you've been miserable for years. Always trying to be like the kids in school. Learning the same shit over and over again, just so you can make believe you're mortal again. Don't you ever get bored talking to twelve-year-olds? Lord, you're over a century old; how can you stand those infantile brains?"

"They like me," he answered. "Most of them like me. There's always a bully who thinks I'm too smart."

"The bully is right, Roger. You don't belong with twelve-year-olds. You can outdo Dad at chess. Fix Mom's computer. Use psychology on Chuckie to make the little worm reasonable. Don't you want to do more than skateboarding and Little League?"

"Adults see us only as children, you know that. We're no more than our parents' property. Dad could slap you or me in a store and no one would say anything. Maybe Chuckie could get a rise out of onlookers, only because he's so small."

"Chuckie," she growled. "Amaze people, Roger. Go out and be a child genius."

"You mean a child prodigy."

"Yes. Make everyone admire you."

"What about the fact that I'll never grow old?"

"Tell them you have some physical condition that keeps you young."

"Great. They'll instantly dissect me. Besides, I'm not looking for fame."

"What are you looking for?" Vanessa asked.

Roger carefully mulled over his sister's question. He even began pacing the room.

"I know what you want, Roger. You want to be unvampirized. You don't want to live forever. You want to be part of society. A good, productive citizen having friends, raising a family, watching the grandkids take over for you, and finally meeting the Lord in heaven. You are a bore, Roger." Vanessa kept shaving the broomstick in her hand into a sharpened point.

"Don't you miss any of that, Vanessa?"

"Give me tits and an ass, and I'll be happy."

"That thing you're making looks like a stake."

"Right. See, you're as smart as I said." Vanessa blew wood chips off her lap.

"Do you intend to get rid of our guests?"

"Aunt Marie and Uncle Louis? Nah, they don't bother me."

Silence smothered the room while Vanessa admired her work.

"You know, Chuckie kinda has it worse than us. I mean, he's so small, and there's something creepy about a toddler with an adult mind," said Roger.

"Sure is."

"Is that stake for Chuckie?" he asked.

Vanessa looked into Roger's eyes and gave him a broad smile.

"Mom's not going to be happy about losing Chuckie."

Vanessa's grin drew wider and she raised the other half of the broom, and Roger could see that she had already whittled it into a fine point.

Chapter Twenty-eight

Cindy skipped down the road. She had orders to fill. Orders that had been made months ago. Most of the neighbors had been generous and bought more than one box of cookies. Several houses had been empty, and she wondered whether she should knock on those doors again. The contest was over, and she had already won, but there were cookies to sell year-round.

She came upon a leaning picket fence with most of the white paint worn off the old slats of wood. Small bushes anchored the landscaping on both sides of the fence. The house was white, with forest-green shutters decorating the windows. Lace curtains filmed the glass panes. A large doormat had curlicues of ivy trimming its borders.

This house had been vacant on the several tries

she had made. No one knew much about the people who lived there. They seemed quiet, and had a slim twelve-year-old who played on the school's softball team. Twelve, an older man. She'd have to wait another four years before she'd turn twelve, and by then he'd be interested in sixteen-year-old girls. Cindy sighed.

A bush rustled to her right, and she stopped to peer into the branches. A toddler was digging in the soil and hadn't noticed her presence.

"What'cha doing?"

The toddler quickly looked up into her face.

"Who the he . . ." The toddler stopped talking and began to gurgle and giggle.

Again she asked her question. This time the toddler gave an answer.

"Digging up lunch."

"Oooo! That's a fat worm you have in your hand."

"Care to join me?" The toddler stood and jabbed the worm into her face before she had time to back away.

Cindy's eyes went round and her stomach pumped the vestiges of her breakfast into her mouth. She managed to swallow several times, and by the time she stepped away from the toddler her stomach had calmed.

"Do you live here?" she asked.

The toddler nodded his head.

"So you have a brother named Roger?"

"So what?"

"Do you think your mother would like to buy some cookies?"

"Go knock at the door and ask."

"I won't be disturbing her?"

"Everything bothers Mom right now, including me sometimes."

"Then maybe I should wait." Cindy turned to face the road again.

"No, don't go away. I've . . . I've got some money; maybe I could buy your cookies."

"How old are you?" she asked.

"I look younger than I am, and besides, I take money out of Mom's pocketbook all the time."

"That's terrible. You shouldn't be doing that."

"Why not? It saves time having to ask her."

"But she may not want you to have the money."

"Why not?"

"Ma says children should always ask permission." Cindy lifted her head righteously.

"I'm special."

"I think you're just being a bad boy." She folded her arms across her chest.

"Do you want to sell cookies?"

She nodded.

"Than why do you care where the money comes from?"

"Because I shouldn't be encouraging you to do something bad."

"You want to meet my brother?"

Cindy felt her face flush. Roger never noticed her, and they had nothing in common, so this might be her only chance to at least be introduced.

"You've got a crush on my brother, don't you? You look all icky, the way older people get sometimes."

"I have to go pick up my cookies, and I have a lot of orders to fill."

"Before you go, how about coming into the house? I can at least show you his room."

Cindy shook her head. "He probably wouldn't like that."

"He'll never know. He's not even home."

"I thought you said you were gonna introduce me to him." She creased her forehead into a frown.

The toddler suddenly rubbed his nose violently. When he finished, he looked much calmer.

"Could you walk me to the house, at least?"

"Why? You're only a short walk from the front door. Are you trying to get me to follow you into the house?"

"I'm alone and wanted some company."

"Where's your mother?"

"There was an emergency, and she had to run off."

"And left you alone? You're too young to be alone. I'd never leave my baby sister alone. How could she do that? Want me to go get my mother?"

"Naw, just come into the house and spend some time with me."

"I'm not allowed in other people's houses." She thought for a few seconds. How dangerous could it be to spend some time with a toddler? After she played a game with him, maybe he'd let her call her mother, and she'd know what to do.

"I'll come in for just a little bit."

The toddler's eyes sparkled, and he made a stubby run for the garden gate to let her in.

"Thank you," she said. "I'm Cindy, and what's your name?"

"Chuckie."

Chapter Twenty-nine

Babette watched the children from her bedroom window. She hid behind the folds of lace, making sure that neither child could see her. Chuckie obviously had decided that it was time to taste human blood. She had never seen such a thin little girl; but then, the girl hardly ever remained still. Even with her arms folded, she managed to hop around in place. *Eager* would describe the little girl. Eager to die.

The foolish girl patted Chuckie on the head as if he were an innocent pup. Stupid child deserves to die; can't live long in this world when you're so vulnerable. Chuckie pulled on the girl's pleated skirt when she started to pick wild flowers from the front of the house. He tugged so hard that one side of the skirt waist slipped down onto the girl's shapeless hip. Annoyed, the girl almost turned to go, but Chuckie managed to squeeze out a few tears—just enough to make her feel like a heel for leaving.

Babette watched the predator-and-prey game closely until the children disappeared onto the porch. The front door slammed. Babette moved to her door and put her ear to it. Too silent, she thought. Kids should be making more noise, unless you were a child doing what your mother had told you not to do. Should she scare the girl away and offer him her blood? Marie had warned against that. Marie believed the Hugheses' tolerance would vanish if one of their children were to be destroyed. Was the girl's life worth potentially losing her opportunity to rid the world of Sade? She could scare away the girl and only give Chuckie a verbal warning.

She heard a crash and undid the lock on her door to investigate. In the hall a glass vase lay shattered on the pine floor. Water seeped into the crevices between the slats, and flowers wreathed a dark scene.

The girl lay on the floor, barely moving, and Chuckie lay atop her sucking the blood out of her neck. He looked like a plump spider feeding.

Barefoot, Babette stepped on a shard of glass and squeaked out her pain and surprise. Without removing his mouth from the girl's throat, he looked up at her. He snarled like an animal, showing baby teeth that did not suit the situation. The girl weakly kicked her legs, and her eyes rolled back in her head.

Babette dropped to her knees and reached out to touch Chuckie's shoulder, but his growl warned her off. The girl reached up and grabbed a chunk of Chuckie's hair, attempting to pull him off. The hand weakened and eventually came away from his skull with his thin blond hair wrapped around several fingers.

"What do you do now, Chuckie?" Babette asked.

Sucking noises became louder. The girl was dead. Her parents would go to the police, and they would comb the area.

"Chuckie, what do you do now? She's dead. What will you do with her body?"

Finally he took his mouth away from the flesh. Tears had formed in his eyes. His bloodied bottom lip began to quiver. The small baby teeth were caked with blood. His small fat fingers touched the girl's skirt, her blouse, and finally attempted to lift her by the shoulders.

An earthworm wiggled out of his pants pocket. It slid down the denim material and wrapped around his naked ankle. Chuckie reached for the worm and gently petted it.

"I have to take the worm back outside. Let it live." He rose to his feet and very carefully carried the worm down the stairs. He disappeared, and then the front door clicked open.

Babette didn't hear the door close.

"The next time will be easier," she whispered, thinking about the vampires she had destroyed in

136

the past. But they had fought harder and longer than the little girl. Their bodies had twisted into deformed shapes with the cramping caused by her blood. Some had promised to share their gift, and their eyes reflected disbelief even as their bodies emptied. They had offered to make her one of them. They would have gifted her with a new existence. Others raged when they realized that their kill had escaped. And then they were still, just like the little girl. Not peaceful, but still, the contorted faces frozen into grimaces forevermore.

Chapter Thirty

"What are you doing?"

Marie stood hovering over Babette and the dead body.

"I'm keeping vigil," answered Babette. "She's dead. Someone should watch over her."

"If she's dead, it's not necessary. How did she die?"

"Chuckie."

Marie burst into laughter.

"The baby punk is really going to need my help," Marie said. "Does he know you saw him?"

"He spoke to me. Said he had to go out to free an earthworm. He won't be back for a long time."

"Yes, he will." Marie stomped down the steps, calling out Gillian's name.

Babette encircled the child with her own body

and lay still beside it. *Where do they go?* she wondered. When they close their eyes, or even when they refuse to let the sight of earth disappear, where do they go? Did her victims share the same heaven as this little girl? Or did they disperse into the air, becoming part of the earth? Where did they go?

"Liar," Gillian screeched from the kitchen. "Bitch" was the next word.

Babette put her fingers to the girl's neck and tried to close the open wound. A pink tint smeared across the girl's neck. The body remained slightly warm. Pounding footsteps drew Babette out of her reverie.

Gillian screamed as Marie kept pushing her toward the body.

"Just see what your baby boy did."

"He's sorry," Babette said. "I know he is. He went outside to return a worm to the earth."

Marie laughed. "He certainly returned this poor girl to the earth."

"Babette, did you see what happened?" asked Gillian.

"She witnessed the entire act," stated Marie.

"Did you?" Gillian's eyes narrowed.

Babette nodded.

Gillian grabbed for Babette and kept asking, "Why didn't you stop him?" Gillian's fingers bit into Babette's flesh, making indentations into bleeding cuts.

Babette didn't fight back. She waited. Would this woman's rage cause her to feed? Would her tongue touch the flesh and blood under her fingernails and spawn a hunger that would make her feed?

"What the hell is going on?" Stephen grabbed his wife's shoulders and lifted her off the entwined bodies on the floor. He wrapped his arms around his wife and held on with all his strength. Gillian had always had spurts of strength that had frightened him, but this seemed worse than every other time. "Dammit, Marie, explain what's going on. What did your bitch do to rile Gillian up like this?"

"Nothing, really. Chuckie is the one responsible for the dead body on the floor."

Babette rolled over, revealing the little girl. The girl's body was colder, but there still was no peace on the child's face.

"This makes no sense. What the hell did Chuckie do? He couldn't . . . Damn, did that boy sneak some human blood for himself?" He looked at Marie, and she nodded.

"She watched it happen and didn't stop him," Gillian kept repeating.

"That does surprise me, Babette. Why did you let him finish?" Marie asked.

"He wasn't a child but a beast. An animal doing what animals naturally do. Devour their prey."

"My son is not an animal, you freak." Gillian tried kicking at the bodies on the floor.

"Calm down," Stephen said. "We have to find out whether anyone saw her come into this house. If so . . ."

"If so . . . what?" Gillian was tugging at her husband's hands.

"We should move on. It's time."

"If we run, they'll suspect us."

"Yes, Gillian, but if we stay, we may all be destroyed. I should go back to doing my job . . ."

A wild scream broke from Gillian's lungs. "Leave us, you bastard."

"I'm not abandoning my family, Gillian. We need to make our lives seem as normal as possible. Perhaps even send the boy away." Another scream from Gillian caused Stephen to let her go. "Calm down."

Gillian stood in the center of the group and looked at each face. Her rigid body seemed immovable. Her flesh had a bluish tinge, and her tightly closed fists emphasized each white knuckle of her hands. Her eyes saw only strangers. Her nostrils flared wide like an undomesticated animal's. She worried her bottom lip, causing some of the skin to peel off and dangle around the edges of her mouth.

"Mom?"

Roger's voice took her away from the strangers. "Mom? What's wrong?"

Gillian turned to her son and pulled him into a hug. Freeing him, she wrapped her palms around his face. "Where's your brother?"

"I don't know. He was in the front yard when I last saw him."

Gillian released him and ran down the stairs, leaving the strangers to explain what had happened.

"It couldn't have been Chuckie. He's the littlest

one." Roger looked from face to face, hoping to find an answer.

"Chuckie is strong, Roger. Stronger than a little girl." Stephen couldn't reach out to his son. Couldn't hold the boy he had fathered. He hardly knew the boy. He simply passed in and out of his son's life.

Babette had her arms wrapped around the little girl and rocked her back and forth.

"Maybe it's time to run away from home, Roger. We haven't done much for you as parents. And now it seems Chuckie will bring the law down on this neighborhood, and probably on us in particular, since we don't tend to socialize much."

"I can't leave Mom now."

"When will you be able to leave, Roger? If everything were going smoothly, you wouldn't want to leave."

"But Mom's not going to be able to accept this."

"She'll have Chuckie as her consolation prize, son."

"Don't tell Vanessa, Dad."

"Why not? Wouldn't you be angry if I kept a secret like this from you?" Stephen laughed. "What the hell am I talking about? This will never be a secret to anyone inside this house."

"I'm certainly not good at keeping secrets," Marie said.

Chapter Thirty-one

Chuckie ran around to the side of the house and tripped on the mesh screen that usually covered the entrance to the crawlspace. *Usually* wasn't the correct word, he thought; *occasionally* suited the situation better. His dad would spend ten to fifteen minutes fiddling with the screen, announce that it was repaired, and within the next few days they could hear cats meowing from underneath the house. Once a gray speckled cat gave birth to nine kittens in the crawlspace, and as a treat, Chuckie's mother didn't tell the other children, so every one of the kittens was his. The mother abandoned her litter once she saw his head poking in through the hole. He hadn't even found it necessary to go all the way under the house, since the mother cat had placed her litter within his own mom's reach.

No one would look for him in the crawlspace. No one beside himself would be able to comfortably move around in it. He didn't like the idea of dirt, but he couldn't face his mom right now. As he crawled through the opening, his denim jeans caught on a nail and ripped. Toddler jeans just weren't made to last. He managed to fit himself between an old ladder and a rake that was missing several teeth. He peered into the depths and realized that there was a lot of crap stored under the house. None of it belonged to his family. A daddy longlegs brushed against Chuckie's hand on its way to hiding under the ladder. Chuckie grabbed the spider before it could disappear.

"Where are you going? I could use a good guide, if you wouldn't mind spending time with a murderer."

He mentally kicked himself. He was a vampire. It was his job to kill. It wasn't his fault that he needed blood from other living beings. He only followed his instincts. A sigh escaped his lips as he thought about how he had killed Cindy. He wished she hadn't told him her name. He didn't even get a proper taste of her blood, because he was in such a frenzy. All he knew was that the blood seemed to sit like cement in his tummy. He burped and wished Mom was there to pound on his back.

The spider climbed up his arm. When it reached Chuckie's elbow, it either fell or jumped down onto the dry soil, where Chuckie stomped his booted foot on it.

He continued to go deeper into the crawlspace.

He hoped he could find an area in which he wouldn't be seen. A small rat peeked up through the inside of a skull. An animal skull, he knew. It had the shape of a cat's head.

"That's called getting even, all right."

The rat's nose shivered, catching Chuckie's scent, and it reburied itself under some loose debris.

"Yeah, you know it's the mighty Chuckie coming through."

His foot slipped on something squishy. He reached down with his right index finger to wipe up the crud and brought it to his mouth for a taste. Squirrel, he thought, and carried on with his travel.

He was almost to the other side of the house when he spotted several skeletons clustered together. On closer inspection, he realized the bones were human. Two adults and a child, he mused. People just didn't crawl under a house to die, he thought, no, they were probably murdered. One adult had a huge crack in the skull. The other two offered no indication of how they had died.

Chuckie rubbed off the film of webs that had collected on his hair, wiping the goo onto his jeans.

"Chuckie!" His mother's voice reached him. "Chuckie!" And then, on the third "Chuckie," he heard his mother's voice crack. The sound of sobs followed.

Should he yell out and let her know where he was? Should he hold out, hoping that the longer she missed him, the less pissed she'd be? He wasn't above lying and saying that he hadn't heard her.

A second voice had joined his mother's in a chorus of yelling his name. Roger sounded almost as desperate as his mother. Why? Probably because he wanted to help his mother. He certainly had never demonstrated a strong love for Chuckie himself. Chuckie inched his way to the back wall. A pentagram was painted on the wall in a red-tinted color. Blood? he wondered. He stuck out his tongue and ran it over the pentagram. Tasteless, except for a few ants that happened to be wandering by. He wished he could remember the flavor of Cindy's blood. He might never have the nerve to take that kind of chance again, especially after his father paddled his bottom raw.

Would his family move away and leave him all by himself? He'd better be prepared to turn on his toddler charm. What little was left of it. People mentioned noticing something in his eyes, a maturity way beyond his years. His mother always covered by saying he tested on the genius level. He doubted anyone bought that.

Chuckie sat down and heard a crunching sound.

What the hell did he sit on now?

Lifting himself slightly, he caught sight of a skeletal hand.

The place was infested with dead bodies, or at least what was left of the bodies. The renter before them must have been a serial killer, or maybe he ran some crematory business and saved money on fuel by storing the bodies under the house. How could he use this knowledge to save his own ass? Great! *We can stick Cindy's body under the house,*

146

and when it starts smelling, the police can come and find her body. Everyone in the family could act shocked and claim some stranger must have been storing bodies here for years. He knew there was a flaw to this idea but allowed himself to block out the truth.

"Chuckie!"

Damn! His father was out searching for him, too. He didn't want Dad to be the first to find him, so he leaned back against a cement block and waited.

Chapter Thirty-two

"What shall we do with the body?" Babette asked.

"Nothing. Leave it there. It's the poor family Hughes's problem. Nothing to do with us."

"But the police will come and check us out also."

"Who said we were staying, Babette? Do you think I'm stupid enough to support a bunch of imbeciles like the Hughes family? I want my casket out of here as soon as possible."

"What about Sade? How will we destroy him?"

"If not here, then someplace else. You'd better get your things together, unless prison appeals to you. Doubt any vampires live in prison. You'd get awfully bored."

"We brought trouble into this family. We should help in some way."

"We didn't do a thing except pay a friendly visit."

"That's not true. You planned to have a confrontation with Sade inside this house."

"But I didn't tell the grubby little brat to drink another kid's blood. The family is at fault. They should have taught him to be cautious. Banning an action doesn't prevent it from happening. Parents should prepare their children for worst-case scenarios."

"Did you prepare your daughter for her marriage with Sade?"

"I wasn't the perfect mother, but I protected her in my own way. And I made sure my grandchildren spent as little time with their father as I could arrange. Seeing to it that Sade bounced from one prison to another to finally the insane asylum wasn't easy. Bribery and favors became daily activities for me. My poor husband hardly ever saw me."

"Why don't we kill the Hughes family ourselves? Leaving them here could bring up a lot of questions if the police point a finger at them."

"You're dying to seduce Stephen, aren't you? I must say he's worth the effort, but the final outcome would be such a waste. You'd never be able to bed him without giving up some of your blood. I can attest to that. His teeth biting into my neck, his penis inside my . . . But I'm going off to memory lane."

"Sounds like you're the one who wants to bed him again."

Marie stood taller and took the time to measure the width of her hips with her hands.

"Horrid wife would make such a fuss. She's such

149

an uptight prig. Yes, it's because of her that the family finds themselves in so much trouble now. Didn't teach her children the importance of dining away from home.

"By the way, has Sade taken any interest in you, Babette?"

"He knows I'm poison."

"How?"

"He senses that there is something strange about me. He would like to take my blood but fears that he may have to pay the consequences."

"He's always been astute about things like that. Actually, this trait arose after he had been incarcerated a few times. I guess he learned his lesson. Mmmm. Why don't you tell Sade what has happened? Elaborate a bit. Talk about the pain the girl went through and the way Chuckie attempted to fuck her."

"He didn't."

"Elaborate. Didn't you hear me the first time? Fondle his appetite to the ultimate climax."

"What if my blood doesn't poison him?"

"Then you've failed and will suffer the penalty of death, since he'll drain you dry."

"He'll still come after you."

"By then it won't be your problem."

Babette looked down at the dead child. Still, there was no peace. The child's face stayed frozen in fear. Babette wondered whether the child now worried about where she would end up. In heaven, smiling down on her family; in purgatory, hoping the family could offer up enough prayers to free her; or in hell, cursing the toddler who led her there?

"Don't you wish the dead could talk, Marie?"

"I'm dead, and I talk."

"No, you're the undead. I mean those who will not walk the earth again. If they could speak . . ."

"They have nothing to tell me." Marie's voice was raw with disdain.

"That's right. Vampires are bound to the earth."

"I can tell you what it's like to be in the world but unable to touch, smell, or change it. No, it is you who must worry about an afterlife. But don't let that stop you from fulfilling our bargain. Pray that Sade has no special power to ward off your gift."

Chapter Thirty-three

Sade brooded over the female lying next to him. She had a plumpness that would have been appreciated in the 1700s. So many women starved themselves today. While they had sex, some milk had flowed from her breast. Such a taste. It had almost appeased his blood hunger. Her belly, still distended from the birth of her fourth child, had been soft and pliable. Her thin brown gilded hair flowed down across her breasts. Her face held not a touch of makeup.

He had forgotten about this kind of woman, since he had been traveling in a very different society. Peasant women were always the best lovers. No airs, no fear of appearing too easy or too knowledgeable. They simply enjoyed each moment of lust.

TAINTED BLOOD

There would always be the problem of what to do with the brats they squirted out from time to time. Even this woman had set the clock so that she would be reminded to pick up her children at school. The baby, at least, she had left with Grandma.

Since he was only a few houses from the Hugheses' home, he never considered taking too much blood. Just a little nip that made her giggle and warn him not to do it again, because hubby could be quite observant. Hubby, the gross character with the belly hanging over his belt. Yes, Sade had seen him on several occasions. Perhaps that was why he had chosen this woman to fuck. She had a right to at least one good lay in her life. Maybe two, if he found the time.

Her body jiggled deliciously when she turned over. He reached over to touch her nipples, and she automatically spread her thighs, even though she was asleep.

The sheets had been clean and white when they first got into bed. Now the sheets were stained with sex and blood. Would she notice how much blood stained the sheet, even though she didn't have her period? Well, it was something that she certainly wasn't going to complain about to her husband.

He looked around the room and found it full of photographs, memories: Her husband with the eldest boy. Herself displaying a tiny infant in her arms. Children caught enjoying all sorts of games and birthday parties. Amusing, but not stimulating.

He opened the nightstand on his side of the bed

and found fur-lined handcuffs. He chuckled and wondered whether he had time for another go and another drink. She had enjoyed the paddling, even cried out for more. Her rear was now the color of red beets, just starting to darken a shade. How would she explain that? he wondered. Not his problem. Yet.

He weighed the handcuffs in the palm of one hand and meditated on the possibility the woman would reveal her lover. He hadn't finished with Marie, and she seemed firm in her desire to stay with the Hugheses.

"Will you be a nuisance, madam, or can I trust you with our secret?" He pulled back the hair from her face and she awoke.

"Louis, you're still here."

"Madam, I believe I've not had enough of you." He waved the handcuffs. "Perhaps another . . ."

"Oh, Lord, no." She checked the time. "I must get ready to pick up the children. They'll expect to see some cookies and milk on the table when they come in. They have such fierce appetites."

"So do I, madam."

She smiled and promised a rain check.

Sade smiled and shook his head.

"I'll not be put off like a commoner, madam."

"A bit full of yourself," she said.

He brought his hand to her throat.

"My hungers are ravenous. My time is precious. Raise your hands above your head."

She complied with his orders. At that moment he knew she would never reveal his identity to anyone but would always pray for his return.

Chapter Thirty-four

"If I find that kid . . ."

Gillian interrupted her husband. "He ran away. I'm sure of it. He thinks we'll be mad at him."

"Gillian, we have a dead body . . ."

"Shush! Don't speak of it out in the open."

"I'm ready to wring the little bugger's neck."

"I hope you mean Chuckie." Vanessa had just arrived home after hunting her lunch. The dog she had chosen was the loudest barker on the block. He barked whenever she walked past his house. A vicious animal, she had decided. Beside his owners, no one else in the neighborhood would miss him.

"Vanessa, what happened to your hand?" asked Gillian.

"A dog bite. It's not bad, though. I'll take a nap, and it'll heal quickly. So, what is Dad upset about?"

"That rotten little bastard . . ." Gillian's hand covered her husband's mouth.

"Go in the house. Aunt Marie and Babette are there; they can tell you what happened."

Vanessa walked toward the front door but stopped to make a side trip to visit her brother, who was beating some bushes.

"Swing the stick harder, Rog, and knock the little twerp out. I take it you, too, are looking for Chuckie."

"Yeah. He's in big trouble." Roger looked sideways at his sister.

"What did the twerp do?"

Roger pulled closer to his sister and looked around to make sure neighbors were not standing too near.

"He killed a little girl."

"Sucked the blood out of her?"

"Yeah, and now Dad is roaring mad and Mom's worried that Chuckie ran away."

"I knew we needed to destroy him. I told you that all along, and no one would listen. Now we'll probably have to move again. But I guess that doesn't bother you, since you planned on running away."

"Can't now. Mom needs me."

"She'll always need you, but she'll always love Chuckie more."

"That's because he's the baby."

"He's no baby. The twerp has a whole repertoire of curse words handy at any given second. He's spiteful. Whenever he can, he makes fun of me, and the twerp isn't even as tall as I am. Mom takes him

156

out on hunting trips. The only things he manages to catch on his own are those stupid earthworms that don't even have blood. What does he munch on those things for? Just to annoy us, probably. He looks disgusting with those things dripping out between his lips. Ugh! On several occasions, he's tried to bite me, and Mom chooses to ignore that. Now Mom should feel guilty." Vanessa looked over her shoulder at her mother.

Gillian was trying to talk Stephen into going back inside the house.

"Stupid doesn't even get it yet. Look how she's trying to cover for Chuckie. Dad's right to be fuming. We all should be." Vanessa turned back to her brother. "Even you."

"He doesn't do anything to me."

"Come on; he tells on you all the time. Mom and Dad know about everything you do in the house. You spent most of yesterday jerking off in your bedroom."

"No, I didn't."

"Well, a good part of the day. Chuckie found a little hole in the wall where he can peer in at you. Didn't know that, did you? He's been watching you for over a year."

"If that's true, then why didn't you tell me?"

"I'm not your watchdog."

"No, but you've listened to every story he's had to tell, I bet."

Vanessa chose to ignore Roger's observation.

"I'm going into the house to get the stakes, and as soon as I've found the twerp . . ." Vanessa made a hand movement, as if she were staking someone, and turned away.

Roger grabbed her shoulder and turned her around.

"It's not up to you, Vanessa. Mom and Dad will decide what to do."

"Mom's a wuss."

"You can't hurt her like that. She loves Chuckie, especially since he does have limitations."

"What about us, Roger? Don't we have limitations? You've been going to school forever, it seems."

"Because I want to."

"Because you're limited to having other twelve-year-olds as friends. You put up those stupid sexy posters on your wall but know none of those women would look twice at you."

"Probably wouldn't look twice at most guys."

"You'll never know whether you could have grown up to be a Don Juan. Maybe they would have fallen at your feet. Dad doesn't do so badly. You might have followed in Dad's footsteps."

"I wouldn't have wanted to."

"Naw, I guess it's more fun closing your eyes and pumping yourself to orgasm."

"Don't be spiteful, Vanessa. We both could fling mud at each other."

"That's the point, Roger. You and I are just as limited as Chuckie, but does Mom spend extra time with us?"

"She spends plenty of time with us. I think you're jealous."

"What?"

"Yeah. You'd like to have Mom's body, and probably Dad to go with it."

"Please, Dad is slime, aware slime that knows how to live, but still nothing to drool over. Yes, I would like to have reached maturity before being made a vampire, so I envy Mom that, but not the life she lives. I'd be doing her a favor to put her out of her misery. Just think how lost she'd be without Chuckie. That second stake will come in handy." She flashed a grin at her brother and walked into the house.

Chapter Thirty-five

The vent covering the entrance to the crawlspace popped out of place. Chuckie closed his eyes and hoped it was accidental and no one had the brilliant idea of checking for him under the house.

"Chuckie."

Chuckie opened his eyes to see Roger's head poking in through the hole. Should he say anything or stay quiet? Trust no one, he told himself, and pulled himself farther into the shadows.

"Chuckie." Roger sighed and began pulling himself into the crawlspace.

Go away. Go away, Chuckie kept repeating to himself. The word *Ma* pressed against his lips, but she'd never hear him.

Roger was all the way in now and orienting himself to the darkness.

"Chuckie, come out of that corner now," he yelled.

Chuckie shook his head.

"I swear I'll drag you out of here if I have to. Mom's going nuts looking for you."

"And Dad wants to beat me up, I bet."

"True, but you can't stay in here forever, and Dad's temper is only going to get hotter the longer you stay away. Mom's blaming him for what you did."

"Him?"

"For not setting a good example. But we know it wasn't Dad's example you were following. It was your own hunger. I feel the same way, Chuckie."

"You do?"

"It's in our nature to lust after human blood. Only I never acted on it like you did. I couldn't, because Mom didn't want us to get caught."

"Are we going to get caught now?"

"Dad's talking about going back on the road. Aunt Marie is looking for another place to store her coffin."

"And Mom?"

"She's obsessed with the idea that you've run away."

"I wouldn't do that."

"I know. That's why I'm under the house. If Mom and Dad were able to calm down, they'd be able to figure out where you were, too. I didn't trip over the vent as usual; that's how I figured it out."

"Klutz," Chuckie said.

"Come out for Mom's sake."

161

"What about Dad?"

"He's a minor problem. Stay away from Vanessa, though."

"She's pissed at me, too?"

"Kinda."

Chuckie moved away from the wall.

"Roger?"

"Yeah."

"There are dead bodies down here."

"Doesn't surprise me."

"You know about the bodies?"

"Makes sense. This stupid vent never stays in place. Lots of animals have either been trapped down here or came here to peacefully die."

"Nope. I'm not talking animals. Yeah, there are a few strays here, but I'm talking humans. Somebody's been knocking off people and storing them in our crawlspace."

"But we would have smelled them."

"Considering how long we keep dead animals we've fed from in the house, I doubt we'd notice."

"How far back would I have to go to find one of these bodies?"

"Go a little bit to your right and crawl a couple of paces."

Roger followed his brother's instructions. Finally he saw the outline of a skeletal profile. When he touched the skull, the cheekbones caved in.

"They've been here awhile." He moved his hand down over the skeleton and noticed that there were no signs of clothes. "The place is hopping with ants."

The brothers heard the vent being slammed back into place.

"That damn thing is always tripping me. I don't know why you don't just board the whole thing up. I bet you never go down there anyway. The place is falling apart, Stephen. Doesn't Gillian do anything but coddle her brood?"

"Aunt Marie," whispered Chuckie.

Roger put an index finger to his lips, and Chuckie fell back deeper into the shadows.

"That brat is no major loss, Stephen. My God, he even wanted to steal your body."

"Shit!" Roger quickly covered his brother's mouth.

"He planned on taking everything. Your body, your wife, and let's not forget she's his mother. The child's a pervert."

Roger felt Chuckie's lips move under the palm of his hand. Roger glared at his brother, and Chuckie shut up.

"No, he's not. He's sad," said Babette.

"A sad pervert. Actually, he makes a poor pervert. He doesn't even have the flair of a committed pervert. No, he hides behind his mother's skirts every time the wind blows in the wrong direction."

Chuckie's shoulders drooped. His right hand attempted to pull away his brother's hand from his mouth, but he didn't have the strength.

Chapter Thirty-six

Babette found Sade spread across the leather wing-back chair in the living room. One leg fell over the bulbous arm of the chair; another rested on the matching ottoman. A modern French novel lay in the palm of his hands. The wrinkled linen peasant shirt he wore fell open to mid-chest, and his leather jeans clung snugly to his muscular thighs. He was barefoot, and she could see the pronounced veins on the upper side of his feet.

She moved quietly into the room. The cushioned carpet gave lots of insulation. A window was open, and she could hear rush-hour traffic wending its way home from work, blocking the voices of the songbirds.

"Yes, Babette, what do you want?"

"Monsieur Sade, I see you've isolated yourself from the troubles of the house."

Sade glanced up at Babette, who stood in front of him.

"Yes, Babette? You have something to tell me?"

"You don't seem interested, Monsieur Sade. Do you ever worry about being caught off-guard? Perhaps an enemy or hunter might have an opportunity to outmaneuver you someday."

"Is this the day, Babette?"

"It could be very soon, and you probably won't know from which direction the enemy will come."

"I have you in front of me. That gives me one hint. Any other directions I should be checking?"

"I'm the one who will truly overpower you, Monsieur Sade. Still, you should be guarding against other human enemies. Many would want you dead."

Sade chuckled. "I know of at least one husband who would. Considering the shape of his belly, I don't think he could possibly catch me."

"There's a dead body upstairs on the landing."

"There are dead bodies scattered throughout this house."

"I'm not talking about the undead. This is a little girl who lived in the neighborhood. She wandered in with what she thought was a playmate, not expecting more than simple games."

"We're all playing simple games, and I don't like the one you're playing now. Tell me, dammit, what you are so eager and yet so slow to tell me."

165

"Chuckie killed a child today."

"Bang the child over the head with some toy, did he?"

"Why do you take this as a joke?"

"Because of the way you're telling it to me, *ma femme.*"

"Chuckie killed the child, and no doubt the authorities will be making house-to-house calls. She was a pretty little girl. I'm sure you would have liked her."

"*Ma chére,* small children should be put to bed early. It's their mothers that interest me."

"Marie thought . . ."

"Marie sent you. Is there any truth to this story? Gillian keeps her goslings so close to her that this is hard to believe."

"He wanted to taste human blood. Desperate. I found him and the girl on the floor in the hall. He was crouched over her. His little arms and legs seemed to grow extensions to hold the girl in place; his mouth was fastened to the white flesh of her throat. Tiny drops of blood slipped from the sides of his lips and spoiled the thin yellow blouse she wore. He was a fiend when he looked at me. No more a toddler, but instead his true self."

Babette had been staring into the distance, reliving the horror she had witnessed. When she came back to the present, Sade stood in front of her.

"Where is Chuckie now?"

"No one knows. Gillian believes he's run away. He couldn't. Where would he go? The animal in him is scared and dangerous, but he'll not leave his nest."

"Did anyone else witness this beside you, mademoiselle?"

"You think I'm lying."

"No." Sade sighed and glanced over his shoulder toward the doorway before looking back at Babette. "I think Gillian must be in a great amount of pain. You couldn't guess the worry and agony she feels right now. You've never been close to anyone. Someone you trusted drove you into a cocoon that you're very unwilling to leave." She had left the top two buttons of her blouse open. Sade reached out and closed them. "I'll not force you out, mademoiselle; you must want out. Kicking and screaming is only fun when its consensual."

"Is that how you got the scratch on your chest?" She raised her right hand and let her fingertips lightly skim his flesh.

Sade moaned. "You'll give yourself to me only to lay a curse, *ma chére,* not for our mutual satisfaction. Such a shame, because in my arms you would learn about ecstasy."

"You, too, have a lesson to learn, yet you stall because your giant ego is in the way."

"You are a *sorcière,* mademoiselle. If I were tired of this world, you are the woman I would choose to take me out of it. What is the dark secret you possess? How can it be banished?"

She allowed her palm to rest heavily on his chest and stepped closer to him.

"Your flesh is cold, Monsieur Sade. Beneath the

surface, however, I feel the pumping of a weak heartbeat. The heart is so tired. It's been too long since it could rest. It flutters now as I speak, wanting to be free of this body that you've forced to live on."

Sade placed his hand over hers and pressed her closer.

"My heart stopped beating long ago. Before I became what I am it found no reason to beat. It will never pump or flutter again. As for my body, it takes pleasure freely. Living is a minor trial for it to bear. I will have you one day, Babette. You'll writhe and call out my name, and all you'll hear back are echoes."

As she opened her mouth to answer, his lips sealed hers shut. Both their hands fell away into an embrace. Her body pushed forward into his, forgetting the pact she had made with Marie.

It took her a minute or two to realize he had released her and was walking away.

Chapter Thirty-seven

Sade found Gillian in the attic, fingering a jumble of antique toys.

"Chuckie's toys from when he was truly a *bébé?*"

Gillian remained seated on the floor but looked up to frown at Sade.

"He *is* my baby," she said.

"He'll always be your son, Gillian, but not your *bébé.*"

"He's *my* baby."

He rested a hand on her shoulder. "And you'll always be my lover."

She pulled away from him.

"Figuratively, I mean. I can't hold you to my side forever, nor can I expect you to jump to my commands."

"What do you know about having children? You

spent most of your time in prisons and an insane asylum, protesting the hypocrisy of your own class. Your mother-in-law basically raised your sons and daughter."

"She influenced them, *oui.*"

"She turned them against you." Gillian's eyes were full of spite.

He sat on the floor next to her and reached out to clear a strand of hair from her forehead. She immediately recoiled.

"You are a stupid *femme.* Beautiful, but stupid. You could have spent the past century with the taste of fresh blood on your lips and tongue. Instead you waste your time in matronly tasks that will provide you with nothing."

"The love of my children."

Sade laughed. "The love of grown men is far superior to wiping the ass of a male infant, *mon amour.* You've missed so much that I could have taught you, if you hadn't wanted to return to the children of a man who's not even faithful."

"He protects and cares for his family, Louis. You wouldn't understand. You've always been too wrapped up in your own desires, forgetting that others have needs different from yours."

"You're hiding behind your family, Gillian. I recall when we fucked . . ."

"That's all we did, and it was empty."

Sade reached out and grabbed the top of her right arm and held it firm.

"We fucked like animals, and you never once thought of your children. Your pleasure was foremost. Remember the feel of my touch." His hand pressed tighter against her flesh. "Remember the softness of my silken ascot wrapped around your wrists, the crack of the whip, my hands exploring your body, the throbbing sensations gifted by my prick, and the twinge of pain when I finally took your blood." He pulled her closer and covered her mouth with his own, tasting the sweetness of her saliva as she allowed him to battle with her tongue.

While still kissing her, he swept away the tired toys and pushed her back onto the floor. The smell of dust and moldy wood covered them in a private world where no other could see or intrude on their lust.

Gillian allowed his hands to disrobe her and waited in anticipation as he removed his own clothes. He licked her body until the warm saliva cooled her flesh. Her legs parted, and he stooped to bring his lips close to her right ear.

"Beg," he whispered. "I want to hear you whimper with need."

Her hand wrapped around his penis and moved slowly, gently, his flesh delicate and yet powerful with its urge. Her lips curved up into a smile as she said, "For this I never have to beg."

Sade roared with laughter and drove deep inside her.

Chapter Thirty-eight

"Where is Sade?" asked Babette."

"I don't care where he is," responded Marie.

"You should. What if he is plotting something against you? You are taking his visit very lightly, for a woman who supposedly fears him."

"I fear him more when he's not near. Strange. I hate the man, but oddly enough I feel safer when he's near. The man who destroyed my body and drove me into the vacuum from which I escaped can make me feel . . . That's it! He makes me feel something. Most others are just bodies to fulfill my needs. He is hell on earth for me, and yet he sparks my desires more than anyone else. Perhaps it's because he's also the person who could take everything away from me.

"He's a strange man, Babette. A true lunatic. Do

you know my daughter, his wife, died in a convent with her own daughter by her side? Ugly creature, my granddaughter. I have no idea who she took after. At least Louis is not unattractive, although slightly short. Most people never even notice his height. They're too busy being taken in by his charms and his strengths. He couldn't be all that much in bed, given that my dear daughter chose the convent over him. Of course, she didn't have a big choice, since I made sure he couldn't remain safely at home for too long. At one time I would have jumped into bed with him."

"And you still would."

"Not jump. I'd have to think about it. I've always been curious about his prowess, given the number of women who took chances to be with him. My younger daughter went off with Louis for a while, even though her sister was married to him. Such an embarrassment." Marie shook her head and kept packing her suitcase. "Everyone knew, of course. Including his own children. No wonder they didn't want much to do with him."

The door to the bedroom swung open, and Stephen walked in.

"Leaving?" he asked.

"I hope to beat you to the door, Stephen."

"Can we talk without the bitch being present?"

"Watch your language, Stephen; you're starting to sound like Chuckie. Babette, you should be packing instead of glowering at Stephen. I'll let you know when it's time to leave."

Babette sullenly walked to the door but stopped

short of opening it. She turned back to Stephen. "What are you going to do with your son when you find him?"

"None of your business."

"Give him to me."

Stephen's face creased into many lines. "What the hell do you want with Chuckie?"

"I'll punish him for you. A father shouldn't have to do what is necessary here. He looked so like a spider sucking the life out of a fly. The image made me hesitate. I won't hesitate again; not for any of you."

"What is this mad bitch talking about, Marie?"

Marie shrugged and pointed the way for Babette.

After the door had closed, Stephen allowed himself to fall onto an ancient rocking chair that had missing spindles. His toes slowly rocked him back and forth. He sat several minutes in silence while Marie packed.

"What did you mean, Marie, when you said Chuckie wanted my body?"

"You certainly can figure it out. The little brat is tired of being little. He heard about my transformation and approached me about helping him."

"You'd never stake me, Marie." He sought her eyes, but she avoided his. "I'm like a son to you."

"I've never had a son; only two girls. They weren't bright, but I guess anyone could be taken in by an attractive rogue. They're both dead and I'm childless, Stephen."

"But you created me."

174

"I simply aided in your transition, and you were quite willing."

"We share the same vampire blood, Marie. If I were to be destroyed, wouldn't you grieve?"

"Don't be melodramatic, Stephen. Gillian is the one who would kneel at your grave, not me. You were a fling for me. A really good one, but only a fling."

"Do you care about anyone besides yourself, Marie?"

She stood still for several long moments, thinking about everyone she knew who still existed on the earth. The numbers astonished her. So many naked and clothed bodies, but the differences were minor. They all fit together in a numbing box in her brain.

"Wil. He's a man I met before I changed into this body. Had a father with a terrible disposition. Got on my nerves so bad that I blooded him. Probably the son has never forgiven me for that. I wonder, though, if I had made Wil mine, would I have yearned for him as much as I do now? I doubt it. The fact that he fought me intrigued me. He's another one I aided in his transition, Stephen. I have a long list, and I would probably bore you if I went over the names. Some names I may have even forgotten, like their faces. You're not of my flesh. You exist because of a hunger for your blood and a need to rule over you."

Stephen stood. "I'm a free man, Marie. No one tells me what to do."

"I don't frighten you?" She moved closer to him,

and the room became quiet, as quiet as a room full of dead people can be. The inanimate objects frozen in place. The dead waiting.

"Not anymore, Marie. You've ruined my life, and my family's. You took away our ability to truly love. Instead we go day by day as zombies, freaks. That's what you made us. You've stolen not only my blood but also my ability to protect my family, and worst of all, you've taken my children's love from me."

"Chuckie will steal more than that from you."

Chapter Thirty-nine

The little girl's body lay at Babette's feet. The wound on her neck had attracted a pair of flies. Babette knelt on the floor and reached out to chase the flies away as she heard steps coming down from the attic. She turned and saw first Gillian, followed immediately by Sade. Gillian's clothes were in disarray and Sade wore only a smirk.

"Ah, Babette," he called. "My fate lies in your hands. Will you work your witch's incantations on me or show me mercy?"

Babette stood. "Are you drunk?"

"Sated. Rapturously sated."

The door opened to Marie's room, and Stephen stopped in the doorway.

"He's mad, Stephen; he wanted to throw both

our clothes out the window. I managed to keep mine, but his he tossed to the winds."

"Were you wearing your clothes, Gillian, or simply clutching them in your arms?"

"Tell the truth, *mon amour.*" Sade had grabbed Gillian by the hips and delightedly rubbed himself against her.

Stephen lunged for the naked figure, and Sade swung a blow to Stephen's throat, forcing him backward. Stephen gained his balance and once again attempted to grab Sade. Louis turned imperceptibly and obtained a choke hold on Stephen's neck, twisting the man around to look at Marie standing in her doorway.

"Tell him what I can do, Marie. Tell him how I broke your neck, leaving you helpless to the blows of my ax. She watched, Stephen, as I fed bits and pieces of her into the fire. The smell of her roasting was like perfume to me. A rich, full intoxicant that drove me to save one bit. Her head. It festered at the foot of my coffin, and I watched the flesh fall free of the bone. The drippings stank, but I wouldn't give up her head. Ah, now she smells of lavender, so feminine." Sade flung Stephen into Marie's arms. The two toppled over onto the carpet, Stephen attempting to stand and Marie holding on, preventing him from gaining his footing.

"Babette, *ma chére,* come into my arms and share all Marie's evil secrets with me. Let my lips play at your neck, and my hands free you of the dreary garments you wear." Sade spread his arms wide, but Babette didn't budge. "You remain faithful to this vengeful woman?" he said, nodding his head in Marie's direction. "Or are you awed by our humanity? Yes, we still have the same old emotions. We can hate, love, despise, appease, even lust, as you can see." He looked down upon his own erection. "Take me in your mouth, Babette. Suckle at my manhood."

"Do it," screamed Marie.

Babette slid her body over to the top of the staircase, and, barely raising herself, raced down the stairs.

"Must you always ruin my fun, Marie?" Sade lowered his arms to his side. "And she's called you priggish, *ma gentille* Gillian. Ah, your wife, Stephen, is far more lustful than you can imagine, when properly primed."

Again Stephen fought to stand, but Marie overpowered him.

"You're a horrid person, Louis." Gillian confronted him, feeling naked and chilled by a cold worse than the death she experienced when she slept within her coffin.

"Was I so much the beast in the attic? Wait, I guess I was, and I recall you liking it."

"Get out of here before my children see you."

"Gillian, I explained already that they are no longer *enfants*. Like lovers, they must blossom and grow away from us, so that they can be far better educated when they return."

Sade regally walked to the staircase, gave them all a small bow, and descended the stairs.

179

"You'd never be able to defeat him, Stephen," said Marie.

"You don't care what happens to me anyway."

"I don't want to waste an ally."

"Are you all right?" Gillian kneeled next to Stephen, exploring his body for possible injury. "It was a mistake. I'm so overwrought by Chuckie's disappearance, I allowed him . . ."

Stephen reached out a hand and clamped it over his wife's mouth.

"You heard him. One's lover needs to learn outside the relationship to keep it from getting boring. And for us it's been the same old for some time now."

Chapter Forty

Babette fell down on the hard earth and vomited. Inside her head, her thoughts roared objections to everything she had done. With both hands covering her face, she sat quietly, her stomach calming a little more each moment. She hadn't realized how warm it was, but now waves of heat struck her shivering body.

"Babette?"

She looked up and saw the twelve-year-old boy who wasn't really twelve.

"Roger, did you find your brother?"

He ignored the question and proceeded to ask his own.

"Are Mom and Dad in the house?"

"Don't go in there, Roger. Stay out here with me a while."

"I need to know what's going on." He started walking toward the front door.

"No, Roger. They're very upset. Sade has caused a rift between your parents, and Marie isn't helping to improve the situation. Sit with me over there on the porch swing. We can talk and imagine ourselves as different people elsewhere in the world." Babette stood and started for the porch.

"I don't want to be someone else," he said.

"You should," she said, sitting herself down on the wooden planks of the swing. "You can't be happy being what you are. Chuckie's not happy."

"Chuckie's been spoiled."

"Spoiled? To be made into a vampire is to be spoiled? No, Roger, he's being tortured by his parents for as long as he walks the earth. I bet he's scared right now and thinks he may never be able to return home. He can still taste the blood on his teeth and lips. He hungers for more now and will always want more now that he's tasted human blood."

"He's all right."

"You've hidden him, haven't you? Where is he, Roger?"

"Were my parents arguing?"

"They were too stunned to argue."

"What did Uncle Louis do?"

"Uncle Louis. That sounds so odd. 'My dear Uncle Sade has just plugged my mother.' Do you suppose he tied her down? I'm sure if he did it was consensual." Babette heard a tiny gasp to her right. "Do we have leprechauns in the yard? Little fairies toddling around, ducking in and out of the shadows?" Babette used her feet to push herself back and forth, a slow summer-day kind of pace, allowing the breezes to catch her hair. "I once was a child. A pretty child. Everyone told me I was pretty. I had a daddy and a mommy like you do, Roger. Only they weren't vampires. They were worse than vampires. They freely contracted with the devil. But there was a clause they never took note of. Why should they have? It didn't effect either of them. No, it was their pretty little girl who paid the price for their glory. You, too, Roger, paid the price for your parents' selfishness."

"They couldn't help themselves," Roger said.

"Did they even try? Do you remember them agonizing over what would become of the children if they shared their blood? Or one night did they rush into your bedroom, seemingly deranged, and clasp you to them, drinking in your innocence and blood?"

"Our father took Vanessa and me. Mom wanted Chuckie."

"And always has. Come out, come out, wherever you are, Chuckie. The game just ended."

"You were telling me about when you were a little girl."

"Still protecting your brother. I had no sibling. I guess I was better off than you. There was no one for me to protect. No one to lie next to when the screams found my ears." She closed her eyes. "They were loud. They got louder as I grew older."

"Are you nuts?" Roger asked.

"Ever since I was very small." Her smile seemed empty. "The devil used to ride me on his knee and promise me gold and silver and sweets. Especially sweets, for I didn't know the worth of his presents. My parents always left us alone. And when he was done, he tucked me into my own bed. He'd pull the covers up under my chin and show me his true face, but only for a split second. He was a patchwork, Roger, a patchwork of dreams that would never come true. A patchwork done in multiple colors. The shiniest, brightest colors covered the muddy film that could never be true flesh."

"Where are your parents now?" Roger asked.

"Inside me, always inside me. Telling me what to do and how to act. Warning me to be faithful to the devil."

"Have you really seen the devil?"

Babette nodded. "He visits when I am bad to reward me."

"He knows where to find you?"

"He sends me wherever I go. He took the guise of Marie and brought me here."

"You think Aunt Marie is the devil?"

"He took her form briefly. Now he's taken a different shape. Small. Clumsy. He spews foul language and dodges from me." She looked up at Roger and smiled. "Ever dream of tasting my blood?"

"I only allow myself to dream."

"Good, because the dream could quickly become a nightmare. Come out, come out, wherever you are." She said those words for several moments, stopping only when she saw Chuckie peek around the corner of the house. She cocked her finger and eagerly encouraged him to come sit on her lap. She watched his eyes veer from hers to his brother's.

"Stay there, Chuckie. Let me quiet things around here before you come out. Shouldn't you be getting ready to leave?" he asked Babette. "It sounds like Marie is planning to abandon us."

"Come out, come out, wherever you are." She sang the phrase in a soft whisper.

"I'm going into the house. Don't go near Vanessa or . . ." He nodded his head toward Babette.

185

Chapter Forty-one

Roger turned into the kitchen and found a naked Sade rummaging through the refrigerator.

"Ah, a boy. I haven't had one in a long time."

"Uncle Louis, do you know where my parents are?"

"Uncle Louis. Why do you call me *uncle?*"

"Because we were told to. We always have."

"Hmmm. And are we related?"

"Through Dad?"

"You don't sound very sure of that."

"Mom said I should call you uncle because you were some sort of cousin to Dad."

"That wouldn't make me your uncle."

"Okay, we did because . . ." Roger hesitated. "Because we were children once."

"And now you're a midget." Sade pointed an index finger at the boy.

There was a loud scream, and Roger ran upstairs. "Mom?"

"It was me, not your mother," cried Marie.

He found her at the end of the hall, holding the knob of the door behind her.

"I didn't think you could scream, Aunt Marie. At least not a scream that sounded like fear."

"The spawn of the devil is in this room."

"That's Vanessa's room. What does she have to do with the devil?"

"She's standing in the middle of the room, lunging forward with two stakes."

"She's practicing." Roger looked wistfully at the door and wished he could change his sister's mind.

"On whom is she going to use those stakes?"

"Not on you; don't worry, Aunt Marie."

"Sade?"

"No. Chuckie."

Marie relaxed and let go of the doorknob.

"That makes sense."

"No, it doesn't. He's her brother. She should . . ."

Vanessa whipped open the door.

"I should what? Play along with his stupid humor? Let him tease until he's satisfied, which he never will be? And you, Aunt Marie, what's the screaming about?"

"She thought you were planning to stake her," Roger explained.

"I don't have the time." Vanessa slammed the door in their faces.

"Have any of you ever been spanked?" Marie asked.

"We're too old for that." Roger walked away and went downstairs a level to knock on his father's bedroom door. "Dad?"

His father opened the door. "I thought you were running away from home. What are you stickin' around for?"

"Dad, Chuckie didn't mean to kill the girl. He explained that he just wanted a taste of her blood but couldn't contain his thirst once he started. Can I tell him he's forgiven?"

"By all means, tell him he's forgiven. I can't wait to get my hands on him."

"Where's Mom?"

"Try the basement with your Uncle Louis." Stephen flipped the door closed.

Roger froze in midstep. Nothing made sense. Everything seemed to be in upheaval. His sister was preparing to kill his brother. His brother had killed a little girl. Aunt Marie, who was afraid of nothing, was terrorized by the sight of his little sister. Babette was bonkers. His father wanted to kill his brother, and his mother might be in the basement with a naked Uncle Louis.

Chapter Forty-two

Vanessa flung the stakes onto the brocade spread resting on her coffin and walked to the window. A faint breeze wafted through the window, so faint that she had almost forgotten it was open. She decided to take a break and kicked the wooden footstool over to the window. She stepped up on the stool and stretched her body out the window. Earlier in the day the neighbors had had a barbecue, and the nuggets of charcoal were smoldering in the Weber. The fireflies were out in full force, with their rears lighted up to make it easier for her to catch a few. She'd play with one a while within her palms before smashing it between her hands.

Where was Chuckie? she wondered. Where was Mama's baby boy? She imagined that every one of the fireflies were Chuckie. Chuckie with his baby teeth just barely descended. Chuckie with his little legs trying to run away from her. *The miserable little brat.*

Vanessa stood on her toes so she could reach farther out the window. And then the vision of Chuckie became a reality.

Minutes later, Vanessa ran past Babette and around the corner of the house, coming in full contact with her brother. Chuckie landed on his behind and stared up at his sister.

"Where'd you come from?"

"Chuckie, I was so worried about you. Are you okay?" She grabbed one of her brother's arms and helped lift him up. "Mama's worried sick. Dad will be worried too when he cools off."

"Is he raging mad?"

"I've never seen him this angry, but you must admit you deserve it."

"No, I don't. I didn't do anything Dad wouldn't have done. You know that."

"But you're not Dad. You're his baby boy."

"Damn, I'm tired of being thought of as an infant. I want respect."

"Are you going in the house to demand that of Dad?"

"Not yet. Roger told me to wait here." His brow furrowed. "He also said I should stay away from you."

"Why?"

"He didn't tell me."

"He's being overprotective. What harm could I be?"

"You tried to bite me the other day."

"Only after you bit me, creep." Vanessa smiled. "Listen to us fight. Right now you need people standing behind you."

"Or in front of me, if Dad comes."

"Give me your hand, Chuckie."

"What for?"

"I'm going to sneak you up the stairs to my room and hide you."

"Why?"

"Because you're my brother and I love you."

"You never told me that before."

"I never appreciated you the way I do now. You did something that was quite brave. You defied our parents and fulfilled Roger's and my dreams. We desire human blood, too, you know. However, we've never had the courage to actually drain a human dry. Was it good?"

"I have a tummy ache. I think I made a pig out of myself. Doesn't help my digestion, knowing everyone hates me, either."

"I don't hate you, Chuckie. I love my scrumptiously cute little brother." Vanessa chucked him under the chin.

"Babette's on the porch waiting for me."

"I noticed her as I came around the corner. We do have a back door, you know."

"It's all cluttered with vines and stuff."

"We can clear them away, and then I'll run into the house and unlock the door."

"I need my soil in order to rest."

191

"We were buried in the same soil. You can rest in my casket."

"Not big enough," Chuckie said. "I'm too plump and you're too gangly."

"Thanks, little brother. How 'bout you resting in my coffin, and I'll rest in yours?"

"Won't they wonder why?"

"I'm not going to make a public announcement. How will they know? Besides, Mamma only bothers to tuck you in. She thinks Roger and I are old enough to tuck ourselves in. At worst, she'll pay a visit to your coffin, but she won't want to open the lid and see it empty."

"I don't know. Roger is trying to smooth things over for me."

"That could take days, maybe weeks."

"Or never. What if I have to sleep out here in the open all by myself? Should I dig a hole and bury myself? I've never slept in a grave before."

"You'd love it. Those icky worms would keep you company."

"Would you help cover me over, and at night dig me up again?"

"Come rest in my coffin for one night and think this over. You shouldn't rush into any decisions, since you're already in deep trouble."

"Thanks," he murmured, with a sadness that sickened Vanessa.

Chapter Forty-three

Just before he climbed into his coffin, Stephen heard a pounding on his bedroom door.

"Go away, Gillian. Not tonight. From the way Louis talked, you should be exhausted."

The pounding continued, so strong that the door vibrated.

"What the hell did he do, give you an aphrodisiac?"

When the kicking began, he gave up and opened the door.

"What the hell do you want, Marie? I thought you were too special to bother with someone as lowly as me."

"Don't be offended, Stephen. All I did was tell you the truth. Not even mentioning that I saved your meager life. Louis would have broken you in two."

"Nah. I award you the prize for doing that."

"Only your ego; the rest of you is quite sound. Besides, I'm not here for a quick fuck. I want to know what you're going to do about the dead body laying near my door."

"I was hoping to forget about it for a while."

"I can't. I must pass it every time I come and go."

"Marie, it's not like you're not used to dead bodies."

"It's esthetically deplorable to leave dead meat lying around. Shall I bring it down here and toss it into your coffin?"

"You wouldn't do something like that to me. My own smell is bad enough. Daily the damn coffin fills with the noxious fumes released by my body while asleep."

"I want the body gone. Not after your nap. Now!"

Stephen knew of an ideal place, a place he didn't want to share with anyone else. It would be too much to hope that they all would be away at the same time. However, if at least most were away or embroiled in one of their feuds, he could stealthily carry the body away.

"You know we don't deal with dead bodies at home. I've only performed my kills when traveling, and Gillian has seen to it that nothing disrupts this house. Until now . . ."

"Dead bodies bring trouble, Stephen. I'm not saying you should carelessly dump the poor creature anywhere. Heavens, the poor little soul deserves a respectable burial."

"Oh, come on, Marie. You'd dump her down the toilet if she'd fit."

"Stephen, sarcasm is not going to solve the problem, and I don't believe one of your naps will, either. I'm sure you're completely brain-dead once you settle your body down in that thing."

Marie walked past Stephen into the room. She circled an ornate antique coffin.

"Where did you obtain this monstrosity?"

"Gillian gave it to me for one of my birthdays. I don't even remember which one it was. I used to sleep in a bed and spread a few handfuls of dirt across the sheets. Gillian felt I should face what I am. I think what she wanted to say is, let this remind you of the ruin you brought to your family. Anyway, it's certainly nothing I would choose. She polishes the thing every week. It gleams at me every day. She's repaired the lining several times. Secretly I like to make little holes into the satin and lace lining the coffin. Too feminine for me."

Marie lifted the lid and spied an embroidered name and date. His, she realized. His name and the date he supposedly died. She recognized Gillian's delicate hand at work. The words and date had been done in blue thread, but the coffin was naturally lined with a peach hue that hinted at the pink of roses.

"Did she ever tell you where she found it?"

"I didn't ask. Came home from a trip, my bed

was gone and the coffin had taken its place. Touching, eh?"

"It's called passive-aggressive." She let the lid fall with a thud. "Most appropriate for a little girl, though."

"You want me to give up my coffin for some strange kid who was stupid enough to wander into my house with that detestable son of mine?"

"Bit too large," she said, evaluating the coffin from a slight distance. "Getting it out of the house without being seen wouldn't be easy. Much easier to shove her into a large garden bag. You do have those bags that are used for dead leaves, don't you?"

"Gillian has everything. A perfect housewife."

"Then get one, and I'll meet you on my landing."

Chapter Forty-four

Vanessa and Chuckie worked hard at clearing the ivy and brush away from the back door of the house. Vanessa had scratches up and down both arms. She kept imagining Chuckie asleep inside her coffin, his hands resting across his chest. She'd have to brush them aside. Maybe she'd even undo his overalls and pull up the T-shirt. After taking careful aim, she'd jab the stake into the center of his heart. Oh, the grimace on his face, the shiver that would carry throughout his body, the ash that would mess up her coffin.

"Hey, want this?" Chuckie threw her a dead rat, which she managed to catch before dropping it to the ground.

It would be worth it, she decided.

"Are you sure the back door unlocks and we're not wasting time?" Chuckie asked.

"I'll force the lock if I have to," she said, ripping away another long branch of ivy.

"Children at play. I love the sight." Sade stood behind them in his long velvet robe, his naked feet spread wide apart and his hands resting on his hips.

"Go away, you stupid old man."

"Vanessa, hasn't your mother taught you to speak properly? I can't imagine she'd approve of calling me names."

"I didn't call you any names, although I could think of quite a few. I merely spoke the truth. You're an old man."

"I sometimes wish I were," Chuckie said, wistfully pulling a fistful of weeds from a crack in the stairway cement.

"Your mother's worried about you, *mon petit*. Perhaps you should go to her," Sade suggested.

"Go away," screamed Vanessa, spinning around to face Sade.

"Have you ever felt the heat of a good paddling, *ma chére*? Or perhaps a slap to bring roses to your cheeks?"

"Mama would be angry at you."

"She already is." Sade waved his hands in the air. "What do I have to lose?"

He took several steps toward the children. With a piercing yell, Vanessa dropped the detritus in her hands and ran around to the front of the house.

Babette still sat on the porch, the swing barely moving.

Vanessa threw the door open and didn't bother to close it behind her. She ran to her mother's bedroom door, then stopped abruptly.

What would she tell her mother? How could she explain what she and Chuckie were doing? Vanessa wanted Chuckie destroyed, yes. Did she want everyone to know who did it? She'd be considered a pariah within the vampire community.

She scrunched herself into a ball on the floor and sulked.

"Oh, get out of the way, Vanessa."

She looked over her shoulder and saw her father carrying a brown heavy-duty garbage bag. Aunt Marie followed behind him and seemed to be tying the end in a knot.

"What's that?" Vanessa asked.

"Get out of the way, child. Your father has something very important to do."

"That's the little girl Chuckie sucked dry, isn't it?" Vanessa stood.

"Do you expect me to step around you, Vanessa? Please move before your mother sees what we're doing."

"What are you doing, Dad?"

"I'm sure you'd like this kid's company, but she has to leave. Would upset your mother to have her hanging around, you know."

Vanessa backed up against her mother's door and allowed the two adults to pass.

"Where are you dumping her?" Vanessa called.

"In the utility room, for the time being. Aunt Marie didn't cotton to having dead bodies lying in front of her door."

The utility room. What if Mom faced Chuckie's kill again? If Mom disappeared first, Vanessa wouldn't have to worry about getting rid of Chuckie. Dad would take care of that.

Vanessa tried the doorknob to her mother's room. She was locking Dad out again, dammit.

Chapter Forty-five

Chuckie smiled weakly at Sade. "I envy your age," he said. "I envy anyone older than me."

"I thought you told your mother that my body was too old for you." Sade spread the robe beneath him and sat.

"I thought your hair was starting to thin. Since then, I've seen it's not. Guess the light was shining funny on your head."

"So now you want my body."

"Aunt Marie promised me Daddy's."

"Do you think Aunt Marie will come through for you, *enfant?*"

"Not anymore." Chuckie gave up on his work. Not even Vanessa would help him now. "Why was what I did so bad?"

"I didn't know that it was." Sade stretched his arms behind him and leaned back.

"Everyone's mad at me."

"Have you asked everyone whether they're angry?"

"I hid before asking."

"Ah, you're assuming everyone is mad at you. Your mother is worried about you. She told me that herself. She never mentioned being mad at you."

"Dad's mad enough to . . ."

"Destroy you?"

Chuckie nodded solemnly.

"Would that be so bad? You don't like being a toddler anymore. Perhaps you could join a circus and make believe you're a midget. Have you ever thought of doing that?"

"You're making fun of me, Uncle Louis. You're telling me I'm a freak and should be part of a sideshow."

"This family could be an entire sideshow, *mon enfant.* But you . . ." Sade sat forward. "You would be the saddest specimen of them all. An old man in shrunken skin with a pathetic pain clouding your eyes. Poor *petit* Chuckie. *Un fil* whose mother refuses to throw him into the garbage of the world. Instead she pampers an old man who imagines there's something better.

"I passed Babette on my way out. She was dreaming in her own private world and didn't take notice of me. She's unhappy, too, Chuckie, but she doesn't expect any joy. You expect a balloon to fill with air and carry you away. She knows her balloon will always burst."

"But she's grown up."

"Only superficially. Her arms and legs are longer than yours. Her genitals have matured. That's all."

"You think she's as miserable as I am?" Chuckie asked.

Sade nodded.

"That's stupid. She's all grown up and can do whatever she wants. Nobody's going to pat her on the head and expect her to giggle with delight."

"No one expects you to think like an adult, but you do. No one assigns adult responsibility to your actions. *Petit* Chuckie, the toddler, what does he understand?"

"Plenty. I use the baby ploy all the time to get around all sorts of stupid rules. Why can't I use it now? Come back all sad and hungry. Better skip the hunger part. Come back all sad and contrite, climb into Mom's lap, lean against her breast, and sigh. Dad will be the tough one."

"Especially since he knows you wanted to transfer into his body." Sade stood. "By the way, Chuckie, stop calling me uncle."

Chuckie watched Sade brush the grass from his robe and retie his belt. Sade walked up to the back door, ripping away the remaining foliage as he did, and with a fluid motion opened it.

Chapter Forty-six

"There you are, Chuckie. I told you to stay by the entrance to the crawlspace in case you had to hide."

"Roger, I'm not hiding anymore. I'm as good as ash."

"What are you talking about?"

"Dad knows I coveted his body. I asked Aunt Marie for help in stealing his body while he slept."

"She planned on staking him?"

"And me. Except I thought I could overcome his spirit and come back in his place. Hell, he could have my old body, although maybe not. What if my spirit wouldn't transfer unless my body was burned up? Dad wouldn't have had any body. Neither would I, if I was unable to overcome Dad. Shit, Roger, I wish Aunt Marie and Un . . . Louis hadn't come here."

"The house is in chaos. I don't think we'll make it out in one piece," said Roger.

"Dad won't forgive me?"

Roger looked at his brother with a painful grimace.

"Mom?"

"Can't find her."

"Probably out wandering the streets looking for me."

"Dad didn't think so."

"Where'd he say she was?"

Roger scratched his head and mumbled incoherently.

"What? You suddenly have marbles in your mouth. Mom's not even looking for me, is she? She doesn't want me back. You and Vanessa have been lying to me to make me feel better."

"Vanessa?"

"She was here a while ago, trying to help me."

"You didn't turn your back on her at all, did you?"

"What is she going to do, spit at me? Why are you so hyper about Vanessa? Don't shrug your shoulders! For once give me a direct answer. You're such a wimp about everything. You don't even know whether you want to stay or go. Hell, go. Who's going to miss you? Clunking around, trying to act like a preteen for almost a century. Get up some nerve. Do something beside living in a make-believe world. You're not a preteen anymore, Roger. Maybe you need a special announcement to understand that."

"Don't get riled at me; I'm helping."

"Helping. I'm in the same situation I was in hours ago when you found me in the crawlspace. You achieved nothing, except probably making Dad even angrier at me."

"Don't raise your voice or he'll know you're out here," said Roger.

"Here I am, Dad," Chuckie screamed. "I'm in the backyard talking with a moron."

"He'll think you're talking to yourself," grumbled Roger.

Chuckie fiercely ran into Roger's legs, gripping them so tight that they both lost their balance. Chuckie attempted to pound Roger's kneecaps to a pulp. He couldn't move any higher, because Roger's hands pressed down on his head.

"Take it back, Roger. I'm smarter than you are. I've tasted human blood. You haven't even figured out a way to do it."

"Yeah, and now you're scared to go back in the house."

Chuckie picked up his head and spit at his brother. Roger rolled away.

"Babette's right; you're a beast. An animal. You don't belong in this family. You still act like a toddler, wanting your own way and refusing to curb your urges."

"That's what you all expect of me, isn't it? You treat me like an infant and think I'm going to make all sorts of rational adult decisions. Mom still slaps my hands when I get near the stove. By this time, I know about fire. I'm not a little infant caveman."

206

Chuckie jumped to his feet, waving his arms wildly to keep his balance.

"I'm going back in the house, Roger. I'm going to face Dad and make it clear to Mom that I'm no longer a little baby, even if I look like one." Chuckie started up the back stairs.

"Sneaking in through the utility room. That doesn't seem so brave to me."

"One step at a time, Roger. I'll change how you all treat me one step at a time."

Chapter Forty-seven

Gillian heard the mumble of voices outside her room. Inside the coffin, she was free of family responsibilities for a while. Her hand instinctively reached for the collection of photographs she had tucked into the lining on the right side. Pictures of her children and husband before the entire family was changed. Birth, first steps, birthday parties, holidays wrapped inside a lace handkerchief. Her grandmother had given her the handkerchief on the day of her wedding to Stephen, when Gillian was certain her life with him would hold happiness.

The darkness inside the coffin bathed her with peace. Perhaps one day she would find true peace inside this wooden prison. She couldn't die a natural death; no, it would have to be violent. Her blood and all the blood of her victims had to be spilled before she could rest.

What had Stephen been thinking when he allowed a stranger to steal his life and put at risk his family's? The truth was that on his trips he didn't think about family. He didn't trouble himself with letters to her or the children. He took his pleasures easily, never worrying about consequences. Home was far away when he was on the road. Hotels and brothels took the place of their house. Prostitutes and low-life replaced his wife and children. Oh, how he used to brag about the poor souls he met and helped, never considering that his closest relatives were in need.

The high pitch of Vanessa's voice tickled her ears, drew her away from the memories. She couldn't make out what the child was saying, and the little girl's voice was interrupted by her father's.

Gillian lifted the lid of her coffin. The room was softly lit by a single candle that she had left burning on the windowsill. What for? she wondered. For Chuckie's return, she remembered painfully. Stephen's and her baby boy. The one who appeared to suffer the most from the change. He was always on the edge of hunger, overeating and seeking more food. Nothing could fill up his tummy. Was he sated now? Had the taste of human blood been as marvelous as he had expected? Did the lingering saltiness make him even more thirsty? Had he become the wild beast Babette had described? Was he killing another as she sat hiding inside her room?

Gillian stepped out of the coffin, her feet settling into the plush carpet. Earlier she had disrobed completely in order to bathe her body clean of Sade's odor. But she had been too tired to turn on the faucets and collect fresh towels. Sade, Stephen; they weren't very different. At least Sade had not turned his own wife and children into vampires, maybe because Marie had made sure he had limited access to them. Hard to think of Marie as anyone's protector.

She heard something brush against the door to her room. The outside world called, but she didn't want to answer. All she could think about was climbing back inside her coffin and sleeping forever. She had tried that already and found that too many memories ran through her mind. Too many happy and sad remembrances that would never be relived.

There was a light tap on the door. Gillian stood still, her arms at her sides, her hands unfurled from the tight fists that had twisted them earlier.

The tap grew a little louder. Could it be Stephen wanting to make up? His hands could never be gentle and tenuous enough to make so soft a knock.

Someone twisted the doorknob.

Roger, Vanessa, never Marie or that idiot Babette.

One of her children wanted her, and she ignored the request. One of her children had the courage to face her now, knowing the kind of mood Gillian would be in. She had eliminated Chuckie as a possible visitor because he would demand admittance, not request it. But would he now, after the error he had made?

Gillian walked to the door and rested her ear against the wood.

"Chuckie," she whispered.

She heard the huff of a sigh outside the door. Gillian reached for the doorknob but couldn't rest her hand on the faceted glass. Her hand hovered, as if fearful of getting burned. Fearful of what would be revealed to her on the other side of the door.

"Mother."

Vanessa wanted inside. Her only daughter. The child who didn't trust Chuckie and had wanted to destroy him before he had made this serious error.

"Open the damn door, Mother. I can sense that you're leaning against it. Open now."

Her daughter's voice sent a chill through Gillian's body. The little girl didn't belong to Gillian anymore. She could hear the callous timbre of the girl's voice.

"Father has removed the body from the upstairs landing. He and Marie are taking it down to the utility room. They don't know where else to stash it for now. Chuckie has done a terrible thing, Mother. I warned you more than once, and you refused to see what was obvious. You are at fault. You can't allow him to roam the neighborhood killing again. You can't hide from the sin you committed. Taking a baby's blood and feeding him

211

yours is evil, Mother. Come out and at least try to atone for the horror you've brought down on this house."

"And your father, my sweet child, what responsibility does he have in this?" Gillian slid down to sit on the floor. There were several moments of silence.

"Father knew who could handle the gift Marie gave him. He erred only in letting you have your way with Chuckie."

"We could all be sleeping quietly in our graves, sweetness, and instead we're plotting against each other and hating those we should love."

"Only you could love Chuckie. He's all you ever wanted."

Gillian rested her palms against the door. She wanted to reach out to Vanessa, convince her that she was wrong. Reach out to a child she had abandoned long ago. Reach out, trying to pull Vanessa back into the circle of love Gillian thought she had created. Gillian didn't know how, had never known how to love them all equally. Chuckie was last in both birthing orders: the last to be given human life and the last to be turned. He always needed more help. At least that's what she had thought. None of the children survived the change well, but she had assigned degrees of neediness right away.

"I'm sorry, Vanessa."

There was no reply. Gillian's hands searched the door, attempting to find her daughter's presence. Not there anymore. Not waiting for a mother's love.

Chapter Forty-eight

Chuckie used two hands to shut the back door behind him. He was relieved to be back inside the house, even if it was only the utility room. The linoleum was dull from years of use. Mops, buckets, and rags were scattered about the room. Even a big bag of garbage lay near his feet.

The next step was to open the door leading to the hallway that would take him into the family living area. With his luck, he'd probably run into Dad first. He sat on the floor and scratched his head. Maybe Vanessa had had the better idea. Who knew how long he could have hidden inside Vanessa's coffin?

He heard a movement. A weak movement. Suddenly something sounded as if it jerked into life and then went dead again. Rats? he wondered. At least he wouldn't go hungry. He looked around the room, trying to locate the source of the movement. The garbage bag jolted. How the hell did a rat get inside a sealed garbage bag without making a hole? Unless it made such a tiny hole he couldn't see it. He shifted his rear across the linoleum until he was right next to the garbage bag and leaned over to find an entrance. Something scratched against the bag. He found the mound making the noise and grabbed it. He heard a yelp, but it didn't sound like a rat. He squeezed what he held and felt five fingers. There was someone hiding inside their house. Maybe the killer of all those skeletons in the crawlspace. If he could hold on and call for help, maybe he'd be viewed as a hero. A smile brightened his face.

"Help, help," he screamed, and nobody came. Shit, he could scream louder than that. Once again he called out his alarm.

Roger opened the utility door. "What are you playing at now?"

"Quick, get some help. I've found the person responsible for all the skeletons in the crawlspace."

"In a garbage bag?"

"Yeah, hurry up. I don't know how long I can control this thing."

"What is it?"

Chuckie sighed and frowned at Roger, who took no note but instead walked over to the bag and Chuckie. He was unknotting the top of the bag when Chuckie screeched and ran around the utility room, looking for a weapon.

"Chuckie, you can put down the mop. You've already defeated this monster once." Roger rolled down the bag to reveal Cindy, just coming back to life.

"I didn't kill her?"

Roger shrugged as the girl reached out and punched him in the chin.

"Wait, wait," Roger said, grabbing the girl's arms. "No one will hurt you. Chuckie, take that mop out of her face."

Chuckie stepped back and lowered the mop.

"She was dead. She wasn't breathing. I still have her blood on my clothes."

"Get Dad," Roger said.

"Me? Are you kidding?"

"Don't you want to tell him that your victim isn't really dead?"

"I'd rather someone else do that."

"Then get Marie or Mom, but get someone who can help us decide what to do."

At this point, Cindy seemed fully awake and was fighting furiously.

Chuckie ran blindly out of the room, dropping the mop only when it caught on the banister. He cursed his little legs that were so slow to climb the stairs. He had watched Roger taking them two at a time in awe.

He came first to his mother's room, where he pounded on the door and tried the doorknob, but got no response. Next came Dad's room. Again he pounded on the door. Nothing. He turned the knob and the door opened slowly, revealing his father's ornate coffin. Since the coffin lay on the floor, the lid was within his reach. Should he open the coffin? Should he go away and look for a friendlier face? Maybe Dad wasn't even inside the coffin, but what a jerk he'd appear to Roger if he had to admit not trying.

His little hands were far more powerful than they looked, and he attempted to spread his arms wide to gain leverage. He gave a big heave upward, and the lid came up halfway, then fell back down with a loud thump. The smell coming from his father's coffin made him dizzy. If Dad was in a deep sleep, his body would be partly decayed, he knew, but the smell made him believe someone had staked the old man.

Again Chuckie spaced out his arms. This time he took a couple of steps backward. When he was ready, he ran forward, using the motion to feed into his upward thrust. The lid flew up and tilted in mid-air, but before it could fall back down, his dad's decayed arm grabbed hold of the lid.

"Dad," whispered Chuckie.

His father rose up to a sitting position, his flesh sagging, some even peeling off, since he was in the midst of renewal. The bones in his fingers almost protruded through the thin skin that flaked off. His head turned to face Chuckie, and when his eyelids opened there was a whirlwind of colors instead of his blue pupils. The nose was melting back into shape after swelling up in his sleep. His mouth had partial lips that gradually grew new skin and covered the frightening sight of his teeth.

"Do we all look that bad, Dad?"

The eyes transformed into white, with a familiar shock of blue in the center.

"But you won't have to worry about that anymore." His father threw back the lid and reached for his son. A prepared Chuckie quickly stooped low to the floor and crawled away to a distant corner.

"Dad, I didn't kill her. That girl, she's alive, and Roger's holding on to her downstairs to prove it to you."

Once he was mostly whole, his father stepped out of the coffin.

"I looked at her. I put her in a garbage bag and dumped her into the utility room. She's dead. She's probably been inside that bag long enough to be dead from asphyxiation, if from nothing else."

"Then you tried to kill her," Chuckie said in amazement.

"Stupid brat, she had no pulse when I picked her up off the floor. Everyone could see she was dead."

Chuckie shook his head adamantly.

A little girl's scream came from the first floor, and Chuckie and his father fought to be the first one out of the room. Chuckie crawled out between his father's legs and received a bad bruise on the side of his forehead.

By the time they reached the utility room, Marie, Babette, and Vanessa stood in the doorway.

"Get out of the way," Stephen shouted, pushing the women clear of the door. Chuckie had managed to get into the room first and immediately sat down next to the child, staring into her face in wonder.

"I want to go home to my mother," Cindy cried out.

"What the hell is going on?"

Chuckie looked up and saw his mother's face. Her mouth hung open for a moment before she shouted, "My baby." Suddenly Chuckie was embraced in a bear hug, the scent of his mother's sleep still clinging to her body. He was glad he hadn't awoken her first, because he didn't think he could have accepted his mother with major flaws.

"Can we just send her home, Mom?"

The adults all looked at each other.

"I'm thirsty," Cindy announced.

"I bet you are, my dear, and I doubt she wants milk," Marie said, looking in Gillian's direction.

"Is she one of us?" Chuckie asked.

His mother nodded and said, "I don't know what we should do with her."

"Stake her," Vanessa shouted.

"Her parents have probably already reported her missing to the police. We need to send her home before the police knock on our door."

"Won't that give us away?" Gillian asked.

"She doesn't understand what she's become. All she knows is that she's thirsty."

"Perhaps you could prepare a glass of . . . something special for our little guest, Gillian." Marie smiled down at the child.

"Mom, maybe this time Vanessa's right."

"About what, Chuckie?"

"Staking her," yelled out Vanessa.

"She survived, and we should give her a chance to continue with her life for as long as she can."

"You think her parents would destroy her, Dad?"

"No, but eventually they'll detect some oddities about her."

"I want my mother. I don't know what any of you are talking about. That stupid toddler jumped me in the hall and knocked me down. I must have passed out, and the next thing I knew I was being prodded by . . ." The girl looked up at her attacker and smiled. "Roger."

"She's got the hots for you, Roger. I saw it in her eyes, and she blushed when I mentioned your name."

"No taste," muttered Vanessa. "I still believe we should stake her. We already have Chuckie running around giving us a bad name."

"Vanessa, have you ever seen anyone staked?" asked Marie.

"No."

"Be careful it doesn't happen to you before you get to actually see one. It's amazing to watch, and the pain seems to enter everyone in the room. Right about there," Marie said, poking Vanessa in the chest. "That's where I'd stake you if I had to. But why would I have to? You're such a well behaved, quiet little girl."

"Mom wouldn't let you."

"Don't be so sure, my sweetest." Gillian put Chuckie on the floor. "Come, sweetness, you can help me get some . . . libation for our thirsty company."

Chapter Forty-nine

"Vanessa, did you see how disgusting Cindy looked swallowing that blood?"

"Unfortunately I did, Chuckie. I was holding the glass, remember. She almost bit right through the glass, she was so out of control."

"Do you suppose we look that way when we're feeding?"

"Not me, Chuckie. I'm in complete control."

"Then why don't we ever drink blood together? Yeah, we eat food together. Every holiday Mom's got to make her turkeys or fresh hams. But we always drink in private. I mean, you never see me sucking on a rabbit or a rat, do you?"

"Mom has."

"But she's Mom. She'll forgive us anything."

"She'll forgive you. Mom's still mad because I wanted to stake that little girl."

"That's only because it was a dumb idea."

"You agreed with me, Chuckie."

"Only briefly."

"Brief counts."

The children were stretched out on the grass in the backyard, staring up at the stars and wondering what story their parents would be telling Cindy's parents right now.

"*Mon Dieu,* you children are always in the backyard. What is it that you are planning?" Sade's voice caught Chuckie in the gut.

"We're dreaming about what life will be like when you and Aunt Marie leave," Vanessa said.

"Ah, life was peaceful before we arrived?" Sade looked directly at Chuckie, who simply shrugged his shoulders in reply.

"Holy shit!" Chuckie jumped up to his feet. "I forgot to tell Dad about the skeletons and the pentagram."

"Have you been hanging out at the cemetery again? I told you, we were never buried anywhere. We have no family headstone."

"No, Vanessa, under the house. We have skeletons under the house, and they're not all animal skeletons. Some are human. Ask Roger; he saw them, too. Hell, go and look yourself if you don't believe me."

"This prank isn't going to work on me. You just want to lock me under there somehow."

"No, really. Mr. Sade, you believe me, don't you?"

"Since when have you started calling Uncle Louis mister?"

"Someone has been storing dead bodies under the house. One of the skeletons had a crushed skull, but I couldn't tell how the others had died."

"It doesn't surprise me, *mon fil.* Your father is a careless man."

"He can't help it if the door to the crawlspace keeps falling out. Who'd ever think that people would be storing bodies under their house? Besides, Dad's away most of the time. It would be more Mom's responsibility."

"Every problem ends up at your mother's door. What a very sad life she has, *mon fil.*"

Sade stared up at the window to Gillian's room.

"She's not up there, Mr. Sade. She's returning the girl I killed to her parents."

Sade's body stiffened. "Alone?"

"Dad went with her."

"What do they expect to accomplish?"

"They want to prevent the police from knocking on our door. After drinking the possum blood, Cindy quieted down. They made me apologize for knocking her out, so to speak."

"*Mon fil,* you have confused me."

"She bit the dimwit on the arm while he was taking her blood. She drank enough of his blood to come back as a vampire. Only she doesn't know she's a vampire," Vanessa clarified.

"*Mon petit,* I am proud of you. You have made your first disciple."

"Hey, she belongs with me now, and not with her parents. I'm her new parent." Chuckie was delighted with the idea that he could have power over someone else.

"*Oui.* I bet if you try hard enough, you can call her back to you."

"Uncle Louis, why are you causing trouble?" asked Vanessa.

"*Moi?* I offer only assistance. It is Chuckie who must decide whether he wants to cause friction within the family. Hate to think of it as trouble. He's such a cute *petit fil.*"

Chuckie had lost the flow of the conversation. He was too busy thinking about being a leader of vampires. Maybe he'd be able to steal the body of one of his creations. He'd search for the perfect man. Not too tall, not too short, handsome but rugged. Intelligence didn't matter, since Marie had retained her own mind in the switch. No beer gut, possibly a body builder. Yeah, that would be nice. No one would dare order him around or make fun of him again.

Vanessa nudged her brother. "You're not going to seriously consider his suggestion, are you?"

"Suggestion? What did you . . . Where'd he go?"

"He became bored with us when he heard the front door slam and Babette call out for Marie."

"What did he suggest?"

"I'm certainly not going to tell you, runt. We'd all be in trouble."

223

Chapter Fifty

Sade watched Babette walk out into the middle of the street, calling for Marie. Panic seemed to be overcoming her as she called. He wouldn't be surprised if she burst into tears.

"Babette, standing in the middle of the street making a spectacle is what I'd expect of Chuckie, not you."

Her eyes were still clear. Her hands didn't shake when she raised them up in his direction. However, her walk did not appear to be steady. She came close to him, leaving her search behind.

"Have you taken her away again?" she asked.

Sade took both her hands in his and envied the warmth that flowed through them.

"Has La Maîtresse abandoned you?"

"She may have fled and left me to my doom. You

are my doom, Monsieur Sade. You will be the last.
I can sense that. I didn't understand until now. You
were made to destroy me."

"*Ma femme,* hold back your melodrama. I have
killed many; you wouldn't be outstanding."

"Yes, I will, because I will take you with me."

"There is one who took the last of my love with
her. All that is left is a wizened shell that refuses
to be destroyed. Even my niece, Liliana, couldn't
make this body give up. This ring I wear I gave to
her. I took it back when I found it among her scattered body parts. She was eaten, Babette. Eaten by
her own kind. I will never part with this ring again,
mademoiselle. There will never be anyone worth so
much to me again." Sade dropped her hands and
turned.

"Wait. I don't expect you to treasure me, Monsieur Sade. You only need to desire me for a night."
Her hands reached out and touched his shoulders,
and her cheek rested against his back.

"Mademoiselle, I believe you have crossed the
boundary Marie has set for you. You must not want
me for myself, but for what I am. Isn't that true?"

"Marie wants you destroyed."

"And you, mademoiselle?"

"I have never felt so alone or so confused. Even
Satan has abandoned me. He doesn't come to speak
to me anymore when I'm alone. He wants me to
make a choice. But it isn't between himself and
God. You are the one he now contends with."

"Your dreary nightmares don't frighten me, mademoiselle. Not even the delicacy and scent of your

flesh can make me believe in Satan. I don't believe in evil. And if it did exist, it would be God's gift to us, not the devil's."

Babette circled his body. "Then I am pure enough for you?"

"Not pure, mademoiselle, just not evil. You try to save the world in your own way, and yet the world keeps running away from you. The real world, that is."

"You think I am a lunatic?"

"If you were completely insane, I wouldn't fear you so much. No, there's a true power that sparks your madness. To bed you I would leave myself open to attack by Marie. Oh, not by her hand, but by yours." He turned and took both of her hands in his. "I look at your hands and know they would be soft against my skin, and yet powerful enough to properly wield a whip. Mmmm. I am erect before you, mademoiselle, in more ways than one."

"Let temptation rule. Take my blood, but fuck me first."

"And how will you fulfill La Maîtresse's wishes?"

"I will not. You will."

"A frustrating game that only Marie could start." Sade laughed. "And I thought I would be making her life hell. She has chosen a beautiful agent in you." He kissed her forehead, and she moved against him, her hand finding his swollen penis. "You make it difficult to avoid Marie's trap." He lowered his head to smell her skin. "Your blood boils hot, mademoiselle, and I thirst to taste it." His tongue slid up her neck and followed the curvatures of her ear. He sensed the blood grow hotter as his flesh flushed from the flow. A simple taste. A few drops. The trap was somehow mixed in with her blood, he knew. "Mademoiselle, your blood, it is impure."

"This once I wish it were not," she said, pulling away to kiss his lips.

He gently held her tongue between his teeth. A touch harder and he would taste that tainted blood. If only he could trust himself to take her body and leave his thirst behind.

Chapter Fifty-one

"La Maîtresse."

Marie spun around and found Stephen standing in the doorway to her room.

"You haven't called me that in a long time."

"I've refound my need for La Maîtresse."

"No one ever loses the need, my dear; you only tamped it down for a while."

Stephen moved into the room, closing the door behind him. He dropped to his knees before her.

"Did you return the child to her parents?"

"Yes; they were so happy to have her back, they gave us no hassle. Said they understood how children's games can become too frantic. Yes, that was the word they used, frantic. Not violent. The fact that our son knocked her out cold was frantic. Isn't that strange, La Maîtresse?"

"Some of us enjoy violence, Stephen, and prefer to call it by a friendlier name."

Marie reached behind herself and lifted a matchbook from the dresser. She struck a match and threw it at Stephen, hitting him on his right cheek.

"Remember Florida, Stephen. The flash of pain that lasted days, weeks, as I recall."

"I was bad, Maîtresse."

She caught a glint of fear in his eyes before he looked away from her.

"And have you been bad again recently?"

"Bad enough to require your attention, Maîtresse."

"You require nothing. You beg for whatever I will give you."

Stephen bowed his head and asked for forgiveness.

She hadn't had the pleasure of marking a man in a long time.

The room was not soundproofed, she reminded herself, pulling out a pair of silk stockings. She rolled them into a ball and shoved them inside Stephen's mouth.

Decorative ropes sashed the velvet curtains on the window. She would use them, of course. He dared to look at her, and she spat in his face. When he reached up to touch the saliva, she kicked him sharply in the ribs, sending him sideways onto the floor.

"I didn't say you could move. It's been too long, Stephen. You don't remember the rules. I shall enjoy teaching you all over again." She took a folding knife from her bag and snapped it into place. She bent down and dragged the blade across his cheek. "Remember when I shaved your body clean with a knife similar to this one? I recall the taste of your blood that night. Clean blood, unsullied by my vampire blood, but that didn't last long, did it, Stephen? I could have blooded you and let you die. You wouldn't have fought me, even if I hadn't used those wicked chains to keep you still. I had mercy on you and gave you a taste of my own blood. Will I be as kind this time, I wonder?" Marie pulled the blade down the front of his body, ripping apart his clothes. She whacked his erection with the side of the blade and teased a drop of his semen onto her thumb. She tasted the salty milk on her finger and smiled down at him.

"And what if Gillian should walk in, or possibly hear the sounds of my whip? What will you tell her, Stephen?" She pulled the stockings out of his mouth.

"That I am finished with this family."

"What will you do? Travel from place to place, hoping to find peace? There is none, you know. There are only lulls."

"Roger no longer wants to live here. Vanessa has a strange obsession with staking one of us. And Chuckie was never mine."

"Do you mean biblically?"

"He was born of my sperm, but not out of desire. Gillian loves babies, and she produced one that would last an eternity."

"What a disappointment for Gillian should he find a way to become an adult."

"He wants her as a man wants a woman. She, in turn, sees only a small boy needing protection."

"Should we go public, Stephen? Should we take our pleasure in the living room so that no one doubts our relationship?"

"I don't hate Gillian. I only want to be free of the children who hate me."

"How dreary, Stephen. A father's love repulsed by his children. We've all had loved ones, Stephen, who we have sacrificed to save ourselves."

"Who have you sacrificed, Marie?"

"Many, including Louis. You look surprised, Stephen. Louis can be charming and sensual. I briefly thought about seducing him myself, before my daughter married him. I knew he would never be faithful to her. She was too reticent and he too passionate."

"Then why have them marry?"

"My daughter was not a beauty, and we had money but lacked nobility. The Sade family had not been careful with their money. Women, drink, and gambling drove them into near desperation."

"You make marrying your daughter sound like true desperation."

"She was sweet and docile. My dear daughter covered for many of Louis's escapades. Foolish girl couldn't see that she had his title and could now dispense with her husband."

"Maybe she loved him."

"And he loved his pleasures." She used the knife

to shave away clumps of hair from Stephen's chest. "Where is your heart? Here," she said, pricking his skin with the knife. "Shall I cut it out for you?"

"I hope you still realize that I lie under your knife, and not Sade."

Marie gave him a small smile. "I have made that mistake before and suffered the nasty consequences of my error."

She saw the fear again in his eyes. He wanted to move away from her but feared she would stab him before he got away. The point of the knife was inside his flesh, but still far from his heart.

"No, tonight you will be a client, Stephen. I can even assign a safe word for you to use. Would that make you more comfortable?"

"Not if you ignored me. Not if you didn't recognize my voice. Not if you buried yourself in your fantasies."

She rammed the stockings back into his mouth. She lifted the knife and began shredding his clothing. She flung strips of cloth around the room.

"Go to your wife and beg her for what you want from me. When she refuses, go find Babette, and she will know what to do."

Chapter Fifty-two

Stephen left Marie's bedroom and stood in the hall. A soft breeze blew down upon him from the attic, forcing him to acknowledge how naked he was. Marie hadn't bothered to close her door and hadn't remained in the doorway to watch him fulfill her wishes. She trusted that he was slave enough to follow her orders. He went down one flight of stairs and stood in front of his wife's door. He raised his right fist to knock.

"What the hell are you doing, Dad?"

Stephen turned to see a wide-eyed Chuckie looking him up and down.

"I want to be alone with your mother. Go away and play."

"More likely she'll tell you to go away and play with yourself."

Stephen spun around and quickly tried the door. It opened with an eerie slowness that made him hesitate before crossing the threshold.

"Gillian," he called.

Her coffin lay in the center of the room; a sewing machine sat in the right corner, and a mountain of clothes lay next to it. Nothing else invaded the seclusion of the room.

"Dad, I have something to tell you. We've got skeletons in the crawlspace."

Stephen halted for a brief moment before walking into the room.

"Dad, don't you want to do something about it?"

Stephen slammed the door in Chuckie's face. *Yes,* he thought, *I want to destroy every cell in your body. Why must any of my children suffer for what I have done?*

"Gillian," he called again, hoping she would not be inside the coffin. Hoping that his entire life had been only a nightmare and he would wake in a crib wailing as loudly as babies do. His mother would pick him up. She would attempt to feed him, to change him, to pace with him, and she would never understand why her baby cried so much.

Gillian had a plain pine coffin, and the lid easily fell back when he pushed it.

Instead of the stink he expected, he imagined rose petals. Waves of the flowery scent arose in visible spirals from the coffin, spreading a smoke screen across the room. Pines flourished and sank their roots deep into the carpet. Gillian sat not in a coffin but on a boulder. Her hair was long again, as in her youth, and her skin fresh, unmarred. Her breasts rose and fell as if she needed to breathe. The ancient, snug dress slenderized her waist. He wanted to say *I love you, Gillian,* but the words were buried under his strong emotions. He wanted to tell her of her beautiful eyes, her narrow nose, her succulent lips. If he said all this, she would forgive him.

"What the hell do you want, Stephen?"

Her voice shattered the dream. Stink worse than a sewer took the place of the roses. Her dress faded into a ragtag sweat suit, which revealed nothing about her body. The pines burst into flashes of fire, mixing their ashes with the dirt of the carpet.

What did he want? He tried to remember.

"If you think I'm going to be seduced by your running around naked, forget it. Go pay a visit to that whore who ruined our lives."

The door creaked open behind him.

"Mom, I've been trying to tell Dad about the crawlspace. I hid down there when I thought Cindy was dead, and there're all these human skeletons. One has his head bashed in. I don't know how the others died. Somebody has been storing dead people in our crawlspace."

"Stephen, what are you going to do about the crawlspace?" Gillian asked.

What was it that Marie had told him? Ah, yes; after Gillian rejected him, he should seek out Babette. Stephen turned and walked to the door, where Chuckie stood.

"Stephen, don't you think we should check out Chuckie's story?"

"No."

"Why not?" asked Chuckie.

"Because I put the bodies there." Stephen closed the door and heard his wife scream.

"Why did you put them there, Dad?"

"Because I fed from them, and when they were dead I needed a place to hide the bodies."

"Mom thinks you never feed from humans when at home."

Gillian's door opened, and she grabbed Stephen's arm.

"You've been putting us all in danger," she said. "How could you do that?"

"You expect me to abstain from human blood, sex, and whatever else you deem reprehensible."

"Let's discuss this in private, not in front of Chuckie."

"Ah, Mom, I know all about this stuff. You two could use my opinion, since neither of you are going to want to apologize. Now, if I should mediate . . ."

"Go struggle back into that crawlspace, Chuckie, and stay there." Stephen began feeling good about being naked. He didn't even listen to the words spewing out of his wife's mouth. He'd stay naked if he wanted. He'd find Babette and take his pleasure there. He jerked away his wife's hand and walked past Chuckie, who leapt for one of Stephen's legs. Chuckie's nails bit into his flesh. The toddler wrapped his legs around his father's calf and held on, while his father stumbled to the head of the stairs.

"A wonderful family sight." Marie laughed.

Gillian streaked into Marie's midsection, knocking Marie down. Gillian twisted free of Marie's hands and started tearing at her hair. Stephen stopped to watch the women, but only to watch. Chuckie lost his grip and fell down the flight of stairs. A piercing scream came from his baby lips as Vanessa plunged a stake into his heart. Stephen turned immediately but couldn't move when he saw the blood splattered across the entire front of Vanessa's dress. Chuckie's legs waved in the air as his small hands attempted to pull out the stake. Vanessa reached out to hold the stake in place.

Stephen barely heard Chuckie call for his mother, who still writhed on the floor with Marie.

The toddler's legs stopped waving about; his small hands weakened and sagged down onto his chest.

"Vanessa," Stephen called.

The little girl looked up with fiery eyes.

He wanted to ask why but didn't have to. The little girl removed her hands from the stake.

He wondered why he couldn't descend the stairs and save his son.

A loud crash alerted him to the fight taking place behind him. Marie had managed to kick Gillian across the landing.

"No," he said, grabbing hold of Marie.

"This woman isn't going to rule over me, Stephen."

"Look down the stairs, Marie." She did.

Vanessa was gathering stacks of newspaper and laying the sheets across and around Chuckie's body.

Enraged, Gillian stood but paused in her attack, sensing the two others were watching something harrowing. She looked at the two faces that didn't even notice her when she stumbled onto the floor. Her body was incredibly heavy. She had to stand, but her body didn't want to. Her soul burned inside her while her eyes lost focus on the two at the head of the stairs. She made attempt after attempt to gain her footing but failed every time. After crawling several feet across the floor, she reached out, expecting to touch either Marie or Stephen. Instead, her hand caught hold of a handrail spindle. Her hands climbed it as if it were a mountain, until she reached the banister, where she was able to pull herself to her feet.

"Gillian."

She heard her husband's voice; her eyes fixed on the direction of the voice, trying to focus.

"He didn't want to be a toddler forever," Stephen said.

His hands wrapped around her waist and held her close to his naked body. He was not erect.

Bit by bit a smell crept up from the first floor, a familiar odor. Blood. Her baby's blood, mixed with the hint of burning fibers. Paper crackling in the silence. Gasoline was always stored in the garage.

Why should she smell it in the house? she wondered.

"Chuckie," she whispered, and with all her might she pulled away from her husband. Cautiously she descended each blurry stair. When she looked ahead, she saw orange and blue and soot. Gillian almost toppled over at the last step. Meat cooked. Bloody meat. The heat scorched her hands, and she heard her daughter scoot away.

"Chuckie?" She screamed and blindly searched for a blanket, a throw, anything that could smother the flames.

Stephen watched his wife run in circles. Her sweats were singed by the bonfire Vanessa had set. It took only a moment for her to fling her own body atop her son's. Her hands became torches. Her body seemed to fuel the fire instead of smothering it.

Finally a massive rug was thrown over them, blocking his view and muffling her cries.

"The entertainment is over," stated Sade from the bottom of the staircase.

"Pity, Louis; you should have let the flames take the entire house," said Marie.

"With you in it I hope, *ma chére.*"

"My wife . . ." Stephen said.

"And child," Sade reminded him.

"Hardly a child, Louis, more like a spirited little demon," interrupted Marie.

A huff of smoke rose up from the carpet, lingered in the air, then dissolved. Sade moved around the edges of the rug, stomping out stray embers.

Stephen drifted down the stairs. Sade grabbed him as he took the last step.

"He didn't do it, Louis," Marie cried out.

"Who did?" Sade held a firm grip on Stephen, and with one hand reached up to grab a hank of hair, pulling it far back so that it appeared Stephen's back would break.

"My daughter," Stephen admitted.

Sade looked up at Marie, and she nodded.

"Actually, she set her little brother afire. Gillian merely wandered into the flames."

Sade tossed Stephen down on the smoldering rug. He felt the warmth of the wool, the former plushness now in cinders. The mixed smell of wool and flesh caused him to gag. A movement under his left hand brought him to life, and he rose and pulled back the rug.

An ashen hand felt for the toddler.

Where was her son? she wondered. She could feel nothing but pain. Her eyes ached only from the soot; she realized her sight was coming back. She twisted her body, and a sharp stab halted her movement. The sweatshirt had risen and her midriff lay bare. Her hand pulled at the small bone that had stabbed her. A tiny bone lay in her hand, whitish and gray. Burnt scraps of denim speckled her ashen palm.

"Gillian."

Her husband attempted to pull her up. She rolled over and presented him the bone. He instantly swept it from her hands, and she followed its path until she saw the blackened stake.

"He's your son," she told her husband, but the words did not come clearly. Her lips and tongue stung.

Her weight had crushed Chuckie's body so that he lay split through the chest where his ribs were revealed broken, singed around a hallow chest. Her son's face had his own caked-on blood circling his mouth and on his chin. His own.

"He's only a little boy," she said. "Only a small child." The voice wasn't hers. No, the voice came from a defeated, battered woman she didn't recognize. The flesh on her arm folded back like a slab of cooked meat. It was wet with blood. Hers or her son's. She didn't know.

"Where will we put him until he heals?" she asked. "He can sleep with me. I don't mind making room for him. He'll need months of rest, Stephen. Months of care from us."

"He's gone, Gillian. Let him rest."

"He'll come back to me because I want him to."

"No, Gillian. He is badly damaged; let him go. His life has been prolonged for way too long."

"We will take the stake out, and he will wake."

"In unbelievable pain."

"I'll never let him go, Stephen."

Stephen pulled closer and whispered in her ear. "Read your own body, Gillian; what is the pain like? He is mangled far worse than you."

Some of the ashen paper had melted into his face. His features had leaked into each other. His hair

241

existed only in patches. His eyes were swollen and sealed.

Gillian faced Stephen, and he peered into her face, a mask of suffering now. The tangible parts of her would heal. The flesh would flake away into whole skin. The suffering, however, would never go away.

"For heaven's sake, lift her up, Stephen, and get rid of that brat."

"Which brat, *ma chére?*"

"The both of them would be fine with me," Marie answered.

"If we bundle the soil around him, maybe he'll heal faster," Gillian said.

Stephen looked at the son who had wanted to steal his body. Had wanted Marie to stake his own father so that he could finally grow up.

"How can I love the boy?" he asked Gillian.

"I would never have permitted him to harm you, Stephen. We were playing a child's game of make-believe. He made a wish. Our dreams made the wish come true."

"I love only you, Gillian. The others have distanced themselves from us. They're no longer children. Not even of our flesh anymore. They are gnomes destroying our future together."

"You'll help me carry him upstairs, Stephen. We'll collect extra soil."

Sade kneeled next to Marie.

"Strangely, I think your husband is correct, madam. Your son should not be brought back. We can finally bury him in his grave. You will bring flowers when you visit, until one day you'll be relieved that he's gone, and you will not need to bring flowers anymore."

"You're the one who must rest, Gillian. Come, and I will lay next to you until the blackness of slumber overcomes you," said Stephen.

"Never! If you won't help, I shall do this myself." Her hands patted along her son's body, trying to gauge how solid he was. "Get me a blanket, Stephen." His hand did not leave her shoulder. "I want it now."

Sade stood and climbed the stairs. Within moments he returned with a cashmere throw. She grabbed at the throw and proceeded to wrap the toddler's remains in the softness of the wool. Her hand reached for the stake.

"Gillian, he feels nothing now. If you remove the stake, he will be screaming in pain. I will help take him up to your room. Mourn him for a day and a night, then give him back to God."

"God wants nothing to do with us." Marie chuckled. "I know what Chuckie is thinking. He wonders how this happened. What had he done to Vanessa? He merely used her as the butt of his sick humor. Stephen is right; he feels no pain in his world. He may long for his body, but it doesn't really torture him. He longs for a friend who has gone away for a while. He envies his father's body. The maturity of it. The solidity of it. He envies the love Stephen can capture with it. Someday I believe the little fellow will find his way back. Maybe not inside your body, Stephen. Then again, who knows? I wouldn't rest very soundly, Stephen. I wouldn't let my soul wander into the deepest pits you have traveled; you might find yourself trapped in a home you cannot control."

"Are you saying that I'm safer if I allow him to return in his own body?'

"You'll never be safe from him, Stephen. Whether he retakes his body or not, he will always haunt you inside your own coffin."

"Help me, Stephen," Gillian said.

Sade scooped up the remains and climbed the stairs. When he reached Marie he stopped. He turned to look at Stephen.

"She's right. He will haunt you inside the coffin. He will cause you to tumble out of nightmares with your flesh still rotted and your bones still aching. The only delight you'll have is knowing he suffers far more than you do." Sade smiled at Marie and carried the remains into Gillian's room.

Chapter Fifty-three

Gillian watched Sade lay her son inside her coffin.

"Take the blanket from him," she said.

Without looking at her, Sade unfolded the blue cashmere and gently pulled it away. Black soot and body fluids covered the blanket where it had touched the toddler's body. Bits of the child's flesh fell away onto the softness of the satin lining his mother's coffin.

"This is crazy, Gillian. Let me put him in his own coffin, at least. You can sit with him, and tomorrow . . ."

"There will be no burial, Stephen." Her hand waved him away from her so that she could reach inside the coffin and tuck her son in properly. "He's strong, Stephen. He'll bear the pain."

"His bones are broken, his flesh melted enough

to make him unrecognizable. Don't put him through the agony of being worse off than when he began. Say good-bye now and let him sleep."

"You heard Marie. He'll never be able to rest."

"Lord, don't listen to that woman."

"She has been there, Stephen. She knows what he feels."

"Shit, Gillian, all she knows is what she imagines."

"Gillian, *ma chére . . .*"

"Get the hell out of here, Louis, and take that old battle-ax with you."

"May I ask, Stephen, why are you undressed?" asked Sade.

"Because it's my birthday. Get out."

"But I am curious, Stephen. I come into the house and find your wife and son aflame, with you naked at the top of the stairs with Marie. I wonder what you and Marie could have been doing. I also think it strange that you did not come to your wife's assistance. Now Marie I understand. She enjoys tragedy. Pain stimulates her appetite for more pain. But you, Stephen, what were you thinking?"

Gillian faced her husband.

"Is it true, Stephen? Did you do nothing to help us?"

"Chuckie was past being helped. You were inconsolable. There would have been no way to stop you."

"Ah, but I did manage to put out the fire with the rug," said Sade.

"You wanted us to burn. The bodies in the crawlspace. You put them there knowing that they would someday be found and your family would take the blame."

"Nonsense, Gillian. It was a stupid thing to do, that's all. I didn't plan for the bodies ever to be found. I placed them far back in the crawlspace under an old pentagram painted on the foundation. It had been drawn in blood and . . ."

"Whose blood, Stephen?"

"Hell, I don't know. It was just there."

"Whose blood, Stephen? One of your victims?"

"Two of my victims, Gillian. I hadn't left enough blood in the first to finish the design."

"Witchcraft. You were going to accuse your family of witchcraft."

"There are easier ways of ridding myself of you and the children. I purposefully drew the pentagram so that we could claim it had been there before we moved in."

"Stupid. The authorities could date the remains."

"Yes, I am guilty, Gillian; of stupidity and carelessness, that's all."

"Why would you watch as your wife was turned into a torch?" Sade asked.

"I was stunned. I couldn't believe what was happening, first to my son and then my wife."

Vanessa appeared in the doorway.

"I smell him." She sneered while looking about the room. "It didn't burn all the way. There's some of him left. I don't like that."

"Leave, Vanessa. Get out of my room." Gillian barely contained her anger.

Vanessa walked into the room, sidling up to Sade. "You reek of his odor. He is on your shirt, on your hands." She turned and set herself on tippy-toe in order to look inside her mother's coffin. "Ugly. Cut off his head and cast it away." She reached into the coffin.

Gillian struck Vanessa across the face.

"Get out now, child, or I will destroy you."

"She's not a child, Gillian. We spawned a monster."

"And he's lying in Mother's coffin," Vanessa said. "Look how ugly he is. Let's put him out of his misery. That's all I was trying to do. He wasn't happy or bright, and he could be vicious."

"Sibling rivalry. Ah, I am glad I no longer must deal with that emotion." Sade stepped away from Vanessa.

"You don't have to deal with any of us, Louis. Get the hell out of here."

"Uncle Louis threatened to hurt me." Vanessa's voice carried a lilt.

Stephen flew toward Sade's throat, wrapping his fingers around the windpipe. His arms went limp, his hands wilted away from Sade's flesh. His arms were nearly broken by Sade's force.

"Bit by bit, Stephen. I will break you bit by bit." Sade immediately left the room.

"I knew they would bring horrors that we've never had to deal with before. They have turned us against each other," said Gillian.

"I never really liked Chuckie." Vanessa ran out of the room when she saw her mother raising a fist.

Chapter Fifty-four

"Why destroy this family, Marie?"

She turned and saw that her son-in-law had quietly entered her room.

"Why not?"

"Because you came here for refuge from me."

"They never should have created vampire children. Actually, I had expected to find Stephen beyond help. Instead, that demon boy has been eliminated. Doesn't matter which one, eh?"

"His mother may attempt to save him."

"What a fool! Don't they have a Social Service Agency to take care of such cruel parents?"

"Do you remember how you treated your daughters?"

"Oh, I've regretted having my poor daughter marry you. At the time, it seemed to service our needs. We wanted a title and your family had one. It made my grandchildren nobles."

"And you showed perfect timing."

"My grandchildren survived the Revolution. I saw to that."

"You are incredibly selfish, Marie. Even I abhor the way you encourage this family's rivalries."

"To hell with the family, Louis. Here we are facing each other. What is it that you want from me?"

"I want the years I spent incarcerated back. Can you give them to me?"

"Can you give me back my daughter's reputation? Can you take away the laughter that exploded behind fans in ballrooms as she entered? My grandsons came home with bloody noses because of their father's sins. My younger daughter—can you give her back the virginity you stole? The child she bore?"

"I will not speak of her." Sade turned to leave.

"Run away, Louis. Bury your head in your hands and pine for your greatest love."

"I've destroyed you before."

"But you never will again. I dare you to wipe out all your memories again, because that's what I carry with me."

"And why do I want to remember anything from my past?" Sade gave a soft chuckle.

"Because Liliana is part of it."

He turned. "I look at you and no longer recognize the face or the body. This is a new woman before me. One who has no connection to my past."

"It isn't my flesh that you need to see. It's the

memories I share with you. They are all there. Not a single one was lost in the transition."

"Your memories are warped, Marie. They don't meld with mine."

"I know about your single weakness, Louis. A girl. A sweet girl you turned. She hated her life."

"She never hated me."

"No, but there was a secret we kept from her."

"Never utter the words, I warn you."

"She listens to us once in a while. Do you feel her now? Shame, I don't. I have no reason, then, to speak the truth."

"Causing Liliana pain will gain you what, *ma chére*? She only knew that I was her uncle and nothing more."

Chapter Fifty-five

Alone with her toddler son, Gillian gently rubbed his scarred brow. She fingered the wound surrounding the stake. His small hands were missing several fingers that had been burned away. His feet had barely been touched by the flames. She touched him where the baby skin was still fine and smooth. A smile spread across her own bruised face. The stinging pain made her feel closer to her son. Nursery rhymes played their music inside her head. A nursery with blue tint on the wall and hints of blue in the small rug that was spread in front of the crib. The carved bureau was covered with stuffed animals, one especially made for him by a grandmother. He hardly ever cried. He giggled and cooed delightfully, teasing her heart away.

Why had she blooded such a precious gift? He

should have been laid in the arms of the reverend father. *Keep him safe, Father. Keep him within God's protection. And when he asks of his mother, tell him I loved him far too much to keep him with me.* She imagined herself a saint. She could never be one. Her selfishness stole her children's lives away. Each forever hindered, never reaching maturity, to remain a child for eternity.

Stephen had refused to turn the youngest child. The older ones he had taken without a thought. The youngest he would not touch. She had demanded that they take Chuckie to the priest and let him grow up without their love.

However, at the doorstep to the rectory she faltered. The bundle in her arms squirmed for release from the blanket she had tightly wound around him. He started to speak, repeating words over and over to hear himself. His conversations were made up of real words and baby talk.

The scent of his blood encouraged her to walk away from the rectory. Even when the door opened, she didn't stop descending the stairs. No, no, she said to the housekeeper at the door. She didn't wish to bother them.

The path back to the car had been long and protected by shrubbery that blocked the outside view. He wiggled in her arms, wanting to walk. If she put him down, she might never pick him up again. He could be lost in the bushes, run from her into the arms of a stranger. Chuckie's legs kicked as much as they could inside the blanket. A few feet ahead and Stephen would have seen her. Her legs stopped working; her arms squeezed the toddler tighter. Gillian bit into the sensitive area around her wrist and blood spurted out. She tried to get him to drink, but he fussed. The smell of her own blood fed her hunger. She buried her head in the blanket to make it all go away, but it wouldn't. The smell of blood, the familiar scent of the toddler, drove her crazy. Her head jerked, and without thinking she was feeding from her own son. After a while he willingly lapped at her injured wrist.

Again she had the opportunity to free his soul, to send him back to God. She remembered Marie saying that a vampire's soul was forever bound to the earth. She saw him wandering through the shadows of the in-between world, calling for her, sniffing his tears back, and wanting to be brave.

How could such a little one understand her choice? He'd believe she had abandoned him.

Several times she circled her own coffin, catching different angles of her son's face and body. No movement from the coffin. The stake was a seared slice of wood, barely stable in the tiny chest. Her hand reached for the stake, and as soon as she did, her husband's warning reverberated inside her head. The unbearable pain would hit his entire body, making movement impossible and speech incoherent. Her hand slid down the wood and fingered the blackened wound.

Vanessa had hated her little brother enough to fiendishly destroy him. Jealousy, hatred; was there a difference between them? Did Vanessa hate Chuckie, her brother, or did she hate the way Gillian appeared to favor him over her two other children? Vanessa was jealous of Chuckie and hated her mother.

Gillian climbed into her coffin. Staring up at the ceiling, she remembered Chuckie's birth. The other children had been happy to have a baby brother. Vanessa wanted to dress him in all sorts of outfits, even in the dresses she offered to hand down to her baby brother.

Gillian pulled the lid closed and felt for the open wound on her son. Her fingers rested lightly on the wound, and her eyes closed; seeking peace in her sleep.

Chapter Fifty-six

Babette first heard then saw Sade and Marie arguing inside Marie's bedroom. Neither opponent took notice of her. Instead they rambled on about the Hughes family, drawing similarities to their own personal dispute, a dispute that seemed to extend far back in time.

She noticed the flicker of candlelight coming from the attic. Moving closer, she shivered, feeling the blast of cold air hitting her flesh. After climbing the stairs, she pushed against the partially open attic door. Without a sound, the door swung back, barely missing the wall.

"Vanessa," she called.

The child looked over her shoulder with unchildlike eyes. The eyes reflected too many years to belong to an eight-year-old. The shine had left them.

Joy had gone long ago. Now the eyes were callous and full of deception.

"What do you want?" Vanessa asked, the smudge from the fire's soot on her nose the only symbol of her childhood.

"I saw the candle and wanted to know who was up here."

"Just me." Vanessa turned away from Babette.

"Are you sorry for what you've done?"

Vanessa giggled, shaking her head.

"You seem to be hiding."

"There are far better places to hide than the attic."

"I guess there's the crawlspace." Babette moved closer to the child.

"The brat's hiding place."

"Chuckie is in very serious condition. Most are encouraging your mother to destroy him completely. She hesitates."

"He stinks. Did you get a whiff of that creep's body? He'll only smell worse the longer they keep him around. They could bury him in the backyard. The soil is soft enough that even I could dig."

"Are you offering to dig a grave for your brother?"

"My last gift." Vanessa's voice was sardonic. She stretched out her legs in front of her and leaned back on the palms of her hands. "Do you like my nightgown?"

Babette looked at the black transparent cloth that covered the child's body. The front dipped so low that the flat breasts were exposed.

"I think you are too young to wear that outfit."

"A century old and I'm too young to be a woman and always will be too young. I get up every night, and you know what? My measurements never change. I never gain or lose an ounce. I have no character lines. My teeth are perfect, not a single cavity. My flesh never sags, even when I've not gotten enough rest. I remain looking like an innocent child."

"No, Vanessa, you're wrong."

Vanessa folded her legs and sat straight.

"Name a spot that shows my age." Vanessa said this both in defiance and hope.

"Your eyes are ancient. They show how tired you are. Evil flashes in them at unexpected moments. There's not a bit of innocence in the shadow of your eyes."

Vanessa perked up, enjoying the conversation at last.

"Can you see my thoughts? Do they speak to you through my eyes?"

"I see pain, jealousy . . ."

"You could have guessed that about me," Vanessa interrupted.

"Your hunger goes beyond the passion for blood. The need for sex is a deception. The slutty clothes are a disguise to hide the greater power that rules. You've coasted all these years, waiting for recognition, and you've been ignored. You're a coward, Vanessa."

The child's eyes slitted, her bottom lip shivered,

and her nostrils flared as her entire body became rigid.

"Say it, Babette."

"You're the greatest evil existing inside this house. Joy disgusts you. The dreams you have are filled with wounds both shallow and deep. You curse those closest to you. The rest of us aren't worth your time. For you blood isn't for drinking but for spilling. Red stains on a bit of cloth, or better yet excised flesh, thrill the blackened soul that hides within you. You're too scared to admit to what you are. Instead you flounce around, acting the child/woman, engaging in petty games with your brother."

"What I did to him wasn't petty." The edge in Vanessa's voice caused a chill to shake Babette's entire body.

"Not brave, sweetness. Sweetness; I've heard your mother call you that often, usually when her nerves have been frayed by your behavior. I know and she only guesses what you really are."

"The devil." Vanessa leered at Babette.

"No, even the devil is terrified of what you think."

Vanessa giggled. "And do you personally know him?"

"He's touched me many times during my life."

"Where? Here!" Vanessa lunged forward and grabbed Babette's breast. "Or maybe he's tickled your snatch." Vanessa's hand glided slowly down Babette's body. "Perhaps you're the devil's own concubine." Vanessa raised herself up onto her knees. "He may be the only one in the world who would miss you. You haven't a parent down the street waiting supper for you. No one in this house likes you. You can't even get my randy Uncle Louis to have sex with you. Don't worry; I'll make sure none of your blood is wasted."

Babette watched Vanessa creep up on her. The small fingers pulled at Babette's cotton shirt, seeking a firm purchase. Vanessa brushed back Babette's hair, watching the strands spring out in the air before gently falling down to cover Babette's back.

"Why have these fools allowed you to flourish in our midst without tasting the sweetness coursing through your veins? Do you have a secret, Babette? One that can be smelled and tasted?"

The child's head buried into Babette's neck. The prick of tiny teeth tickled rather than pained Babette's flesh. The soft lapping was delicate and slow, signaling that they had much time to savor.

A sharp screech made Babette open her eyes. The walls resounded with screams. Pain felt tangible in the air. Babette's gut ached and she heard Vanessa retch.

Chapter Fifty-seven

He lay next to his mother's rotted flesh, actually savoring his awareness of her. Her shaking hand covered his mouth, and he bit into the flesh to assuage the pain. His skin crawled with tiny pellets of steel that embedded his flesh. Open sores feeding off the acid of the awakening. *Mom,* he wanted to say. *Mom, what's wrong with me?* Her blood spilled into his mouth and he suckled. She didn't pull away from him.

"You have to be brave and endure the long renewal that you must go through, Chuckie. Do it for Mama."

Her voice soothed his mind but could do nothing for his flesh that burned and roared with heat. He wanted to cry out again. He wanted to dump out his pain and let it ride through the air and carry his

261

plea to every ear in the world. *Toddler Chuckie hurts and is miserable. Mom, when will the pain go away?* He remembered her words, telling him to be brave and endure the *long* renewal. How long? A day? A day and a half? No more than two days, he hoped.

Brightness seared his eyes shut. His mother had pushed open the lid of the coffin. Gradually he peeked through slitted lids and saw only the soft glow of a candle that split his head in two and robbed him of vision.

"My little boy has come back to me. I knew you would. You'd never leave your mother."

His hand reached up to feel her cold flesh, but he couldn't find her.

"Mama's going to take these nasty bits of sooty cloth off your body and wash you down."

He screamed so loud that his throat ached. His hands waved in the air, warding off imaginary arms reaching out for him.

"No, no, don't fret. Mama doesn't want to hurt you."

His hands kept waving in the air, not chancing a possible intruding arm.

"What the hell did you do, Gillian?" Stephen rushed into the room.

Chuckie sensed that his father was near his mother. This made him nervous, considering the threat Chuckie had posed to his father.

"You couldn't let the boy rest in peace."

"There was no peace for him. You heard Marie."

Was that quiet, dark vacuum peace? Chuckie

wondered. He had been riding the air, feeling not even a whisper of a breeze. There had been no weight holding him down, forcing him into the gravity's pull. He had been floating through the air alone, but within earshot of voices, familiar voices that had made him smile.

"Do you believe everything that woman says?"

"She should, Stephen." He heard his aunt's voice, sprinkling sugar along with salt.

"He's our baby, Stephen. We can't abandon him. Look at his face."

"It's horrid," Stephen said. "The child is nothing but agony and fear. The face isn't the face of our little boy. Instead he looks like a tortured prisoner on the verge of death."

Chuckie dared to lower his hands to his face. His nose wasn't in the right place, his eyes seemed swollen twice their normal size, and his mouth . . . Where the hell was it?

"He'll heal, Stephen."

"It'll take months."

Oh, shit, Chuckie thought.

"If it's any comfort to you, Chuckie, you no longer look like a cute little toddler. There's nothing cute about your looks anymore," his Aunt Marie said.

"Get the bitch out of here, Stephen."

"Oh, Gillian, if you had listened to me, you wouldn't find yourself in this mess. Kids running away from home, attempting to do away with a sibling, jumping playmates. There's nothing but chaos in this house. I don't know how you've all lasted this long. During the French Revolution you all would have been hunted down and guillotined, each of your heads flopping into straw baskets."

Gillian tried to fight her way past her husband to reach Marie.

"She's purposely riling you, Gillian. You should know better than to let her see that she's getting to you."

Chuckie wanted to snuggle next to his mother in the coffin. He wished everyone else would disappear.

A hand brushed his sensitive skin and he cringed.

"Look! his skin flakes off in my hand," Marie said, lifting her hand for the parents to see. "You know, Gillian, he may never be the same little boy. Maybe his features will return, but he'll always dream about the pain. He'll wake from his sleep before it's time, and he will endure the last melding of flesh, the repair seeming to take longer each day. I pity the boy. There's no safe place for him. Unless he is able to steal another body the way I did. Any volunteers, Stephen?"

"I volunteer Marie." Sade joined the family scene.

I don't want to be a girl, Chuckie thought. He wanted to get a hard on, chase pretty ladies, and bed his mother.

"Can you believe, Louis, that this woman is making her child exist as a freak?"

"Chuckie isn't a freak." Stephen grabbed hold of Gillian before she could reach Marie.

"We are all freaks, *ma chére*. We should be

crumbling in our graves. At the very least laying in our coffins the way your *fils* is. He does look natural lying on that white satin, except a funeral home would probably advise a closed casket."

"All of you get out of here. My son is not on display."

"What will you do, Gillian, lock him away until he is whole again?" The sarcasm in Marie's voice triggered Gillian into action.

Stephen allowed his wife to pummel his arms and shoulders while he ordered the other two out of the room. Slowly they walked to the door. Marie turned for a final glance at Chuckie.

"Months, perhaps years will pass before he's ready for display."

Chuckie screamed out all the pent-up pain and fear, piercing their ears with his sorrow.

Chapter Fifty-eight

"Why do you suppose Stephen married her?" asked Marie as the door slammed behind her.

"She's an excellent lay," Sade answered.

"Is she? She seems too uptight to enjoy sex. Will she do more than the missionary position?"

A ghastly ghost waited for them in the dark part of the hall.

"Babette, is that you?" Marie stopped for only a moment, then continued walking toward the pale spirit.

"You've given up your blood. To whom?" asked Marie.

"To my ward." A weakened Babette fell against the wall. Her eyes barely stayed open. Her legs seemed spongy, ready to flop her body onto the floor. The whiteness of her flesh turned her into a supernatural waif waiting and wailing in dark old homes.

"Roger? Vanessa?"

"The one who wanted me the most," Babette said.

"And I thought I was the one suffering blood lust whenever I saw you," Sade said.

"Louis, she's killed one of the children. This isn't good."

"Which *enfant* did you rip from its mother's bosom?"

A child's dry heave called their attention to the attic.

"The child isn't dead yet."

Marie followed Sade up the stairs. Pools of blood spotted the floor of the attic.

"Quite disgusting," Marie commented.

Vanessa leaned against an old nonworking rocking horse. The paint was mostly peeled off, and the horse leaned a bit to the left because of the child's heavy body.

"Vanessa, why would you take Babette's blood?"

The child swallowed down several heaves before speaking. "No one would miss her."

"I would, child." Marie came closer to check Vanessa's color. "She's pasty, Louis; I would guess she's lost most of her blood and taken a good portion of Babette's."

"No bedtime snack for me this morning."

"Louis, don't be sarcastic."

"*Mon Dieu,* I would have thought you'd be joyous just to think that I would be considering that girl's fetid blood."

"That's why none of you drank from her," Vanessa's eyes narrowed. "Who did you mean to trick?"

"Not you, child. You aren't worth Babette's precious time and blood. Why did the stupid bitch let you drink, anyway?"

Vanessa retched again. This time, a small amount of blood dribbled from her lips and down her chin.

"What will happen to me?" Vanessa asked.

"I've never seen the final results. I imagine you will puke all your blood and shrivel up into the corpse you really are."

"I don't believe she likes your answer, Marie. Her eyes detest the sight of you right now."

"It's not my fault, child. You've been warned not to take human blood. You even attempted to do away with your own brother because he had disobeyed."

"No one would miss her." Vanessa's voice spoke in a whisper.

"I would have, dear, and I'd never have forgiven you."

Vanessa sneered up at Marie.

"You've failed, child. You haven't taken all of Babette's blood. There's still some left for another."

"Thank you, Marie." Sade smiled down at Vanessa.

"And your brother is back. Not in one piece, obviously, but ready for the long haul of getting well.

You, unfortunately, look worse second by second."

"I need blood." Vanessa reached out a hand toward Marie.

"Does she really believe I'd stoop to help her, Louis?"

"Ah, *ma chérie*, we've already established that she is stupid."

Marie laughed until she heard footsteps creeping up behind her. "Your mother is joining us, Vanessa. If that gives you comfort."

"Mom, all this blood is mine," she said, waving her hand in the air. "I need to be refreshed or I may shrivel."

"Become a dry, dusty corpse, actually, Gillian. She should never have attacked my Babette. I know you've told her many times not to drink human blood. And to think of the vengeance she took on poor Chuckie for committing the identical offense," Marie tut-tutted.

"Gillian, consider what you should do before acting," Sade said.

"Mom." Vanessa raised her arms up to her mother. "Come here and give me some of your strength."

Gillian searched the attic while the others watched.

"Oh, Mom, I can't wait for you to catch a rat. Its blood will not heal me as yours can."

Gillian reached behind a trunk and brought out a saber.

"Vanessa, this is a saber. It was used by men in

the cavalry. You must have had one, Louis, when you were in the military."

Sade nodded his head.

"It has but one sharp edge. It was meant to cut down or wound the enemy defeated in battle. The former owner of the house left it behind. Matter of fact, when we first moved in, it hung in the dining room. I thought it crude and a danger around children, so I brought it up here and hid it behind that old trunk, filled with silver. I knew you children had no interest in the antique silver. I was sure it would be safe there.

"I tried very hard, Vanessa, to protect each of my children. I allowed no blooding of members of the household, and I banned drinking from mortals." Gillian laughed. "I thought I was in complete control. Instead your father slipped his victims under the house. Chuckie grew impatient to taste mortal blood. And you, Vanessa, plotted against us all. If I had fallen down those stairs, Vanessa, what would you have done? Did it matter whether it was Chuckie or me? I found a second stake hidden in the closet of your room. Who was it for? Couldn't have been for Daddy, because he would have trained you in his ways. And you knew that. Did you know about the skeletons under the house, sweetness? Did Daddy ever throw you his leftovers? He did. I can see it in your eyes. Not guilt. No, scorn for my gullibility. All these years you've been Daddy's little girl."

Gillian unsheathed the saber. The metal sparkled in the candlelight. She dropped the sheath on the floor and raised the saber into the air with both hands.

"Chuckie meant no harm to any of us. Yes, he teased, but never with evil intent."

"Gillian . . ."

"Shut up, Louis," Marie interrupted.

"You plead for my blood to make you whole again. Instead I will set you free, sweetness." Gillian swung the sword. The blade passed through her daughter's neck, separating the head from the body.

Vanessa's lips moved slightly before Marie kicked the head across the attic.

"I could have sworn she was saying *bitch*. I can't stand children who don't respect their elders," Marie said.

"Louis, bury them far apart and deep."

"Why not burn the child, Gillian? Make sure she doesn't have the opportunity to return, as I did." Marie touched Gillian's arm and the mother recoiled. "If not, Louis, you could shove her under the house with the other skeletons."

"I want my child buried. Her head can never again be joined to her body."

Chapter Fifty-nine

Sade wrapped the small body in a crocheted shawl he had found in her room. He covered the gaping hole on the shoulders and lowered the body into her casket. The satin lining of the coffin was a pale pink, with touches of white lace on the empty pillow.

He hadn't shut the door to Vanessa's room, but he sensed Stephen's quiet step drawing closer.

"I'll bury my child," Stephen said.

"Gillian requested that I . . ."

"I know what she wants. Even if my wife doesn't see fit to care for her daughter's last needs, I do."

Stephen ran his hand over the shawl.

"Where's the head?" he demanded.

Sade turned to the bureau. Vanessa's head sat atop the marble counter, her eyes staring into her father's, her flesh sagging, losing elasticity and decaying before the two men.

"Gillian wants the head to be buried separately."

"I'll take care of it."

"Separately," Sade repeated.

Stephen looked at Sade and said, "I'll lay the head at her feet."

"I don't think . . ."

"She'll not find her head. Do you still believe in the old legends that she could lift up her head and replace it upon her shoulders?"

"At one time I wouldn't have believed that a skull could reclaim its vampire life simply by laying with a staked corpse. Now whenever I see Marie I'm reminded that every impossibility is possible."

Stephen walked over to the bureau and stooped to open the bottom drawer. He pulled out a small pink-and-white-plaid blanket.

"Her baby blanket," Stephen explained. "Her very own, not a hand-me-down from her big brother. We were excited to have a girl. Gillian refused to use any of Roger's clothes for the baby. Everything had to be shiny, new, pretty, frilly, be the most feminine article she could make or buy. Roger would sit fascinated near his sister, watching her play with her fingers and toes. He even guided her path when she started to crawl. He loved her as much as we did. He didn't seem to mind giving up his only-child status. Maybe he was glad to be free of doting parents."

"And when Chuckie came?" Sade asked.

"She was spoiled rotten by then. And not very

long after that, all our lives changed, thanks to Marie."

Stephen leaned over to kiss his daughter on the mouth, but drew back quickly when he found a few gnats stuck to the blood around and on her lips.

"I haven't had a chance to wash the head yet. I'm sorry, Stephen. Just give me a second and I'll have her cleaned. . . ."

"No, I want to cleanse my own daughter for her burial. I never got the chance to do that before. The children went to sleep and woke a short time later little vampires. Do you think we're horrid for what we did?"

"I think you were inconsiderate, Stephen, never giving them the choice."

"What kind of choice could an eight-year-old and a toddler make? I explained what would happen to Roger."

"Did he understand?"

Stephen looked over his shoulder at Sade.

"Probably not. All I can remember is the fear in his eyes. I never gave him the chance to say 'yes' or 'no.' Gillian and I kept telling ourselves that there wasn't anything else we could do. Abandoning our children to strangers was not a viable solution. Stealing normal lives from them was."

Stephen left the room for several minutes and came back with towels and a washrag.

"May I help?"

"No, Louis. The children mean nothing to you. You've always considered them annoying.

"I was never able to spend any kind of extended

time with my own progeny. I suppose I'm simply uncomfortable with children, since I didn't have the practice."

"I have . . ." Stephen stopped for a moment to select the proper words. "I have one-and-a-half sons left. One is planning on running away from home, and the other wants to see me staked. He covets my well-used body. Louis, how did it feel to destroy your mother-in-law?"

"There is a lot of bad feeling between myself and Marie. I don't think it can be compared to what has happened here."

"Still, you knew her well, and even if only related by marriage, she was a member of the family."

"A relative who always played power games with me. She won when we were mortal. Now I am in control."

"Or you think you are. How do you think destroying Vanessa will affect Gillian?"

"Initially she'll run from it," said Sade, gazing out the open window. "She'll never quite believe she did it."

"You wanted to keep something belonging to Marie with you after destroying her. Gillian has asked for nothing and doesn't want to know where Vanessa will be buried."

"Someday she'll ask. Better it be me to have to tell her than you."

"Why?"

"You'll never find a good place to bury your child, Stephen. You feel that now. And you'll live these feelings all over again when Gillian asks."

"I won't tell her." Stephen's hands worked to clean the blood from Vanessa's face, and finally he noticed the smudge on her nose and rubbed the dirt gently off. He laid the plaid blanket over her face and carried the head to the coffin. He hesitated.

"At her feet," Sade reminded.

"I would think you'd offer me some privacy."

"What neither you nor Gillian understand is that your children are better off in the in-between world."

Stephen placed her head near the tiny naked feet.

"Do you know any prayers, Louis?"

Sade laughed. "What do I need prayers for?" Sade stepped through the doorway and heard the door slam at his back.

Chapter Sixty

Babette lay in her bed, unable to sleep, unable to get up. She had never destroyed a child before. Quickly she reminded herself that Vanessa was no child. The girl had lived far longer than Babette and had no qualms about taking Babette's life.

No one had come in to ask how she was doing. She'd had to use the hall wall for support until she reached her own door. Opening it, she immediately fell into the room and onto the floor. After several tries, she managed to stand and shakily walk to the bed, throwing her body down on the mattress as if she had run a two-day marathon.

She rolled from side to side, waiting for the silence to die down. In her imagination she saw pairs of feet tiptoeing past her bedroom door. Did the residents expect her to jump out and attack them?

No, she never attacked first. All her victims had willingly come to her, begging for her blood, leaving her always close to death but not dead. Marie had warned Babette that Sade might succeed in killing her, but she doubted he had the ferociousness of that horrid child. The door opened. The squeak frayed her nerves.

"You really did meet the devil, didn't you?"

Roger was standing next to the bed, leaning over to whisper in her ear.

"I thought you were crazy, but I believe now. The attic floor is covered in blood and still you live. That should be impossible. My sister is gone."

Babette wanted to open her eyes, wanted to see the boy, but her lids were too heavy.

"Dad is burying Vanessa. He didn't want anyone's help. Seems she shared some of Dad's victims with him while the rest of us . . ." Roger faltered.

Daddy's little girl is no more. Unless Daddy should . . .

"Burn Vanessa," Babette whispered. "Burn her into white dust."

"Can't. Mom and Dad want her buried."

"He will bring her back." Babette's throat kept tightening, allowing only a few words at a time.

"No, he knows the pain she would suffer. Mom brought Chuckie back. No one is sure whether he even knows where he is. Tell me about the devil, Babette. Tell me where to find him."

Slowly she raised an index finger to her lips to hush him. They sat for a long time in silence. Finally Babette reached out to find Roger.

"I'm still here," he said, taking her hand in his.

"It wasn't a curse," she said. "The contract was plain and simple. A hand covered my heart, and I felt the blood heat up within me."

"The devil's hand?" Roger asked.

"His hand. One night he put me to bed, and I smelled him on my flesh. But it was when he touched my heart that I felt the change."

"Did he cut open your body?"

"He didn't have to. My heart was already exposed."

"Did he love you and did you love him?"

"No one mentioned love. Do you know love?"

"My mom and dad love me, I think."

"How do you know?"

"They've said so once in a while."

"But how do you know they love you?"

Roger kept silent for a few minutes.

"I want to believe they do," he finally answered.

"No one loves."

"You're wrong."

"No one loves. They only desire. They want. They take. And disguise their selfishness as love."

"Did the devil disguise himself when in front of you?"

"Never. But he never spoke of love. He had a desire for my flesh. He wanted my soul. He took away what made me human. He gave me instead a weapon."

"Why won't you tell me where to find the devil?"

"He doesn't want to see you. You haven't anything to offer."

"I could become his disciple."

Babette's hand tightened on Roger's.

"Don't," she whispered. "He'll give you a gift that will make you hate yourself."

"Do you hate yourself?" he asked.

"I no longer am myself. I was once a little girl, and he was godlike." Babette strained to open her eyes. She wanted to look into Roger's eyes. "Come closer, Roger."

"I'm not sure it's a good idea. Will you make me drink your blood?"

Babette smiled. She wished she had the strength to laugh at his assumption.

"I can't make you drink, and even if you should want to, I doubt there's enough left to destroy you."

She felt the boy put his ears to her lips.

"I have died over and over. My tainted blood is an elixir that poisons and gives life. Already the elixir is multiplying in my arteries and veins. I can't die unless every drop is taken from me."

"And a vampire can't do that because he becomes too ill," Roger said.

She smiled and found that her lids fluttered open. Roger's face was close, his eyes wide and sorrowful.

"Don't look so pained for me," she said. "I am vulnerable to time and disease. Someday my blood will be trapped in a corpse. I pity you. Disease and time no longer exist for you."

"The stake does. The hatchet to cut off my head does. Fire does. And you do. Someday one will get me." He smiled and rubbed her cheek with his fingers. "I hope it's you."

Surprised, she asked, "For the sex or the strange taste of my blood?"

"Neither. Because you understand."

Chapter Sixty-one

"A carrion crow sat on an oak
Fol de riddle, lol de riddle, hi ding do,
Watching a tailor shape his cloak;
Sing Heigh-ho, the carrion crow,
Fol de riddle, lol de riddle, hi ding do!
Wife, bring me my old bent bow,
Fol de riddle, lol de riddle, hi ding do,
That I may shoot yon carrion crow;
Sing Heigh-ho, the carrion crow,
Fol de riddle, lol de riddle, hi ding do!"

Chuckie lay patiently, listening to his mother reading through the Mother Goose book. Hour after hour she read to him, played music for him, cleaned his body, and encouraged him. Lord, was he bored. One more nursery rhyme and he would ask for the stake back again.

Somehow in her eyes he had reverted back to being an infant. She had even tried to carry him downstairs with her, but his screams of pain dissuaded her. He didn't need a mother anymore. Yes, those many years of being the baby had been good, but now he was ready to move on.

> *"Jack Sprat*
> *Could eat no fat,*
> *His wife could eat no lean;*
> *And so,*
> *Betwixt them both,*
> *They licked the platter clean."*

How many times had she recited that one? That one she had memorized. He had it memorized. He imagined everyone in the world had that rhyme memorized.

For days he had seen no one beside his mother. The special attention grated on his nerves. Worse on the nerves in his flesh than on his mind. He knew they were intertwined; when one gave him hell the other would follow closely behind.

"Mama," he whispered.

"Baby, don't talk. Rest. I only want you to become whole again. I'll take you to the zoo as soon as you are strong enough to walk, or I can carry you if you are hungry for the wild animals."

All he had wanted to say was "Shut up. Don't torture me with any more rhymes or lullabies." But she gently kissed his lips and silenced him. He wondered if he would have the strength to stick his tongue into her mouth the next time. Maybe she would get the hint.

He lifted his hands to look at them. New flesh was covering the blackened waste that slipped off his hands and onto the coffin's pristine satin.

"Is Mama's little boy counting his fingers and toes?"

Shit! Mama's little boy is wondering when the hell he'll be able to get out of this box and back on his feet. When he'll be able to feel things again. The numbness had begun to subside in the palms of his hands, but the fingers craved the sense of touch.

"The girl in the lane, that couldn't speak plain,
Cried, 'Gobble, gobble, gobble':
The man on the hill, that couldn't stand still,
Went hobble, hobble, hobble."

He couldn't drift into the sound sleep he needed. He would close his eyes and see his sister, her hand pushing down the stake, preventing him from tugging it out. His eyes would pop open, and Mom would start with the rhymes all over again. She had sung so many lullabies he wondered why she wasn't hoarse.

Visions of his sister, his pain, and his mother's doting kept him from sleep. Awake, the healing process would take years. He had to sleep. Mom had promised that Vanessa would never come near him again. How could she be sure? Sometimes Mom left him alone for a few minutes for her own feeding. What if Vanessa timed it just right and opened the door to this room while she was gone? He barely could whisper. If he allowed himself to drown in his pain he could scream. He wouldn't stop screaming then. He had no idea where the sudden strength would come from. His throat would grow hoarse and painful.

Every cell of his body would prickle with pain. It felt like tiny pins puncturing his flesh.

"Close your eyes, my little baby, or you'll never get better," his mother said, laying her hand across his open eyes.

He didn't want to be in the dark. There were monsters waiting to stake him and roast him. Even when his mother came to take her own sleep next to him, he could not sleep. He liked having her near, but she would go away and her flesh would decay. A truly dead body lay next to him. Where did she go during those hours of rest? He didn't sense that she stayed in the coffin with him. She would suddenly take leave and her body would instantly dry up and shed that day's skin. But she wasn't there when it happened. Where did she go? He didn't even know where he had gone when he had slept.

She always came back to him, though. Her hands would reach for his small body and her careful touch would be reassuring. And another day would have passed for him without sleep.

He heard his mother recite another rhyme.

"Tommy's tears and Mary's fears
Will make them old before their years."

Chapter Sixty-two

Roger was passing through the kitchen when the doorbell rang. Since he was nearby and knew the others were likely to ignore it, he went to answer it. When he opened the door, he found a rotund man of thirty. The man's belly stretched out the oil-stained T-shirt he wore. His shorts came down almost to his knees, and his sockless feet were tucked inside thong style sandals.

"Can I help you?" Roger asked.

"Kid, I want to see your grandfather."

"He's dead," Roger answered honestly.

"Come on, kid, don't give me that. Who's the old guy who lives here?"

"Old? Oh, you mean my Uncle Louis."

"Whoever the hell he is, I want to see him. Go get him now, kid."

"You don't want to talk to my uncle."

"Oh yes I do."

"He's kinda sick and grouchy," Roger said.

"I don't want to talk to him, kid. I want to rip his head from his shoulders."

"Have you ever met my uncle before?"

"No, but my wife has."

Instantly Roger understood.

"I don't think he's at home."

The man placed his hands on the frame of the door and leaned toward Roger.

"When will he be home?"

"I don't know. Sometimes he has these doctor appointments and we never know when to expect him."

"Bullshit!"

"You really don't want to have anything to do with my uncle, believe me," Roger pleaded.

The man pushed Roger aside and walked into the house. Under his arms yellow sweat stains darkened his T-shirt.

"Big old house you got here, kid. Do you want me to go through every room until I find the bastard?"

"You can't do that. My brother's sick upstairs, and Mom won't allow anyone near him."

"Is what he got catching?"

"Yes! It could be the plague. A new form, that is. We've even had the government doctors here. Everyone is supposed to stay clear of him."

"Then how come this house isn't off limits?"

"You mean quarantined. Did the sign fall

288

down?" Roger was making his way back to the front door when he heard the man climbing the stairs.

"Wait! I told you, my brother can't be disturbed. You could catch what he has."

The man paid no attention to Roger, continuing his climb to the second floor.

"Guess I should begin at the top and work my way down." He started up the next flight of stairs.

Roger started to think that this was the ideal time to run away from home. Mom had disappeared behind her bedroom door and was seen only briefly when she needed food for herself or Chuckie. She had no need for a second son. Hadn't she made a clear choice when she destroyed Vanessa? What if he accidentally hurt his brother? He'd probably suffer his sister's fate. When it came to Chuckie, Mom didn't wait for explanations.

Chapter Sixty-three

Marie thought she heard an elephant walking down the hallway outside her bedroom and popped the door open for a peek. Elephant was close, she thought, viewing an overweight stranger heading for the attic stairs.

"Excuse me, sir."

When he turned, she saw the most belligerent face she had ever seen.

"May I ask what you're doing in this house? Are you the plumber or some other sort of service person?"

"Hey, lady, don't get on a high horse with me," he said.

"My two feet are on the floor, so it's impossible for me to get on any kind of horse at all."

The man sneered at her and turned to continue his journey up to the attic.

"Sir, who let you in?"

"Some kid," he said, placing his foot on the first step leading to the attic.

"There's only one mobile child left, so I suppose you mean Roger."

He stopped on the third step and turned around to look at her.

"I didn't bother to ask the kid his name. Seems, though, that I'm looking for his uncle."

"Uncle Louis?" Marie burst out laughing.

He shook his head and was about to turn back to his chore when she interrupted.

"But he's not up there."

"Listen, that bastard screwed my wife."

"No! How unheard of for Louis. Are you sure?"

"She had bite marks on her body, and she didn't get them from me. The neighbor next door has been telling me about a visitor who comes around in the afternoons, and we both agreed the description fit the guy who lives here."

"Two guys live here."

"I want the older one. I plan on kicking his ass."

"He'll enjoy that."

"Who the hell are you, anyway?" he asked.

"I'm a guest in this house. Perhaps not a very welcome guest, but still, the occupants all know me. That is certainly something you can't say. I believe you are trespassing."

"Hey, screwing someone's wife is trespassing. So I got every right to be here."

"I don't understand your logic, but . . ."

"I couldn't stop him," yelled Roger from the opposite end of the landing.

"I really don't care. Even though he is quite rude. However, your parents are going to have a different point of view. I guess we should direct this . . . man to your Uncle Louis."

"Oh, no, Aunt Marie. Don't do that."

"This man has been insulted by your uncle. He deserves to meet Louis face-to-face."

"Where the hell is he?" roared the man.

"Please don't, Aunt Marie. I don't think my parents will be able to cope with finding another body."

"What the hell is the kid talking about?" the man asked.

"He's sputtering out words. Simply doesn't want to get caught letting a stranger into the house. Go downstairs, Roger, and see if you can find your uncle."

"Honest, mister, you should get out of this house. Nothing good ever happens around here anymore."

"I thought we've been having a wonderful time the past few days, Roger. There hasn't been a dull moment," said Marie.

"Please, mister. This isn't worth the awful things that can happen."

"I insist you go down and get your uncle, Roger." Marie's face turned stern and her voice had the edge of a threat.

"This sucks," said Roger, descending the stairs with heavy footsteps.

"Why don't I continue my search until you find the old guy?" The stranger turned back to the attic stairs.

"You'll not find anyone up there. Why don't you come wait in my room? Roger shouldn't take long."

"Okay, to show you I can cooperate, I'll give you fifteen minutes; then nothing's going to stop me from rampaging through this house. And I'm going to check every nook and cranny." He descended the stairs.

"Come have a seat in my room," Marie said. She smiled seductively, but his frown indicated he wasn't interested. "No sense standing in the hall."

"Are you helping him to get away? Maybe I ought to go down and check on that kid." As he passed Marie's room, he peeked in. "What the hell is that?"

"What?"

"That casket."

Marie faced her room.

"Oh, you're right. There's a coffin in the center of the room."

"Hey, don't try to tell me you hadn't noticed it."

"Perhaps that's where Uncle Louis is hiding," she said.

"What the hell would he be doing inside a coffin? Ain't there a local law against in-house wakes?"

"I'm not from here."

"Yeah, I can tell by that Southern drawl of yours."

293

"Shall we take a peek inside?"

"Hell, I don't care what you have in there."

"Even if it is Uncle Louis?"

"If he's dead, he ain't going to be a problem anymore."

"A good reason to check," she said.

"Shit, just open the lid; I can see from here."

Marie sidled up to the stranger.

"What if I told you we could have some fun." She winked at him.

"With a dead body?"

"I'm talking about you and me," she whispered.

The stranger took one long look at her, turned his back, and shouted, "Where the hell is that old man and his freakin' nephew?" He walked to the head of the staircase.

"You ingrate," shouted Marie, rushing forward to tackle the stranger to his knees.

Chapter Sixty-four

"Roger said someone was here to see me." Sade immediately spotted a touch of blood coloring Marie's lips.

"Yes." Marie stared back at Sade.

"Yes, there was someone here to see me, or yes, what do you want?"

"Yes to both." Marie smiled.

"Where is this man Roger told me about?"

"Don't worry, Louis, I rescued you from the brute." Marie was about to close the door to her room when Sade reached out an arm to stop her.

"And how did you do that, *ma chére*?" Sade reached out with his other arm to dab at the blood on her lips. He presented his red-stained finger to her, and she immediately licked it off.

"Where is he, *ma chére*?"

"Where he'll do no harm," she said.

Sade looked over her shoulder and saw the open lid of the coffin. He pushed past her to view what was inside.

"Ah, Marie, another dead body. This is the last thing the Hughes family wants to find."

"He'll be up and around in just a bit," she said.

"You shared your blood?"

"Why not? As you said, the Hugheses don't need to find a dead body, and I was hungry and the man was rude. He got what he deserved."

"How will you feed him when he wakes?"

"Lord knows Gillian keeps all sorts of blood in the refrigerator. I can offer him possum, rat, or something special, like kitten or puppy blood. Must have been a run on births, from what I see in the refrigerator."

"Then you will send him home to his wife?"

"You scoundrel, you recognize him, don't you? Did his wife keep his photo on the bedroom dresser? I hope you were able to ignore it and have a good time."

"Half the neighborhood will be vampires before you leave, *ma chére.*"

"It'll be good for the Hugheses to have friends. They spend way too much time with each other. Except for Stephen, of course."

"He has spent way too much time with you, Marie."

"He would have learned more if he had. Gillian would be dust, and the children would be out of their misery. What on earth possessed him to stay with his family?"

"Love, perhaps?"

"I think they're all scared to live their true personalities. Stephen mixed very well at the parties I invited him to. He could have had his own little tribe of vampires. Imagine the power he would have had. All Gillian did was nag him and curb his hungers. And the children are simply a burden. Thank heavens he's rid of one of them."

"He doesn't think that. I watched him care for Vanessa's body. He was gentle, sad, and I'm not sure he'll let her go."

"What is wrong with this family?" Marie shouted.

"They never lost their humanity. You, Marie, never had any to begin with."

Chapter Sixty-five

"You should really eat all of this, but I'll be satisfied if you finish the eggs."

Babette looked up to see Roger holding a great wooden tray filled with poached eggs, juice, bacon, and English muffins with butter dripping down their sides. He plopped the tray across her thighs and waited for her to begin eating.

"I certainly can't eat all this. Not even half of it. A little broth would have been better, Roger."

"I can always open a can and bring broth up, but I personally think this food will get you on your feet faster."

"So I can get the hell out?"

"I've decided I'll never leave this house on my own. I need a companion."

"Me? You expect me to travel with a vampire?"

"You already are. You came with Aunt Marie, didn't you?" Roger lifted a spoonful of egg and brought it to her lips. When she opened her lips to speak, he shoved the food into her mouth. "Salt or pepper? I forgot to bring them up, but I can run downstairs and get them."

Babette swallowed the egg and grabbed Roger's hand when he went for another spoonful.

"I can feed myself, Roger." He let the spoon slip into her fingers.

"Has your father buried your sister yet?"

"Doesn't seem like it. Her coffin is still in her room, and I know he placed her body there."

"Help him, Roger."

"Dad's already told me to go away. I'm not stupid enough to cramp him."

"He's not going to bury her and you know it."

"Listen, I'm ambivalent about this whole mess. She's my sister, and I couldn't imagine doing to her what Mom did. Yet I understand why Mom did it. Before Vanessa did what she did, I was hoping you and Aunt Marie would leave. Uncle Louis would follow, and we'd be able to go back to the way we were living before." Roger sat on the mattress. "I don't blame you for what happened, but I do blame Aunt Marie and Uncle Louis."

"Why not blame me?" she asked.

"All you did was sit and talk to Vanessa. She didn't have to take your blood."

"I could have tried to fight her off. I knew what my blood would do to her."

"Served her right for attacking you."

"You do want to meet the devil, Roger." Her eyes narrowed, enabling her to catch the subtle changes in his expression.

"If the devil happens to call on you while we're together, I wouldn't mind being introduced."

"What do you want him to do for you?"

Roger shrugged his shoulders. "I want something different than what I've been experiencing for the last century. Besides, I still have doubts about your sanity. Wouldn't you like to prove that you know the devil?"

"How could you not believe me after what you've seen me do?"

"Don't get so excited. I've seen plenty, and the devil had nothing to do with any of it. Maybe you're wrong. Your devil might be of this world and might never have seen hell."

Chapter Sixty-six

Stephen needed to see his little girl whole again. He unwrapped her head and set it gently down on the lace pillowcase inside the casket. He had closed her eyes earlier but was now sorry that he had. One last look at her open eyes would have given him peace.

Who the hell was he fooling? Nothing would give him the strength to bear the torture of burying his little girl. On moonless nights he used to take her trolling for prey, she the bait that made strangers stop and he the brawn that broke their necks. Sometimes they brought their catch home, allowing the danger to add flavor to the blood. They had sat in the backyard, not far from Gillian, with their private feast right under Gillian's nose. How Vanessa had enjoyed those nights, enjoyed not only the taste of human blood but the joy of knowing she was doing wrong. He understood that feeling, that getting away with something that had been banned. He had often found the same joy in women's beds while on the road. Gillian never asked questions, but he knew she cared. She always made a point of being extra sexy before one of his departures, obviously attempting to ensure his return. And he always did return, but it had become less and less clear to him why.

His hand brushed Vanessa's cheek, and the head rolled down the pillow to touch her shoulders. He straightened the head, balancing it carefully on the open wound.

"Stephen, where the hell are you?"

Marie's voice jolted his hands into immediately closing the lid of the coffin.

"There you are, pining away over a casket that should have been buried a century ago."

"What do you want, Marie?"

"I wanted to be sure you were carrying out Gillian's orders."

"Gillian doesn't give me orders. We consult with each other, Marie."

Marie gave out a bark of laughter.

"I could almost swear you planned to carry out her order without a second's hesitation. That's what you're doing in this room, right?"

"I'm here saying good-bye to my daughter." His teeth clenched, and his hands drove deep into his pants' pockets.

"Gillian doesn't seem to be worried about any

good-byes. Think that's because she has her pint-size son back?"

"Why do you enjoy antagonizing me?"

"I enjoy irking everyone. That's why I make a good dominatrix. Are you going to continue keeping your back toward me, Stephen?"

"I'd like to spend some time alone with my daughter."

"You're not going to bury your little girl, are you?"

"Marie, my family isn't your concern. You came here to escape or deal with Sade; I can't figure it out." He turned and saw the smirk on Marie's face. "I take it back. You came here to ruin the stability of my family, didn't you? Now I know what you put Louis through back in the seventeen hundreds."

"You don't know the half of it, darling. You still have your freedom. Now, if I took that away from you . . ."

"You'd never succeed. You can't have me put in jail or an insane asylum."

"I could do much worse. I can make you crawl and beg. Get on your knees, Stephen."

He felt his body tremble. His knees ached to bend. His flesh wanted his pain muted by another very tangible pain. He could ride out the burns, cuts, and bruises; they made him forget the emotional horrors he was forced to endure. He watched Marie's right hand move up and down her thigh. Her hands itched for the whip.

"You were a bad boy, Stephen. I told you to find

your pleasure with Babette, and you didn't."

"Then it would have been me instead of my daughter lying in a coffin."

"Maybe not. But isn't it a parent's job to give up his or her life for the next generation? Vanessa would be here standing in front of her coffin instead of in it. Wouldn't that have been worthwhile?"

"I'm not a martyr. And I can't believe that you ever suffered for your children."

"But I did. It caused me great stress to have to constantly worry about Louis."

"That wasn't stress, Marie, that was a thrill for you. Since you won't leave me, I'll take myself back to my room." He walked past Marie and stopped in the doorway. "Are you coming? I'll not leave you alone with Vanessa."

He watched her eyes shift back and forth between him and the casket.

"I could always slip back in here," she said.

"Why would you want to? Leave us alone, Marie. Take Louis and that bitch back to Paris with you."

"You're so pathetic, Stephen." Marie shook her head and crossed over the bedroom threshold. "You didn't say when and where the burial will be."

"I'm going back to my coffin to rest. When I get up, I'll take Vanessa to the local cemetery. Instead of being a graverobber, I'll be adding to the population."

"Pathetic, Stephen. Your life has become so dreary that even a burial takes all the energy you can muster. I remember when I could drive you way into the night, and you'd still want more at dawn." Marie turned away from Stephen and went up the stairs.

Chapter Sixty-seven

She felt the noose around her neck tighten. Her throat burned. So much pain that she couldn't open her mouth to let it out. Thirst, a horrible need for liquid. Blood! Water! Dry. She had never been this desiccated. Her tongue searched her parched mouth but found only cracking flesh. Her tongue lunged out of her mouth, tasting the air for liquid.

It took her a while to realize that the low moans she heard came from her. Her throat gagged on the grumble exploding quietly deep inside her, until there was finally silence.

Her lips formed the word *Mama*. Fear sparked within her, and she banned the word from her lips. That woman had . . .

"Oh, my God, where am I?" she asked herself hoarsely.

The saber in her mother's hands sweeping through the air, cutting through . . .

Vanessa lifted a hand and felt the deep indentation, not a wound. But her mother had severed her head from her body, she remembered. And Aunt Marie had kicked her head to the far wall. She felt again the sharp thump when she hit the wall.

She dug her fingers into the flesh around her neck and found no gash, just an even indentation circling the entire surface of the skin.

Her eyes opened to blackness, but she felt safe. Her other hand fingered the satin above, to the sides, and below. Her own casket. Did Mother just want to teach her a lesson? No, she'd heard her mother's voice demand that she be buried. The head separate from the body. She felt her chest, her arms, her waist, and her childlike tummy that hadn't had a chance to flatten before the turning.

"Separate," her mother had said. Had her mother relented? Vanessa's hands pushed against the lid, and she saw a hint of light. No, she wasn't underground.

She pushed harder on the lid, opening the casket. Slowly she moved into a seated position, her skin feeling like crisp dried leather.

This was her own room. Looking down at the palms of her hand, she saw how cracked and dry the skin was.

Babette had done this to her. Babette had purposely seduced her into drinking. Had Babette survived? Vanessa remembered drinking lots of Babette's blood, forcing herself when her stomach heaved against her will to feed. Then there was so much blood that Vanessa had thought it was coming out of her own pores.

"I hate you, Babette." Her gravelly voice cut through the silence of the darkened room.

Her brother, Chuckie, she despised. He had survived and lay at their mother's bosom, lapping at her blood for sustenance while Vanessa thirsted.

She looked over the side of the coffin that rested on a long oaken table. How was she to climb out?

Tired and weak, she wanted to lie back down again, but if she did that, she might never taste blood again. They would leave her for eternity inside this prison she had once loved.

Vanessa threw her right limbs over the side of the coffin and allowed herself to fall. Dragging herself to the door, she noticed that it had not been closed all the way. Her small hand slid into the opening and quietly opened the door.

She rolled her body back and forth on the carpet, trying to tamp down her thirst. When the desire had barely abated, she lay still for a minute, driving herself toward revenge.

"Roger," she whispered. Their rooms had been on the main level, but since Uncle Louis had arrived all the children had been given rooms on the second floor. Roger's was to the right of her room. Would he be asleep?

"Roger," she whispered, again feeling the ache in her throat.

Her hands gripped the carpet and pulled her onto the smooth hardwood floor of the hallway. Like a viper she slid her body toward Roger's room. She felt a thin outer layer of skin slough off, leaving a trail behind her.

At Roger's door she knocked softly.

"Roger," she whispered.

A hand touched her shoulder. Her body stiffened, and the thirst drove her almost mad.

Chapter Sixty-eight

Feeling her fright, Roger knelt and rolled Vanessa onto her back.

"It's only me," he said.

Her lips smiled, and he watched the flesh around her mouth start to disintegrate.

"Roger, hide me. Don't let anyone else find me."

As he rose he lifted his sister into his arms and took her into his room, closing the door quietly behind him.

He placed her on a beanbag he had bought through a catalog.

"I hate this thing," she said.

"Would you rather lie on the floor?"

"No. My limbs feel out of my control on this beanbag."

310

"I don't think your limbs were doing all that well when I found you in the hall."

"Thirsty, Roger." She laid her hand on his shoulder and weakly tried to draw him closer.

"You can't feed from me."

"Why not?"

"Mom would be furious with me. Maybe I could get you some blood from the fridge."

"What? Animal blood? Stinking animal blood won't make me stronger."

"Yes, it will, Vanessa. You'll slowly grow stronger."

"Do you think I can wait? How many people don't want me around, Roger? I have to be able to defend myself."

"Will you still go after Chuckie?"

"Think Chuckie means more to me than my own life? No, Roger, I've learned my lesson. If the family wants to stand dumbly by while he leads the enemy to us, what can I do?"

"Vanessa, I'll get you some blood." He tried to rise, and she gripped his shirt tightly.

"Haven't you heard me? Haven't you witnessed enough to know that they want to do away with all of us?"

"Nonsense. Mom acted out of rage. The others . . ."

"Did nothing to stop her. Babette begged me to take her blood. She wanted to be joined to us."

"No, she didn't."

Vanessa's eyes narrowed.

"What did she tell you?"

"If you were going to make her one of us, you would have given her some of your blood, and you weren't going to do that, Vanessa."

"My body burns and aches. I need relief and only your blood can take away all the pain."

"I can't, Vanessa. Mom would be furious with me. I couldn't face her. Eventually Mom will be able to tolerate you again. It's better that you hide and slowly get back your strength."

"Like Chuckie? Mom's feeding him, isn't she? She's sharing her blood with him. She wouldn't share it with me when I asked her for help. Mom turned away from me to find a weapon. A saber, Roger. She split my neck open with a saber. See?" Vanessa raised her hands to the top of her shirt and pulled it down so that he could see the scar.

"It will heal, Vanessa. The scar will disappear with time."

"Touch my skin, Roger; touch it."

He lowered his right fingertips to her neck.

"Feel the indentation it makes? I don't know how I made it back . . ."

"Dad."

"What?"

"Dad wouldn't let anyone else near you. He must have reconnected your neck to your shoulders."

"Then why didn't he stay to give me blood?"

"Maybe he didn't expect you to come back so soon."

"But how could I not come back this fast? It

couldn't be more than a few days since this happened."

"A day, really."

"Then my body hadn't deteriorated much."

"You look so awful, Vanessa. Let me get you some blood from the kitchen."

"Your blood," she whispered. "I'm your sister; I need your blood."

"I can't face Mom."

"Then go away after you've given me some of your blood. You've wanted to leave. Here is a reason to go while feeling proud that you rescued me. Just a little." Her hand searched his. Her fingers lingered on the protruding veins of his wrist. Her index finger traveled the distance of one vein, then backtracked to follow the winding of another.

Chapter Sixty-nine

Chuckie lay nuzzled against his mother. She had gone away again, and he realized he was in the arms of a rotting corpse. But that was all right, because he knew she would come back to him when she finished with her dreams.

His fingers entwined with her thin skeletal fingers. The skin barely covered the bones, but that would change when it was time for her to wake. Her flesh would blossom and the stink would disappear.

He shut his eyes and ordered himself to sleep. The pain crept up on him. The ache of his burned skin. The smell of cooked meat encircled him like an invisible cocoon. He recalled his mother many years earlier telling him he was good enough to eat.

Now he was cooked enough to be served up for dinner.

His eyes popped open when he heard the lid being lifted and felt the cool draft from the outside world.

"Are you okay, Chuckie?" Roger stared down at him. His eyes looked tired. His complexion seemed sallow. Hadn't he been eating enough?

"What's wrong?" Chuckie asked.

"I'm leaving."

"You mean you're running away from home?"

"I don't think any of us can be accused of running away, Chuckie. We're too old."

"Won't you be frightened by yourself?"

"Babette is coming with me."

"What for?"

"Because I asked her to, and she's tired of being used by Aunt Marie. We'll help each other survive. Maybe even go to Paris. She misses the place a lot."

"Wow! I guess I can't come."

"Chuckie, you must stay here and heal and help Mom. You'll be an only child finally, unless . . ."

"Unless what?"

"Keep guard against Vanessa," Roger said. "I couldn't . . ."

"Couldn't what?"

"She's our sister, Chuckie. I know she put you in all this pain, but she's had her own agonies to deal with. Maybe they taught her a lesson."

"What agonies? You mean because she doesn't have tits and an ass?"

315

"No. Mom tried to destroy her. She cut off Vanessa's head."

"Sounds good to me. But why didn't Mom tell me? I could sleep a lot better knowing that."

"Dad couldn't let Vanessa go."

"Shit! Dad and Vanessa against me. I'm done for, Roger. Take me with you. I'll heal in the backseat of a car or something."

"Mom will take care of you."

"She can't always. She's asleep now." Chuckie turned his head to face his mother's corpse. "You could drive a stake through my heart, and she wouldn't be able to protect me."

"Vanessa's weak. She'll need to crawl away and heal for a while. Has Mom been giving you some of her blood?"

Chuckie nodded.

"Fine; than it shouldn't be long before you'll be able to take care of yourself."

"Roger?"

"Yes."

"Go to hell."

"I'm sorry, Chuckie, I can't stay here any longer. You didn't want my help before . . ."

"So now you'll screw me by leaving me here."

"I've done all I can do. I find myself caught in the middle trying to make peace with everyone. I'm not going to get used up like this." Roger lowered the lid of the casket, leaving Chuckie in the dark.

Chapter Seventy

Vanessa licked each of her fingers. She had taken a lot of Roger's blood. She had resisted when he attempted to pull away from her. Finally he was able to detach her clinging hands and sucking lips from his neck.

Yes, Roger, I would have finished you had you been weaker or had you let me.

Seated on the floor of her room, Vanessa leaned back against the wall and smiled up at the ceiling. Inebriated. She had often wondered how that would feel. Now she knew. Vampire blood had to be the best. She giggled. Dad had always drunk most of the blood from his victims and had left only a teensy-weensy bit for her. Now she knew the high Dad would feel. For the first time since she had become a vampire she felt warm. Warm and comfy. Sleepy even, she realized.

She looked at her hands, but they were spotless. No more blood staining her skin or under her fingernails. Be so nice to have more blood, she thought. More vampire blood.

She lived in a house full of vampires; shouldn't be difficult to find herself some more of their wonderful blood.

Vanessa stood. She thought she heard shuffling movements in the hall, but when she reached the door and peeked out there was nobody there. She staggered to the next floor, where all was still. The attic stairs were in front of her, and she climbed them languorously, filled with the sweetness of Roger's blood. The attic door was open, and the smell of blood was strong. Rancid blood, she thought. The very blood that had made her vulnerable to her mother's wrath. Disgusting, vile blood that even now made her gag. She swallowed several times and entered the attic. She knew what she wanted. All she had to do was direct herself to that object and ignore the stench surrounding her.

Marie stood at the bottom of the attic stairs. What did that child want? What had led that stupid boy to give her his blood? Roger and Babette had quietly quit the house shortly after Vanessa had blooded her brother. Babette tiptoeing, thinking she was putting one over on Marie, Roger offering to carry little Babette's satchel. *Disgusting!* They had skipped off just before Vanessa giggled and planned her way out of the room and up to the attic. The attic still filthy from the blood meant to destroy Louis.

Marie heard objects being moved around in the attic, as if Vanessa was searching for something. Something to . . .

Ah, yes, thought Marie. Vanessa will not quit until she has won out over Chuckie and her pathetic mother. A mother who couldn't carry through with what she had begun. Instead she left the men to bury Vanessa. Never trust someone else with something so important that it could mean one's own existence.

Marie pulled back into the shadows of the hall, aligning her body with the alcove to Stephen's room.

Chapter Seventy-one

Chuckie heard his own small voice give out with a moan. Roger and Babette were gone. His father and Vanessa were out to destroy him, and his mother would sleep through all of it. He lifted one of his mother's hands, and when he let go the hand flopped back down onto her chest.

Wake up and tell me some more nursery rhymes. Sing a lullaby to me. I'll listen for hours to your sweet voice, Mom. I can recite most of the nursery rhymes and lullabies by heart. We could sing together and lull each other into ... What, sleep? No, not that. Rowdy tunes are what we need. Sailor songs and wild stories about dangerous adventures. Mommy, please wake up and save me.

His skin tingled again. The pain spread in waves across his body. A premonition of some danger drawing closer. He looked at his mother and willed her to wake. He called to her in a soft, birdlike voice. And the smell inside the coffin never changed. Her body was still breaking down. His mother was nowhere near the building-up process.

His small, aching fingers twisted around the cloth that covered his mother's body. He tugged gently at first, then harder, while repeating her name over and over.

There were monsters beyond this peaceful darkness. Others walking in the light, finding their way to Mom's coffin.

He reached up and touched the satin lining of the lid of the coffin. He tried to grip some of the material in his hands. Maybe he could hold the lid shut. Maybe he could fight off the monsters until his mother woke. He couldn't find a hold in the satin. It was so smooth and stretched-out that there was nothing to grip on to. His burnt fingertips were too desensitized to dig into the satin.

"Mom loves me," he said, as if reciting a spell that would ward off those who hated him. "Mom loves me."

"But I don't," shouted a voice.

The lid flew up and Vanessa smiled a vicious grin down on him.

"Mom loves baby Chuckie, does she?"

Vanessa raised the saber into the air and lopped off Chuckie's head.

Vanessa watched the blood flow from her brother's neck, saw the head tilt awkwardly to the side, and felt a deep relief pass through her body.

To his left lay her mother, putrid with the daily sleep upon her. But she'd still have her blood in her veins. The blood never went away. It stayed locked inside the husk, waiting to give life anew to the corpse.

Vanessa reached inside the coffin and touched her mother's throat. Soft, gel-like, due to the putrefaction. The blood still lay within.

Vanessa grabbed onto the side of the coffin and hoisted herself in on top of her mother. She didn't mind the smell, because she knew the feast that awaited her.

She slithered her body up along her mother's clothes until her lips could touch her mother's neck.

Yes, she could smell the blood just under the surface. *How delicious!*

"It's all mine now," she said, glancing over at her brother's staring eyes. "And you can't have any." She reached over and grabbed her brother's nose in order to turn his face away.

Turning back toward her mother, she licked her lips, saliva dripping from her mouth as she closed in on her feast.

"You little freak!"

Vanessa felt her shoulders grasped from behind, and she was pulled back and thrown onto the floor.

Spinning around on the floor, she faced her enemy.

"You are scum, Vanessa. Stealing your own mother's blood, and I imagine you planned on taking it all. Ridding yourself of your little brother is one thing, but disrespect for one's elders is another."

"Get the hell out of here, Aunt Marie. You don't belong here. Go back to your petty arguments with Uncle Louis."

"Petty! I have good reasons to hate and even dread Louis. He destroyed . . ."

"Your old body. And what did my dear Mama do? Do you remember? You were there. You kicked my head across the attic floor."

"And I'll kick your ass, my dear, if you try to destroy your own mother. I'm a mother, and I know what children can drive their parents to do. The years of tolerating that man Louis."

"You've never tolerated anyone or anything, Aunt Marie. You're here because you like to interfere, like to be in control and warp the world into what you want it to be. Uncle Louis is the only person you can't control, and that drives you to control others even more."

Marie squatted down to be nearer Vanessa.

"And what do I plan to do with you, Vanessa? Can you guess? In what weird and twisted way am I going to crush your world? I've already prevented you from growing stronger on your mother's blood. Little brother was a fly you swatted. Gillian is more important prey, isn't she, little girl?"

Vanessa lunged at Marie's throat, and Marie easily flung the girl off. The child rose to her feet and ran out of the room.

Standing, Marie pressed her lower back with her

hand, muttering about how she expected more from this new, young body.

"Nothing's perfect," she reminded herself. She heard feet pad down the stairs. "You can't stay free of me, little girl, because I have special plans for you."

Chapter Seventy-two

Gillian woke to a moon-filled room. The lid of her coffin was already open. Immediately she sought her son, but he wasn't there.

He couldn't have been strong enough to lift the lid and leave, she thought. Someone else would have had to come and take him away.

Instantly Gillian was out of her coffin and rushing down the hall to her husband's room. She swung the door open. His coffin lay before her, the lid closed, the moon spilling its light on the waxed varnish.

She opened the lid and saw that her husband was close to awakening, the skin on his face taut and his eyelids flickering. She looked down his body and saw her husband's hands holding bits of Chuckie's clothing.

She screamed and lunged forward, battering her husband's body. He woke and covered his face from the blows.

"Stop, Gillian. What do you think you're doing?" Marie forced Gillian to step away from the coffin.

"He took my little boy. Our little boy," she screamed at her husband.

"No, no, you're wrong. It was Vanessa. He stopped her."

"What?"

"It was too late; Vanessa had already burned most of the body; and all poor Stephen found were a few shreds of clothes left behind."

"Vanessa! I destroyed her."

"I'm afraid, just as you couldn't give up your little boy, Stephen couldn't give up his little girl, and, well . . . he reattached her head to her body. But don't be angry with him, Gillian; he intended to keep them separated. He merely stepped away for a few minutes. I'm afraid I'm the guilty party who begged him to come and help me find Babette. I didn't realize Vanessa could gain so much strength in such a short time. Only vampire blood could have healed her." Marie looked over her shoulder at Stephen. "You didn't give Vanessa any of your blood, did you?"

Stephen sat up, started to say something, changed his mind, and shook his head.

"I didn't think you would be that stupid or that generous," Marie said.

"Where's Vanessa now?" Gillian asked.

"We don't know for sure. Hiding, I presume. My

Babette is missing too. I don't understand . . ."

Gillian pulled away from Marie and ran out of the room.

"Get up, Chuckie. You can thank me later, after we've disposed of that wicked child Vanessa."

Chapter Seventy-three

Chuckie felt clumsy in his new body and tumbled out rather than climbed out of his father's coffin. His hands were too big; his feet clobbered along with each step he took. He didn't know what to do with those great big arms, and his legs took him way up off the floor.

"Chuckie, if you stand around looking like an idiot misfit, your mother will figure out the game right away. Make peace with your body."

"How . . ." Chuckie's voice boomed, or rather Daddy's voice did. He had gone from being barely able to whisper to having a deep, almost confident voice.

Marie patted Chuckie's body down, including his privates.

"Ah, everything is working just fine. Remember,

you answer to the name Stephen. Chuckie is your poor, lost little boy. And your guilt for the way you treated him weighs heavily on your conscience."

"Did Dad have a conscience?"

"Good point, Chuckie . . . I mean, Stephen. Don't overdo the guilt, but show some remorse for having lost your son. Actually, both your sons."

"I know. Roger said good-bye to me before Vanessa . . ." His hand went up to touch his throat.

"Yes. I don't know what happened to your head. After I staked your father . . ."

"When did you do that?"

"While Vanessa was retrieving the saber. I knew what she intended to do. That girl has no imagination."

"Where is Vanessa?"

Marie was about to speak when they heard Gillian's scream.

Marie pulled Chuckie by the collar and half-ran down the stairs, hampered only by Chuckie's clumsy movements.

"What is it, Gillian?"

Chuckie stared down at what was left of his body.

"You see, she burned him to a crisp," Marie said.

"His head. If we can find his head . . ."

"Gillian, I think you should take a closer look at your son's body. Certainly doesn't look repairable to me."

"His head. We must find his head."

"My guess is that Vanessa would either have it or know where it is," said Marie.

"Don't just stand there, Stephen. Find Vanessa. You know her better than anyone. Where would she be?"

"In the crawlspace under the house," he said.

Gillian ran for the front door.

"In the crawlspace? Why would she be stupid enough to hide in the same place you did?"

"You said she had no imagination."

"Marie, I wish you wouldn't set your victims free to prey on others," Sade said, walking through the open doorway.

"What the hell are you talking about, Louis?"

"The hubby you blooded. He was wandering around the house. Must have been a quick learner, because he jumped me and tried to bite."

"Whose husband?" asked Chuckie.

"None of your business," Marie replied.

"He's destroyed, and I buried the bits and pieces," Sade said. "But not deeply. The next rainstorm should wash his remains back up into this world. I suggest we leave and continue our vendetta in a safer locale."

"Mom can't stay here," Chuckie said.

Sade walked circles around Stephen's body.

"This is Chuckie, I take it. And it's your doing?" asked Sade.

Marie sighed. "I felt sorry for the boy."

"You were that bored?" Sade asked. "Where's Gillian?"

"Probably in the crawlspace under the house."

"Your doing again?" said Sade.

"No, it was . . ." Marie hesitated. "It was Stephen's idea. He thought Vanessa might be there."

"As a matter of fact, she is. I saw her scrambling into that hole a short while ago, *ma chére*."

"Why are they so predictable?" Marie said, waving her hands in the air.

"Will Mom destroy her again?"

Marie put a hand to Chuckie's cheek. "No, she'll want to get 'your head' back so she can stick it atop those bare bones." Marie pointed at his remains on the floor and shivered. "Why she would ever want to get that heap up and walking around and talking is beyond me. Anyway, Vanessa will be your problem. And let me warn you, Vanessa will know our little secret. She'll know you're not Stephen. Gillian is too upset to tell. Of course, when she finally calms down, you'll have to work hard at keeping our secret."

"You're not leaving, are you, Aunt Marie?"

"Lord, after all the trouble your family has caused me. I haven't dared take a decent sleep since I came here."

"Stephen, make her tell us where his head is," screamed Gillian, shoving her daughter into the house.

Marie and Sade quietly retreated.

Chapter Seventy-four

"I wish you had used some restraint, Stephen."

"I couldn't help myself, Gillian. As soon as I saw her I wanted to rip her apart. My own daughter, can you imagine that?"

"But you literally ripped her body apart."

"Yeah. I mean yes. But I didn't know what I was doing. I completely blanked out until you screamed when I, in a fierce, blinding rage, smashed her head in with the poker from the fireplace."

"I still think we should have tried putting the remains back in her coffin; maybe they would have regenerated into something that could have given us the information we needed."

"Gillian, we forced those children to eke out an existence they never asked for. Someday, if we see

Roger again, we should put him out of his misery, too."

"What? Maybe he's happy."

"Wandering around with a female with tainted blood who could kill him?"

"You're assuming they went off together. We don't know that. Babette may have run off on her own. I doubt she could take much more of Marie. Thank heavens she and that son-in-law of hers left. I know I couldn't have stood one more minute with that woman."

"I don't know. She grew on me."

"She grew on you in Nice, too. That's how all this came about."

"What I meant is that I began to understand the problems she had dealing with Louis." Chuckie silently thanked Sade for telling him to stop calling him uncle, or else that little slip could have done him in.

"And I can understand what Louis has to put up with." Gillian slammed her hand down on the steering wheel. "Maybe you should drive, Stephen."

"I told you, eventually I'll drive again. For some reason I now freeze behind the wheel. It's as if I've never driven before. Maybe you could teach me all over again."

"You don't seem the same, Stephen. I keep feeling that Chuckie is standing between us. I want to forgive you for what happened, but Chuckie is always on my mind when I'm with you. After we make love I feel dirty, as if I've just committed some horrible sin against Chuckie. We're awkward now when we make love, as if we have to learn each others' needs all over again. Rationally I know, Stephen, that we have to move on and let our children rest in peace, but Chuckie always seems to be present."

"Don't worry, Gillian. Give it time." He leaned over and kissed Gillian on the cheek and patted her knee. "We'll go far away from our old life."

"Can we run from all the pain?"

"We have lots of time to try. We'll go to different places and share new adventures." *Hell,* Chuckie thought, *maybe we'll even go to Paris.*

MARY ANN MITCHELL

Ambrosial Flesh

Jonathan's favorite sacrament was always Communion, the eating of the body of Christ. Since he was taught that we are all made in the image of God, it seemed natural to him to take it one step further—to eat actual flesh from a living body, starting with small bits of his own. . . .

But now Jonathan's an adult. His religious belief may have faded, but his taste for flesh remains as strong as ever. He's long since moved on, from eating his own flesh to eating that of others. But when his wife discovers his secret, Jonathan is faced with a problem. And his solution leads him not only to new extremes, but also to a meeting with a mysterious stranger—a stranger who holds the key to an evil force far greater than any Jonathan ever dared imagine.

___4902-3 $5.99 US/$6.99 CAN

Quenched

MARY ANN MITCHELL

An evil stalks the clubs and seedy hotels of San Francisco's shadowy underworld. It preys on the unfortunate, the outcasts, the misfits. It is an evil born of the eternal bloodlust of one of the undead, the infamous nobleman known to the ages as . . . the Marquis de Sade. He and his unholy offspring feed upon those who won't be missed, giving full vent to their dark desires and a thirst for blood that can never be sated. Yet while the Marquis amuses himself with the lives of his victims, with their pain and their torture, other vampires—of Sade's own creation—are struggling to adapt to their new lives of eternal night. And as the Marquis will soon learn, hatred and vengeance can be eternal as well—and can lead to terrors even the undead can barely imagine.

___4717-9 $5.50 US/$6.50 CAN

IN THE DARK

RICHARD LAYMON

Nothing much happens to Jane Kerry, a young librarian. Then one day Jane finds an envelope containing a fifty-dollar bill and a note instructing her to "Look homeward, angel." Jane pulls a copy of the Thomas Wolfe novel of that title off the shelf and finds a second envelope. This one contains a hundred-dollar bill and another clue. Both are signed, "MOG (Master of Games)." But this is no ordinary game. As it goes on, it requires more and more of Jane's ingenuity, and pushes her into actions that she knows are crazy, immoral or criminal—and it becomes continually more dangerous. More than once, Jane must fight for her life, and she soon learns that MOG won't let her quit this game. She'll have to play to the bitter end.

___4916-3 $5.99 US/$6.99 CAN

AMONG THE MISSING
RICHARD LAYMON

At 2:32 in the morning a Jaguar roars along a lonely road high in the California mountains. Behind the wheel sits a beautiful woman wearing only a skimpy nightgown. She's left her husband behind. She's after a different kind of man—someone as wild. daring, and passionate as herself. The man she wants is waiting patiently for her . . . with wild plans of his own. When the woman stops to pick him up, he suggests they go to the Bend, where the river widens and there's a soft, sandy beach. With the stars overhead and moonlight on the water, it's an ideal place for love. But there will be no love tonight. In the morning a naked body will be found at the Bend—a body missing more than its clothes. And the man will be waiting for someone else.

___4788-8 $5.99 US/$6.99 CAN

B|TE RICHARD LAYMON

"No one writes like Laymon, and you're going to have a good time with anything he writes."
—**Dean Koontz**

It's almost midnight. Cat's on the bed, facedown and naked. She's Sam's former girlfriend, the only woman he's ever loved. Sam's in the closet, with a hammer in one hand and a wooden stake in the other. Together they wait as the clock ticks down because . . . the vampire is coming. When Cat first appears at Sam's door he can't believe his eyes. He hasn't seen her in ten years, but he's never forgotten her. Not for a second. But before this night is through, Sam will enter a nightmare of blood and fear that he'll never be able to forget—no matter how hard he tries.

"Laymon is one of the best writers in the genre today."
—*Cemetery Dance*

HEXES
TOM PICCIRILLI

Matthew Galen has come back to his childhood home because his best friend is in the hospital for the criminally insane—for crimes too unspeakable to believe. But Matthew knows the ultimate evil doesn't reside in his friend's twisted soul. Matthew knows it comes from a far darker place.

___4483-8 $4.99 US/$5.99 CAN

Dorchester Publishing Co., Inc.
P.O. Box 6640
Wayne, PA 19087-8640

Please add $1.75 for shipping and handling for the first book and $.50 for each book thereafter. NY, NYC, and PA residents, please add appropriate sales tax. No cash, stamps, or C.O.D.s. All orders shipped within 6 weeks via postal service book rate. Canadian orders require $2.00 extra postage and must be paid in U.S. dollars through a U.S. banking facility.

Name_____
Address_____
City_____State_____Zip_____
I have enclosed $_____ in payment for the checked book(s).
Payment <u>must</u> accompany all orders. ☐ Please send a free catalog.
CHECK OUT OUR WEBSITE! www.dorchesterpub.com

THE DARK FANTASTIC
ED GORMAN

Seventeen stories. Seventeen slices of terror. Seventeen trips into the shadows. Whether it takes place in small-town America, a lonely highway at night, the near future, or the Old West, the real setting of each tale is the realm of nightmare, the place where imagination and fear reign.

No one knows this eerie realm more intimately than Ed Gorman, award-winning author and master of dark suspense. Now, for the first time, his greatest tales of horror and the unknown are collected in one volume, a compendium of the fantastic and the terrifying, the chilling and the grotesque. Brace yourself as you get ready to experience . . . the dark fantastic.

RICHARD LAYMON
DARKNESS, TELL US

It starts as a game. Six college kids at a party. Then someone suggests they try the Ouija board. The board that Corie has hidden in the back of her closet and sworn never to touch again. Not after what happened last time. Not after Jake's death. . . .

They are only playing around, but the Ouija board works, all right. Maybe too well. A spirit who calls himself Butler begins to send them messages and make demands. Butler promises them a hidden treasure if only they will follow his directions and head off to a secluded spot in the mountains . . . a wild, isolated spot where anything can be waiting for them. Treasure or death. Or Butler himself.

NIGHT IN THE LONESOME OCTOBER
RICHARD LAYMON

Everything changes for Ed that day in the fall semester when he gets a letter from Holly, the girl he loves. Holly is in love with someone else. That night, heartbroken and half mad with despair, Ed can't sleep, so he decides to go for a walk. But it's a dark, scary night in the lonesome October, and Ed is not alone. . . .

There are others out there in the night, roaming the streets, lurking in the darkness—waiting to show Ed just how different his world could be. Some of them are enticing, like the beautiful girl who wants to teach Ed about the wonders of the night. Some are disturbing and threatening. Some are deadly . . . and in search of prey.

In keeping with the season,
Harlequin Superromance is delighted to bring
you three very special stories celebrating
Christmas past, present and future.

"Just Like the Ones We Used To Know"
by Brenda Novak

Who can deny a child her only Christmas wish?
Not Angela Forrester. A caring foster mom,
she'd even risk losing Kayla to give her the
father she's never known.

"The Night Before Christmas"
by Melinda Curtis

A modern-day Scrooge falls in love over the
course of one unexpected Christmas Eve and
learns what he's been missing out on as a
workaholic all these wasted years.

"All the Christmases To Come"
by Anna Adams

It takes a festive train ride and shared memories
of holidays past to convince a pregnant woman
to chance everything for happiness.

"And it was always said of him, that he knew
how to keep Christmas well…. May that be
truly said of us, and all of us! And so, as Tiny
Tim observed, 'God Bless Us, Every One!'"
—Charles Dickens
A Christmas Carol

ABOUT THE AUTHORS

Christmas is still a magical time for Brenda Novak, who grew up the youngest of five and has five children of her own. On Christmas Eve she loves to make, decorate and deliver homemade frosted sugar cookies with her family. Charles Dickens's *A Christmas Carol* has long been her favorite holiday story, so for the past twenty years she's collected Dickens village pieces, which remind her a great deal of the architecture of Virginia City, where this story is set.

During the holidays, Melinda Curtis fills her house with decorations and ornaments made by her three children. Someday—between her children's college years and becoming a grandparent—she plans to decorate like an adult. Until then, it's cotton-ball snowmen beside popsicle-stick mangers and clothespin Santas with globs of bright glitter.

Anna Adams loves to see snow flying in the movies, snowy holiday mugs and snow painted on her windows…because she lives in a hot climate and longs for an old-fashioned—you got it—snow-covered holiday.

ONCE UPON
A CHRISTMAS

Brenda Novak
Melinda Curtis
Anna Adams

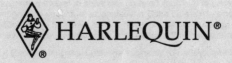

HARLEQUIN®

TORONTO • NEW YORK • LONDON
AMSTERDAM • PARIS • SYDNEY • HAMBURG
STOCKHOLM • ATHENS • TOKYO • MILAN • MADRID
PRAGUE • WARSAW • BUDAPEST • AUCKLAND

ISBN-13: 978-0-373-71380-6
ISBN-10:   0-373-71380-0

ONCE UPON A CHRISTMAS

CONTENTS

JUST LIKE THE ONES   9
  WE USED TO KNOW
Brenda Novak

THE NIGHT BEFORE   121
  CHRISTMAS
Melinda Curtis

ALL THE CHRISTMASES   215
  TO COME
Anna Adams

Dear Reader,

Virginia City is a place out of time. When I first visited there, I was completely taken with the look and feel of it, the sense that it has remained unchanged for so long. It immediately caught my imagination and begged to appear in one of my books. I'm glad it was this story, a story about Christmas.

Hopefully, as you read "Just Like the Ones We Used To Know," the town will come alive for you as it did for me.

Have a wonderful holiday season!

Brenda Novak
www.brendanovak.com

JUST LIKE THE ONES
WE USED TO KNOW

Brenda Novak

To my husband and five children,
because they make every Christmas special.

CHAPTER ONE

"Mrs. Forrester?"

Seeing Kayla's teacher smile expectantly as she held the door, Angela swallowed hard, then straightened her spine and walked into the sixth-grade classroom. On the Friday afternoon before Christmas break, it was empty of students, yet it still smelled of pencil shavings and chalk, which evoked pleasant associations. Growing up, Angela had been a good student. But the girl she'd taken in a year earlier was struggling in school, in life.

Angela had become Kayla's caregiver so late, could she really make any difference?

That was the big question and had been from the beginning. Angela was afraid she couldn't. And she was afraid Kayla's teacher had called her in, once again, to let her know just how badly she was failing.

Trying to ignore the helplessness that engulfed her so often lately, Angela perched uncomfortably on the chair next to Mrs. Bennett's battle-scarred desk—she knew her place in this room well—and smoothed the skirt of the designer suit she'd worn to work that morning.

"I'm sorry to bother you again," the teacher began, peering at Angela over her bifocals.

Angela pulled her heavy trench coat more tightly around her and forced a smile. "It's fine. You know I want what's best for Kayla."

"I want the same thing."

"Of course." They just approached it differently. Mrs. Bennett could be stern and rather severe. She often indicated that she felt Angela was letting pity about what had happened in the past interfere with good old-fashioned discipline. But Angela had been a foster child herself—had spent several years living in the same house as Kayla's mother, in fact—so she understood Kayla's situation well. Besides, this was Angela's first attempt at parenting. She was twenty-nine, but she wasn't married. Maybe she wasn't the best person in the world to finish raising Stephanie's daughter, but before Stephanie's mother had died, she'd given Angela guardianship because she was a better choice than any of Kayla's other options.

"What seems to be the problem, Mrs. Bennett?" She decided to ask the question and get it over with. "Isn't Kayla turning in her assignments?"

Angela knew Kayla finished her homework because they did it together. But only last Wednesday Mrs. Bennett had informed Angela that it'd been two weeks since Kayla had handed in a single paper. Angela had been shocked and worried, of course, but what made the situation more mystifying was the fact that Kayla couldn't tell her *why* she wasn't turning in the work.

"She's improving there," Mrs. Bennett said. "I'd like to see her test scores come up, but that's another issue. I called you in today because I wanted you to see something she's written."

Written? The crisp Denver winter settled a little deeper into Angela's bones. Kayla was generally excluded from the tight cliques of other girls. She kept to herself and rarely associated with the kids in her class, which had been the subject of yet another parent/teacher conference. So…had Kayla finally decided to get even with the ever-popular but cruel Barbie Hanover, who'd stolen her notebook and shown Jordan Wheeler the poem she'd composed about him?

Angela half expected Mrs. Bennett to smooth out a note detailing Barbie's lack of good qualities or some other manifestation of the intense humiliation she'd caused Kayla. But Mrs. Bennett presented her with what looked like a regular English paper. And, even more surprisingly, written across the top in red ink was a big fat A.

It was probably Kayla's first A, which should've been reason to celebrate. Except Mrs. Bennett's sober expression indicated that Angela should still be concerned.

"What—"

"Read it," Mrs. Bennett said.

Angela glanced at the heading.

All I Want For Christmas
By Kayla ???????

"She wouldn't put her last name?" Angela asked in confusion.

Mrs. Bennett gestured that Angela should keep reading.

She returned her attention to the small, cramped writing.

I suppose you want to hear that Christmas is my favorite time of year. That's what everyone else says, right? There's candy and presents and parties. There's baby Jesus and Santa Claus. Even for girls like me.
So why am I finding this stupid paper so hard to write? I should just copy someone else, someone normal. I can hear the people all around me. I want this…I want that…I'm getting a new cell phone, a new TV, a new dress. Barbie sits next to me and wants an iPod. Not any old iPod. It has to hold about a billion songs and play videos, too. Nothing but the best for Barbie, and we all know she'll get it. Her friend Sierra is asking for a snowboard. That's not cheap, either, so I wouldn't ask for it even if I wanted it. But Sierra's parents are rich, which means she'll be pleasantly NOT surprised to find it under the tree on Christmas morning. They're lucky. Not because they get

what they want, but because they want what they get. A boy I know wants a new basketball. He's—*the next part had been heavily erased and written over*—He's even luckier.

Was Kayla writing about Jordan at this point? Angela wondered. She thought so. He was the only person not named, which was significant, and there was emotion behind all those eraser marks.

Angela frowned and kept reading.

Tyler Jameson is asking for an Xbox. *Tyler was Jordan's best friend, which seemed to offer more proof that she'd segued from the boy she liked to his best friend.* He's always making a list of the games he wants—at $60 apiece. His Christmas isn't going to be cheap. Money. I wish it could buy what I want. I wish I could be satisfied with an iPod or new clothes, or even getting my ears pierced. But I don't care about any of that. I want something Santa can't pull out of a sack. I want a real last name. The kind that came before I did. Not, "We'll just call her…" I want to know what my name should've been. I want to know who I belong to. I want my father. Then I could ask him why he loved my mother enough to make me but didn't love me enough to stay.

If I knew him, I think even I could be happy with an iPod.

By the time she finished, Angela's throat had constricted and she doubted she could speak. She didn't know what to say, anyway. As tears filled her eyes, she felt Mrs. Bennett's hand close over hers.

"Heart-wrenching, isn't it?" she said softly.

Surprised at the empathy in the teacher's voice, Angela nodded. Evidently Mrs. Bennett wasn't quite as stern as she appeared. But Angela wasn't sure why she'd called her in to read this essay. Angela couldn't give Kayla what she wanted. Kayla's father didn't even know she was alive—and, because of what had happened thirteen years ago, Angela couldn't tell him. This letter only made her feel worse because now she knew that nothing she could buy Kayla for Christmas would make the girl any happier.

"She's a...a deep child," Angela managed to say.

"She understands what really matters."

Angela sensed that Mrs. Bennett had more to say, but the teacher wasn't quite as direct as usual. She seemed to choose her next words carefully. "You've already shared with me the situation that motivated you to take her in. Have you heard from her mother lately?"

"Not for a few months." Angela had had little contact with her friend since Stephanie had turned to prostitution in order to support her drug habit. Angela had tracked her down a number of times and tried to get her off the streets. She'd planned to put her in yet another drug rehab center. But during their last encounter, Stephanie had spent one night with them, stolen all the money out of Angela's purse and disappeared before she and Kayla could get up in the morning. Without so much as a goodbye or an "I love you" for Kayla.

The incident had upset Kayla so much that Angela had decided she didn't want to see Stephanie again. She had to let go of the mother in order to save the daughter. Which was why she was selling her house. She couldn't have Stephanie dropping in on them whenever she felt like it, disrupting Kayla's life. Kayla had refused to come out of her room for nearly three weeks after the last visit.

"You've never mentioned her father," Mrs. Bennett said. "Do you know anything about him?"

"I'm afraid not," Angela lied.

"Do you think a little research might help? Even if the circumstances surrounding Kayla's birth weren't good, the information might assuage the terrible hunger I sense in her through these words— and in some of her other behavior, as well."

Angela sensed that hunger, too. But telling Kayla about her father would start a chain reaction that could disrupt, possibly ruin, a lot of lives. Besides, Angela had promised Kayla's late grandmother—the woman who'd provided a foster home for Angela after her parents died—that she would *never* tell.

"There's no way to find him," she said. "I've tried."

"Recently? Because now that we have the Internet—"

"It was a one-night stand. Her mother didn't even know his name." Another lie, but Mrs. Bennett seemed to buy it.

"I see." She shook her head. "I'm sorry to hear that."

"It's unfortunate." The whole thing was unfortunate—and only one person was to blame.

"Okay, well, we'll continue to do what we can to make Kayla feel loved, won't we? Thanks for coming in. I hope you both have a wonderful Christmas."

"Same to you," Angela said and stood as if nothing had changed. But a thought she'd had several times in the past was stealing up on her. What if she were to take Kayla back to Virginia City for a visit? It'd been thirteen years. Surely, Matthew Jackson would never guess after so long. It would give Angela a chance to assess the situation, determine where Matt was now, what he was doing—and whether or not there was any chance he might be receptive to such a shocking secret.

"WHEN WILL WE GET THERE?" Kayla asked.

"Sometime tomorrow." Gripping the wheel with one hand, Angela turned down the Christmas music she'd put on as soon as they'd set off and glanced over at the girl who'd come to live with her fifteen months earlier. With long brown hair, wide brown eyes and a spattering of freckles, Kayla wasn't the prettiest girl in the world. She had the knobby-kneed clumsiness often seen with lanky children who were poised for more growth—she was going to be tall, like her father—but Angela had no doubt she'd grow into a beautiful woman. Kayla held herself with a certain grace and dignity that Angela found impressive, considering everything she'd been through.

The girl had spirit. Her mother hadn't broken it. The

kids at school hadn't broken it. Even Kayla's wish for something she'd probably never get hadn't broken it.

Angela was going to make sure nothing ever did. "MapQuest said it'd be about fifteen hours. Is that okay?"

"It's great," she replied. "I didn't realize Denver was so far from where you grew up."

Kayla's excitement lessened Angela's anxiety about returning to Virginia City. Maybe their second Christmas together would be everything she'd hoped. It certainly couldn't be worse than the first, when Stephanie had shown up completely wasted and without a gift for Kayla. "I wish we could drive straight through, but we started too late this morning." Last night they'd stayed up late packing, so they hadn't gotten up as early as Angela would've liked.

Kayla took a rubber tie from her wrist and pulled her thick hair into a ponytail. "We can go as far as possible before we stop, right? I'll help keep you awake. I love long car rides."

Angela smiled. "So do I."

"Is that why we didn't go on a plane?"

"Partly. That and the fact that Virginia City's a very small town. If we'd flown, we would've landed in Reno and then had to rent a car. And since we'll be staying for two weeks, I'd prefer to have my own transportation." Angela liked the flexibility having her car would provide. She and Kayla could head home anytime they wanted, without notifying anyone.

If she found Matt happily married with a few kids, she'd probably do that sooner rather than later.

"What if we run into a storm? Will we have to stop?" Kayla asked.

"That depends. I brought chains, but if it's snowing too hard, we might want to get a room and wait it out."

Kayla adjusted the seat belt so she could turn toward Angela. "Are you excited to see all your old friends?"

"The few who still live there," Angela said.

"Almost everyone moved away?"

"A lot of us did. Unless you run a restaurant, a store or a hotel—or you're willing to commute twenty-five miles to Reno—it's not easy to make a living in Virginia City."

"So who do you think is still there?"

"Sheila Gilbert, a friend of mine and your mother's from high school, according to last year's Christmas card. Other than that, probably just a few teachers I had when I went to school and some of the older, more established folks."

"What about boys?"

Angela switched lanes to go around a semi. "What about them?"

"Won't you want to visit some of your old boy-friends?"

"I didn't have a lot of boyfriends." When her mother had died eight years after her father, Angela had only been ten years old. She'd gone to live with her aunt Rosemary, until Rosemary had fallen and broken her hip. Then Angela had moved to Virginia City to live with Betty, who was a distant relative of Rosemary's husband and also Kayla's grandmother.

From then on, Angela had spent most of her time trying to keep Stephanie, Betty's real daughter, out of trouble. But she didn't add that. Neither did she admit that the one man they probably *would* see was the person who made her the most uneasy. She doubted Kayla's father had moved on, like so many others, because he came from some of the earliest Irish miners to settle in Virginia City and had a lot of family in the area. And, if he'd married Danielle as everyone had expected, he'd have even more reason to stay. Her parents owned one of the nicest hotels in the Comstock region.

Kayla studied her for a moment. "Whoever sees you is going to be impressed."

Angela chuckled. "Why's that?"

"You're still so pretty."

Still? Actually, Angela had bloomed late. She'd been tall, skinny and reserved, a foil for the boisterous and impulsive Stephanie. But at least her acne was gone, she knew how to apply a little makeup and she'd gained fifteen pounds in the places she'd needed it most, so she was no longer flat and shapeless. Overall, Angela was satisfied with her appearance—and grateful to feel comfortable in her own skin. Maybe her years in sales had done that for her. She'd been marketing large office buildings since graduating with a business degree from the University of Colorado at Denver and dealt with a wide variety of people. That experience had endowed her with confidence poor Stephanie had always lacked.

"You dress nice," Kayla was saying, continuing

her list of Angela's assets. "And you have a really great car. I *love* this car."

"Fortunately, it's easier to make money in Denver than it is in Virginia City," Angela said.

"Is that why you moved away?"

No, they'd moved because they'd had to leave. In a hurry. "Your nana wanted a change of pace," she said.

"And you were still living with her?"

"I had my senior year to complete. But I would've gone even if I'd already graduated. It was time for college, so I had to go somewhere. And I wanted to help take care of you."

Kayla made a face. "Since my own mother can't do anything."

Angela didn't respond. She never complained about Stephanie, but she didn't overreact if Kayla made an occasional derogatory comment. The girl had a right to her anger. Stephanie had let them all down in the worst possible way. Sometimes Angela couldn't believe that the friend she'd loved like a sister had made the choices she'd made.

They drove in silence for several minutes. Angela was about to turn the music back up when Kayla spoke again.

"Do you think you'll ever get married?"

"Maybe."

"You don't date much." The words sounded almost accusatory.

"I'm too busy with work."

"Most people go out *at night*," she said. "You're usually home by six, remember?"

Angela shrugged. She didn't like leaving Kayla home alone. "I'll meet the right man eventually."

Kayla seemed thoughtful, almost brooding. "What if you find someone, and he doesn't like me?"

"I can't imagine anyone not liking you."

Kayla's attention shifted to the scenery flying past her window. "You've forgotten Barbie and her friends," she said bitterly.

"Shallow, mean girls don't count."

"What about Jordan? He was nicer than everyone else. Until they started teasing him about me." Her tone turned glum. "Now he won't even look at me."

"That could change as you get older."

"Still. I know you feel like you owe Nana for taking you in, but I don't want to be the reason you don't have a life of your own. You're not the one who got pregnant at sixteen."

Angela reached across the seat to squeeze Kayla's hand. "Kayla, I love you. You're a central part of my life, and no one will *ever* change that."

"But don't you wish I had a father who'd come and take me off your hands?"

"No, I don't," she said, and she realized as she spoke that it was true. As difficult as the past year had been, she didn't want to lose Kayla. Kayla was her only family.

CHAPTER TWO

MATTHEW JACKSON SAT with longtime friend and fellow firefighter Lewis McGinness at a table in the bar and restaurant on the first floor of the Old Virginny Hotel. With wooden oak floors, flocked wallpaper, a dark, ornately carved bar and a tin ceiling, the place had been restored to the glory it had known as a saloon in the booming silver era that had once made Virginia City the most important settlement between Denver and San Francisco. There was even a man dressed in nineteenth-century costume playing lively Christmas carols on a piano in the far corner, next to a Christmas tree adorned with paper chains and popcorn strands.

It was all for the benefit of the tourists, of course— a group of whom stood brushing the snow from their coats and marveling over the glass case by the register, which contained a few items originally owned by the famous 1860s soiled dove, Julia C. The display was designed to generate interest in the Bullette Red Light Museum down the street, where folks could see more *intimate* items, as well as some nineteenth-century medical instruments, all for a buck.

It was worth a buck, right?

Matt shook his head. Heaven knew *something* had to stimulate new interest in this town. Cut into the side of a mountain almost two miles above sea level, with its houses and businesses sitting on as much as a forty-percent grade, it wasn't a convenient place to live. Although, at its peak, the town had boasted nearly thirty thousand citizens, it was down to about fifteen hundred and had been struggling since the early 1900s, when the mines had played out. But Matt had never thought of it as desperately hanging on to what once was. It was home, pure and simple. And yet, as the snow piled higher and higher outside, he had to acknowledge that Virginia City had seen better days, even in his lifetime.

In any event, it was turning out to be a long, cold year. After his older brother, Ray, and his wife had pulled up stakes and moved to Reno last October, Matt was beginning to feel a little like a stubborn holdout—which was how he'd begun to view the town. He wasn't experiencing much of the Christmas spirit today, despite the snow, the lights that trimmed the buildings, already twinkling in the storm-darkened sky, the music.

"I should move to Arizona," he said, sipping some of the foam off the top of his beer. "If I lived in the desert, I'd never have to shovel another walk."

McGinness didn't look up. He was too busy settling his giant, bear-like hands around the half-pound burger he'd ordered for lunch. "Good idea."

Matt glanced at him sharply. "Did you just agree with me?"

"Then I'd get your job, right?" he said, a mischievous twinkle in his eyes.

Tipping back his chair, Matt scowled. "You could at least act as if you'd be sorry to see me go. I've been your chief for what, ten years?"

"I'd miss you," he said, but shrugged. "In between spending the extra money I'd be making off my raise, of course."

Matt righted his chair. "Remind me to fire you when we get back."

"Why are you putting it off that long?"

"It's your turn to pay for lunch, remember?"

McGinness swallowed his first bite and managed a grin. "Come on, you're not going anywhere, Chief. This place is in your blood." He took another bite and spoke with his mouth full. "And then there's Kim."

Matt started in on his French dip sandwich. "What does Kim have to do with anything?"

"She keeps your bed warm at night, doesn't she?"

Not anymore. The moment she'd begun talking about marriage, he'd backed off. He wasn't eager to make their relationship permanent, and getting any closer risked a messy breakup. He'd had a couple of messy breakups in his life, enough to know that even one was too many. "I like Kim. She's a nice woman. But there's something missing," he admitted.

"Like your ability to commit?" McGinness stuffed a couple of fries into his mouth.

"You're a regular comedian today, you know that, Lew?" Matt said.

"Just trying to be helpful."

Matt was about to tell him to shut up and eat when the door opened and a woman stepped into the saloon. She had shiny black hair cut in a style that hit a fraction of an inch below her chin—definitely too sophisticated for these parts—and a smooth, olive complexion. She also had a girl with her, who appeared to be twelve or thirteen years old. But it was the woman who caught his attention. She was *gorgeous,* but that wasn't it. He was pretty confident he recognized her.

He leaned over to get a better look. Sure enough. It'd been thirteen years since he'd seen her, but he was almost positive she was the girl who'd come to live with Stephanie Cunningham when they were in junior high. What was her name? Angela? That was it—Angela Forrester.

"What's the matter?" McGinness asked.

"Nothing." Matt quickly controlled his expression. He didn't want to say anything that might make Lewis gawk at her and draw the woman's attention. Their last exchange hadn't been good. She'd been there the night Stephanie had caused him to lose the only girl he'd ever really loved. He was fairly sure Angela was partly responsible. But he didn't know how she'd participated or why, and the last thing he wanted to do was relive the humiliation and embarrassment. Luckily, Stephanie had moved away only a few weeks after that incident and had never contacted him again.

"Let's go," he said, tossing twenty-five bucks on the table.

McGinness held on to the rest of his hamburger as though he'd rather part with his left hand. "*What?*"

Matt fixed his gaze on his plate before Angela could catch him watching her. "Never mind," he muttered, settling back in his seat. "Just hurry so we can get the hell out of here, okay?"

MEMORIES PELTED ANGELA like the snow blowing thickly outside. She'd missed Virginia City more than she'd realized. Closing her eyes, she took a deep breath, reveling in the familiar scents of food, coffee, pine trees and wet leather. Because of the cold, Denver could smell fresh and clean in winter— but no place smelled as authentically "Old Fashioned Christmas" as Virginia City. Maybe that was because it hadn't changed much since it had been rebuilt after the great fire of 1875. Standing in the largest federally designated historical district in America made Angela feel as if she'd just stepped out of a time machine. She'd gone back into her own history. To Christmas, the way it used to be.

"It's great here, isn't it?" she breathed to Kayla as they crossed to an empty table.

"I like it," Kayla replied, but she kept glancing over to another table, where two firemen were having lunch.

"What is it?" Angela asked above a lively piano rendition of "Deck the Halls."

"That man was staring at you when we walked in."

Angela opened her mouth to say that after so long, chances were slim they'd know each other. But then she caught a better glimpse of him and felt her jaw drop. Surely they couldn't have run into Matthew Jackson the moment they'd pulled into town....

"Do you know him?" Kayla asked, peering closely at her.

Angela had no idea what to say. They'd chosen a table less than fifteen feet from Kayla's father!

"Angie?" she prompted.

Angela found her voice. "Yes, I—I knew him as a...a guy in high school." Although she had to acknowledge that he'd improved quite a bit. With dark whiskers covering his prominent jaw, and smile lines bracketing his mouth and eyes, he'd matured into a man who appeared rather rough-hewn. And while his sandy-colored hair had darkened, the unusual ice-blue color of his eyes hadn't changed at all.

"He's handsome, isn't he?" Kayla whispered.

He was so handsome Angela almost couldn't stop staring. And it wasn't just his face. He'd put on maybe thirty pounds since graduation, but none of it had gone to his middle. He filled out that uniform to perfection, looking larger than she remembered him, and far more powerful.

Angela tried to gather her wits, but she was suddenly so nervous she was afraid to remain in the same restaurant. *He doesn't know,* she told herself.

But the doubts she'd wrestled with from the beginning crowded in. *What if he guessed? Would he? Could he?*

On the drive over, Angela had convinced herself that the answer to those questions was *no.* Matt had been with Stephanie only that one night, when they were sixteen, and he hadn't really *chosen* to be with her even then. He wouldn't expect a child from one brief encounter, especially a child he'd never heard about. Besides, Stephanie had trouble carrying Kayla and she'd delivered two months early. That alone would make it difficult to figure out the dates.

Which meant it didn't matter that Angela had suddenly shown up with a twelve-year-old girl in tow.

Reassured by her own reasoning, Angela immediately turned to the menu. But, inside, she couldn't help grimacing at the terrible trick Stephanie had played on Matt. Angela felt partially responsible, but once it had happened, there was no way to fix it—other than doing what Stephanie's mother had done. Angela didn't think she could've stopped Stephanie, anyway. She'd never seen a girl so single-mindedly determined to get what she wanted. And what she'd wanted was Matt.

Ironically, she'd also never seen a man, who—before and after that night—had so studiously avoided Stephanie. It was almost as if Matt had sensed the halter she had waiting to slip around his neck....

"Look, here they come," Kayla said.

The words suddenly registered, as well as the accompanying movement behind her and, turning, Angela realized that she also recognized the second man. He was a beefier version of the boy she'd seen with Matt so often in high school—Lewis McGinness, who'd been one of the best linebackers on the football team.

A smile curved his lips as he made his way toward them. Matt followed, seeming much more reluctant.

"Hello," Angela said warmly and stood. A lot depended on her acting ability. She wasn't about to raise suspicion by revealing how shaken she felt. She'd wanted to figure out what kind of man Matt had become before bringing Kayla into direct contact with him. But it was too late; she had to improvise.

"Hey!" Lewis swept her into a hug as if they'd been good friends in high school instead of mere acquaintances. "What brings you back to Virginia City?"

"I'm here for the holidays."

"Where are you staying?"

"We just got into town, so we don't have a room yet. But we'll probably end up at the Gold Hill Hotel." That was the hotel owned by Danielle's parents, but neither man brought up her name when Angela mentioned it, so she still didn't know if Matt had ended up marrying the girl he'd dated for so long.

"They've made some improvements, but the new Silver Queen is closer," Lewis said.

Angela kept her smile firmly in place, even though she was acutely aware of Matt and his steady gaze. "We'll have to stop by and take a look."

Lewis waved a hand toward Matt, who seemed perfectly satisfied to stand in the background. "You remember Matt, don't you? Or maybe you don't. He went out with Danielle all through school."

Did that mean he wasn't with her now? Angela knew they'd reconciled after the incident at the party, but if their relationship hadn't progressed beyond high school, Stephanie was probably a large part of the reason.

"Hi, Matt." She held out her hand because he made no move to hug her as his friend had.

He shook hands with a definite lack of enthusiasm. "Good to see you again."

I can tell you're thrilled about it, Angela thought sarcastically. But she could understand that. Because of Stephanie, she couldn't possibly evoke pleasant memories for him.

She put a hand on Kayla's shoulder. "This is my daughter, Kayla."

If Kayla was surprised at being introduced like that, she didn't let on. Nodding shyly, she slipped an arm around Angela's waist, acting more relieved than shocked. Angela knew her real mother was an embarrassment to her.

"She's beautiful," Lewis said. "Like her mother."

"Thanks."

"How long will you be staying?"

"A couple of weeks."

He shifted to make room for Matt, but Matt didn't come any closer. "Are you here to see anyone in particular?"

"No, I just wanted to show Kayla the town."

"Where do you live now?"

"In Denver. I'm in real estate." She glanced conspicuously at their uniforms and badges. "And you're both firefighters, I see."

"That's right. Matt here's the chief. Unless he moves to Arizona." He tossed his friend a meaningful grin. "Then I'm taking over."

"Now you'll never get rid of me," Matt grumbled.

Angela tried not to notice that Matt was even better-looking up close. He'd always been attractive; that, and his popularity, was why Stephanie had wanted him so badly. But the past thirteen years had added a few finishing touches.

"So…is your husband stuck at home, working over the holidays?" Lewis asked.

She shook her head. "I'm not married. You?"

"Tied the knot nine years ago, already got three kids."

"That's wonderful," she said. "And…what about you, Matt?"

"No." He didn't elaborate, but Lewis quickly filled in.

"He's asked quite a few women, but the poor guy can't get anyone to take him."

Lewis wore such a falsely pitying expression, that Kayla laughed out loud and Angela laughed with her.

"How's your friend?" Lewis asked. "What was her name… Stephanie?"

Kayla's arm tightened around her, and Matt's mouth turned grim. "She's fine."

"Where's she living now?"

Angela had no idea. Stephanie partied with one person or another, then drifted on. "In…Colorado."

"What does she do for a living?" Lewis asked.

"Um…she's in sales," Angela said and felt some of the tension leave Kayla as the girl smiled more easily.

Lewis stepped aside to let some people pass through to the exit. "What about Stephanie's mother? She used to babysit me when I was four. Only for a few months, but I still remember her. Does she live in Denver, too?"

The merry music and Christmas atmosphere lost some of its charm. Angela missed Betty, who'd been such a part of this place. This Christmas couldn't be like the ones she used to know. Not without Betty. "No. She had a heart attack and passed away a little over a year ago."

"I'm sorry to hear that."

Angela nodded politely. "It was tough to lose her. She was a nice woman."

There was a respectful pause, then Matt said, "We'd better get back to work."

"See what a slave driver he is?" Lewis teased.

Angela smiled. "It was great to see you again," she told him and meant it. But she wasn't sure she felt the same about Matt.

"Would you and your daughter like to join me and my family for dinner tomorrow night?" Lewis asked. "Matt will be there, too, right, Matt?"

Matt blinked, as if Lewis had caught him off guard and he didn't know how to escape.

"I wouldn't want to impose," Angela said.

"It's no trouble," Lewis insisted. "You might remember my wife. Peggy Sutherland?"

"Was she my age?"

"She's four years younger."

"I can't quite place her," Angela admitted.

"Maybe you'll recognize her when you see her. Anyway, I know she'd love to have you over. She likes to entertain."

By now Angela could see a muscle flexing in Matt's cheek, but if Lewis bothered to notice, he completely disregarded his friend's less than eager response. And, with the goal of getting to know Matt better, Angela chose to do the same. She'd come for a reason, after all. "If you're sure…"

"I'm positive," he said and Angela gave him her cell number so they could make the arrangements.

CHAPTER THREE

AS SOON AS THEY were inside the fire station, Matt pulled Lewis to a stop. "What the hell were you doing back there?"

"When?" His friend's eyes widened as if he really was as innocent as he pretended to be.

"At the restaurant!"

"I was doing you a favor, buddy. Didn't you see how beautiful she is?"

He'd been reluctant to acknowledge it. She and Stephanie must have slipped him something that night when they were juniors. He knew it. He'd never wanted Stephanie before. So how had he wound up in bed with her? And at a party, no less? "I'm not coming to dinner."

"Why not?" Lewis said. "I know you're thinking about...*what happened.* I was there that night, too, remember? At least I was there later on, when Danielle walked in and caught you. But that was thirteen years ago. It's time to forgive and forget. Danielle's married and has two kids. And you heard Angela. She's not attached."

"She said she's not married. That doesn't mean she's not attached."

"I got the impression she's not seeing anyone."

Matt stomped into his office. "She doesn't even live here!"

"You might not be living here either, right?" Lewis called to him. "Maybe you'll want to move to Denver instead of Arizona."

Matt cursed under his breath.

"What did you say?"

"Now I'm *really* tempted to fire you."

Lewis stood in the doorway. "You don't want to do that."

"Why not?"

"Because I have your best interests at heart."

Matt slumped into his chair. "Yeah? Even my mother isn't as meddlesome as you are."

"It's time for you to settle down. Being a father is awesome. You're missing out, my friend."

Matt said nothing. He wanted a family. He'd just never cared about anyone the way he'd cared about Danielle.

"Besides, wouldn't you like to know what happened that night?" Lewis went on. "You've always said you don't remember how you ended up in that room with Stephanie."

"I remember bits and pieces, but mostly it's a blur."

"Well, Angela might be able to explain it."

Matt shoved a hand through his hair. Even if she could provide the answers he'd long craved, what was done was done. They couldn't go back and change anything.

Lewis came into the room and leaned on the desk. "So, what do you say?"

Matt still felt a little resentful despite the passing years. But maybe he was overreacting. Angela seemed nice enough as an adult. And there was a slight chance she hadn't been a party to his downfall. Stephanie had certainly never needed her help to try and corner him before.

But every other time, he'd managed to get away. That was the difference!

"Something about Stephanie chilled me to the bone," he said, recalling her overeager smile, the way she brushed up against him at every opportunity, her attention-hungry eyes.

"Angela isn't Stephanie." Lewis bent lower to peer questioningly into his face. "You're not going to back out on me, are you?"

Matt sighed. What the hell. He could survive one dinner. And, as Lewis said, maybe she'd be able to tell him what had really happened so he could finally understand why he'd let Danielle down so badly.

ANGELA SHIFTED NERVOUSLY as she waited next to Kayla on the doorstep of Lewis's wooden A-frame. Set a couple of blocks off C Street, the main business district, it looked like so many of the other homes and businesses in Virginia City—as if it had been built in the late 1800s. It probably had been. But it was recently painted, a muted yellow with white trim, and obviously well-maintained.

She wondered where Matt lived. While they were

growing up, his parents had owned a jewelry store called Comstock Silver and Turquoise. She'd watched for it when she and Kayla had driven through the slushy streets—the weather had warmed enough to melt some of the snow that had fallen the day before—but if his parents still had the store, they'd changed the name and the location. An old-fashioned soda shop now resided where the jewelry store had been.

The door opened and a child of about five, with bright red hair and a few freckles, gazed out at her.

"Hello," Angela said.

He continued to stare, but Lewis's voice rose from behind him. "Derek, those are our dinner guests. Invite them in, okay?"

The boy stepped back and opened the door wider just as Lewis crossed the room, obviously intent on making sure his son followed orders. "Hi," he said when he saw them. "I'm glad you could make it."

Dinner smelled like roast turkey. "Thanks for inviting us." She handed Lewis the bottle of wine she'd bought.

He checked the label, smiled as if it met with his approval and asked to take their coats.

Kayla removed her parka and Angela shrugged out of her trench coat. "Thank you. It looks like the weather's clearing up," she commented.

A short, slightly plump woman with hair the same color as the little boy—and lots more freckles—stepped out of the kitchen. "I think we'll have a white Christmas. They're expecting a big storm next week."

She sounded relieved, and Angela guessed that a white Christmas was very important to her. Judging by the many decorations adorning the yard outside and the two Christmas trees—one in the living room and one in the adjoining dining area—she took her holidays seriously.

"Angela, this is my wife, Peggy," Lewis said from the coat closet.

"Nice to meet you." Angela didn't recognize her, but she seemed friendly.

"And this—" he turned and grabbed the boy who'd answered the door, pushing him to the floor in a playful tussle "—is Derek."

The boy squealed and giggled as he struggled to get free, and Lewis finally released him. "He's the youngest of the kids. The older two are with their grandma tonight."

"I wanted to go, too," Derek sulked.

"Grandma takes gingerbread houses to a professional level," Peggy confided, her voice a half whisper. "According to her, he's not old enough."

Hearing this, Derek climbed to his feet and folded his arms. "I can do it!"

"Next year, honey," she promised and returned to the kitchen.

"Have a seat." Lewis motioned to an antique floral couch and matching chair. The living room resembled a Victorian parlor. "Matt isn't here yet, but he'll be along soon. Can I get you a drink?"

Angela accepted a glass of wine; Kayla asked for a soda. "Are Matt's parents still in town?" Angela asked.

"Yeah. But they've upgraded the store. It's now called Virginia City Treasures and Gifts and is located closer to Taylor Street."

Angela opened her mouth to ask about the rest of Matt's family. As much as she believed Betty had done the right thing in taking Stephanie away when she had, the decision affected many more people than just Matt. Would they be angry to learn they had a twelve-year-old granddaughter/niece? In a way, Angela felt they had a right to know. And yet—

A knock interrupted her thoughts. Tensing, she waited for Lewis to answer the door. But he didn't bother. He was setting the table, so he merely barked out, "Come in!"

Matt strode into the room as though he'd done it a thousand times. And he probably had. He and Lewis had been friends forever.

"Hi, Matt," Peggy called from the kitchen.

"Uncle Matt!" Derek charged him and threw his arms around his knees.

"Whoa, hold on, buddy. Let me set this pie down," Matt said.

The mention of pie brought Peggy hurrying into the living room. "Did you say pie? What kind?"

"What kind do you think?" he teased. "Your favorite."

"Pumpkin?"

"Of course."

She rose up on her toes to give him a hug. He put one arm around her and used the other hand to pat the head of the boy who was squeezing his leg. It was very apparent that he loved these people. But when his eyes met Angela's curious gaze, she could tell those warm feelings didn't extend to *everyone*.

Clearing her throat, she looked away.

"Can I help?" he asked Peggy.

"Yes." She waved him toward the couch. "You can sit down and entertain our guests while I finish up. Lewis will pour you a glass of wine in a minute."

Instinctively, Angela slid over to allow him more room, but it wasn't necessary. He sat at the far end and focused on Kayla.

"How old are you?" he asked.

"Twelve."

His eyebrows went up, and he glanced subtly at Angela. She knew he had to be doing the math, thinking she'd gotten pregnant awfully young. But he didn't say anything. He let Derek climb into his lap and addressed Kayla once again. "Do you like school?"

Angela sat there, rigid with tension, as father and daughter conversed. She'd been crazy to bring Kayla here, she decided. The truth suddenly seemed so obvious. She could see the similarities in their faces—the slightly square shape to Kayla's chin, the high cheekbones, the broad forehead.

But Matt didn't seem at all suspicious. He did seem reluctant to get to know *her,* and even more reluctant to like her, but he had no qualms about Kayla. Of course, she'd said Kayla was her daughter, they'd bumped into each other during a chance meeting, and Lewis had instigated this dinner. It wasn't as if they'd appeared on his doorstep or rung him up out of the blue.

"Not really," Kayla said, answering his question about whether she liked school.

"Why not?"

"It's—" her eyes shifted momentarily to Angela "—it can be tough to fit in."

"For someone as pretty as you?"

She blushed. "Sometimes," she hedged, and Angela guessed she didn't want to appear too pathetic.

"It's tough for everyone sometimes," he said, even though, as far as Angela could remember, it had never been very tough for him. He'd always been one of the most popular boys in school. "What do you want for Christmas?" he asked.

"I'd like to find my dad."

Angela nearly gasped at Kayla's answer. She'd never heard Kayla admit this to anyone else. Until she'd read that essay, she hadn't realized how deeply Kayla missed having a father.

But the words were already out, and there was no mistaking Matt's surprise. "He's not part of your life?"

She shook her head. "No, he—he left us a long time ago. He said he loved my mom, and he promised her they'd be together forever. But then he couldn't handle a crying baby in the house and changing diapers and all that." She wrinkled her nose, basking in Matt's attention. "So he walked out, and left my mom to raise me by herself."

Angela had stiffened at "he left us a long time ago." Kayla had never been told any such thing. This had to be some kind of fantasy, something she figured would be more acceptable than the reality.

Angela wanted to stop her before she could embellish any further but couldn't say anything in front of Matt. A correction might cause Kayla to make some remark that would give them away. *She* was the one who'd lied first, when she'd introduced Kayla as her daughter.

But, in a way, Kayla *was* her daughter now.

"He was older, then?" Matt asked.

"Yeah, uh…a lot older," Kayla said. "We have no idea where he is."

Matt seemed to look more kindly at Angela, probably because he felt sorry for her.

Only sheer will kept Angela from dropping her head into her hands. How had she *expected* this to go? Certainly not the way it was going…

"I'm sorry to hear that," he said sincerely. "But he's the one who's missing out. You know that, don't you?"

"Time to eat!"

Peggy's announcement brought the conversation to an end, and Angela nearly cried in relief.

MATT COULDN'T BELIEVE that someone had taken advantage of Angela when she was so young. He knew she didn't really have a family; everyone knew that. A foster child wasn't common in Virginia City then or now, so her first appearance at school, when they were in the seventh grade, had caused quite a stir. If he remembered right, Betty Cunningham had given her a home because of some tenuous connection with Angela's family, and Betty hadn't wanted to see her become a ward of the state.

But Betty, a widow herself, had already had her hands full. A bit eccentric, she'd taken in any stray animal that had crossed her path, so she'd had something like three dogs, a couple of cats, some hamsters and a ferret. Matt knew because Stephanie had lured him over to the house once with the promise of showing him the animals. When she'd come on to him, he'd gotten out of there right away, but he'd stayed long enough to see that the situation was unique. Besides caring for all those animals, Betty had had to deal with Stephanie, who'd always been getting into trouble, and Betty herself had been sick a lot.

Suddenly, Matt felt guilty for being so hard on Angela. If Angela had helped to corner him the night he'd had sex with Stephanie, her involvement could only have been in a peripheral way, and it had no doubt been Stephanie's idea. Anyway, Lewis was right—they'd all been so young.

He caught her watching him from across the table and smiled. He hadn't been very friendly to her so far, but it wasn't too late. According to what she'd told him and Lewis, she was in town for two weeks.

He had half a mind to make sure they were the best two weeks she'd ever known.

CHAPTER FOUR

"ANGIE!"

Angela rolled over to find Kayla standing at the side of her bed. "What?" She squinted in the light streaming through the sheers at the hotel window. They'd chosen the Gold Hill Hotel because Angela remembered it so nostalgically from when she'd lived in Virginia City before. "What time is it?"

"It's only eight. But I just talked to Matt. He's off work on Mondays, and he says we want to get an early start."

"Do we have plans with Matt?" she asked, confused. The last thing she recalled was the charming way he'd walked them to their car after the dinner party was over. She'd been terrified he was going to ask her out. Kayla's story had really affected him, and she'd felt his eyes on her all night, had felt him shift closer to her while they'd been watching the movie after dinner. But at the car, he'd kept his hands in his pockets and had merely told them to get a good night's sleep, then had waved as they'd driven off.

She'd thought that would be the end of it, at least for a few days. They'd had an enjoyable night, established a friendship. And now she had a lot to think about. Matt wasn't married, and as far as she could tell, he wasn't involved in a serious relationship. He had a steady job, family in the area, a solid reputation—what appeared from every angle to be a very normal life.

Which made telling him about Kayla a real possibility.

But Angela wasn't sure he'd thank her for the news. His jaw tightened anytime Stephanie was even mentioned. What if he grew angry at the deception and rejected Kayla? Angela couldn't subject Kayla to any more hurt. And Angela was equally afraid of the opposite possibility—what if he decided to take his daughter away from her?

"He wants to know if we'd like to ride the train," Kayla said. "And afterward, he said we could help him pick out his Christmas tree."

Kayla sounded thrilled. She and Matt had gotten along famously last night. He'd taught her how to play chess while Angela had helped Peggy clean up and had even given her advice about boys. How could Angela say no?

She wouldn't. She'd go and make sure he was everything he seemed to be, and *then* she'd figure out whether or not to tell him.

THE TRAIN RIDE HAD been fun, but short. It was a narrated thirty-five-minute ride through the heart of the Comstock mining region, after which they went to pick out Matt's tree. Angela liked tramping through the snow; it was cold, and she was getting wet, but she felt so *alive*. She tried to convince herself that the flutter of excitement in her stomach was the result of returning home. But she knew it wasn't just Virginia City. Every time she looked at Matt, she felt a sudden warmth.

How long had it been since she'd kissed a man? she wondered as he tied the tree on top of his truck.

Since before Betty's death. Angela hadn't dated in more than a year.

She missed the male-female contact. She also missed the experience of feeling desirable and desiring someone else.

"Are you staring at his butt?" Kayla murmured, her voice scandalized.

Angela hadn't realized that Kayla was watching her. She considered pretending otherwise, but she could tell by the knowing gleam in Kayla's eyes that the girl wouldn't believe it. Regardless of any embarrassment, she decided it was better to acknowledge the truth. "I've never seen a pair of jeans fit quite so well," she said, using her mitten-covered hand to shield her mouth so Matt wouldn't hear her.

Kayla giggled. "You should go out with him."

"No, we leave in two weeks."

"Why not have some fun while we're here?"

"We are having fun—"

"Hey, what are you two talking about?" Finished, Matt faced them with one eyebrow cocked.

It probably wasn't too difficult to tell they'd been talking about *him*. But Angela refused to admit it.

"What we want for Christmas?" she said as innocently as possible.

He wiped his sleeve across his forehead as if he'd worked up quite a sweat. She and Kayla hadn't been much help. They'd chosen the biggest blue spruce they could find and left him to it.

Angela figured firemen liked doing tough stuff. She'd definitely enjoyed seeing him wrestle that tree into submission.

"And what do *you* want?" he asked doubtfully.

Angela shook her head. It was the first time she'd thought about sex in ages, but now that the idea had crossed her mind, she couldn't seem to forget it.

"I'm waiting," he reminded her.

"Um…a purse?"

He scooped up a loosely packed snowball and hit her with it. "Come on, you just made that up."

She scooped up a snowball of her own. "Are you calling me a liar?"

He grinned as if unconcerned about the threat. "I guess I am."

She launched her snowball, but he dodged it easily and hit her with another one. "Are you going to tell me what you were saying to Kayla?"

"No."

"I'm pretty sure I can get you to change your mind," he warned.

"You couldn't torture it out of me," she said and laughed when Kayla managed to hit him while he was distracted.

"That's it," he said and then snowballs began to

fly from all three of them. Angela could hear Kayla laughing as she held her own in the battle, and quickly created a small arsenal of snowballs behind a fallen tree. Then, when Kayla drew Matt's fire, Angela took careful aim and *bam!*

He'd taken off his parka while cutting the tree, so when her snowball smacked him in the back of the head, it showered snow down the neck of his thermal T-shirt.

It was more of a direct hit than she'd intended. As he turned toward her, the look on his face told her she was in trouble.

With a frightened squeal, she began running as fast as she could in the knee-deep snow, but it wasn't thirty seconds before he tackled her.

"Tell me you're sorry," he said.

"She thinks you're handsome! She said she likes your butt!" Kayla called and seized the opportunity to save herself by scampering into the truck. Angela heard the click of the locks only seconds after Matt brought her to the ground.

"Thanks a lot, Kayla," she muttered.

He grinned, obviously pleased that Kayla had just handed him total victory, but he didn't let that distract him from his punishment. "Say 'Chief Jackson, I'm terribly sorry to have caused you any discomfort.'"

"No way! You started it!"

"Fine. Then I'm going to finish it." He shoved snow down her jacket, laughing as she bucked and writhed beneath him. But she wasn't feeling nearly as cold as she should've been. And it wasn't long before she could tell that her movements were arousing him, too.

She stopped struggling, but he didn't get up. He smoothed the snow and disheveled hair from her face. "You're beautiful, you know that?" he said passionately.

The fact that she could feel the physical proof of his appreciation didn't seem to bother him. He kept his body snugly against hers, putting pressure on a very sensitive spot—so sensitive that she wished he'd push a little harder.

Her chest rose and fell while she tried to catch her breath. "You never even looked at me when we were younger."

But he hadn't looked at anybody, had he? Except Danielle.

He didn't mention his old girlfriend. "I didn't know what I was missing."

"What do *you* want for Christmas?" she asked. She was grasping for anything to change the subject, to lessen the tension.

His gaze lowered to her lips, and his voice grew slightly rough. "To catch you under the mistletoe."

MATT HELD HIS WINEGLASS loosely in his hands as he lay on the rug, staring at the lights on the tree they'd just decorated. Kayla had done most of the work, but now she was in the other room watching a Christmas program on television. Angela sat a few feet away, petting Sampson, Matt's German shepherd.

As her hand moved over the dog's fur, Matt was

dying to scoot closer to her—if only to thread his fingers through hers. But after their encounter in the snow, she'd been acting spooked. Whenever he sat near, she backed away. And yet she'd been responsive when he tackled her. The flush in her cheeks had come from more than just physical exertion. He could tell by her eyes.

Maybe she needed more time before she'd consider a romantic relationship. She'd be going back to Denver soon, and long-distance relationships weren't easy, but he couldn't help wanting to get to know her better in spite of that. He felt a sort of…excitement he hadn't experienced in years. He hoped she'd stay, hoped they could explore the possibilities. If nothing else, they should make the most of the time she had left.

"What happened to your parents?" he asked.

She'd been sitting with her legs stretched out and crossed at the ankles, leaning back on her hands to admire the tree. But at his question, she changed position so she could reclaim her wine. "My father died when I was two. My mother died when I was ten."

"That's too bad," he said. "How'd it happen?"

"My parents were older when they had me. They'd been told that my father was infertile. And then, at forty-eight, my mother suddenly conceived."

"They must've been thrilled."

Sampson sat up and barked, but when she scratched him behind the ears, he laid his head in her lap. Matt had never seen the dog take to anyone so readily.

"I suppose, in some ways, they were," she said.

"But the fact that it was a little late in life probably tempered their happiness, you know? And two years later, my dad died of cancer. Pneumonia took my mom eight years after that."

"Is it hard to talk about them?" he asked softly.

"No, it's…okay."

He didn't want to bring up any subject that might be painful for her, and yet he wanted to hear the details of her life. "Wasn't there anyone else in your family who could take care of you?"

"No. My parents' brothers and sisters were even older than they were and had finished raising their families. One lived in Belgium. Another was a widow. She tried to take me, but then she fell and broke her hip."

She'd indicated it didn't bother her to talk about her past, but she'd tensed up. He could see it in the way she held her body.

Despite his determination to give her more time, Matt moved toward her.

She watched him warily. But when she finally met his eyes, he saw that she wasn't unaffected by the chemistry between them. He couldn't tell what was holding her back, but he knew it wasn't a lack of interest.

Taking her hand, he began stroking her slim fingers. "So you went to live with Betty."

She stared at the places where he touched her, as if mesmerized by his movements. "She was my aunt's husband's second cousin," she said slowly. "When she heard Aunt Rosemary was going to have to put me up for adoption, she knew it wouldn't be easy to find a good home for a ten-year-old, that I'd probably be bounced around in the foster system until I turned eighteen."

"So she decided to take you in."

"Yes." She shivered as his fingers moved up the inside of her arm. Liking the reaction, he immediately imagined her in his bed, and wanted more. But she was still sending him inconsistent signals. Her body responded eagerly, yet she seemed reluctant.

"Do you like this?" he asked.

She nodded.

"What about this?" Lifting her hand, he caressed the sensitive tips of her fingers with his tongue. Then, one by one, he took each finger into his mouth, gently sucking on it.

She didn't answer. But he heard her quiet gasp. She was breathing faster, too. He was willing to bet her heart was pounding right along with his.

Leaning closer, he brushed his mouth lightly across hers.

Good. Better than good. He was just going back for another pass, hoping to claim one deep, wet kiss. Her daughter was in the other room. He didn't want to make Angela uncomfortable; he only wanted to show her what could happen if she gave in to what she was feeling.

But she pulled away before he could show her much of anything.

Matt frowned. "You're not interested?" he murmured in confusion. Surely he couldn't be that bad at reading her responses. He'd never misjudged a woman's receptivity before.

"It's getting late," she said. "We—we'd better go."

She tried to get up, but he held her fast. "Why are you running from me?"

"I'm not running from you."

"What are you afraid of? Why won't you give me the chance to really know you?"

"I'm not afraid of anything."

"I want to spend some time with you, Angela. I want to *be* with you," he said. "*And* I want to touch you."

"I—" She seemed at a loss. "Matt, listen. This…isn't right."

He scowled. "Are you married?"

"I already told you I'm not."

"Are you committed?"

She tucked her silky hair behind one ear. "No."

"What is it, then?"

"I don't even live here," she said.

"*That's* the reason?"

"Isn't it enough?"

"No. Not if you're feeling what I'm feeling. We have two weeks. Who knows where it could go beyond that? We wouldn't be the first people to try and manage a long-distance relationship."

"I'm not feeling anything," she said quickly. "I— I have too much going on in my life. I can't get involved right now."

She was lying about what she felt. The excuse of a busy life sounded flimsy, too.

He opened his mouth to argue. But then he

stopped himself. He'd be stupid to press her. She was in full retreat. Pushing harder would make her run that much faster.

They sat still for several seconds, staring up at the tree. "Okay," he said at last.

"I'm sorry," she whispered.

"Will you do me one favor?"

Her gaze moved over him, as if she were committing every detail to memory. "If I can."

"Tell me what happened that night. With Stephanie."

"It's over, in the past—"

"I want to know," he said stubbornly.

She pulled her legs in close and propped her chin on her knees. "Stephanie was always so…impetuous," she said reluctantly.

"Impetuous?" he echoed. "She was the most sexually aggressive girl I've ever met!"

"She had a terrible crush on you."

"Calling it a crush makes it sound normal," he muttered. "It was more like an obsession."

"I know. I tried to get her to leave you alone. So did her mother. She wouldn't listen. She never listened—to *anyone*."

The bits and pieces he could recall began to filter through his mind. "I remember seeing her at the party when I arrived," he said. "You were there, too. She asked me to dance, followed me around. The typical stuff. I was annoyed, but not too worried, you know?"

"Yes."

"It was Danielle's mother's birthday," he

explained. "She'd gone out to dinner with her parents and was supposed to meet me later. I can still hear the music, see the people. Someone offered me a beer, but I knew I'd be driving her home that night and said no."

"Is that all you remember?" she prompted when he stopped.

"No. I remember the way Stephanie was touching me, my eagerness to let her. What doesn't make sense is *why* I did what I did. Things got out of control, and I didn't seem to care. Then, in the middle of everything, I'm lying naked on the bed, and Danielle's staring down at me, screaming and crying. Stephanie's there, too, holding the sheets to her bare chest and smiling smugly, as if she'd *wanted* us to be caught."

"I'm sure she did. That would've suited her purpose."

How manipulative was that? He shook his head in disgust. "She told Danielle I'd just *made love* to her, when, regardless of what happened, there was no love involved, and she knew it." He winced at the memory of Danielle vomiting afterward.

"Anyway, I couldn't deny it," he went on, embarrassed all over again. "I really had…you know. But, for the life of me, I can't figure out why I didn't stop. I would never have hurt Danielle that way. I'd had plenty of opportunities to be with Stephanie, if that was what I wanted."

"Did you eat any brownies?"

"Is that where it was?" he asked.

Angela nodded.

"What was it, exactly?"

"Betty's sleeping pills."

"*Sleeping* pills?"

"They were strong. Because of her aches and pains, the doctor prescribed some sedatives. Stephanie simply stole a few from the medicine cabinet and mixed them in when she frosted a couple of the brownies she brought to the party."

"The ones she made for me."

"Yes."

He considered Angela for several long moments. He was relieved to finally have his suspicions confirmed, to know he really wasn't the callous jerk everyone had thought he was.

But that raised another question, one that seemed far more important now than it ever had before. "Did you know what she was planning before you went to the party? Did you help her?"

"No. I only knew that she had hopes of getting with you. She said you'd 'be hers' by morning. But she always talked like that. I didn't realize, until she admitted it the next day, that she'd drugged you."

He sighed. "I'm just glad she didn't get pregnant. Can you imagine? It would've ruined my life."

She said nothing.

"Angela?"

"That would have been terrible," she said quietly.

He chuckled without mirth. "I don't know many guys who've had to worry about being seduced against their will, especially at sixteen. Do you?"

"Stephanie was determined. When she wanted something, she stopped at nothing to have it."

He studied her carefully, wondering why she was keeping him at arm's length. "What about you?" he asked.

"What about me?"

"What do you do when you want something?"

She gazed up at the tree. "I try to think about how it'll affect others."

He knew her answer was significant. He just didn't know in what way.

CHAPTER FIVE

"SO…DO YOU LIKE HIM?" As soon as they reached their room, Kayla sat cross-legged on the end of Angela's bed and smiled eagerly, obviously expecting a girl-to-girl chat.

"He's nice," Angela replied, trying not to sound too enthusiastic.

"Just *nice?*"

Angela stepped into the bathroom to undress. "No, he's cute, too."

"Oh, my gosh!" she called back. "Cute? He's like…Jake Gyllenhaal. Are you blind? I sat in there watching stupid television shows so you could be alone, and now you're telling me he's *cute?*"

"When I said he had a nice butt, you told on me," Angela accused, trying to put Kayla on the defensive.

But when Angela emerged in her pajamas, she found Kayla stretched out on the bed, grinning unrepentantly. "Yeah, but he liked hearing it. He hasn't been able to keep his eyes off you since."

Angela's head hurt from all the conflicting emotions. When she'd first decided to return to Virginia City, she'd expected to find Matt happily married with a few kids. She couldn't show up on a man's doorstep, a man who had a wife and children, and tell him he had another daughter he'd never even heard about. Not when the child had been conceived the way Kayla had. He wasn't responsible for what had happened, so how could she justify disrupting his life and the lives of those he loved? Knowing she couldn't do that had made her feel safe. She'd come here to put to rest the unsettling "what if" scenarios that had plagued her, even before she'd read Kayla's essay. She'd wanted to validate the decisions that had been made in the past and gather more strength and determination to continue with things as they were.

Now she didn't know what to do. She'd never bargained on Matt's being single. Neither had she guessed that she'd be so attracted to him. Their interest in each other confused an already difficult issue. But with or without Kayla, she saw little chance that what they felt would ever turn into a committed, long-term relationship. They were both single at twenty-nine. That had to say something about them. Her life and her business were in Denver; his were here in Virginia City.

She wouldn't tell him, she decided. Not yet. She didn't know him well enough. Besides, as much as Kayla thought she wanted a father, Angela wasn't sure the sudden upheaval and total change of situation would be good for her.

And yet…she felt guilty for keeping the secret. How could she deny Kayla the chance to know the man who'd fathered her? Especially when Angela had discovered it was Kayla's deepest desire?

Smothering a sigh, Angela sat next to Kayla on the bed. *What would be best for this girl?* She'd promised Betty she'd never tell. But Betty had only been trying to right Stephanie's wrong, to make sure others wouldn't be hurt by it. When Betty had asked Angela for that promise, she'd been assuming Matt wouldn't *want* to know he had a daughter.

Now, Angela wasn't so sure. "What do you think of him?" she asked and tried to listen beyond the actual words.

"I think he's great," Kayla said. "Perfect."

"In what ways?" she prodded.

"He listens when we talk. He's patient and funny."

"We've only known him a couple of days," Angela said.

"That doesn't matter. He won't change."

Angela pulled Kayla into an embrace. She thought the same thing. But she had to be positive. And, as she stroked the girl's hair, she couldn't help wondering—was Matt ready for the shock of his life?

CHRISTMAS WAS IN FOUR DAYS and Matt hadn't bought a single present. He was reminded of that when his mother called him at work the following morning.

"You're coming to the gift exchange, right?" she said.

He rolled away from his desk and locked his hands behind his head, stretching his aching back. He'd been doing paperwork since he'd arrived at seven, and it was nearly noon. "Why aren't we having the party on Christmas Eve?" he asked.

"Because your uncle Jim's leaving for New York. He and Don have wanted to see the city for years, and that's their Christmas present to each other."

"I see. So…" Matt rummaged through the stacks of papers on his desk to unearth his calendar. "When is it again?"

"Tomorrow night. At seven."

"Okay. I'll be there." He jotted it down and started to hang up, but his mother was still talking.

"And do not have that friend of yours make Grandma any more eggnog," she said.

He lifted the phone back to his ear. "Why not? She likes it."

"It gives her gas."

"Then why does she ask me for it?"

"The taste. Haven't you ever liked something that wasn't good for you?"

He was beginning to wonder if Angela fit into that category.

"You know how stubborn she is," his mom added.

"What else should I get her?"

"What about one of those firemen calendars you and the other guys posed for?" It had been a local effort to raise money for burn victims.

"You're joking, right? What would an eighty-year-old woman want with pictures of me and a bunch of other half-naked firemen?"

"She likes Lewis."

"*Lewis?*"

"She says you're never too old to pretend."

He kneaded his forehead. "Mom, that's not creating an appealing mental picture."

"You're not the only one who likes sex in this family," she said. "Your father and I—"

"Mom! Stop!"

"Have always been crazy for each other," she finished. "Oh, and bring some calendars for your aunt. She wants to give a few of them away."

"I've got to go," he said.

"When are you planning to do your shopping?"

He scowled. "How do you know I haven't done it already?"

"Because you always wait till the last minute. You need a wife, Matthew."

"You've been saying that for years."

"And you've been ignoring me for just as long. You think I want to die without grandkids?"

He rolled his eyes. "You're barely fifty-five."

"And I feel every year of it. Your brother and his wife say they don't want children. Can you imagine that? You're my one hope, and you haven't had a steady girl-friend in years." She hung up, sounding thoroughly disgusted but, after a few seconds, Matt called her back.

"Can I bring a couple of people to the party?"

"Lewis and his family?"

"No. A woman and her daughter."

There was an intrigued silence. "You've never brought a woman to the gift exchange before. Do I know her?"

"She used to go to school with me. Now she lives in Denver."

"*Really*... Would she ever consider moving here?"

"I don't know."

"Has she seen the calendar?"

He waved as one of the guys called out to him from his open door. "What does that have to do with anything?"

"Bring an extra one just in case," she said and disconnected.

PULLING HER MINISKIRT down as far as it could go—to mollify Angela's nosy neighbors, two of whom were staring out their windows at her—Stephanie promised the cab driver that she'd pay him in a second and hurried up the walk. The house looked empty, and there was a For Sale sign in front, but Stephanie could see that the furniture was still in the living room. Angela might be planning to move, but she hadn't done it yet.

Her barely there sweater was more effective at attracting customers than keeping her warm, but she wrapped it around herself as well as she could and knocked on the door. Meanwhile, she could feel the neighbors' eyes boring holes in her back. A cab in this exclusive area drew too much attention. She should've had the driver drop her at the corner so she could walk, but he probably wouldn't have done it anyway. He didn't want to let her too far out of his sight; she hadn't paid him yet.

No one came to the door. "She's got my kid. But do you think she'd give me a number or tell me where the hell they're at?" she grumbled. She knew she'd made Angela mad the last time they'd seen each other. After that, her friend's numbers had all changed without warning. But Stephanie hadn't wanted the help Angela had offered. She could live her own life, thank you very much.

Glancing at the waiting taxi, she waved to reassure him and hurried around to the gate. She felt jittery, shaky, ill—and she knew it wasn't related to the bronchitis she'd had for over a week. She needed some junk before her symptoms got worse. But if she couldn't get inside the damn house, how was she going to get any money?

The back door was locked as tight as the front. Stephanie could see a single light shining in the living room, the typical "sorry, we're not home but don't want you to know it" light, and considered breaking a window. She didn't have any choice, did she? She had to get in, find a few bucks and get out. Before the neighbors could stop her.

Her mind was fixated on the quarters and dimes Angie threw in a big jar on a shelf in her closet. There had to be thirty, forty bucks in there.

Angie didn't need it. She never used it. Stephanie knew that was all it would take to carry her through the night. It'd be different if she'd been able to work. But what man wanted to pay for a woman with a raging fever and a hacking cough?

Finding a rock in the planter area next to the French doors, she bent to pick it up. But her hand was shaking so badly she could hardly lift it, and by the time she'd managed, the man from next door was standing less than ten feet away.

"Can I help you, miss?"

She dropped the rock and ducked her head so he couldn't see the black eye she'd sustained from a particularly rough customer four days earlier. "Angie, she—she's my friend. She said I could borrow forty bucks, to—to come on over and get it. But I—I got a cab waiting out front. And she's not here."

"She told you to come over."

It wasn't a question. He was looking down his nose at her, like all the other rich bastards in this neighborhood.

"That's what I said, isn't it?" She knew her voice had grown belligerent, but she couldn't seem to control it any more than she could control the shaking. She couldn't think straight. The terrible need inside her was eating her up....

"But that couldn't possibly be true," he replied. "As you can see, the house is closed up. She's gone for the holidays."

Gone for the holidays? Angie never went anywhere for the holidays.

"She—she said she'd give me forty bucks," Stephanie insisted.

"I think maybe you should seek a shelter and some professional help," he said.

Finally, she faced him squarely. "Listen, buddy, I—I'll give you a blow job right here for twenty bucks," she whispered. "I'll do anything else you want for forty."

He didn't take her up on her offer. He shook his head sadly, reached into his wallet and gave her the money.

ANGELA WAS PRETTY SURE that attending Matt's family's Christmas party was not a good idea. She would've said no—except that he'd asked Kayla first. And Kayla had, of course, immediately accepted. Kayla was playing cupid. She liked being around Matt. A lot.

"Matt told us you two went to school together," Ben, Matt's father, said after they'd been ushered in and offered a drink. He was doing his best to make her feel comfortable.

Angela glanced over at Matt, who stood by the punch bowl. He was talking to his brother and sister-in-law, who'd come from Reno, and a couple of uncles or cousins. Angela had been introduced to everyone, but Matt had such a big family, she was starting to lose track of who they were and how they all fit in. "That's right. I lived with Betty Cunningham."

Matt's dad was an older version of Matt, except there was gray mixed in with his dark blond hair, and he had brown eyes. Matt's mother was almost as tall as his father, and significantly overweight, but she was jovial and warm.

"Betty was a wonderful person," Ben said. "Loved jewelry. Came down to the store often."

Angela liked the rustic log home Matt's father had built. A mile or so from town, it was cut into Mount Davidson, like the other homes and businesses in the area, and smelled of the fire crackling in the hearth. Scrupulously clean and well-decorated in rustic browns and reds, it had a wall of windows in front. The Christmas tree stood before the windows, reaching all the way to the center beam of the polished wooden ceiling, its lights reflecting in the glass. Angela guessed that in the daytime, the Jacksons had a lovely view of the Como Mountains.

"I miss her," she admitted. Somehow, the hustle and bustle of the party and the easy camaraderie between all these people only added to Angela's sense of isolation.

"Your daughter is such a nice girl." Sherry, Matt's mother, joined them now that she'd finished whatever errand had sent her scurrying to the kitchen with Kayla as soon as she and Angela had arrived.

"Thank you."

"I've got her decorating cookies with my sister's kids," she confided. "She's a natural."

"I'm sure she'll like that." Angela caught Matt watching her. She smiled as if she were having a good time, but she wasn't. She didn't want to be here. This showed her what Kayla could have—without her.

"WHAT'S WRONG?" Matt asked.

Angela had left the party and stepped onto the extensive deck that wrapped around his parents' home. A chill wind was blowing—possibly the beginning of the storm Peggy McGinness had predicted—but there was a full moon and when he came up next to her, he could see the snow glistening far below. It was beautiful. But not half as beautiful as the woman staring forlornly down at it.

She glanced over at him. "Nothing, I just… needed some fresh air."

"Are you overwhelmed by the crowd?"

"No," she said, but when she met his knowing gaze, she instantly recanted. "Yes."

He chuckled with her. "You get used to the chaos."

"They're great. You're very lucky."

He knew he shouldn't touch her. He'd promised himself he'd take the relationship more slowly, so she wouldn't rebuff him again. But she looked so lost standing there, he couldn't help trying to comfort her, include her. Moving behind her, he gripped the wooden railing, penning her between his arms. He was hoping she'd lean back and let him hold her, but she didn't. "They really like Kayla," he said.

She had a strange expression on her face when she twisted to peer up at him.

"Angela?"

She studied him for a moment, then seemed to relax. "She likes them, too. She—she's never had anything like this."

He slipped his arms around her, pulling her into full contact with him. He wanted to shelter her from the cold, close the emotional distance she kept putting between them as easily as he could close the physical one. If she'd let him… "Neither have you."

She didn't answer.

Lifting her hair, he pressed his lips to her neck. "Why not open up? Give it a try?" he asked softly.

"Matt, I—" He stiffened, afraid she was going to pull away again. "I have something to tell you."

The tone of her voice didn't sound promising. "What's that?"

"It's about that night, with Stephanie."

He could tell by how rigid she'd gone that this wouldn't be good. Could she have warned him and hadn't? He no longer cared. That was thirteen years ago, and Stephanie had probably dragged her into it. He wasn't going to allow what had happened then ruin what could happen now. "I don't want to talk about that night," he said. "As far as I'm concerned it never took place."

"But Stephanie—"

"Doesn't exist."

"Is that what you want?" she asked fervently. "To forget? To live your life just as it is?"

"This is what I want," he responded and, keeping their backs to the house in case anyone glanced out, he slid his hand up her smooth, flat stomach.

CHAPTER SIX

ANGELA KNEW BETTER than to let their relationship get physical. Matt claimed he didn't care about what had happened thirteen years ago, but he didn't understand. There was a living, breathing person as a result of that night. Surely, he'd want to know.

Or maybe not. Maybe he liked his life exactly as it was. That was what he'd implied.

But now wasn't the time to dwell on her worries. His fingers were lightly caressing one breast through the thin fabric of her bra, sending shock waves of pleasure cascading through her.

"Matt," she murmured, still torn. Her conscience demanded she stop him, but her body begged her to close her eyes and forget. She'd tried to say his name in a commanding tone—but it came out choked and eager, and she could feel how deeply it affected him.

Pulling her along the railing to a set of stairs, he led her down to a small guest room. Set off from the rest of the house, it had a bed and its own bath.

"Let me see you," he whispered as he shut and locked the door behind them.

In the house above, they could hear Christmas

music, laughter, the tramping of feet. But it seemed far removed from them. Angela imagined Kayla grinning from ear to ear, licking frosting off her fingers. For the moment, everyone was happy. There was no need to ruin the party by blurting out the truth *or* to deny themselves these few stolen minutes. What would that really change?

Slowly, Angela slipped her red sweater over her head, watching carefully for Matt's reaction as it dropped to the floor—and was gratified when his eyes darkened and his jaw sagged.

"God, you're more beautiful than I imagined." Bending his head, he cupped her breasts, kissing the swell of one, then the other.

Angela let her head fall back. She wouldn't think, she told herself. Not about Denver or Virginia City. Not about the past or the future. She'd only *feel*— the feverish excitement building inside them; his deft hands unhooking her bra and sliding around to touch her; his warm, wet mouth closing over the tip of one breast; his muscular body pressing her into the mattress.

MATT COULDN'T BELIEVE he'd brought Angela into his old bedroom right in the middle of his parents' Christmas party. He'd meant to kiss her, to catch a tantalizing glimpse of her body, to touch her briefly. But the situation was quickly spiraling out of control. And he couldn't stop it for fear she'd never let him have another chance. His craving was too great. He had to feel her body's quivering responses, acquaint himself with all the little things that made her moan and writhe and cry out.

He hoped to make this as memorable as possible for her, but he didn't dare take it slow. There wasn't time. He didn't want to embarrass her by being gone so long someone would come looking for them. And the way she was tugging impatiently at his clothes told him she was as frantic as he was.

Once they were undressed, he pulled her down on the bed with him and pinned her arms over her head while he rolled on the condom he kept in his wallet.

She watched him with heavy-lidded eyes, her lips wet and slightly parted. But the gentle kiss he meant to give her quickly turned savage. Soon he was driving into her with powerful, rapid strokes. Minutes later, they were both damp with sweat and gasping for breath. And just when he thought he was too far gone to hold back any longer, it happened. She groaned, met his gaze as if he'd given her the most wonderful gift in the world, and shuddered.

He was only half a second behind her.

STEPHANIE LAY ON THE rumpled bed of the cheap hotel room staring bleary-eyed at the television. She could smell urine and perspiration, but it didn't bother her. She squinted, trying to decide if she was actually watching a program. It didn't matter. The flicker itself was fascinating, especially when her mind was floating so freely around the room. Spinning, moving, gliding…

"Hey, get up, bitch."

Slowly, she turned her head and blinked. A man's fuzzy shape appeared. Jaydog? "Hey, Jaydog," she said, the syllables running together.

She tried to make her gaping mouth form a smile, but he didn't seem happy with her greeting. A sharp pain suddenly dimmed her euphoria. Had he kicked her?

He was *still* kicking her. And screaming. He wanted her to do something. He wanted her to get out.

Climbing to her feet, she swayed unsteadily as she walked, heading for an opening that was blinding in its brightness. That had to be the door. She misjudged the distance and ran into a corner, causing an additional glancing blow to her shoulder. But then she was outside and the door slammed behind her.

She didn't know how long she stood there before she noticed that she wasn't wearing any clothes.

HE'D MADE A MISTAKE. Matt realized that almost right away. He'd expected his encounter with Angela to bring them closer, to put an end to her cautious reserve.

But after they rejoined the party, she left his side as quickly as she could. He found his gaze trailing after her wherever she went, hoping for a smile or some reassurance that what they'd done was okay—but he got nothing. She wouldn't even look at him. And if there was any accidental contact, she'd recoil.

What was going on? What they'd shared had been a great deal more than he'd expected. Especially so early in their relationship. But she was leaving in a week. It wasn't as if they had months or years stretching out before them. Even if they maintained a relationship, they wouldn't get to see each other very often. Besides, maybe he'd initiated the contact, but her surprising response had been the match that ignited the powder keg. The encounter had been completely spontaneous. Real. Raw.

He couldn't regret it.

Yet she was even less open to him now than she'd been before.

What had he done wrong? He supposed he shouldn't have taken things so far. But he hadn't *planned* for it to happen—not here, anyway.

He wasn't sure when he should've stopped. Angela had never indicated that she'd wanted him to. She'd acted as if she'd been starved for human touch, love.

He'd wanted to give her both.

He took a seat across the room from her and her daughter as his mother started handing out presents. Angela and Kayla sat with polite smiles fixed on their faces—outsiders looking in, enjoying everyone else's gifts and excitement without hoping for anything themselves.

He glanced over, but Angela avoided meeting his eyes. Again.

Maybe she'd been so hurt in the past that she was scared to let down her guard, he decided. She must've had a lonely childhood, after losing both parents and then living like a guest in someone else's house.

Then there was Stephanie. He couldn't even begin to imagine what dealing with her on a daily basis must've been like. Even as an adult Angela seemed to live a pretty solitary life—just her and Kayla. They were both engaging and polite, and he sensed that they wanted closer relationships than they had but didn't know how to reach out because they had no trust.

He remembered Kayla's story about her father. *So he walked out, and left my mom to raise me by herself. We don't even know where he is.*

The bastard had caused some deep scars.

"Are you going to open it?"

Matt blinked and focused on his sister-in-law, who'd just shoved a present into his lap.

"Sure," he said, and unwrapped a bottle of his favorite cologne.

"This is great. I was getting low." He gave her a hug, then waited for the process to continue around the circle until it was Angela's and Kayla's turn.

His uncle, who was sitting next to him, received a basket of salami and cheese. Matt's father acted excited over a new hand drill.

At first, Grandma had tried to boycott the gift exchange because his mother had put a ban on the special eggnog Matt usually provided. But then she relented, opened his brother's gift, which was a box of chocolate-covered cherries and, with a spiteful glare for his mother, stuffed three in her mouth at once.

"Wow. You go, Grandma," Ray said, sitting taller for Matt's benefit. "I guess I'm your new favorite grandson, huh?"

Matt shot his mother a look that said, "Next year

I'm bringing the eggnog." But he didn't bother to wait for her response. It was Kayla's turn to open her gift, and he didn't want to miss it.

"This is for me?" she asked in surprise when his aunt dug the present out from those that remained.

His mother checked the tag. "Yep. From Matt."

Kayla smiled shyly at him and tore away the wrapping. When she reached the plush blue box inside, she sent him another questioning glance, then snapped open the lid.

Her smile spread across her whole face. "It's a gold locket," she breathed. "I love it!"

Her response filled some of the hollowness Matt had been feeling since he'd left the bedroom downstairs. Especially when she hurried across the room to hug him. Her little arms felt so thin and fragile, as fragile as he imagined her heart must be.

"I'm glad you like it," he said.

She immediately returned to her mother so Angela could help her put it on, but Sherry insisted they let someone else do that so Angela could open her gift.

Angela's eyes flew wide when Sherry set a box in her lap, a box that was much, much bigger than Kayla's. "I'm sorry. I—I didn't bring any gifts," she said self-consciously.

Matt shrugged. "I didn't tell you it was a gift exchange."

She cleared her throat. "You should have."

He hadn't wanted her to feel obligated to go out and buy a bunch of presents. He'd just wanted her to come. "It's fine." Hadn't anyone ever given her a gift she could accept without feeling the obligation to respond in kind?

Probably not. Typically, only parents and grandparents gave gifts like that.

Matt's mother huddled closer to Angela. "Let's see what it is."

"Yeah, open it," Kayla chimed in, her locket now securely fastened around her neck.

Angela unwrapped the box and pulled out the quilt Matt had found in one of the gift shops. Handmade by a local woman, it showed nine historically significant structures in Virginia City—the First Presbyterian Church on C Street, Mackay Mansion on D Street, Piper's Opera House at B and Union, the Fourth Ward School on C, St. Mary's in the Mountains, Storey County Courthouse, the *Territorial Enterprise* Museum, where Mark Twain had begun his career, and the Liberty Engine Company No. 1 State Fireman Museum. In the Fireman square, he'd had the maker stitch *Love, Matt,* along the edge.

"It's beautiful!" Angela exclaimed.

He could tell she really liked it. "I thought it might give you something to remember us by."

"Come on, Matt. Who could forget you?" his brother teased.

"She won't forget you," his mother announced and slapped a square flat present in her lap.

Matt immediately recognized the size and shape, and groaned. "I left those at home. On purpose. How did you get—"

"I have my own stash," she said triumphantly.

Sure enough, it was a copy of the calendar.

"He's May and November," his aunt informed Angela, and just about ripped it out of her hands so she could turn to the right months. "See? Isn't he gorgeous? He's my nephew, but I gotta tell ya, he's the hottest one in there."

He rubbed a hand over his face. "Come on, Aunt Margaret."

His sister-in-law laughed and pointed. "I never would've believed it possible, but I think you're embarrassing him."

Matt scowled. "Why would I be embarrassed? I only did it to help the burn victims."

"Honey, that thing's started more fires than you'll ever put out," his aunt teased.

The whole family had a good laugh at his expense. But Matt didn't mind too much. Not when Angela finally looked up from the calendar and he saw the heat in her eyes.

Maybe she was trying not to acknowledge what she felt. But whatever had caused the frenzy downstairs wasn't gone. Not by a long shot.

CHAPTER SEVEN

SHEILA GILBERT LOOKED much the same as she had in high school. Barely over five feet tall, with shoulder-length blond hair, blue eyes and a curvaceous figure, she'd gained a smoker's voice and somehow lost her ready smile—but those appeared to be the only changes.

"It's wonderful to see you again," Angela said as she and Kayla led the way to a table at the Silver Dollar Café, where Sheila had suggested they meet. A mom-and-pop place that had opened since Angela had left town, the restaurant was located across the street from Matt's parents' jewelry store. Angela had noticed that little detail the moment they'd driven up. Every few seconds, she found her attention drifting to the window—just in case she spotted a member of his family on the street outside. She'd liked the Jacksons. She'd liked them all—

"When did you get in?" Sheila asked.

Angela forced herself to focus. "Last Sunday."

"What brings you back?"

She shrugged as the waitress delivered their water, and Sheila ordered coffee. "I missed it, wanted to see the town," she said when the waitress had hurried away.

"You missed *this* place?" Sheila raised a skeptical eyebrow. "You're kidding, right?"

Kayla's nose appeared above the top of her menu. "You don't like it here, Sheila?"

"What's to like?" she asked.

"Everything," Kayla replied earnestly. "The mountains and the trees and the buildings. And Matt, and his parents and cousins. And his funny grandma."

Obviously, Kayla liked them, too.

"Matt?" Sheila turned to Angela expectantly.

"Matthew Jackson," she said. "We ran into him the first day we got here."

Sheila released a low whistle. "Now I understand. If you've seen Matt, you've seen the very best Virginia City has to offer."

Kayla proudly lifted her locket. "He gave me this at the Christmas party last night."

Sheila held it in her own hand for a moment. "Very nice." She grinned wryly. "See? That's my problem. He's never given me a locket."

"But you like him," Angela said.

"Who doesn't?" Her voice grew dreamy. "He's a tough catch, so be forewarned. But maybe you're better at big-game hunting than I am. Anyway, he's nice, sexy and brave. He keeps us all safe while looking like a dream in that uniform." She leaned forward. "And have you seen the calendar? I have May permanently taped to my ceiling. The mere sight of that picture makes me—"

Angela cleared her throat.

Sheila's eyes darted toward Kayla. "—makes me

proud of our local firemen," she finished. But her smile said what she hadn't been able to say. And Angela completely understood. After Kayla had gone to sleep last night, Angela had sat up staring at the picture that featured Matt with a fire hose slung over one muscular shoulder. He was wearing nothing but a fireman's hat and a pair of pants slung so low on his narrow hips that they revealed the line of hair descending from his navel—the line of hair she'd seen for herself last night, along with what the picture *didn't* show.

The memory of his hands on her body, of his body joining perfectly with hers, played in her mind again.

She pinched the bridge of her nose, hoping to stem the tide of mortification, arousal and embarrassment rising to her face. When he'd brought her home, he'd asked her to call him after she got settled in the room, had murmured that he wanted to talk to her about what had happened between them. She'd mumbled something noncommittal, thanked him for the quilt and turned away before he could give her even a peck on the cheek. But she hadn't been able to make herself dial his number. She felt too guilty for taking advantage of his ignorance where Kayla was concerned, knew it would make him hate her when he found out.

When *he found out...*

Now it was only a matter of time, wasn't it? Because she'd already fallen in love with him and every member of his family. And if Kayla had the chance to be part of them, of what they had, Angela wouldn't let anything stand in the way—least of all herself.

Instinctively, she reached across the table to take Kayla's hand.

"What is it, Angie?" she asked, the question in her voice telling Angela she was squeezing a little too hard.

She *had* to do it, right? She had to tell for Kayla's sake.

The lump in Angela's throat made it difficult to speak. "Nothing. I just—I love you," she said.

Kayla smiled sweetly as Sheila looked on. "I love you, too. I'm so glad you brought me here."

A crushing pain made it difficult to breathe. Letting go, Angela tried to smile. "Me, too," she said, then hid behind her menu because Sheila was watching her strangely, and she knew she'd start crying if she didn't.

God, it's going to be tough to give you up, she thought.

STEPHANIE'S HEAD POUNDED as the voices of the other people droned on and on. She was in a shelter, she realized slowly, lying on a mattress, gazing at the cavernous ceiling. She didn't know how long she'd been there or who had brought her in. But she could tell they'd given her something to help her deal with the spasms that racked her body. She could also tell it wasn't enough.

Getting up, she started for the door. She wanted to go back. Jaydog would fix her up. He always did. For a few tricks, he'd get her exactly what she needed.

A woman wearing nurse's scrubs caught hold of

her arm before she could reach freedom. "Miss, I don't think you want to go out there. The help you need is right here."

"You don't have what I need," she argued.

"It isn't easy, but you can do it."

"Let me go." She tried to jerk away, but the woman's grip only tightened.

"Listen to me," the woman said, her voice low, harsh. "Is this the kind of life you want? Look at yourself!" She handed her a mirror, and Stephanie almost didn't recognize the face that stared back at her. When had she gotten so gaunt and haggard? So old? And what had happened to her hair? Had someone set fire to it? Or had she set fire to it herself?

"I need some sleep," she insisted. "I—I'll get a haircut. I'm not as bad as you make me sound."

"Do you want to *live?*" the woman asked.

Stephanie blinked at her in surprise. "*What?*"

"If you want to make it another year, give me the number of someone I can call."

Stephanie took a second look at the stranger in the mirror. Who was that person? Where was she going? What had she done?

She had no answers. She had nothing.

"Who can I call?" the woman repeated, more forcefully.

Stephanie didn't have Angela's cell-phone number. Their relationship had become so rocky Angela had changed the number and wouldn't give it to her. But Stephanie did remember the name of the place where Angela worked.

"WHAT'S WRONG?" Lewis asked, poking his head inside Matt's office.

Matt yanked himself out of the lethargic stupor that seemed to swallow him whole every time he stopped moving, and shuffled some papers around. "Nothing, why?"

"You're not yourself today."

Angela hadn't called him last night. She hadn't even squeezed his hand or thrown him a quick smile when they'd parted. She'd made passionate love to him for about ten minutes, then…no real interaction at all. "Thanks," she'd said as he'd dropped them off. "For everything." And then she'd gone and he hadn't heard from her since.

He shouldn't have taken her into that bedroom. She probably thought he didn't respect her. Or that he was only interested in what he could get from her while she was in town. Or…

Hell, he didn't know. He'd never gotten so many mixed signals in his life. He was thoroughly confused.

"So how was the big gift exchange?"

Lewis was still standing in the doorway of his office.

Matt tried to rouse himself again. "Great. Fun. Grandma didn't get her special eggnog, for which she'll never forgive me. But other than that…" Other than that, it had definitely had its high points. Like the moment Angela had frantically stripped off his pants and greedily touched him everywhere, arching into him when he'd first covered her body with his.

She'd wanted to make love, too, hadn't she? Because if that was *no,* how would he ever know *yes?*

"I ran into Ray a few minutes ago," Lewis said.

"Oh, really? Where?" Matt could hear the flatness in his own voice, but Lewis didn't comment on his lack of enthusiasm.

"At your parents' store. I stopped by to pick up the necklace I bought for Peggy."

"Peg's going to have a nice Christmas."

"Yeah."

"That's good."

Lewis stepped into the room and leaned on the back of one of the chairs. "Anyway, Peg and I plan to invite Kayla to come to Reno with us tonight."

The mention of Kayla instantly raised Matt's level of interest. "What for?"

"We're going to Circus Circus, you know, for the kids. Then we'll be staying over to have a buffet breakfast and do a little shopping. Christmas Eve is the day after tomorrow, so it's pretty much our last chance. I thought I'd let you know in case you wanted to take the opportunity to be alone with Angela."

Matt felt a sudden flicker of hope. Last night, he'd handled her the way he would a house fire—urgently and without finesse. She must've been disappointed. So…what if he brought her some flowers, took her out for a romantic dinner, spent the evening just getting to know her? If she didn't touch him, he wouldn't touch her. Then maybe she'd forgive him, let him start over… This time, he'd take it slower.

But she hadn't called him even after he'd asked her to.

It was too late.

He shook his head. "Thanks, but I'm not going to bother her again. I don't think she wants to see me anymore."

"CAN WE GET IT FOR HIM? Please?" Kayla begged.

Angela didn't have to ask *For who?* After breakfast, when they'd set off to do some Christmas shopping, Kayla had wanted to find a gift for Matt. Angela did, too. She just hadn't expected to find anything quite like this.

"Please say yes," Kayla said.

Angela lifted the sculpture of a fireman carrying a child to safety and read the plaque at the bottom. *Safe from Imminent Danger.*

Tracing a finger lightly over the face of the child, she took in the details—the smile, the rounded cheeks, the pigtails. It was a girl, which struck Angela as very significant.

"Angie?"

Angela blinked and finally answered. "Yes?"

"It's perfect for him, don't you think?"

It *was* perfect. It was also expensive, but his gifts to them hadn't been cheap, and it said everything Angela wanted to say. *Shelter her from harm. Keep her safe. Be a good daddy.*

She could trust a fireman, right?

WHEN HE HEARD ANGELA at the station, asking to see him, Matt couldn't believe it. He'd just decided she didn't want anything to do with him. And now she was here?

Ruben, one of his men, directed her to Matt's office.

Matt rounded the desk as Kayla came hurrying through the door.

"We got you a present," she said breathlessly.

Angela followed, carrying a large square box wrapped in a paper decorated with little Christmas trees.

"You didn't have to get me anything," he said. But since it had brought them to the station, he was damn glad they had.

Kayla clasped her hands in front of her as if she could scarcely contain the excitement. "Open it!"

He would have, right away. Except Angela's gaze swept over him from head to toe, so hot and hungry it nearly stole his breath. He hadn't made any mistake last night—she wanted him as badly as he wanted her. So what was the problem?

He didn't know, but he'd certainly ask. Because he now understood that his other plan would never have worked. Considering the force of what they were feeling, what they wanted, there was no way they'd be able to let their relationship develop slowly.

"Hi," he said, his eyes locking with hers.

"Hi," she murmured and gave him such a sexy, mysterious smile he got lost in it for a while—until Kayla tugged on his arm.

"Don't you want to see what we got you?"

He doubted it could compare with what Angela

had given him last night. Grinning, he took the package, set it on his desk and tore off the paper.

It was a bronze statue of a fireman saving a child.

"Do you like it?" Kayla asked.

He smiled as he stared at it. "I do. Very much. Thank you."

"Now every time you look at it you'll think of us," she said.

He didn't admit it, but he was afraid he couldn't forget them even if he wanted to.

ANGELA REACHED FOR the phone half a dozen times without picking it up. Tonight was the night to tell him. Kayla had gone to Reno with Lewis and his family, so Angela was alone. She could talk to Matt, explain the pregnancy that had resulted from what had happened thirteen years ago and see what he'd like to do about it before she broke the news to Kayla.

Maybe he'd settle for annual or biannual visits. Why not? He wasn't used to having a child. And it wasn't as if Angela needed him for financial support. She did fine on her own. She'd suggest they share Kayla.

But what if he didn't want to share? He didn't seem like the type to have a part-time daughter. He seemed like the kind of man who claimed what belonged to him and took care of his own.

She wiped her sweaty palms on the old jeans she'd pulled on, along with a sweatshirt. She was scared. But picturing that essay, those question marks that had replaced Kayla's last name, made Angela reach for the handset with enough resolve to get the job done. Kayla Jackson had a nice ring to it. Matt was a father to be proud of.

The phone rang just as Angela touched it. Taking a deep breath, she brought it to her ear. "Hello?"

"I want to see you. Will you come over?"

It was Matt. Of course. She'd known it would be.

Angela bit her lip. Could she really break her promise to Betty? What if he insisted on raising Kayla, and Stephanie managed to get her life together? Would he include her at all?

There were so many variables, so many risks....

"Angela?"

"I'll be there in fifteen minutes," she said and hung up.

CHAPTER EIGHT

STEPHANIE SAT ON HER COT and kept rocking, back and forth, back and forth. It was the only way to deal with the turmoil inside her. The methadone the nurse had given her was curbing her withdrawal symptoms, but nothing could ease her agitation over what she'd just learned.

When the nurse had called Angela's work number, she'd been told that Angela was out of town. Then the nurse had explained that it was an emergency, and some assistant had said Angela had gone to Virginia City for the holidays.

Stephanie rocked faster. Virginia City. Angie had gone home without her. And she'd taken Kayla. After thirteen years.

Why? That was the question. There was nothing left in Virginia City.

Except maybe Matt.

ANGELA COULD SCARCELY breathe as she waited on Matt's front step—and it didn't get any easier once he opened the door.

Dressed in a pair of faded jeans and a blue striped

shirt with a white T-shirt underneath, he was fresh from the shower. His hair was still damp and curled around his collar. She thought he looked better than she'd ever seen him. Especially when his lips curved into a crooked smile as his eyes swept over her, telling her that he liked what *he* saw just as much. "Come in."

She couldn't get physical with him, she reminded herself. They both needed to have clear heads, to make a wise decision uninfluenced by peripheral desires. A decision about Kayla.

But then he tilted up her chin and kissed her softly, and all she wanted to do was melt in his arms and let him bury her fear beneath a torrent of sensation.

"I'm making you some dinner," he said, as she greeted Sampson. "I hope you're hungry."

Angela had been so preoccupied that she hadn't bothered to eat. "I am hungry," she admitted and ignored the voice that was yelling *Tell him!* in the corner of her mind. They had all night, didn't they? She had to wait for the right moment.

STEPHANIE STOOD at the pay phone, cursing the long wait as other addicts called a boyfriend, a girlfriend, family. They were limited to one call a day and Stephanie had already taken her turn, but she didn't care. She pushed in front of several people, brushing aside their complaints. She needed to use the phone again, and no one was stopping her.

Was Angela moving to Virginia City? Was *that* what was going on? Or was she taking Kayla to her father?

After she'd found out she was pregnant, her

mother's reaction was the only reason Stephanie hadn't told Matt. She'd wanted to let him know about the baby, could hardly wait to break the news that he *had* to notice her now. That she had something no one else did, even his beloved Danielle. She'd never seen her mother as angry as she'd been the day she'd learned—thanks to Angela—exactly what Stephanie had done. Betty had promised right then that if Stephanie ever told Matt about Kayla—if she ever told *anyone* the name of Kayla's father—it would be the last straw. Betty would disown Stephanie, and she'd be out on her ass. For real. No family. No friends. No one to catch her when she fell.

Deep in her heart, Stephanie had known she needed her mother too much to sever that tie. And, in her more honest moments, she'd also known that even if Matt had accepted Kayla, he would never fully accept Stephanie. So she'd been forced to stick with her only form of support. She had to save herself one last chance, always. Betty was her ticket to a better life, when she'd finally had enough.

Once she'd grown older, however, she hadn't used that chance and she'd rarely thought of Matt. He hadn't been much of a partier in high school. She knew he wouldn't approve of her and didn't need his arrogant judgments.

But neither did she need Angela thinking she could take Betty's place now that Betty was dead. Angela had told Stephanie she had to clean up if she wanted to be part of her daughter's life. Yet Angela had no right to make such a stipulation. Stephanie had only signed those guardianship papers, giving Kayla to her mother, because she'd been desperate for a few bucks. Angela wasn't even related to Kayla. How could Betty have signed Kayla over to her? Angela was a parasite her mother had picked up long ago, and now the flea thought she owned the dog.

Memories of her friend pleading with her to take control of her life threatened to undermine Stephanie's resolve, as did an underlying knowledge that Kayla was probably better off without a mother like her, but Stephanie wouldn't allow it. As long as Angela had Kayla, Angela couldn't turn Stephanie away.

But Angela's return to Virginia City seemed to confirm Stephanie's worst fear. Was it over? Was Angela *really* giving up on her?

At last, Stephanie reached the front of the line. Behind her, she could hear two women complaining about how pushy she'd been. She knew they might report her. She'd leave the shelter if they did. This call meant that much to her.

She held the receiver, her hands shaking from withdrawal, but also from the emotions pounding through her. Her daughter was the one good thing that had ever happened to her. She couldn't let Angela turn Kayla over to Matt.

"Operator. How can I help you?"

Stephanie drew a bolstering breath. She had to talk to someone who might've seen Angela, someone who might know what was going on. But who?

It took four tries—and all the change she'd won

in a poker game earlier—before the operator actually had the number Stephanie had requested. "I'll put you through," she said.

Then the phone rang twice and Sheila Gilbert picked up.

"I have a collect call from Stephanie Cunningham. Will you accept the charges?"

There was a slight pause, followed quickly by a surprised, "Sure, no problem."

MATT SAT AT ONE END of the couch facing Angela, who sat on the other. Sampson lay contently between them, stretched out at their feet. They'd had dinner and talked about his family, his job, her job, what it was like in Denver, how Virginia City had changed. He'd enjoyed the conversation, felt they'd connected in a way he hadn't connected with a woman in years. She hadn't touched him, but he still hoped the evening would end as he wanted it to. Imagining her as he'd seen her at his parents', her head thrown back in wild abandon as he kissed her neck, bare shoulders and breasts, made his heart race.

He ached to touch her again. Would he get the same powerful reaction?

He certainly didn't want to spook her again. That night at his parents', everything had happened way too fast. This time, he was determined to slow things down. Maybe he could even convince her to stay the night.

He liked the thought of that. But he felt it was important to talk about their other encounter. He had a feeling this relationship could be different from the casual flings he'd had with various women since Danielle, and that made him nervous. For the first time in ages, he wanted something he could lose. Especially because Angela didn't seem receptive to anything serious. And she lived two states away.

Obviously, there'd have to be some kind of compromise if they were going to build anything long-term out of their tremendous attraction.

"About the other night…" he began.

She lifted her eyes above the rim of her glass. She'd refused wine and was having cranberry juice. "What about it?" she asked as she set the glass aside, suddenly cautious.

"I'm confused," he admitted. "I can tell you're not interested in letting me touch you again, and yet…I thought you enjoyed it."

She cleared her throat. "I did."

Frowning, he studied her. "Then why—"

"It's not a matter of *want,*" she said, still guarded.

"So…you're upset because it was too fast? More than you bargained for? What?"

"No." She tucked her hair behind one ear, giving him the impression she was stalling, thinking. "I—having you there, touching me, kissing me…it got the better of me, that's all. I knew I shouldn't let myself be swept away. But it'd been so long since I'd made love…and it'll probably be a long time before I do it again."

Matt felt as if she'd kicked him in the stomach. "You're saying it wasn't necessarily *me* you wanted.

I just happened to come along and I could provide what had been missing from your life?"

"Matt, I'm dealing with a lot right now. I can't worry about my own needs and desires. Like I said, that got the best of me, but now I've got to—"

"The other night you said my name as if I was the only man in the world," he interrupted. "You arched into me as if you'd abandon your soul to me, too, if you could."

Her jaw dropped as she gaped at him. "What do you want me to say?" she replied. "That I wish circumstances were different? That I wish we had a chance? Because I do. I want to make love with you right now. It's all I can do to keep from reliving those minutes, to keep from wanting you again! But—"

Matt's body had reacted instantly to her passionate words. He wanted the same thing. Here on the couch, on the table, anywhere. He couldn't remember ever feeling so desperate for another woman. "But?" he echoed.

"There's something I have to tell you."

The gravity in her voice made him uneasy. But she'd already insisted she wasn't married. Twice. So, as far as he could see, what she had to say couldn't be too bad. Nothing big enough to come between them, anyway. "What's that?" he asked.

She hugged herself as if she were almost too frightened to proceed. He was tempted to reach out and pull her to him, to comfort her, but he waited.

"Kayla isn't really my daughter," she said. "I—I

was lying about that. She came to live with me fifteen months ago."

He blinked. That was surprising but certainly not devastating.

"She *feels* like my daughter. I *love* her like a daughter."

He would've felt relieved, except the tears filling Angela's eyes kept him a little off balance. "Of course you do," he said gently. "I understand."

"No, you don't." She wrung her hands as the tears spilled down her cheeks. "You see…there was no man who walked out on us. She—she's *Stephanie's* daughter."

He tried that on for size. *This* was supposed to be the big shocker? That Angela was raising Stephanie's daughter? He hoped so, because it didn't take longer than a split second to realize he could love Kayla regardless of what he felt for Stephanie. It actually made sense. Stephanie was much more likely to get herself in trouble than Angela, who'd been cautious even back in high school.

"It's okay," he said. "I'm cool with that."

She dashed a hand across her face. "I'm not finished."

Sliding closer, he took her hand. "Whatever you have to say, it's going to be fine."

She closed her eyes. "Kayla's grandmother was raising her. I—I took her to live with me when her grandmother died."

"Why didn't Stephanie step up?" he asked. "You said she was in Denver, in sales or something."

She opened her eyes and her hand gripped his like a lifeline. "Stephanie's a heroin addict, Matt. The only thing she sells is her body. She—she's not the person I once knew. I've finally come to the conclusion that it's not safe for Kayla to be around her."

"Wow." He reached out to smooth the hair from her forehead. "I'm sorry to hear that. Sorry for you and for Kayla. But it doesn't change what's between us."

Her forehead creased in a troubled expression. "Remember that party?" she asked.

"What party?"

"In high school."

That party. With Stephanie naked. Where he'd had one of his first sexual encounters. *Sexual* encounters…

Fear struck and Matt dropped her hand. "*Yes?*"

Angela looked bereft, as if she'd reach out to him, but didn't. "Matt, I brought Kayla here because she belongs to you."

Matt rocked back and pressed both hands to his chest, hardly able to breathe. How had Kayla gone from being *Angela's* daughter to being *his* daughter in just a few seconds? His and Stephanie's, who was now a prostitute and a drug addict!

"It…it can't be true," he said softly because his voice wouldn't go any louder.

"It *is* true," she insisted. "Stephanie wanted to get pregnant. She thought she'd finally be able to have you if she did. But when Betty found out what she was up to, she yanked us both out of school and we moved. Betty didn't want it to ruin your life. She knew how unfair it was to you, your family, your girl-friend, everyone."

He shook his head, still unable to believe what he was hearing. He'd slept with Stephanie *once!* And she'd drugged him to get that far. Now Angela was telling him he had a twelve-year-old daughter?

What do you want for Christmas?... I'd like to find my dad....

God! A blinding rage suddenly took hold of him and he shot to his feet. "You knew and yet...you came here, all the while knowing...You let me—" He stopped. Too many thoughts and feelings were assaulting him. He wasn't sure what he was trying to say. He felt so...manipulated. Then and now.

"I'm sorry," she whispered.

He stalked to the window so he wouldn't have to look at her and stared out. It was snowing again, coming down so thick he couldn't see more than a foot in front of him. What was he supposed to think? *What was he supposed to do?*

"What do you want from me?" he asked after a long silence.

She didn't answer right away. When he finally turned, she was standing and had her purse clutched tightly in her hands. "Nothing," she said. "I—I just thought you should know."

"Does *she* know?" he asked.

Angela shook her head. "I decided it'd be smarter to tell you first. This way...nothing *has* to change. I have everything I need to take care of her. But I...I didn't want to steal anything from you. Or take anything from her if…if you felt differently. That's all."

That was all. She'd given him the most shocking news of his life and now she was leaving with a simple "Oops—never mind."

He tried to focus on the act of breathing. He kept seeing Stephanie that night, her triumphant smile as Danielle had wept—and he felt sick.

He'd gotten her pregnant. He'd fathered a child at sixteen. And now that child was twelve years old and didn't know who her own daddy was.

CHAPTER NINE

NOTHING HAS TO CHANGE. Those words seemed to echo in Matt's head long after Angela left. They were so ridiculous. If what Angela had told him was true, if Kayla really belonged to him, *everything* had changed. Regardless of the way Kayla had been conceived, he couldn't simply go on as if he didn't know he had a daughter.

He'd get tests, of course—for his own peace of mind. Stephanie was the one behind this, and he didn't trust her one bit. But he was fairly sure DNA would confirm what he'd just been told. Kayla was his. Stephanie had been so obsessed with him, he doubted she'd so much as looked at another boy that entire year. And when he pictured Kayla, he could see the family resemblance. It was a wonder he hadn't noticed it before. Or maybe not. Why would he? He'd never even entertained the thought. Not after one incident he could hardly remember. And not after such a long silence.

I want to find my daddy....

Still at the window, Matt shoved a hand through his hair. *I'm your daddy.* The reality of that was overwhelming. And yet he felt a strong sense of responsibility. He had to tell Kayla. He couldn't let a child of his go through life feeling lost and unloved.

But how did he explain what had happened? And where did they go from here?

He needed to call Angela, get her to come back so they could talk. Now that the initial shock was beginning to wear off, he could see that she was in a difficult situation, as well. She wasn't to blame for Stephanie's actions thirteen years ago. And yet she was standing in for the absent parents, taking care of a child who wasn't even hers.

His child.

He wasn't convinced he'd ever get used to the idea.

Reaching for the cordless phone, he dialed the hotel. No answer. He tried her cell.

"This is Angela Forrester. I'm out of town until after the holidays, but if you'll leave your name and number, I'll return your call as soon as I can. If this is an emergency, please contact my assistant, Lisa Burton, at Pierpont Realty."

The beep sounded in Matt's ear. "This is an emergency, but your assistant can't help me. I need you. I'm sorry if I didn't react the way you'd hoped I would. I admit that I'm still…reeling. But I need to talk to you, to discuss this. Can I come over? Or if you find that too threatening, you can come here."

Frustrated, he punched the off button and was about to toss the phone across the counter when it rang.

"Thank God," he muttered and answered immediately, although caller ID said Unknown. He assumed Angela had her cell number blocked. But it wasn't Angela.

"I have a collect call from Stephanie Cunningham."

Matt stiffened. *Stephanie* was calling him? After thirteen years of silence? That scared the hell out of him. He hadn't even decided what he was going to do about Kayla and already Stephanie was back in his life!

"Will you accept the charges?" the operator asked.

He cursed silently to himself but agreed. Then Stephanie's voice came across the line.

"Matt, don't listen to her," she said in a rush. "It's a lie."

He expected to feel a wave of intense hatred, especially now that he knew the real consequences of what she'd done to him, but he didn't. A variety of other emotions surged through him instead—anger, pity and disgust. He'd never imagined Stephanie as part of his future. Had he just stepped into some alternate reality?

"*What's* a lie?" he asked, pacing in agitation. Sampson whined, obviously sensing something wrong, but Matt ignored him.

"You don't need to give Kayla any locket. She's not yours. She's from…someone else, a—a guy I met after I left Virginia City."

Matt wished he could believe her—so his life would return to normal. He almost asked her for Kayla's birthday so he could compare the dates. But he didn't need to. The hard edge of desperation in Stephanie's voice told him she was the one who was lying. And now that he'd heard the truth, there was no hiding from it. "What are you hoping to gain by telling me that?" he asked.

"I'm doing you a favor. You're off the hook. You're not the father. Tell Angela she has to come home now. She—she can't leave me here. She can't take my child away from me."

So he wasn't the only one frightened by recent developments. They were all scared, he realized. His involvement upset the delicate equilibrium. And yet Angela had risked it.

"Where are you?" he asked.

"None of your business," she said, but he could hear others talking in the background—"Get off the phone, bitch. I get to make my call, too"—and imagined her in jail or some sort of community shelter.

Briefly, the temptation to take Stephanie at her word, skip the paternity test and pretend he'd never met Kayla reasserted itself. He didn't need to be part of this mess, did he? It wasn't his fault. Angela would take care of Kayla. She'd be fine.

And yet...

He focused on the statue he'd brought home from the station, the one Kayla and Angela had given him for Christmas. It was a fireman rescuing a child. *Safe from imminent danger.*

With a mother like Stephanie, what child needed him more desperately than his own?

"I'm sorry, Stephanie," he said. "But there are going to be some changes."

"What changes?" she cried.

His eyes still on the statue, he drew a deep

breath. "If Kayla's mine, I'll be taking care of her from now on."

ANGELA'S HEART BEGAN TO RACE the moment she heard Matt banging on her door. What now? She'd managed to avoid his calls, but she could hardly let him wake all the other hotel guests at one o'clock in the morning.

Dropping his quilt, which she'd been hugging around her since she'd finished packing Kayla's and her belongings, she hurried across the room and opened the door to find a rumpled-looking Matt.

"Let me in," he said, his voice terse, his eyes intense.

Angela didn't want to. She regretted telling him about Kayla and longed to go home, to pretend that what they'd said and done here in Virginia City had never happened. Tomorrow night was Christmas Eve, but she'd drive straight through. She couldn't wait.

"Matt—"

He peered over her head at the luggage. "It's too late to run," he said.

Someone across the hall peered out, wearing a disgruntled expression, and Angela quickly waved Matt inside.

"I'm not running. I'm—"

"Heading home." He glowered at the bags. "Two states away, which probably sounds like a pretty safe distance."

"I thought maybe we should…you know, take the next few weeks to consider the situation. You can call me in Denver when—"

"I've considered it," he interrupted.

The determination in his voice sent terror shooting through Angela. He had something to say already? She'd only left his place a couple of hours ago. "What have you decided?" she whispered.

He reached over to run his thumb along Kayla's name, which was embroidered on the backpack she'd brought for her beloved books. "I want her. She's mine. I'll take care of her from here on out."

Tears sprang to Angela's eyes. "Matt, wait. Please, I…" The lump in her throat choked off her words. She wasn't sure what to say, anyway. She knew Kayla wanted her father more than anything and that Matt would be good to her. She also knew he could offer her a loving extended family, the roots she craved and greater protection from the influence of her mother. The distance alone would be a plus, because Stephanie couldn't stop by every time she was down and out and wanted money for drugs.

Angela should let Kayla go, shouldn't she? But the thought of driving home without her, of packing up all her belongings and shipping them off, broke Angela's heart. She'd hoped to convince Matt that they could share Kayla, despite the thousand miles that separated them, but the words wouldn't come. It wasn't a realistic idea, anyway. One of them would have to play a very minor role in Kayla's life. And she knew which one that should be.

She breathed deeply, trying to absorb the pain, and felt his hand at her elbow.

"You okay?" he murmured.

Fresh tears fell as she looked up at him. "No," she said. Then his arms went around her, as his quilt had a few minutes earlier, and his mouth touched hers in a kiss that spoke of warmth and comfort—but quickly changed to driving passion and escalating need.

MATT WOKE UP IN Angela's bed. He could smell the clean scent of her hair, feel the softness of her bare skin as she continued to sleep with her body curled into his side, and knew that he'd gained more than a daughter last night. He wanted Angela, too. He wasn't sure how they were going to work out the logistics—where they'd live and who would change jobs—but he was hoping she'd marry him so they could become a family.

He smiled wryly at the thought of that. A *family?* A week ago, he hadn't even had a girlfriend.

He adjusted the quilt they'd used to cover themselves, the quilt he'd given Angela for Christmas, and his smile widened. Just when he'd begun to think it would never happen…

"You're awake?" Angela murmured.

He'd been cautious with his movements so he wouldn't disturb her, but now he slid his hand up over the curve of her hip to her breast, as he'd wanted to do ever since he'd opened his eyes.

"Aren't you tired?" she asked, covering a yawn. "We were up all night."

"I feel good. What about you?"

She gave him a sexy smile. "Fishing for compliments?"

He chuckled. "You kidding? Your screams were enough. I'm surprised our neighbors didn't complain to the management."

"I didn't scream that loud!" She tried to sit up in mock outrage, but he pressed her back, too busy enjoying what his fingers had found.

"Okay, but you groaned a lot," he said. "I loved it. And the way you looked at me right before you—"

She tried to brush his hand away. "Do we have to go over the details?"

"Why are you embarrassed?" He laughed as he moved her beneath him. "I told you I loved it. And the marks on my back will heal."

She narrowed her eyes. "I didn't leave any marks on your back!"

"Yet," he said. "There's always this morning." He kissed the indentation beneath her ear. "And the morning after." He kissed the pulse at her neck. "And the morning after that." He let his mouth drift lower, enjoying the fact that he could so easily make her quiver.

"No, I'm going home today…remember?" She gave a little gasp on that last word because he'd hit his real target.

"It's the holidays," he said, blowing cool air on the breast he'd just suckled.

She was getting lost in his lovemaking. He could tell. But she fought it. "So?"

"So you're spending Christmas with me."

"Trying to get another gift out of me?" she teased.

Leaving her breast, he kissed a trail down to her navel. "No, something better."

"What's that?" she asked, but he knew she was having a difficult time concentrating. He was making sure of it.

"A promise."

"What…kind…of promise?"

He didn't answer. He was too busy.

"Matt!" Her hands clenched in his hair.

He wasn't sure if she'd said his name by way of question or encouragement. But she seemed pretty interested in holding him right where he was, so he guessed she'd been encouraging him—and waited until just the right moment to answer. When her eyes closed, and her muscles tensed, she said his name again, only this time with power and more than a little urgency, and when the moment passed, he told her what he really wanted.

"Marry me."

ANGELA SAT IN THE living room of Matt's parents' home, enjoying Christmas morning. Outside, sunlight glistened on the snow and the world around them appeared crisp and bright, silent and peaceful. Inside, Christmas music played softly in the background as Sherry handed out mugs of hot chocolate and Kayla helped Matt's two younger cousins sort the Christmas presents, which they planned to open in a few minutes. Angela had brought some gifts for Kayla, so Kayla had a small pile of her own, but Matt had something far better waiting for her. Today was the day she'd get exactly what she wanted for Christmas: She'd learn the identity of her father.

"You nervous?" Matt murmured. He'd been sitting next to Angela since she and Kayla had arrived a few minutes earlier.

Angela nodded. "Dying. You?"

"Yeah."

He seemed excited. He also seemed intent on making them a family. Angela had asked him not to mention the possibility to Kayla. She needed more time to think. She had a home and a career in Colorado. Pulling up stakes and moving back to Virginia City was a big decision. Especially so soon. And then there was Stephanie…

When Matt had told Angela about his conversation with Kayla's mother, Angela had made some calls, trying to locate her. It was so difficult to give up hope. She'd thought maybe Stephanie was ready to get clean at last. But when she'd finally made contact with the shelter where Stephanie had been staying, she'd been told that a man named Jaydog had picked her up late last night.

That was where the trail had gone cold. Stephanie was probably right back on the streets, doing anything she could to feed her addiction. Angela had been through the cycle enough times to know that—and yet she felt so guilty for loving Matt, for wanting to be with him. Could she really move back to Virginia City with Stephanie's daughter and agree to marry the boy Stephanie had wanted so desperately?

She didn't think so.

"He's asked her to marry him," Angela heard Sherry whisper to Ray, Ray's wife and Claudia, her sister, in the kitchen. "Can you believe it? He's in love!"

Angela glanced worriedly at Kayla, afraid she might overhear. But Kayla didn't even look up. She was too busy burrowing under the tree.

"What did she say?" came Ray's murmured response.

"She's thinking about it." Sherry lowered her voice, but Angela could still make out the words. "So be really nice to her."

Evidently, Matt had heard his mother, too, because he squeezed Angela's hand and Angela couldn't help laughing softly to herself.

"So where would they live?" Claudia asked.

"I'm praying it'll be here. What good is getting my first granddaughter if I never get to see her?"

Matt's mother had a point. If they got married, they'd live in Virginia City. Angela knew that already. But even if they didn't marry, Kayla would stay with Matt. Angela felt certain she'd be happier here than she'd been in Denver. The only decision left was whether or not Angela could allow herself to be part of the idyllic picture. Could she say yes? After everything Betty had done for her, did she have that right?

"We're ready!" Kayla shouted.

Sherry ushered in the group from the kitchen, while Claudia's children rounded up their dad and

Matt's father, who'd been checking out the new computer in the other room.

Matt let go of Angela's hand and leaned his elbows on his knees, watching Kayla as she sat next to her presents.

"Do we take turns like before? Or do we all open at once?" she asked.

When Matt stood, Angela knew he couldn't wait any longer. "Before we get too carried away with all the gifts, I have something to say."

Sherry grabbed her husband's arm excitedly, Ray grinned at his wife and Claudia motioned for complete silence. Obviously, except for the children, they all thought they knew what he was about to announce. But this would be a surprise.

Angela clasped her hands tightly in her lap.

"I have a special gift for Kayla. One I'd like her to open now," Matt said.

Kayla sat up straighter. "But you already gave me a gift, Matt." Her hand went to her throat in search of her locket but, finding it missing, she turned worried eyes to Angela. "My locket! It's gone!"

"You haven't lost it," Angela said. "I took it last night. Matt's giving it to you again." She cleared her throat to help steady her voice. "Only this time it has your father's picture in it."

Silence as thick as the snowdrifts piled outside descended on the room as everyone stared at Kayla, who was still gazing in shock at Angela. "That can't be true," she said.

"It's true," Angela said.

Matt crossed the room and pulled the plush blue box from his pocket.

"Are you sure I should open it here?" she asked him.

He knelt down beside her so everyone could see. "It's okay," he murmured. "Go ahead."

Kayla's trepidation showed in the stiff set of her shoulders. With a final glance at the people watching, she slowly, carefully withdrew the locket.

Angela's pulse raced as Kayla opened the tiny clasp. Then the girl's jaw dropped and her gaze flew to Matt, who was watching her with so much hope that everyone in the room could feel the poignant emotions inside him.

"*You're* my dad? I mean, my *real* dad?"

Tears glistened in Matt's eyes. He kept blinking, obviously struggling to hold them back, but he nodded. "I just found out myself the day before yesterday. I'm glad I know," he said and gathered her in his arms.

Angela didn't realize she had tears rolling down her own cheeks until they began to drip off her chin. She wiped them as Kayla squeezed Matt tightly.

"Merry Christmas, Kayla," he said. Then he released her and turned her to face all the others in the room. "And these people—they're your family, too."

Sherry had nearly fainted at "You're my dad?" Now she leaned heavily on her husband and waved a hand in front of her, as if she couldn't get enough air. "Does that mean you're going to marry him?" she asked Angela hopefully.

She still believed what she'd originally been told—that Angela was Kayla's real mother. They could explain the details later, Angela decided. She had enough going on right now. Everyone's attention had shifted to her, even Kayla's.

"Marry him?" Kayla murmured.

"That—that's one option," Angela admitted. "We've been…talking about it."

"And what are the other options?" Kayla asked.

Everyone's eyes cut back and forth between them. Angela hoped no one could tell how badly she was shaking. "You could live here with…with Matt."

Some of the excitement fled Kayla's face. "Without you?"

"I don't know yet, Kayla. I have a house in Denver—"

"We're selling the house, remember?"

"And a job."

"Can't you work here?"

"You wouldn't have to. I can support you," Matt said.

His mother moved closer to him. "He'd make a good husband."

"And you've seen the calendar," his aunt added. "You know what kind of fires he can put out."

Angela didn't have a chance to answer any of them. Kayla's eyebrows were drawing together in hurt and anger. "You said I'd always be a central part of your life, and no one would ever change that. Now you're giving me away?"

"I'm not giving you away," Angela said. "I—I'm letting you live where I think you'll be happiest."

"I can't be happy without you!"

Angela turned to Matt, expecting him to help her defer answering. But he didn't. "I can't be happy without you, either," he said softly, honestly.

"Do you love him?" Sherry asked.

Angela didn't want to admit the truth. She knew what would happen. But Matt was watching her so intently, she couldn't lie. "I do."

"So say *yes*... Marry him...It's Christmas," everyone said, pressing closer.

Angela let her uncertainty show in her expression. "What about Stephanie?" she asked, seeking Matt. "Kayla's *her* daughter. You're the man *she* wanted."

This threw the others, but not Matt. "We'll do what we can for her," he promised. "When she's ready."

Kayla's arms slipped around Angela's waist. "Leaving us won't help her!" she said, hugging her tightly. And it was those words that finally made sense to Angela. Denying herself the joy of being with Matt and Kayla wouldn't help anyone.

The tears started to come again, but Angela brushed them away. "Yes."

"You'll do it?" Kayla cried. "You'll marry him?"

Angela smiled through her tears. "I will."

Matt's arms went around both of them, and he kissed Angela's temple. "I'll make sure you never regret it," he whispered.

The rest of the group hugged and congratulated her one by one, and Angela smiled as she realized that Kayla's new family had just become her own.

Maybe this Christmas wasn't like the ones she used to know. But she knew there'd never be a better one. Except for next year. And the years after that...

Dear Reader,

I've always had a fondness for the story of Scrooge and his journey to become a better person. When Brenda Novak, Anna Adams and I first started brainstorming ideas for this project, I found myself intrigued by the idea of Scrooge (Simon Castle in my story) falling in love with the Ghost of Christmas Present (Emma Roberts). Okay, so Emma isn't a ghost and Simon doesn't wear a full-length nightshirt, but the idea that someone can make a difference in your perspective on life is fascinating. I hope you enjoy my lighthearted take on this classic tale.

I love to hear from readers, either through my Web site, www.melindacurtis.com, or regular mail at P.O. Box 150, Denair, CA 95316. Bah, humbug...er...happy holidays!

Melinda Curtis

THE NIGHT BEFORE CHRISTMAS

Melinda Curtis

As always, to my family, especially my kids, who constantly remind me what's important in life. And for Mom, whose patience and enduring love gave me the strength to reach for the stars.

CHAPTER ONE

SIMON CASTLE NEEDED an exterminator, preferably one with a law degree.

Stepping out of the dark casino into the late afternoon sunlight, he frowned as he scanned the empty circular drive in front of his hotel. Not only was his car missing, but the rat—tall, gray and menacing—was still holed up in the west parking lot, where it had been taunting him since last night.

"It's still there, sir," Carrie, his latest assistant, observed. "Do you want me to call someone?"

"No." Tension rat-a-tat-tatted at Simon's temples.

The fifteen-foot inflatable rat—complete with pointed, retractable claws—was the labor union's latest attempt to bully him. Simon could deflate the vermin or have the truck it sat in towed, but that would only bring bad press. Exactly what the union wanted. If the union wanted to solve the dispute, the reps could come back to the bargaining table. Simon didn't respond to intimidation.

He clenched his fingers, fighting the urge to charge across the parking lot and take matters into his own hands. Instead, Simon issued an order to

Carrie. "Put a garland around its neck. Maybe the guests will think it's a promotion for *The Nutcracker*. Now, where's my car?"

He couldn't wait until the holiday season was over.

Carrie hit the speed dial on her cell phone, turned away and spoke discreetly to Simon's secretary, Marlene, through the headset clipped over her ear. A moment later, clutching her clipboard to her chest, Carrie stumbled as she turned back in her four-inch heels. "Uh, apparently, there was a mix-up, sir. Frank thought we were done for the holiday weekend."

Simon waved off the explanation. "Fine. Have someone else bring the car around." Icy wind whipped at him and he shrugged deeper into his overcoat. He glanced at his watch, ignoring the discreet holiday music and oversize Christmas decorations looming above him. "I have to be in Vegas by morning."

On the twelfth day of Christmas my true love gave to me…

As if some guy was sappy enough to send his woman twelve lords-a-leaping, or a woman would be satisfied with the display. Women wanted money and attention. They were a distraction Simon couldn't afford.

Carrie pressed the speaker to her ear as she paused, obviously listening to Marlene. Then her mouth popped open. Carrie quickly closed it, cleared her throat and said, "Um, apparently Frank took the car."

"Fine. Give him a call and get it back." Simon was already calculating what business he could conduct while he waited for Frank to make the forty-five-minute drive from Simon's home above the Northgate Golf Club to the Castle Hotel. He headed toward the casino where the rat could no longer taunt him.

"Uh, sir?" Carrie trotted up next to him.

"Spit it out, Carrie," Simon snapped.

"Frank took the car to Los Angeles for the holiday weekend."

His temple pounded as he spun to face her. "What? Who gave him permission to do that?" Whoever it was would be fired. And Frank along with him.

"Apparently—"

Simon was starting to hate that word.

"—*you* signed the paperwork, sir. It's dated three months ago." Carrie paused, listening to Marlene read something. "Apparently—"

"Oh, for the love of—" Simon bit back the rest of his curse. Carrie was his fourth assistant in as many months. Turnover was getting damn annoying because the talent pool was sadly lacking in Reno.

"His mother is having surgery. He'll be taking time off until the new year."

"With my car?" Simon snatched Carrie's earpiece. "Marlene, get me on the next plane to Vegas and fill out Frank's termination paperwork." Simon had never been invited to a meeting of the heads of all the best Nevada casinos before, so he wasn't going to miss this one tomorrow morning. He had to prove he wasn't small potatoes to the likes of casino magnates Steven Wynn and George Maloof.

Why did everything have to fall apart today?

"No can do, boss. Everything's booked," Marlene said.

The opportunity to make something of himself was slipping through Simon's fingers as surely as that annoying chorus of "The Twelve Days of Christmas" would haunt him until Judgment Day.

His father's voice boomed ominously in his head. "You can either care for people or make something of yourself, boy. And, in the end, everyone will let you down anyway, so you may as well make something of yourself."

The rat rocked back and forth in the wind as if laughing at Simon. His father would have given it the finger. Simon clenched his fists.

"The rental car agencies are all sold out." Marlene's fingers clacked over the keyboard. "I might be able to get you on a bus with one of those senior tours, sir. I'll see if they have a cancellation."

Simon's back tensed. Had it really come to this? He and sixty shuffling old folks on a bus?

More clacking. "Those are all booked, too. What do you want me to do?"

A shiny, black Lincoln Town Car with a worn wreath strapped to the front grill pulled around the bend of the hotel's driveway.

"I'll get to Vegas on my own." Simon handed the earpiece back to Carrie, intent upon the approaching vehicle.

"HERE YOU GO, LADIES. The Castle Hotel," Emma Roberts announced as she turned off "The Twelve

Days of Christmas" and put the Town Car in park. "It's the best place in town for single men over sixty."

The two seventy-year-old women giggled like schoolgirls when they spotted a pair of gray-haired men who had stepped outside to light cigars. Emma loved driving people around during the holidays, sharing their joy and excitement. Her business had been booming since Thanksgiving and all her fares had been brimming with seasonal cheer. Not a Scrooge in sight.

Grinning, Emma hustled around to open the car door for her two passengers, and then unloaded their luggage, transferring care of the two suitcases and cosmetic cases to the bellboy. She graciously accepted her payment and closed the trunk.

Christmas may now begin.

Not. A suit with his ear glued to a cell phone was sitting in her backseat. He hadn't even closed the door after he'd gotten in.

Emma walked around to his side. "I'm sorry, sir, but I'm done for the day." It was Christmas Eve and she had to get to Virginia City to be with her family.

The suit ignored her.

No one but casino management—the lowest of the low—wore a *suit* in Reno. Emma should know. She had contracts with many of the hotels in Reno. Management tended to be cold, snooty and poor tippers.

A blonde, also in a suit, rushed forward on wobbly stiletto heels. "Excuse me." She pulled Emma away from the car by her arm. "Mr. Castle requires a ride to Las Vegas."

Emma frowned up at the hotel marquee. Castle Hotels was one of Nevada's newer and smaller casino chains. She'd never seen Mr. Castle. And she had no desire to meet him today.

"Don't you mean Mr. Castle needs a ride to the airport? So he can *fly* to Las Vegas?" Emma regained possession of her arm and stepped toward the car, intent on getting rid of the businessman. "I'll drop him on my way home."

"No." Blondie cut off her retreat. "I'll double whatever you normally charge if you *drive* Mr. Castle to Las Vegas." In the fifty-degree weather, even without a warm coat, Blondie's mascara was smudged. She was sweating, not so tough after all.

Emma resisted smiling. "Why don't you drive him? It's Christmas Eve and—"

"I have a little boy," the other woman whispered, clearly desperate. "One thousand dollars. Cash."

Whatever protest Emma had been about to make died on her lips, as she visualized a heartbroken child without his mother on Christmas. Besides, one thousand dollars would keep the Town Car juiced for quite some time. "The price of gas has been eating me alive," Emma mumbled.

"I don't care what it costs. I need to be in Vegas tonight." Mr. Castle leaned forward, not far enough that Emma could see more than his chin, what with the phone glued to his ear and the body of the car blocking the rest of her view. She couldn't see his face, couldn't judge if he was a pretty boy or someone to be reckoned with. But his voice…

His tone demanded she obey without regard for holidays or family plans.

Emma blinked.

Here was a man sadly lacking in the spirit of the Christmas. If she was her father's daughter, she'd turn down the cash and drive Mr. Castle to Las Vegas for nothing more than gas money, showing him the true holiday spirit. Christopher Roberts had been generous to a fault, at the expense of his checking account.

"There are no more flights available and Mr. Castle has to be in Las Vegas for a breakfast meeting."

"I'm sorry. I promised my mother I'd spend Christmas Eve with her in Virginia City."

Blondie's eyes widened. "Virginia City is on the way."

"It's about an hour out of his way not counting any stops I need to make." Emma had some sympathy for the woman, but she'd heard nothing that would persuade her to change her plans.

"Two thousand." Blondie leaned around Emma to sneak a peek at her boss. *Two thousand dollars.*

"Two grand? Just to drive him to Las Vegas?" The lure of the money was strong, stronger than it should have been. She wasn't living up to her father's standards. But if Emma took the job, she'd have more than twenty bucks to donate to the Santa Express charity this year.

And how much will you keep for yourself? It was a mind-numbing question considering Emma lived hand-to-mouth.

Capitalizing on Emma's hesitation, Castle's

assistant leaned into the car and told her boss they'd be stopping along the way.

Something mechanical hummed on the pavement behind Emma. A thin woman with white hair haloed by a phone headset, the cord dangling at her waist, guided her wheelchair to a stop in front of Emma and thrust a wad of bills at her. "Here. I'm Marlene, Mr. Castle's secretary. I think twenty-*five* hundred dollars is fair."

Emma found herself holding the thick wad of folded Benjamins while Blondie sealed Mr. Castle in the car.

"Do whatever he asks," Blondie said. "There's a bonus in it for you if he's happy when he gets there. Mr. Castle can be somewhat exacting in his standards."

"Give me your card, dear, so I can make sure you're compensated for any incidents." The woman in the wheelchair held out her hand for Emma's business card, which doubled as a receipt. "Try not to mention too much about the holiday. It annoys him."

"It's *Christmas Eve*." This was a bad idea. She should just toss those twenty-five hundred-dollar bills back….

She was momentarily mesmerized by all that green in her hand. And there was Mr. Castle, who couldn't be as heartless as he sounded if he employed the grandmotherly woman in the wheelchair. Emma could make Christmas wonderful for a lot of families with that money.

"He's waiting." Blondie's voice sounded a bit strangled.

"He doesn't like to wait," added the older woman, glancing anxiously at the car as she wheeled her chair back.

Emma stuffed the cash in her pocket and got in the car. She would drive Mr. Castle to Las Vegas, stop to check in with her family and donate her profits to the Santa Express.

Now if only she didn't have to tell her mother she wouldn't be home for Christmas.

CHAPTER TWO

"To Las Vegas." On that cheery note, the driver slid into her seat. Her white tuxedo shirt and black pants were acceptable, the red bow tie with green wreaths an unwelcome holiday reminder. "Your assistant did tell you that we're making a stop this evening?"

Damn it, he'd like to get some sleep tonight. Simon didn't have time for delays. He stared at the back of her head as he formulated a scathing reply. Stared at the driver's red-red hair held up in a bun against the creamy skin at her nape. "And if I said she didn't tell me?" he drawled. That came out completely, mischievously, inappropriately wrong.

"We're still stopping in Virginia City," she said firmly. "I hadn't counted on taking another fare today and my family is expecting me."

Simon frowned. Carrie had mentioned that the driver had to make a detour, but Simon had assumed she meant to get gas or to eat or something. Then again, he'd been meaning to check out the possibilities for a Castle property on the outskirts of Virginia City. The small town was an out-of-the-way tourist attraction with only a few small hotels.

"Mr. Castle?" With the sun dropping behind the Sierras, Simon could see the chauffeur's eyes dart to the mirror and back to the driveway. Why hadn't she started the car? "If that's a problem, I can drop you somewhere else." She sounded hopeful.

"It's inconvenient, but it'll do."

"What's with the rat?" she asked, finally starting the engine.

Refusing to look, Simon played dumb. "What rat?"

"Parked in a handicapped space—big, inflatable? Looks like he's on crack?"

"Oh, that." Simon tapped out an urgent e-mail on his BlackBerry reminding Carrie to choke the rat in festive garland.

"You're not presenting a topless version of *The Nutcracker* in your lounge, are you?"

Did the woman ever shut up? "A driver and a co-medienne. It must be Christmas."

"Touchy about your rat infestation, I see." She pulled into heavy traffic. "Is that a symbol for some-thing? Your logo perhaps?"

"It's not my logo." Simon leaned forward, making sure she heard every word clearly. "That's a union calling card. They think I should pay my maids more for working less. And I'm not happy to see that parasite in my parking lot, but I've got a reputation to protect, so I can't just exterminate it." Maybe now that he'd cut to the chase, she'd shut up.

"Are you paying the maids well?"

Through gritted teeth, Simon said. "I'm paying them the same as every other hotel."

"So the union is picking on you for no reason. That sucks."

"Yeah." She didn't need to know about the gripes of the chefs and cashiers.

With a nod, the woman turned up her stereo and began humming along to the music. Simon returned a call from his Reno hotel manager and quickly became irritated when Richard babbled nonstop about his problems on the property. So much for Richard living up to the claim on his résumé of being a problem solver. Why hadn't he said anything to Simon when he was in the office?

On the eleventh day of Christmas, my true love gave to me...

Eleven pipers piping. As if there was anything to be piping up about at this time of year. With a flick of a finger, Simon put Richard on hold. "Turn that down."

"What?" She lowered the sound.

"The music. Turn it down. I need to get work done."

The slant of her eyes in the mirror was disapproving. "Just trying to spread a little cheer. It is Christmas, after all."

"Well, save it for someone else." Someone who had happy memories of Christmas. Someone who looked forward to the holiday.

Simon drew a deep breath and listened as his manager droned on about employees who wanted time off and maids who wouldn't risk the wrath of the rat to come to work. "Richard, it's this simple. The employees either come in on Christmas or they don't come in ever again."

Was it his imagination, or did the driver tilt her head and frown at him in the mirror?

"But you aren't even offering a bonus," Richard continued nervously. "I have five hundred rooms booked and only two maids tomorrow. No one will come in just for time and a half. Not on Christmas."

"Bring in Carrie and the rest of the office staff. Between you and the two maids, you ought to be able to handle it." Simon hung up in disgust. When he went to Carson City next week, he was getting rid of Richard. Simon had come a long way without anyone guiding his every step. He wasn't the hand-holding type. His dad had seen to that.

His cell phone rang again—a Las Vegas area code.

"Mr. Castle, this is Erik Wiseman, assistant to Mr. Maloof. I'm calling to confirm your attendance tomorrow morning." Maloof's assistant spoke with just the right amount of disdain required when speaking to a nobody.

As if he could be seen through the telephone connection, Simon sat up straighter. "I—I—I'll be there." Damn. He couldn't believe he'd stuttered. He must have come across like an idiot.

"Doors close at six-fifteen sharp. Mr. Maloof has private plans later in the morning, as do several other attendees, but this is the only day of the year everyone's in town. Are you sure you won't have a family conflict?"

As if Simon would consider turning the offer down if he did. This was some kind of test that Simon was determined to pass. He shook his head, then realized Maloof's assistant couldn't see him. "No."

"Do you have any questions, Mr. Castle?"

"No. I'm en route." Nothing could stop Simon from getting there on time. "See you tomorrow."

Maloof's assistant broke the connection without so much as a *Merry Christmas*. He was Simon's kind of guy. Why couldn't more people be like that?

His driver pulled onto the freeway, the chorus of the dreaded Christmas song barely audible above the road noise.

"Could you turn that off?"

Her fingers didn't move from the steering wheel. "Are you going to be cranky all the way to Vegas?" She smiled into the rearview mirror.

Smiled. As if he were a child and she was trying to tease him into a better mood, as if they had a relationship other than client and service provider. Simon was momentarily speechless. No one who worked for him talked back. Certainly no one smiled at him like that.

"I thought *I* was paying *you*," Simon said finally, putting enough ice in his tone to frost her windshield.

"I can still drop you off at the airport, where you can stand in line for a flight." There was that optimistic note in her voice again, as if she wanted to get rid of him.

"I'd want my money back," he retorted, calling her bluff. "All of it." Simon wouldn't pay her to be stranded at the airport.

"Okay." She twisted in her seat and tossed the cash back to him.

Bills fluttered to the baseboards.

"What do you think you're doing?" He gathered up the notes. His father would have had a heart attack if he saw someone toss money around like that, as if it didn't matter.

"I'm planning on having a *merry* Christmas."

They were back to the ho-ho-ho crap. "We had a deal."

She merged into the exit lane for the airport. "Mr. Castle, I'm not your employee. I don't need your money."

"Everybody needs money."

She shook her head. "I'd rather spend Christmas with people who care about me than make a buck. Don't you have someone you'd like to spend the holiday with? Mother? Wife? Kids?"

The air in the car was suddenly stifling. Clutching the bills, Simon powered down his window a few inches, sucking in the cold mountain air. "I don't have any... It's none of your damn business."

"I'm sorry," she said in a voice that sounded amazingly sincere. "Do you prefer a particular terminal?" They'd exited the freeway.

"I need to get to Las Vegas!" He sounded about as adult as a five-year-old. Simon powered the window back up and loosened his tie. His driver really was going to drop him at the airport. Who did she think she was?

"I'd like to help you, but at the rate we're going, I'd probably leave you on the side of the road come Tonopah."

They sailed through every intersection as if the

driver had some special ability to turn lights green. Simon was running out of time. There'd be nothing at the airport but lines and run-down local cabs. He couldn't call Maloof's assistant and back out now.

"Are you one of those cheer-mongers?" Simon accused. His driver didn't answer. "You know, the type who live for the holidays—bake the cookies, trim the tree, send out Christmas cards?"

"Did I hear you say *bah, humbug?*" she countered, but she was grinning.

Hell, she was probably ecstatic that she was about to dump him.

The airport, jammed with cars, loomed in front of them. Think. Think. Everybody had a price. He'd wager…double or nothing. "Five thousand dollars!"

"Excuse me?" She spared him a surprised glance in the rearview mirror.

"Five thousand dollars," he repeated at a more civilized volume. "Cash." He'd be offering to buy her car next so he could drive himself.

"That must be some meeting."

"The most important of my career." With the support of the major Las Vegas properties, Simon could take Castle Hotels almost anywhere.

"Wow." His driver had room to get out of the turn lane, but she wasn't budging.

"So, what do you say?"

The light changed green. Cars ahead began to inch forward.

"Are you really good for the money?" She eyed him suspiciously, turning this time.

"Do I look like I'm not?" He had to admire her negotiation skills. He was sweating and he had no idea if she'd accept his proposal or not. It was all he could do to not offer a higher amount.

"Oh, boy." She shook her head and gave a little laugh. "All right, Mr. Castle, I'll drive you to Las Vegas. But you'll have to put up with my holiday cheer."

Simon's lip twitched. "Just drive."

CHAPTER THREE

"DO YOU GET RECEPTION on that gadget everywhere?"

Mr. Castle peered down at his cell phone, which seemed to have more options than a fully loaded Town Car. Her threat to drop him off at the airport had captured his attention for all of five minutes. The man's constant clacking on his handheld device grated on her nerves, as did his desire for silence. She couldn't imagine spending Christmas with him. Didn't he do anything except work?

Emma went back to humming "Let It Snow" loud enough for her passenger to hear.

If he didn't treat her like a nobody, he might have been a welcome passenger. With his dark good looks—not a hair out of place—Mr. Castle could give Christian Bale a run for sexiest man alive. She glanced at him in the rearview mirror. He was all angles and shadows, as interesting to look at as a statue, but about as cold and heavy.

He finished what he was doing and looked up. "Too many people take time off at the holidays. I'm trying to catch them before they go. That's why I want *quiet.*"

It was a real joy-sapping quiet, too. Mr. Castle was

in desperate need of some holiday spirit. She had more than enough to share. "When I'm driving, I like noise. Sometimes I sing, too."

"With passengers in the car?"

"As long as you love me so—let it snow, let it snow, let it snow!" Someday, someone would love her that much. She didn't want gifts, just passion and mutual respect. Someday...

"What did I do to deserve this?" her passenger muttered.

"You asked for a ride on Christmas Eve." She could see him shaking his head in the mirror, could imagine his frown. What would he look like when he smiled? Warm and welcoming?

Startled, Emma concentrated on driving. Lusting after clients was not a good thing.

"You're not going to squander the money I'm paying you on Christmas presents someone won't even remember come Easter, are you?"

"The holiday is about more than presents. You'd have to be blind not to see that." Mr. Castle knew nothing of Christmas.

"Christmas has lost any meaning it may have once had." Without waiting for Emma to respond, he leaned forward, his breath warm on her neck. "Do you want to know why I find Christmas superfluous? Because most people wonder if they've bought enough for their kids so they don't feel guilty Christmas morning. You think I'm blind?" He slapped a hand on the seat back, making her jump. "Well, those families with two-point-five kids are haunted by the ghost of Christmas returns, the ghost of leftover spirit lingering in credit-card debt and the haunting specter of bankruptcy."

"Not everyone's like that." But her protest lacked weight as they drove past a packed shopping mall. Her father would be so disappointed in her. Why had she ever agreed to take Mr. Castle anywhere?

"You haven't been in a casino lately, have you?" He sank back into his seat, taking his warmth with him.

"So now Christmas is a crime?" Emma shook her head ruefully. She couldn't hope to convince this man that beneath all the trimmings, Christmas was a time for kindness and charity.

They drove in silence for several miles while Emma wrestled with her mood, which right about now was far from charitable. She itched to shake Mr. Castle until his teeth rattled.

Her passenger sighed and shifted in the backseat, settled, then shifted again. She heard coins jingling. "What's Virginia City like?"

That sounded friendly. Friendly was a step up from the harbinger of bah-humbug he'd been fifteen minutes earlier. A glance revealed he was staring out the window.

"It's a small town where people take care of each other." Emma loved it there.

"I hear it has a lot of charm. I bet they have a decent number of tourists."

"We get our share." Emma sounded more defensive than she would have liked, but there was something in his voice that struck her as too casual. "The shops are always filled with people."

"I'm more interested in the businesses. Hotels? Restaurants?"

And then she caught on. He was looking for more ways to pad his bank account. The only surprise was that he hadn't asked about casinos. "There are a few bed-and-breakfasts, a couple of small motels, and a handful of restaurants."

"Who's the biggest employer?" Again the casual tone, as if they were talking about the weather, not his potential investment prospects.

"I couldn't say." She wasn't going to help him commercialize her hometown. "Why do you ask?"

"You never know what opportunities a town may afford unless you ask," he replied, unfazed. "How much longer until Virginia City?"

"Hungry?" She gritted her teeth. He was probably going to stake out Virginia City like a con man, looking to milk the quaint town for all it was worth.

"As a matter of fact, yes. Are we there yet?"

"Almost, but you'll have to put yourself in my hands for dinner. Nothing will be open on Christmas Eve." The food wouldn't be anything like what Mr. Castle was used to. She hoped he was polite enough not to complain.

"Put myself in your hands," he repeated so softly she barely made out the words.

But only an idiot would miss the sexy inflection in his tone, respond to the innuendo. Warmth flared deep and low inside her.

Clearly, Mr. Castle and his money had been sent to test her. Emma wished she could send him on a few Santa Express deliveries. Then he'd understand. But they didn't have time for that this year. Not if she wanted to get him to Las Vegas in time for his 6:00 a.m. meeting.

"IS SOMEONE HAVING A PARTY?" Simon asked as his driver parked her car at the end of the block. The neighborhood was old. Cars jammed every space between driveways for blocks in each direction.

"It's the Santa Express." She removed her bow tie and began tugging at her bun. "Every year a bunch of us get together with donations of food, clothing and toys. We deliver them to the area's needy on Christmas Eve."

He'd been right. She was a do-gooder. Simon hit a button to illuminate his BlackBerry screen. There were no replies from any of his e-mails and he hadn't received a call in thirty minutes. The holiday slacking had begun. "How long will you be?"

His driver shook out her red hair, waves tumbling across the white shirt. The glow from a streetlight illuminated her face in the rearview mirror as she looked directly at him. Simon couldn't help but stare back. Her eyes were as green as a Christmas tree. Why hadn't he noticed that before?

"Mr. Castle, I don't think you understand. I told you that all the restaurants are closed. If you want dinner, come with me."

He *wanted* to scribble ideas for transforming

Virginia City into a bigger tourist destination. The main drag had that small-town, snow-blanketed, Victorian charm. He smelled raw opportunity. "I don't want to impose."

"Suit yourself. But the next food is about a hundred miles from here…if the drive-through in Babbitt is open."

Fast food? He paused. "This town needs a twenty-four-hour buffet." And a five-star restaurant.

"The town is fine the way it is." She shuffled papers in the front seat. "You might want to leave your suit jacket in the car. The tie, too."

Simon groaned. He was going to eat with *those kind* of people—those who scraped by but never got ahead, who looked at Simon with envy and always wanted something from him. A favor, a job, money.

The driver came around and opened his door. Cold air swept into the car. "We're pretty casual around here. Without that tie you'll loosen up, maybe enjoy a glass of eggnog."

Their eyes met. Simon identified interest in her gaze, which surprised him along with something else…a heartrending defenselessness. She'd want standing dates on Friday nights, Sunday brunch with her family, midweek lunches. She wasn't his type at all.

"It might make this time of year easier for you if you loosened up," she said.

"I dress for dinner."

She looked Simon up and down, then stepped back to let him out. "*Suit* yourself."

Beneath the clear, starry sky, it was bitingly cold.

Even though she toughed the weather in her white cotton shirt, Simon shrugged into his overcoat and grabbed his briefcase.

"You're going to work during Christmas Eve dinner?" She shut the door behind him and locked the car with a beep of the remote. She was tall and slender, moving with a grace he wouldn't have expected in someone of her profession.

Simon stiffened. What was wrong with him? "I don't go anywhere without my briefcase. If someone calls and I don't have it, I'm screwed." Did he have to choose that particular word? It had been months since he'd been with a woman. Tonight it seemed like years.

His driver demurely looked away.

They walked down the sidewalk toward a house bright with strands of colored lights. A spotlighted manger scene took center stage on the snow-covered lawn, and a huge star outlined in white lights graced the roof. The rumble of voices, laughter and music filled the air. This wasn't a small family gathering. This was a large party.

The cement in the front walk was cracked and uneven—and oddly familiar. Simon slowed his steps. He'd left this all behind. He was Simon Castle, damn it. He wasn't the social misfit anymore and he didn't need anyone wiggling beneath his defenses.

His driver didn't knock when she got to the door. She just opened it and stepped inside, leaving Simon no choice but to follow.

Kids were everywhere. Small ones played with

push cars on the floor. Larger ones darted in and out of the crowd. Teenagers circled around a computer in one corner. The adults looked like the kind of people who lost money they couldn't afford to in his casino, the men dressed in cotton T-shirts and flannel, the women in bright red sweaters decorated with reindeer and snowflakes. They were all packing boxes and wrapping packages. The living room and the dining room beyond it were a flurry of activity.

Everyone seemed to pause when they came in as if they recognized him.

And then there was a wave of excitement... directed at his driver.

"Emma!"

"Em!"

"Emma's here!"

Simon hadn't even known her name.

No one paid any attention to him in their rush to embrace Emma and pull her farther inside the house—which was as hot as a furnace if you were wearing a suit, tie and overcoat. Simon closed the front door and stood awkwardly in the small foyer. No one came to take his coat. No one placed a drink in his hand, although he could see people were drinking. Pink wine and cans of domestic beer. This wasn't his kind of thing at all. A girl ran past him singing.

Six geese a laying...

Looking through the boisterous crowd, trying to figure out what to do next, his eyes fell on the faded red felt stockings trimmed in white hanging from the fireplace, and he froze.

Mom was so sick... It was up to Simon to make sure Santa didn't forget them, so he climbed into the attic to get the Christmas box and arranged her favorite Twelve Days of Christmas figurines on the coffee table. Then he hung his stocking from the wire hook over the mantel.

"What in the hell are you doing?" his father bellowed when he returned from work. "Don't you realize your mother is dying? I'm breaking my back here trying to keep a roof over our heads, and you want a toy?" His dad ripped the stocking from the mantel and tossed it into the cold fireplace. Later that night, Simon carefully pulled it out of the ashes and hung it back up.

A wave of laughter brought Simon back to the present. He was fingering a stocking, standing next to the fire and was warmer than ever now.

CHAPTER FOUR

"Momma, you have to come into the living room." Emma snatched a sugar cookie still hot from the oven and then tugged her mother's arm. "I've never met anyone without an ounce of appreciation for the meaning of Christmas."

The room was warm and smelled of freshly baked cookies ready to be delivered to Santa Express families. Cookie sheets loaded with festive doughy cutouts lined the counter, ready to go into the oven. Round tins were stacked high in the breakfast nook waiting to be filled. Her mother insisted the cookies be baked the day of delivery, even though it overheated the kitchen, using that as an excuse to get out of cooking dinner for fifty people. The dishes laid out in the dining room were potluck.

"Did you bring home another stray? Just like your father, I swear," Donna Roberts said. "Every holiday it's the same thing. One year it was a dog that bit you, another time it was a turtle that wouldn't come out of its shell. What are you going to bring home next?"

"She brought home a *man*." Emma's older brother, Owen, grinned as he took out another tray of cookies. For most of the year, Owen and his buddy, Doc, fought wildland forest fires. But get Owen in a kitchen and he transformed into a woman's dream. To the disappointment of the single women in Virginia City, though, Owen had no interest in settling down.

"A man…" Emma's mother removed her apron and set it on the counter. "Let's meet this man of yours."

"He's not mine," Emma protested, but her mother was off and running. Emma followed her into the living room, where she caught sight of Mr. Castle near the fireplace. He looked about as uncomfortable as a person could be.

"Oh, my goodness. Let's get you out of this coat. Where did you come from? I hope not a funeral." Emma's mother babbled as she bore down on him, grabbing the collar of his overcoat and pulling it down to his elbows.

Emma tried to stop her mother. "Slow down, Momma. He might want to keep that on."

"Nonsense, Emma. Look at him. He's sweating." Emma's mother yanked Mr. Castle's overcoat off the rest of the way. "You went to early church service, didn't you? You must have gone directly from work, and never had a chance to change. But you don't have to worry about that here. It's come as you are at the Robertses' house." Yep, Emma's mom was on a roll. Mr. Castle didn't stand a chance. "We'll just get you settled with a plate, and then you can help pack up boxes for the Express." In less than a minute, Emma's mother had taken Mr. Castle's overcoat and briefcase.

A blank expression on his face, Mr. Castle watched her retreat down the hallway with his things. "What just happened?"

"You'll get used to it." Although it was ten times better to witness it than to be on the receiving end of Momma's whirlwind touch.

Mr. Castle frowned. "I won't be here that long."

Emma was about to explain that time didn't seem to matter where her mother was concerned when Momma returned.

"I do so apologize that I didn't introduce myself. I'm Donna Roberts, Emma's mother." Her faded blue eyes sparkled. "I'm so pleased to meet you…?"

"Castle. Simon Castle."

"Simon," Emma's mother said as Emma rolled the name around her head. It fit the young entrepreneur—classy, cool, distant. "Have you eaten? I'm sure Emma told you that we don't sit down to dinner on Christmas Eve—there's just too much to do. But we do have a large buffet to choose from."

And that's all it took to thaw Simon Castle's cool facade—food.

SIMON LET HIMSELF BE LED to the dining room, where the table was covered with cans of all shapes and sizes—hams, green beans, yams, cranberry sauce. Pairs of adults rotated around the table, one person with a cardboard box, the other loading food into it.

The sideboard was against one wall, laden with platters of nearly demolished piles of food. In the blink of an eye, Simon and Emma had plates in their hands and Donna Roberts fluttered off to wreak havoc with someone else.

"Is she always like that?"

Emma's cheeks were bright pink and her lips twitched suspiciously as she leaned close to him, reaching for the dish of mashed potatoes. "Sometimes she's worse."

"She won't take me by surprise next time," Simon vowed, looking away, toward the sliced ham. He wished he could guard against the surprising effect Emma had on him. He should ignore the unwelcome, growing sense that she needed protection—from *him*—and set the tone for what he wanted once his business in Las Vegas was done—her.

A couple of men in flannel shirts walked by, carrying loaded boxes.

"Lingering under the mistletoe, Em? You know that's an open invitation." The guy with a receding hairline glanced at a sprig of mistletoe taped to a section of ceiling fan before leaning over to kiss Emma's cheek.

Possessiveness gripped Simon and he had to remember to breathe.

The man gave Simon a dismissive once-over and then said to Emma, "Did you hit the guy up for a donation to the Santa Express?"

Simon stiffened. He'd expected this kind of reception. "I only support *legitimate* charities."

That elicited a frigid smile from the soon-to-be baldy. "Hey, they're all tax deductible and that's what's important to a guy like you this time of year, isn't it?"

"How's the ride, Em?" the other man asked, stepping between Simon and the smart ass, clearly trying to defuse the growing tension. "Should we load up your car for a run?"

"No. I've got work." Emma bobbed her head in Simon's direction.

For some reason, Simon was riled that she'd dismissed him as work. The question was: why? He slapped a dill pickle onto his plate and jostled past the three toward the mashed potatoes.

Five golden ri-i-ings—ba-da-baba...

Some kids joined in the song blasting out of the stereo, mutilating it during the fast countdown. Had Simon ever been that carefree? Would he ever be again? With effort, Simon concentrated on filling his plate. He was losing focus. Las Vegas was important. Eating to keep up his strength was necessary. Superfluous romantic fantasies would only slow him down.

Ignoring Emma, the music and the singers, Simon found a place to sit next to a Christmas tree choked with tinsel and decorations that didn't match, and started eating. The food may have been cold, but it was good, even the yams slathered with marshmallows. He hadn't had yams like that in ages.

"It's good to see you have an appetite," Emma observed, sitting next to him on the sofa. Her plate was nearly as empty as his. "I was beginning to wonder if you worked 24/7, drank power meals and never slept."

"Sleep is highly overrated," he finally managed to say. Simon liked women, had always been good at flirting. But he'd never had a problem putting his wants on hold until his business was done. The attraction he felt for Emma was different. Her smile touched him, demanding he notice her, think about her, push his priorities aside.

"Work is overrated, too," she said.

"Work is everything to me." It was all he had. "I'd expect that from someone without ambition, but you seem bright enough to have gone to college and made something more of yourself. Why would you settle?"

"Is that your idea of a compliment?" Her eyes flashed. "I own my own business and I make enough to help others, too. We didn't have money for college. But I wouldn't expect you to understand what it's like to lose a parent, or to know how hard it is to be brave for the rest of the family and carry on a father's traditions."

Simon sat back. His mind filled with questions. How? When? Did she still find it hard to sleep at night? His mother had been like Mrs. Roberts before she'd gotten sick. Back then the house had always smelled of good things…like fresh baking and pot roast. After she'd died, it had just smelled dusty.

"My family is busy." Emma stood. "The sooner I get you out of here, the sooner I'll be able to get back."

"And this Express charity? That's done tonight?" He should be jumping up to leave. Instead, he was toying with the idea of telling her he'd lost someone, too.

"All deliveries are tonight. Over one hundred needy families will have a merrier Christmas thanks to the work of the folks here." She reached for his plate. "It would be great if I could stay and help."

His brain reawakened. "I'm paying you to get me to Vegas, not waste time on frivolous charities."

She froze, her hand above his plate. "Frivolous—"

"People come to expect handouts," Simon cut her off, hearing his father's voice as he spoke. "I'd never take someone's charity. I've always made my own way."

Her eyes blazed as she captured the rim of his plate. "Sometimes you don't have a choice. Everyone here knows that and wants to help." Emma tried to yank the dish from him.

"People who build their own destiny don't believe in charity or a free lunch." He didn't let go of the plate. For some unknown reason, it was important that she agree with him. "The only person you should rely on is you. A fare like mine should go into your savings so you can buy a second car and hire another driver, grow your business. But I expect you'll be giving it away."

"Since there's no free lunch, we'll accept your fifty-dollar donation for dinner," she said, pointedly ignoring his business advice.

"Mister, can you help me wrap this?" A sturdy young boy interrupted them, his shirt tail hanging over his rumpled jeans as he juggled a roll of wrapping paper, tape and a Yahtzee game. "I'd ask Aunt Emma, but she's a girl and I don't ask girls for anything."

Simon was so startled, he let the plate go, allowing Emma to escape to the kitchen.

With dramatic eye-rolling, the kid dumped his items on the couch next to Simon. "My name's Johnny. The quicker we wrap, the sooner we can have pie. Do you know how to wrap? If not, I need to go find someone else." He glanced around the room and Simon followed his lead, taking in all the blue-collar dads and uncles who fit in so well. "My dad's busy and all the good uncles are taken." Johnny turned back to Simon, sizing him up. Based on his frown, he wasn't impressed with what he saw.

"So, you're in this for the pie?" What would Emma say about good deeds and intention if she heard that?

"Aren't you?"

Two giggling girls ran by with tinsel in their hair, twirling empty wrapping paper rolls like batons. Johnny frowned at them, too.

It had been years since Simon wrapped anything. After his mom had died, he and his dad had tried their best to avoid this holiday.

Nevertheless, feeling the boy's eyes on him, Simon began rolling out the paper.

"Grandma's pies are the best." Johnny smacked his lips. "My new best friend, Wallace, he's really good with music, but his mom has to spend money on the doctor bills instead of presents this year. I put his name on the Express list because I don't want Wallace to be sad."

Okay, so maybe Emma was right. Even the kid wanted to help for reasons other than a slice of pie. As Simon wrapped the Yahtzee box, he couldn't remember ever being as caring as this little boy. He'd been too lost in his own pain.

"It's not often you find someone so excited about Christmas," Emma's mom said as she bustled into the kitchen with a load of dirty dinner plates.

"Particularly a CEO," Owen added, following with more dishes.

"You can't be talking about Simon Castle. In his opinion, the Santa Express is *frivolous.*" Emma ripped off a piece of wax paper with a bit too much gusto and worked it into place in a cookie tin. He didn't care that Emma was going to break Momma's heart when she told her they had to leave.

Owen scraped food off the dirty dishes. "You could have fooled me the way he and Johnny are race-wrapping Doc and Teddy."

"The sooner he's done…" Emma couldn't tell her mother she was leaving yet. And then, to her horror, Emma's voice cracked as she blurted, "I really blew it this time."

"What's wrong?" her mom asked, putting her arm around Emma. "You're with family. It's the holiday—"

"And you own a nice car," Owen said. "Ow! What'd I do?" he said when their mother poked him in the ribs.

"Money can't guarantee happiness," Momma admonished Owen, then turned to Emma. "Do you need money, Em?"

The thick bulge of cash in her pants pocket felt as noticeable as a third appendage. "I don't need money."

"Did the CEO get you pregnant?" With a scowl, Owen took a step toward the kitchen doorway.

"No!" Emma grabbed a handful of Owen's flannel shirt and pulled him back. "It all started so innocently," Emma tried to explain. "I was dropping off a fare, fully intending to come straight home when along comes Mr. Castle and he wouldn't get out of my car." She paused to catch her breath, knowing what she needed to say, yet unable to confess she'd have to leave soon. "I've never met anyone so driven. He thinks he's on the brink of getting the perfect life." He was the perfect challenge, and she was surprised to realize that she was attracted to the compelling mix of regret and longing in his eyes.

With an expression that said his sister was nuts, Owen opened the door a crack, presumably to get a better look at Simon.

"Now, Emma," her mother began with that stern expression of hers. "I knew it would come to this someday. You can't *make* somebody believe in the same things you do. You'll end up getting hurt."

Emma turned back to the cookie tin to hide the blush heating her cheeks. "Simon Castle is as cold and uncaring as the rat in his parking lot."

"I don't know about any hotel rats, but I think you're losing it." Owen had always been good at spying when they were kids. "Come here and take a look. He's laughing."

Sure enough, when Emma peeked out, she would have sworn Simon and Johnny were having the time of their lives.

"That doesn't count," Simon challenged Doc, gesturing wildly at a large package. "It's too ugly. I'd be embarrassed to give it to someone."

Emma couldn't believe what she saw. Simon's hair was rumpled and he had a piece of tape on his tie. He sat surrounded by sloppily wrapped gifts.

"It's a work of modern art," Doc protested, his glasses slipping to the end of his nose as he held up the oblong, knobby package wrapped in red-and-green Grinch paper.

Simon scoffed. "But your paper is so cockeyed, you can see what the present is through the seams."

There were calls from the crowd to rewrap. Doc reluctantly tore off the paper from the piano keyboard and started again. Meanwhile, Simon charged toward the kitchen, scattering the three Robertses away from the door.

"We need more tape," Simon said as he barged in and held out his hands imploringly to Emma's mother. "Tape?"

Emma couldn't help but laugh. Owen was right. Simon did have the Christmas spirit. Surely, he'd let Emma stay and help with Santa Express deliveries, and admit there was joy in the season. She wanted to hug someone and shout, "Merry Christmas!"

Introducing himself, Owen shook hands with Simon.

Emma's mother produced a handful of tape rolls from the junk drawer. "I bet we're running out all over the house," she said, hurrying over with the dispensers.

Johnny poked his head into the kitchen. "Mister, come on. They're almost done rewrapping that keyboard."

"Three more presents and we'll be crowned the winner!" Simon pointed at Emma with a tape roll. "Then we're off to Vegas."

"Bit of a competitive streak?" Owen looked from the swinging kitchen door to Emma, and then uncomfortably away as he realized what he'd said.

Simon Castle was competitive, not excited about Christmas.

Emma sighed. "A small competitive streak." Only about a mile wide. That, and an apparent obsession with money, would guarantee Simon a lonely holiday.

"What did he mean 'off to Vegas?'" Momma crossed her arms over her chest.

"You're eloping to Vegas? I thought you didn't like the guy." Owen stood next to Momma and crossed his arms as well.

"No." Emma's cheeks heated. "I've been trying to tell you that I can't stay. I'm driving Mr. Castle to Vegas tonight."

"You took a job on Christmas." Momma sank into a chair. "Why?"

"Is he getting a kidney transplant in the morning? It must be important for you to blow off the Express." Owen brought Momma a glass of water.

"I…uh…" Emma thrust her hands into her back pockets, away from Mr. Castle's money. "He has an important business meeting tomorrow."

"On Christmas?" Owen didn't hide his disdain.

"Are you sure he doesn't have a hot date with a showgirl?"

"Hey, this is one of those make-it or break-it business meetings."

"Stop it, you two," Momma commanded. "There will be other Christmases together, but for now we've got to get through this one."

CHAPTER FIVE

"WE MAKE A GOOD TEAM, KID. When you graduate from college come see me." Simon patted Johnny on the head. He couldn't remember the last time he'd had so much fun, and all he'd done was won a gift-wrapping race. He couldn't wait to get on the road to Vegas. Luck was with him tonight. Hopefully, it would carry through until morning.

"I'm not a dog, Mister." Johnny brushed Simon's hand away. "You high five when you do a good job." He held up his hand until Simon gave him five. "Why do I need to come see you?"

"For a job."

"Jeez, I'm only eight. I'm too young to go to work." Shaking his head, Johnny disappeared into the sea of kids, leaving Simon standing awkward and alone.

"Congratulations. You're the best wrapper I've been up against in years." The young man they called Doc thrust his hand at Simon. "I'm Owen's friend, Jordan Donato. Most people call me Doc."

Simon introduced himself.

"The Robertses know how to make giving a party." Doc knelt and gathered wrapping odds and ends off the floor. "Is this your first time?"

"Hard to tell, I know." Simon reached to help him. "And you come every year?"

"Wouldn't miss it. The food's great and the beer's free, although we only get one until we finish deliveries. And the women love us."

Simon handed Doc the crumpled remains of their efforts. He noticed Johnny in between stacks of cans at the dining room table, eating a piece of pie loaded with whipped cream.

"You know—" Doc lowered his voice "—you've been looking at everyone here as if we're members of a cult or something. We're just a big group of friends lucky enough to be able to give something to people less fortunate."

Emma's brother, Owen, appeared in front of them with a clipboard. "Doc, you brought your truck, right?" When Doc nodded, he turned to Simon with a determined set to his brow. "We need one more vehicle and another pair of hands."

"Don't even think about it." Simon had more important things to do than act as a delivery boy. "I've got to be in Vegas in…" He glanced at his watch. "Eleven hours. And Emma's agreed to drive me." No way was she stranding him in Virginia City for this.

Owen exchanged a glance with Doc, then indicated they should sit on the couch next to the Christmas tree. "We treat everyone who enters our door on Christmas Eve like family, so I'm going to be blunt."

"Good, because neither one of us has time for anything less."

"You won't get anywhere with Emma if you

consider money more important than people," Owen pointed out.

Simon bristled. "The only place I want to get with Emma is Vegas so I can attend a very important business meeting." Somehow he'd overlooked Owen's attack on his character in his haste to deny the attraction between him and Emma.

Doc laughed. "You're going to a meeting? On Christmas Day? What kind of people have a business meeting on Christmas?"

"The kind you and I wouldn't consider doing business with," Owen answered Doc slowly. "I know Emma agreed to drive you to Vegas, but she looks at you as if she was digging through her stocking on Christmas morning."

Simon could picture Emma on the floor with a stocking in her lap, her eyes sparkling as she discovered one small treasure after another. He tried to recall seeing that joy on Emma's face when she looked at him, but couldn't…. But he felt something unfamiliar, distinctly close to male pride, at the thought.

"Emma loves the Santa Express and everyone here loves Emma," Owen added, just in case Simon was a numskull. "We don't want to see her fall for the wrong guy and get hurt."

Simon saw Emma put her arms around Johnny and give him a tender squeeze. Simon couldn't believe it—he actually felt jealous of the kid.

"Emma drove you here, right? You might want to check with her before you turn us down if you want

whatever you've got going to last beyond tonight—
business or otherwise."

"Nothing is going on between us." Simon
scowled, even as he couldn't take his eyes off Emma
clearing dessert dishes from the dining-room table.

His denial only made Doc laugh again. "Dude, all
I'm saying is it's Christmas. Count your blessings
and don't take someone like Emma for granted. You
never know when your luck will change."

Doc and Owen left Simon, who continued to
deny his attraction to Emma even after they were
out of sight.

Someone snorted on the floor next to Simon and
he glanced down. A drooling toddler with a pile of
ornaments at his feet grinned up at him. Then the
child turned to the Christmas tree and took another
ornament off, placed it with a clink on his pile of
sparkly goods and snorted again.

"I don't think these are supposed to be on the floor."
Simon bent and picked up a pink plastic rocking horse
and a red glass ball, returning them to the nearest bare
spots on the tree he could find. Next to one of them,
a Popsicle-stick picture-frame ornament caught his
eye. It was a picture of a smiling girl with braces who
looked just like Emma might have at about twelve.

Simon leaned in for a closer look. His school
pictures had been stiff and bland. In hers, she looked
open, trusting, ready for anything life sent her way.
Simon couldn't keep from smiling.

The tyrant on the floor let out a shriek louder
than a siren that wiped the smile from Simon's face.

He looked around, half expecting a mother in a knit sweater to descend upon him as if he were the Grinch himself.

A redheaded girl was immediately at Simon's side. "Garrett, no, no, no. The orn'ments go on the tree, remember?" She began putting things back.

Garrett made a keening sound and then he shrieked again, his entire body rigid.

"I didn't touch him," Simon said to no one in particular, wishing someone would make the kid stop.

"Don't you want the tree to be pretty, Garrett?" the girl crooned, bending to pick up more ornaments.

Drooly-boy reached nearly glass-shattering pitch. Still, there was no sign of his mother.

"I don't think he likes that," Simon leaned over to shout in the girl's ear.

She ignored him and kept putting ornaments back. "Orn'ments go on Christmas trees." As efficient as Simon could hope for in an employee, she got them all back and then skipped off.

The screaming stopped with a shuddering gasp. Garrett exchanged a long sad look with Simon. Huge crocodile tears tumbled down the toddler's red cheeks. Without thinking, Simon handed the boy the plastic rocking horse.

Garrett stared at it for a moment, clutching it in his fist. He stood on his wobbly legs and then took another ornament off the tree. With a wheezy laugh, the kid placed both at his feet.

The toddler reached for Emma's Popsicle picture, but Simon was quicker, moving her ornament to a safer location higher up. Garrett gave a halfhearted wail, but settled on a nearby ribbon-and-lace angel instead. It wasn't going to take long for him to accumulate another pile. Suspecting the house was in for another screech-fest as soon as the bossy little girl discovered what Garrett was up to, Simon went in search of Emma.

It was time to get back to business.

"MISS ROBERTS?" The woman's voice wasn't familiar.

Emma pressed her cell phone closer to her ear. "Yes."

"This is Marlene, Mr. Castle's secretary." The woman in the wheelchair. "I'm just checking on your progress. Is everything okay?"

"Fine." If you considered ankle-high spirits fine.

"And you'll arrive in time for the meeting?" Worry tinged Marlene's voice.

"Marlene, please enjoy your Christmas. I'll get Mr. Castle where he needs to be." Emma disconnected and put the small phone in her belt clip before returning to the dirty dishes.

"It's getting to be *that time*," Momma announced, plopping a Santa hat onto Emma's head. "We need to load up the sleighs."

Emma dried her hands. She knew Momma wouldn't give up on her so easily. "I've got to take Mr. Castle to Las Vegas tonight."

"He's such a nice man." Emma's mother ignored the ringing telephone. "And it's Christmas Eve. Surely you can ask Mr. Castle to postpone?"

"No. I took the job knowing what I had to do." With a sinking heart, Emma pulled off her hat and reached for the folded bills in her pocket. Even the thought of giving the money to those less fortunate wasn't salve to the guilt she felt for disappointing her family.

Excited male voices began shouting, "Let's go! Hurry!"

Doc burst into the kitchen. "Sorry, ladies. There's a fire at a house south of town. I'm taking the volunteer firemen, including Owen." He gave Emma's mom a handful of car keys and a clipboard. "These are the trucks we've loaded so far and the list of deliveries."

"You can't all leave," Emma protested. There had to be at least eight firefighters in the house…rapidly leaving by the sound of things. "What are we going to do without you?"

"Whatever happened to women who don't need men?" Doc was already heading toward the door, salivating to get to a fire.

With near the same level of enthusiasm, Owen gave his mother a quick kiss. "Mom, you can handle it."

"No." Emma blocked Owen's path.

"Oh, let them go, Emma." Momma splayed the keys on the counter.

"But we won't have enough drivers," Emma said. "We're not done filling the cookie tins. Besides, who'll stay with the kids if we go?"

"The CEO," Owen said, backing out and into Simon, who carried a small piece of pumpkin pie. "We have every member of the volunteer fire department here, plus some. Putting out the fire should be a snap."

"The *CEO* is not a babysitter." Simon bristled. "The CEO needs to be in Las Vegas."

Owen apologized. Horns honked outside. "You'll sort it out, Em. Gotta go."

"It's almost seven o'clock." The Santa hat lay crumpled on the counter. Emma's fingers twitched. "More than one hundred families and six drivers? We'll be delivering until midnight without help."

"Not *we'll* be delivering, *they'll* be delivering, as in without you and me." Simon waved a hand in front of her face. "I hired you to drive me to Las Vegas. Can we go now?"

His attitude fired a single-minded purpose in Emma that had been lacking earlier. Snatching the hat from the counter, Emma jammed it on her head. Her father would never have let the community down. "No. I'll get you to Vegas in time for your meeting. I just need a couple of hours here."

"That's not—"

"This is not negotiable, Mr. Castle." She turned away from him and the deal she'd made. "Momma, we'll have the high-school kids bake, and you and I can make deliveries." Emma picked up the clipboard and scanned it.

"Of course, dear." Emma's mother glanced at Simon with a smile meant to charm. Emma doubted it would have any effect on Simon. "I'll go see if they're ready to load up."

"You—" Emma pointed at Simon without letting him get a word in "—go sit in a corner, eat your pie and check your strawberry for messages."

"BlackBerry," he corrected, a stormy angle to his brows. "I brought the pie for you, but neither one of us has time—"

"You have all the time in the world." Emma ignored the way his pie offering warmed her. "But if I don't get these presents out of here soon, there will be kids who won't have anything to eat on Christmas, much less a toy to play with."

Momma cradled the keys in both hands. "It shouldn't be so hard. We've got four trucks loaded and the cookie tins are nearly full."

Simon followed so close, he almost bumped into Emma as she entered the dining room. "But—"

"No buts. Sit." Emma pointed to a corner chair in the living room before grabbing an empty box and starting to fill it.

CHAPTER SIX

Please confirm your attendance upon arrival. Erik Wiseman.

Didn't Maloof's assistant ever take a break? His brief e-mail sent Simon's blood pressure soaring. He was trapped in Virginia City. The meeting would go on without him. Most likely, Maloof wouldn't even realize Simon wasn't there.

Fuming, Simon sat where he had a clear view of the lopsided, overdecorated tree, a sappy holiday movie on the TV and Emma flailing about the dining room trying to organize the women and teenagers. Emma was a beacon among them, with her fiery hair and high energy. The efforts of the remaining volunteers were lackluster, their enthusiasm drained since the men had left. Emma's charity was as doomed as Simon's desire to be in Las Vegas.

Simon stroked his BlackBerry. This Christmas was turning out to be among the worst ever. Rats. Limo drivers who refused to drive. What else could go wrong?

"Who works on Christmas?" he heard someone say. "Do you see him over there? He could be helping."

"If you were the head of a large corporation, you'd probably work every day of the year, too," Emma said defensively, dodging a kid who bumped the box she was carrying. "All right. That's it. Everyone under twelve needs to go out to the living room and *sit*."

A local newscaster appeared on the television screen, catching Simon's attention. "Who is the Rat of Reno? Tune in at eleven to learn why Simon Castle, founder and CEO of Castle Hotels, has riled employees once more and won't be having a merry Christmas." They flashed a picture of the large sharp-clawed rat in Simon's parking lot on-screen with the hotel logo looming behind it.

If blood could boil…

The couch cushion bounced next to him. "Mom said I was too small to help." Johnny pouted. "Aunt Emma said to come sit over here with the babysitter."

Simon glanced around the room filling with children. His quiet corner was fast disappearing. He waited for an adult or teenager—the babysitter—to come in, but he was the only one in the room older than ten. *He* was the babysitter.

"That's just not right," Simon said under his breath.

A glance showed the chaos whirling about Emma. She was really no good at organizing. He suspected she'd be better watching over these kids than he would.

Someone sneezed, followed by an eruption of loud *eeewwws!*

"Tommy, get a tissue!"

"He got some on me!"

"Hey, don't push me. I didn't sneeze on you."

Scowling eyes swiveled from Tommy, another toddler, to Simon. Boogers were something a baby-sitter was supposed to take care of. When Simon didn't, the kids rose in anger. Someone would have to be sacrificed, most likely Tommy-boy.

Simon had a choice: tackle the Booger Riot or participate in the chaos of Christmas, charity and ho-ho-hos.

Another juicy sneeze. Another chorus of *eeewww*.

"Come on, kid. This isn't the room for us." He dragged Johnny through the raucous group toward the dining room. Maybe the fire would be put out quickly, the men would return and Simon would get out of here and make the meeting. Maybe the networks wouldn't pick up the rat story. And maybe there was a Santa Claus.

"Becky, I need you and Brian to take the south end of town. It's got the heaviest boxes," Emma was saying.

"But I have the smallest car," Becky argued.

"Emma—" a teenage boy popped his head in from the kitchen "—we burned a batch of cookies."

"Do we have any more boxes? I think we're out of boxes," announced a woman with wild gray hair.

"Look at the time," pointed out an older woman wearing a sweatshirt with a holly wreath made out of children's handprints. "We're never going to make it without the guys. And our own Christmas will be ruined. Why don't we wait until morning to deliver this stuff, when the guys get back?"

"We can do this, Dora," Emma countered in a

panicked voice. "Once you see the smiles and hear the thank yous, you won't feel as if your holiday is ruined."

A few of the women muttered, and Simon sensed impending disaster. His pulse raced and, for the first time all evening, Simon felt at home. He thrived on crisis management.

He couldn't resist leaning close to Emma and whispering in her ear, "What happened to merry Christmas and the joy of helping others?" She smelled like cinnamon and spice. Simon breathed in a second time before he realized what he was doing and pulled back.

"We've never had to do this by ourselves before," Emma said with a frown in Simon's direction. "We're short-staffed."

"You didn't have a backup plan?" Simon raised his eyebrows.

"It's a charity, not a business," Emma snapped back. "Next thing, you'll be wondering if we have insurance to cover our drivers."

Simon waved her off. "Organize. Cover contingencies. Plan for the future the same as you would your own life. Nobody watches out for you better than you. That's common sense, not business." Emma opened her mouth to retort, but Simon cut her off. "Show me the list of delivery locations, and you—" he pointed to Becky "—make a list of available vehicles. And you—" he took Dora, the mutinous woman, by the arm and pointed her in the direction of the living room where empty rolls of wrapping paper were being wielding like swords "—can watch the kids."

Simon poked his head in the kitchen where two teenagers were kissing under the mistletoe hanging from the outdated light fixture. "Quit messing around and set the timer. If you can't handle that, Tommy needs help blowing his nose in the living room." He waited until the teens moved to the oven before leaving them alone again.

"You're helping us?" The disbelief on Emma's face should have irritated Simon.

Instead, he laughed. "At the rate you're going, we'll never get out of here tonight."

"We've just hit a rough patch," Emma assured him, ruffled. "You'll get to Vegas in plenty of time."

"Yes, I will." He was going to make sure of it, if he had to make every delivery for the Santa Express himself. "Now, what's this I hear about a box shortage?"

"THAT MR. CASTLE IS a miracle worker," Momma said, clearly charmed. "What does he do for a living?"

"He owns Castle Hotels." Emma had to agree that Simon was a blessing in disguise. He'd taken the bedlam and mutiny and coordinated the volunteers into something resembling a team. He'd organized a group to repack donations for the smaller families into bags so that there were enough boxes to go around. The vehicles were divvied up as well, with one adult and one teen in each. The smaller vehicles held the smaller donations, the trucks and larger cars, like Emma's Town Car, the larger ones. As far as Emma could see, there was just one problem.

"You and I are going together?" she asked again when he passed her way.

Simon nodded, reviewing a list of destinations he'd assigned someone else to write down. Emma followed him through the dining room to the kitchen. "And when we're done, you and I are going to Vegas." He paused in the doorway, one hand on the swinging door.

"You're under the mistletoe, dears," Emma's mom noted with a twinkle in her eye. "You know what that means."

Emma froze, her gaze meeting Simon's. *Say something, stupid.*

To her complete surprise, Simon leaned over and pressed his lips to hers.

Something warm flickered inside Emma, making her want to curl her fingers around Simon's arms and pull him closer. Instead, she stumbled back into the door frame, bumping her head and seeing stars around Simon's face.

"I don't normally have that effect on women," he said, closing the distance between them and running his fingers through her hair as he searched for a bruise.

"I bet you don't normally kiss them under the mistletoe, either." Emma was still too unsteady to trust herself to step away. Who would have thought the unfeeling Simon Castle could generate such feelings in her?

Who was she kidding? She'd wanted him from the moment she'd laid eyes on him in her rearview mirror.

"Gosh, if you marry my aunt Emma, you can help

with the Santa Express every year," Johnny piped up from the dining room.

Cheeks heating, Emma slipped away to retrieve her car keys. She didn't dare look at Simon. This was not the kind of holiday cheer she should be spreading to her client. She groaned. She had to endure eight hours alone in the car with Simon. Maybe he'd sleep on the way to Las Vegas—*all* the way to Las Vegas.

As SIMON WATCHED HER WALK AWAY, he could no longer deny he wanted Emma Roberts. If only the feeling wasn't so inconvenient. After tonight, they'd go their separate ways and she'd annoy another unsuspecting passenger.

Someone tugged on his hand. "Are you?"

Simon looked down in confusion at his temporary administrative assistant, Johnny. "Am I what?"

Johnny rolled his big blue eyes dramatically. "Going to marry Aunt Emma?"

Laughter erupted all around them, even though the work didn't stop. When they were organized, they were an efficient group. Simon wished his employees were that motivated.

Unable to keep from grinning, Simon checked his watch. "This convoy leaves in ten minutes."

"So, the businessman has a heart after all," someone said behind him.

"Everyone has a heart on Christmas," Mrs. Roberts said staunchly, sending Simon an approving look the likes he hadn't seen since his mother was alive.

CHAPTER SEVEN

"TWELVE STOPS AND THEN WE'RE on our way," Simon said, settling into the front seat next to Emma with no indication that he was uncomfortable after their earlier kiss.

Emma couldn't forget it. She'd been counting on Simon sitting in the backseat—keeping his distance.

Without a word—because she couldn't trust herself to speak—Emma drove toward the first stop, a family of five living in a one-bedroom house behind a grocery store.

"How long do you think this will take?" Simon asked, glancing at his BlackBerry, although he didn't work the keys. He'd barely seemed to notice the sights as they'd crossed the center of town.

"Maybe two hours." Emma braced herself for Simon's reaction, which was likely to be colder and more furious than a blizzard.

"And how long to Las Vegas from here?"

"Eight." Barring any snow, accidents or slow drivers, they'd just make it.

Amazing. The blizzard held off.

"It looked as if you were having fun wrapping with Johnny," Emma ventured.

"He's a good kid," Simon allowed. "Was his dad there?"

"Yes. Gerry's the one who looks like a linebacker. He married my cousin, Kate."

"They all look like linebackers."

"Oh." Emma supposed a stranger would look at all the firemen that way. "He's the balding linebacker."

"Ah." Simon checked his BlackBerry again. "I'm sorry you lost your dad. What happened to him?" The question may have been casual, but Emma could feel his scrutiny.

"He was killed," she said.

"I'm sorry." His touch on her shoulder was so brief, she almost thought she'd imagined it. "How did he die?"

Emma spared him a glance, gauging the emotion behind his request. The look in his eyes wasn't polite pity as she so often saw, but curiosity and perhaps... understanding. "My dad was a professor of sociology at the university in Reno. He was studying the impact of America's increasing inner focus as it related to the Christmas holiday."

"Can you say that again in earth-speak?"

Emma almost smiled. "My dad noticed that fewer people were sending Christmas cards, baking cookies, buying real Christmas trees, hosting holiday parties and such. He thought it was becoming something else to add to our to-do list rather than a time to reflect on traditions and enjoy the relationships you have, which translates into more stress, shorter tempers and contributes to health problems."

"That explains a lot about you," he said, "but not how he died."

"He was mugged." It was ten years later, and Emma's eyes still filled with tears when she talked about her dad. "He was going door-to-door for his research in some of the poorer sections of Reno the week before Christmas and someone must have thought he was an easy target." She added quickly, "Please don't make a joke of it. I've heard them all." Her dad, killed by Christmas.

"It's not a joking matter." He kept his hand on her shoulder longer this time.

"It's hard to imagine anyone would kill him for the fifty bucks he had in his wallet. He was such a big, trusting teddy bear of a man."

They pulled onto a street of small rectangular houses lacking even a hint of Christmas decorations.

"You still miss him."

She nodded. "Especially at this time of year."

"Despite that, you'll go out and help others, in neighborhoods like this." Simon gestured to the run-down homes around them.

"Mom, Owen and I decided keeping the Santa Express alive was the best way to honor Dad's memory. He was a real believer in the season and if you gave him two minutes of your time, he could make you a believer, too."

"Like father, like daughter."

It was a good thing Emma had the car in Park because she couldn't tear herself away from the intensity of his gaze. She almost wished the Town Car didn't have such wide seats.

Apparently Simon was thinking the same thing. He slowly leaned toward her and pressed his mouth to hers with a heat that compelled Emma to kiss him back. Lips like his should have a warning label— Caution: May Overheat If Turned on Unattended.

It took Emma a moment to realize his lips had left hers. His palms cradled her face. She held on to his wrists. They stared into each others' eyes in an awkward moment. "Merry Christmas," she finally managed to say, with a tentative smile she hoped said, *Kiss me again.*

"Only if we keep to the schedule, Emma." His words were cool, but his eyes betrayed a longing that matched hers. As they got out of the car, Simon changed the subject. "Do we just leave the packages on the doorstep? The house looks dark."

"That would be quicker, but it's not the way the Santa Express operates. They're expecting us." Okay. If he could play detached, so could she. Kind of. She still had a few surprises for Simon. Emma popped the trunk and pulled out a red hat similar to the one she was wearing. "I can't let you make deliveries without the hat."

Simon stepped back and eyed it as if he were in imminent danger. "You're kidding, right?"

Emma shook her head solemnly. "You can either help or you can wait in the car."

"Which would mean these deliveries would take

that much longer." With a frown, Simon snatched the hat. "I'll carry it."

"No go. It sits on your head. I'm willing to wait here all night until it does." Emma crossed her arms over her chest before adding, "With the keys in my hand."

His eyes narrowed, sending a thrill through Emma. "That's blackmail."

"Yep. I've got a reputation to protect." For the first time since she'd met him, she felt as if they were equals.

Simon pulled the hat over his ears and nudged Emma aside so he could reach inside the trunk for a box. This was priceless. The only thing better would be to see the rat outside his hotel in a Santa hat.

"That must be some meeting," Emma observed, grabbing a sack of presents.

"You don't know what it's like to be the outsider, do you?" Simon asked as he headed up the walk, carrying the heavy box with ease.

"I was born an outsider." Emma couldn't quite achieve the note of levity she desired. "You've heard of the glass ceiling? Well, there's also a *class* ceiling. Not everyone is born into money."

"I grew up in a house a lot like this one." Simon's revelation surprised her. He reeked of stiff-backed, old money. "I'm proof that there is no ceiling if you have a goal you're serious about and pursue it relentlessly every day."

"That doesn't sound as if it leaves much room for anything else." Like a wife or a family. Emma stabbed at the doorbell as she juggled the bags of gifts.

"There's not."

Emma's heart sank. What had she been expecting? He'd made himself into a successful businessman. She was, and would probably always be, content with her lifestyle. He'd drawn lines clear enough for Emma to read. There would be no more pursuit of their mutual attraction.

Emma straightened her shoulders. They both needed to lighten up.

"It's too bad you only think about work. Life doesn't wait around, you know." She couldn't resist jostling Simon in the shoulder. "You have to say 'Merry Christmas' when they answer."

Simon made a growling noise.

"And mean it," Emma added as the door opened, turning to muster a smile.

SIMON COULDN'T REMEMBER ANYONE ever being so happy to see him as that first Santa Express family. He deposited the box of food with the fixings for their Christmas dinner on the wobbly kitchen table and was immediately enveloped in a bear hug from the robust lady of the house.

"It was getting so late, we thought you might not be coming," she said wiping away tears when she finally released him. "Merry Christmas."

"You shouldn't have worried. Nothing stops the Santa Express," Simon said, watching as Emma's expression changed from curious to approving.

There was much more to Emma than he'd first expected. She wasn't an overboard,

Christmas-loving do-gooder. She was honoring her father. It all made sense now. Emma's heart was larger than Simon's would ever be. Unlike him, she'd never want for friends or family. And the way she kissed—with uninhibited abandon—she wouldn't stay single much longer.

"You can put the gifts under the tree," the woman said, pointing to a crooked tree that barely stood two feet tall.

The tree was propped on a scarred coffee table. Emma deposited the gifts with a smile that warmed Simon from his fingers to his toes.

A man appeared in the hallway with a baby cradled in one arm and a toddler snuggled in the other. "Both our little ones went down with bronchitis yesterday, so we had a big doctor bill today. Every time I put them down, they cough themselves back awake." He deposited the toddler in his wife's arms and shook Simon's hand with bone-popping strength. "You don't know how much this helps us, especially since I've been laid off. No one's hiring mechanics this time of year."

"Never you mind, Rueben," his wife said. "You'll find a job in the new year." She could have put her husband down, but instead, she was positive and supportive, as if she hadn't been crying with relief just moments before.

The sentiment and encouragement humbled Simon, who would have been bitter if their situations had been reversed. He certainly hadn't been raised with such compassion. Simon remembered his dad complaining when his mother had become so sick she could no longer work. His father's love seemed shallow compared to this couple's. Someone like Emma would offer that kind of love to her partner and expect—no, demand—it be returned in kind.

Simon looked up to find Emma studying him. She turned, spoke softly to the other woman and pressed something into the woman's hands.

"We need to be going." Simon's voice was unexpectedly thick.

"Thank you, thank you." The big man shook Simon's hand again as he tried to leave. "This means so much to us."

"Maybe next year you can help make Santa Express deliveries," Emma suggested, before following Simon out the door.

"I'd love to," the man said. "I'll keep in touch. Merry Christmas!"

Simon and Emma didn't speak until they were back in the car.

"That wasn't what I expected," Simon admitted, an odd emptiness making him restless. He didn't want to sit in the car. He wanted to...do something. Unbidden, a long forgotten memory of his mother humming while she wrapped presents on her bed came to mind. Simon had been trying to stack bows on the floor at her feet when his father had burst into the room, swept Simon's mother into his arms and kissed her. Then he'd lifted Simon with strong arms, holding him so tight Simon didn't think he'd ever let go.

"You thought we'd be dropping in on cold-hearted freeloaders?"

"No. I expected it to be more like the house I grew up in, with a father too proud to accept help. I just...didn't expect them to be so...grateful. I'm sorry." Sorry for thinking the Santa Express wasn't worth his time or money. Sorry he hadn't realized there were more sides to love than he'd known as a child, because now a woman with expectations was tempting him and Simon had no idea how to be the man she'd want.

"In case no one told you, this is the season to spread joy and give thanks," Emma said in a flat voice.

"So you've told me. I just didn't believe it."

"Do you have any family traditions for the holidays?" Emma asked.

The night may have been chilly, but Emma felt warm. Simon was starting to come around. He'd worn the Santa hat all evening and he hadn't mentioned Las Vegas since they'd left the first house— although it helped that the reported fire had been a bonfire so the men had caught up with most of the delivery teams. Doc and Owen had taken half of Emma and Simon's load.

Simon waited so long to answer, Emma didn't think he was going to. "Christmas isn't my favorite time of year. My mother died when I was a kid." He added almost as an afterthought, "Just after the holiday."

She gave Simon's hand a squeeze, surprised as he held on to her fingers when she would have let go.

"That's a horrible thing to have to grow up with…or without. A mom, I mean."

"I used to think we got by," he said slowly. "But after seeing these families, I'm beginning to think we were luckier than most. We faced tragedy, but we still had a roof over our heads and food in the kitchen."

"And your dad?"

"We don't see each other much. I think we both like it that way." There was a sadness in his voice that said otherwise. He let go of her hand.

"Are you sure?"

"Does Christmas fall on the twenty-fifth of December? My old man doesn't agree with anything I do. He doesn't care for anyone but himself."

"Really?" This last might have described the world's view of Simon Castle, a view Emma now disagreed with.

He reached for his BlackBerry. "I don't have time to do things like this. I'd rather send money and leave the actual giving to the professionals."

"My dad would have loved talking to you." Emma kept seeing glimpses of Simon that she was attracted to. "It's amazing the things we take for granted, like family and a steady paycheck."

"I don't take anything for granted because I've worked so hard to get here. And I got here without anyone else's help." Maybe he had every right to feel this proud.

Yet, Emma couldn't relate. She put the Town Car in Park and turned to face him. "You never asked for advice? You never got an unexpected break? You say you did it on your own, but I bet someone some-where along the line helped you. This is your chance to return the favor."

Simon's expression darkened. "I've never said I was anything other than what I am. I'm not like you. I put my goals and needs first."

Emma had to swallow twice before she was able to speak. "Do you ever stop to ask yourself if you're happy?"

"I'm about to achieve more success than I ever imagined."

"That's not an answer." Not the answer Emma wanted. She knew come morning that Simon would disappear through darkened casino doors and she'd drive back to Virginia City alone. Yet, she'd worry about Simon long after he'd forgotten her because somehow that impossibly driven, vulnerable man had found the route to her heart. Her mother had been right. Trying to make someone believe only led to heartache.

Emma opened her door to get out, angry at herself, angry at Simon. "Why don't you spend your time in a more *productive* manner? I can handle this one on my own."

CHAPTER EIGHT

WAS SIMON HAPPY?

Simon hadn't questioned it until now. What did happiness matter when you were making something out of nothing? Simon sat in the car as the heat dissipated. He could hear Emma rummaging in the trunk. He should help her, but he stubbornly remained where he was.

The surface of his BlackBerry was cold. Nothing new had come in since Maloof's assistant's last e-mail. Undoubtedly, everyone Simon dealt with was home stuffing themselves with turkey, yams and pumpkin pie.

Simon had smiled more this evening than he had in a long time. Emma's family, her charity, the arguments with Emma and her wholehearted kisses, all of it chaotic and unpredictable, yet oddly satisfying—a feeling his money and success had been unable to evoke.

Simon glanced at his watch. There was still time to make it to Vegas, still time to explore these feelings he had for Emma. So what if she was a distraction? He was due a distraction or two. Emma, with her Christmas-green eyes, sparkling spirit and moral indignation was just the kind of diversion Simon needed.

He opened the door and went to help complete these last deliveries.

"How DID WE END UP with this small delivery?" Simon asked. Despite her suggestion he sit this one out, he stood at the rear of the car looking at two small bags of food and gifts Emma was pulling from the trunk.

"I always deliver to Mrs. Brennaman," Emma said. She glanced up at the sky. If it would only snow, it might help her forget that his tender kisses led nowhere. "I think everyone in town had her for kindergarten, but she always told me I was her favorite."

"Merry Christmas," Simon said defiantly when Mrs. B. opened her door.

Emma echoed his sentiment, her smile forced.

"Come in, dearies," Mrs. B. said, peering at Simon through her thick glasses. "You look very familiar to me, boy."

"I'm Simon Castle."

"Of course you are. You must have helped Emma with deliveries last Christmas. Come in, come in." She shuffled to one side of the door so that they could enter her cluttered living room.

Newspapers and magazines were stacked on the floor by the couch, which was draped in a half-finished afghan. Framed photos of Mrs. B. and her husband at various ages crowded the coffee tables. Simon picked one up for a closer look.

"That's my husband." She took the picture from Simon and stroked the frame with her thumb. "People live such fast lives nowadays. Not like Bill and I used to. That man. He loved to surprise me. One night when we were hiking the Sierras, he made me a bed on sugar pine branches. It was like sleeping in a tree."

"You can't get that in a hotel." Simon's voice was gruff.

"No, you can't." Mrs. B. beamed at him. "I know you're in a hurry tonight, so I won't keep you. I'm always grateful for the Santa Express. Make sure you thank everyone for me."

"We'll stay as long as you like." Simon reached for Mrs. B.'s hand.

How could Simon come across as cold one minute, yet charm the socks off Emma and Mrs. Brennaman the next?

"You've stayed long enough already." Mrs. B. patted his hand.

Emma deposited a small bag of gifts on the couch and gave Mrs. B. a careful hug. "I'll come and get you on New Year's Eve. Momma wouldn't want you to miss her party."

"Thank you, honey." Mrs. B. turned to Simon, who stood silently taking in the cluttered apartment, which couldn't have been as big as one of his hotel rooms. "I bet in kindergarten you used to pull someone's pigtails." Mrs. B. gestured for Simon to come closer, and then she said in an audible whisper, "If you had gone to school here, I bet you would have been my favorite student that year."

When Emma gasped, Mrs. B. turned to her. "Honey, you know I tell every former student they were my favorite. I'm so fond of all of you I could never choose just one."

Simon winked at Mrs. B. and laughed, the sound falling over Emma like so many Christmas morning snowflakes, with a hypnotic quality that was impossible to ignore.

"Now, skedaddle. I know you have more deliveries." Mrs. B. shooed them out.

As soon as the door closed behind them, Emma wrapped her arms around Simon's neck and kissed him. She'd be content to be snowed in with this man.

And then Simon was kissing her back, sharing his warmth, pulling her so close she wished their clothes would disintegrate, removing all barriers between them. His hands—those heated, magical hands!— traced their way beneath her jacket and up the curve of her spine before delving back the other way.

"Ooooh."

Emma wasn't sure who moaned. She'd take credit if he asked—as long as he didn't stop kissing her long enough to ask.

A door opened. "Who's out there?" Mrs. B. tapped on Emma's arm. "It's Christmas Eve. Don't you two have someplace else to go?"

Laughing, the pair ran hand in hand to the car as snowflakes started to fall.

When Emma reached in her pocket for the remote, Simon stopped her. "Wait. I haven't kissed a girl in the snow in a long time."

Emma tilted her head for his kiss, accepting his need, disclosing her own.

Someone drove by and honked, sending Emma into a fit of giggles.

"I'm sorry. I'm so sorry. I'm attacking you and it's Christmas and we've just met." She gazed up into Simon's dark eyes, unable to keep from smiling because she wasn't sorry in the least.

"You know me well enough," he said gruffly, and she realized it was true. "Anytime you want to give me another present—" He tugged her hips against his. "Anytime you want to kiss again under the mistletoe, you just let me know."

"It's a long way to Las Vegas," Emma said, already wondering if he'd invite her to stay a few days after he attended that all-so-important meeting, wondering what she'd say if he did, wondering if what she felt for him was love or infatuation. She voted for love. "I'll have to ask you to sit in the backseat."

He buried his head beneath the hair at her neck and nibbled on her skin. "I won't be in that backseat alone again." With his clever hands playing across her skin, she couldn't even articulate an answer.

Another car drove by, reminding Emma that they needed to get on the road as well. There were three more deliveries and many miles to travel.

Reluctantly, Emma backed away from Simon when all she wanted to do was burrow beneath his overcoat and cling tightly to this wonderful man.

EMMA ROBERTS WAS JUST WHAT the doctor ordered for his annual Christmas blues. The holidays were going to be different this year. Hell, the new year was going to start with a bang—successful business ventures and the promise of something that had been missing from Simon's life for far too long.

"Just one more delivery," Emma said, turning down a court lined with rusted, sometimes lopsided mobile homes.

Simon's fingers were linked through hers. One more delivery and they'd be on their way to Vegas. He hadn't expected the deliveries to be so difficult, so joyous.

In companionable silence, they unloaded a box of food and the bulky present Doc had wrapped and carried them to the door.

"This is Johnny's friend, Wallace," Emma said when a small boy opened the door. Wallace stuck out his hand for a manly handshake.

"Johnny told me you'd come," Wallace said.

Simon hesitated a moment when he realized Wallace only had two fingers and a thumb. But he recovered quickly and shook the boy's hand firmly, uncomfortably aware that while his own smile had wavered, Wallace's never had.

"It's all right," Wallace's mother softly reassured Simon.

"Can I open my present, Mommy?" Wallace

asked. "Johnny told me to wait up and I was really good all day, just like you asked." He put both hands up to his cheeks and Simon saw that his left hand only had two fingers and a thumb as well.

How on earth was that boy going to play the piano? There must have been a mistake. Simon tried to catch Emma's eye, but she was watching Wallace.

"It's all right with us," Emma said, smiling as if Wallace had the brightest future ahead of him.

Wallace sat down in front of the big package on the floor and tore off the wrapping paper. For a moment, the boy sat frozen, staring at the box and Simon was sure there had indeed been a mistake.

And then Wallace jumped up and down, ran to each adult in the room and hugged them, shouting, "I asked and I asked and I got it!"

Simon found himself grinning and hugging the little dynamo back.

"Can you get it out of the box for me?" he asked Simon.

"Of course." His throat nearly closed with emotion, Simon's voice sounded gruff. He carefully opened the box and set the keyboard on the kitchen table, plugging it into the wall outlet.

"He plays at school, but hasn't had anything to practice on," Wallace's mother told them, wiping tears from her eyes. "I knew it was a big gift, but I hoped…"

Emma hugged her and pressed something into her hand.

As Wallace plunked his fingers on random keys on the keyboard, his mother unfolded two hundred-dollar bills. She began to cry and hugged Emma again.

Where had Emma gotten two hundred dollars? But Simon knew. He couldn't decide if he was proud of her or angry with her for giving some of her money away. Despite all the advice he'd given her, Emma didn't care about her own future. Simon reached for her, intent on pulling her aside when Wallace struck the first few notes of Beethoven's Fifth Symphony, his face aglow. Simon's jaw must have dropped halfway to the floor. The kid could play better than most people with ten fingers.

"When you first came in, I thought you were someone else." Wallace's mother gave Simon a hug, then drew back with a sad smile. "I used to work as a maid at the Castle Hotel in Reno, but Mr. Castle would never do anything like this."

Simon stiffened, but the woman didn't seem to notice. She only had eyes for Wallace now.

"Mr. Castle put in these lovely new featherbeds that are supposed to be heavenly to sleep on. But they were also heavier to make and it took longer to change the sheets," she explained. "I couldn't make my quota and Mr. Castle didn't care. So I lost my job and came back here to live with my dad."

The reality of her situation hit Simon with a knee-knocking force that almost brought him down. Simon retreated toward the door, letting Emma return their wishes for a merry Christmas as she followed him out. He pulled the hated Santa cap off his head and started to get into the front seat, then thought better of it and tossed the hat there. He climbed into the backseat and retrieved his BlackBerry from his pocket but didn't look at it. "Let's get to Vegas."

CHAPTER NINE

"YOU LIED TO ME." Emma jammed the key into the ignition, then froze, cold for the first time that evening.

She could have fallen in love with him.

It took her a few moments to work up the courage to turn and confront Simon. "That's why the rat is in your parking lot, isn't it? Because it's harder for the maids to keep up now that you've changed the bedding and the union knows it." *Please, please deny it.*

"That's right." He sat in the corner of the backseat, his face in shadow.

"Nothing lasts forever, Simon. Did you know that?" Emma faced forward, blinking rapidly. She'd let desire cloud her judgment. Simon was just another heartless guy who put himself first. She bit her lip. "When you're gone, do you know what will happen to Castle Hotels? They'll be sold and demolished. That's the way it is in Nevada. No one will remember you."

"It's all right, Emma."

"No, it's not. Do you know why men like Carnegie and Rockefeller live on in history and have monuments dedicated to them?" She drew in a ragged breath, trying not to let him know she was breaking apart inside. "Because they *gave back* to the community."

When he didn't fight for her—or himself—she dug into her pocket and threw the remaining bills over the seat. "Here's thirteen hundred dollars. The keys are in the ignition. Drive yourself to Vegas."

"We had a deal." Simon didn't want to go without Emma, which was ridiculous. All she'd done since she'd met him was make him doubt himself and his goals. He caught one of the bills before it drifted to the floorboard.

Without a word, Emma opened her car door.

"You're not like me, Emma." Of course, not. She had a conscience. "You'll regret that you didn't uphold your end of the bargain, either tonight as I drive away with your car, or Tuesday when I ask my lawyer about breach of contract." He might still have the power to keep her with him, at least for tonight. "Think of all that money you'll owe me if you don't."

"It always comes back to money." Emma clutched the wheel, bowing her head.

Simon wanted to pull her into his arms and tell her everything would be all right, but he knew that was a lie. Mrs. B. would continue to spend her holidays alone. Wallace would grow bitter as he realized how handicapped he was. Even little Johnny would find that life wasn't as easily won as a wrapping contest. Simon had made a choice long ago to be the kind of man Emma would never be able to love because that's the kind of man who got ahead in the world.

"I didn't ask for your sympathy about the rat. At the time, I didn't think it was any of your business." Simon's stomach churned. He really was a selfish, heartless bastard. It was best she knew it. "I stand by my decisions. All I ever asked was for you to drive me to Las Vegas." Why wasn't she arguing? Before Simon knew what he was doing, he reached for her. Just in time, he drew back, staring at his fingers as if they'd betrayed him.

He needed something to do with his hands. A punch of a button illuminated his BlackBerry screen and one new message.

Assuming your plane is delayed. Please confirm your attendance upon arrival in Las Vegas. Erik Wiseman.

Steven Wynn wasn't soft. George Maloof wasn't soft. Simon Castle couldn't afford to be soft. And neither could Emma. Anger drowned out his sorrow and pity. "Thirteen hundred dollars? Didn't Marlene give you twenty-five hundred? Did you give two hundred dollars to every family?"

"Yes." Emma closed the door and started the car, shifting gears before the engine fully caught. The Town Car lurched away from the curb with a groan.

"Twelve hundred dollars?"

"Yes." She hadn't missed the hardness in his voice because Emma's had developed something just as edgy.

Good. If nothing else, perhaps this interlude would teach her to be more selfish with herself and her dreams. "We visited six homes. If Doc and Owen hadn't caught up with us, would you have given away another twelve hundred?"

"Yes." Just the way she said it made him believe she saw absolutely nothing wrong with giving away a good chunk of the five thousand dollars he'd promised her.

"You'll never be anything more than a chauffeur, Emma." Simon sank into the seat. "You have to think of yourself first."

"Like when you offered to stay longer with Mrs. B.? Or when you helped Wallace set up his keyboard?" Emma gave him a quick glance in the mirror, but it was too dark to read her expression. "Your trouble is that you don't want to care about anyone but yourself."

"No." If he hadn't cared for the people he'd met tonight, it wouldn't hurt this much. "But I can't help everyone and myself at the same time."

"Everyone? What about a few?" Emma drove through the center of town, past the businesses that had been refurbished into their original Old West charm. "You helped six families tonight, six very special families. You helped a woman who lost her job because of a decision you made."

"And that's supposed to make me feel better?" Emma couldn't possibly understand what he was going through. Simon wanted to be the kind of man Emma deserved, but that man couldn't also earn enough money to buy back his father's love.

Blood roared in his ears, drowning out all coherent thought but the truth.

"Emma, stop the car." He was going to throw up.

"What?"

"Stop the car," he yelled, not waiting until she had completely stopped before getting out.

On unsteady feet, Simon staggered across the asphalt to the icy sidewalk. He stared inside the dark windows of an Old West saloon, wishing it were open so he could down a shot of whiskey and try to ease this frustrating pain. All this time, he'd thought—

"What's wrong?" Emma slid on the ice in front of him, holding on to his arms so she wouldn't fall.

Simon couldn't speak. Not now. Not when he was seeing his mistakes clearly. He stepped back, desperately wanting perspective and for his stomach to stop churning. He could have been happy with one hotel, but he'd called his dad and listened when he'd said Simon's success wouldn't last. "Give me the keys."

Emma looked confused but didn't resist when he pried the keys from her fingers. "What about—"

"Go home, Emma, before I change my mind." Simon had to do this alone. He wouldn't ruin her, too. "You can walk home from here. I'll make sure your car gets returned to you."

"But—"

"Go!"

He couldn't watch her leave him, but he did listen to the soft tread of her feet on the thin layer of ice as he clutched one of her hundred-dollar bills.

Simon didn't know how long he stood there waiting for something—lightning to strike, a ghost to tell him he'd been a fool. Nothing. His nose began to run from the cold. All the money in the world wouldn't bring Simon's mother back. His dad would never love him. He'd lost Emma, probably lost career opportunities in Vegas, and would most likely suffer a severe setback from the inflatable rat choking in garland in his parking lot.

The question was—what was he going to do about it?

Simon curled his hands into fists, squeezing the remote control so hard the car alarm went off, startling his feet right out from under him.

"IS THAT YOU, EM?" Donna Roberts called as Emma let herself in the front door. "Did you complete all your deliveries?"

"Yes." Emma wiped away tears with icy fingers. "Mrs. B. says hello and thank you."

"Did Wallace like his keyboard?" Emma's mom peeked around the corner of the foyer, wearing her red-and-green terry robe. "What's wrong? Where's Mr. Castle?"

"Trying to get to Vegas." *Without me.* Emma should be counting her blessings that she wasn't with him. She swept an afghan from a living-room chair over her shoulders.

"Emma Noelle Roberts, did you leave him alongside the road on Christmas Eve?"

Emma let Momma believe Simon was stranded. "He wants to turn Virginia City into a little Reno, complete with a hotel, twenty-four-hour restaurant and casino."

Momma started to say something, then stopped to

consider this latest development. She straightened her robe. "The jobs would be welcome."

"Momma, he's heartless."

"That's not true." Her chin had a stubborn tilt to it. "I saw him wrapping presents this evening. He reorganized everything and he helped you load up the car."

"Only because he knew I wouldn't leave until after the Santa Express deliveries. The most important thing to Simon Castle is his bank account. All he thinks about is how to improve it."

Momma crossed her arms. "Really? Then why did he leave his briefcase here?"

KARMA REALLY SUCKED.

Stars flashed in front of Simon's eyes. Something terrible had happened and Simon was helpless to stop it. Everything was quiet and cold.

Gradually, he became aware that he was clutching something in each hand. Curious, he unfurled his fingers to find a set of car keys and a one-hundred-dollar bill. A soft breeze sent the money tumbling out of his grasp. Money didn't matter. Emma was right. People mattered. Like his mother, whom he'd never really allowed himself to grieve for. And Wallace with his stodgy determination to follow his heart instead of the logic those around him tried to force on him. And Marlene, who handled every curve he threw her way, in a wheelchair, no less. And Emma, good-natured, eternally optimistic Emma.

Four calling birds, three French hens, two turtle doves...

Now he was imagining things. He heard angels singing.

And a partridge in a pear tree! The song died away. How fitting that he was hearing the last lines when he was at the end of his rope.

"Look! Is that a man on the ground?"

Simon was feeling more like the money-grubber that Emma had accused him of being than a man at the moment.

Footsteps rushed toward him. Shadowy Victorian figures surrounded him. Simon was either dreaming or dead and about to be trampled by the ghosts of previous Virginia City residents. It was nothing less than he deserved.

"I'm a doctor. Are you all right?" A face with fogged glasses swam in front of Simon. Fingers probed the back of his head.

"Ow!" Simon's eyes widened as the man found a tender spot at the base of his skull. He became aware of his back, cold against the icy sidewalk.

"Can you wriggle your toes? Move your fingers?"

"Yes." His digits felt like ice cubes.

A spotty-faced teenage boy leaned into Simon's line of vision, a top hat on his head. "Is this your money? You shouldn't walk around with so much cash." He waved Emma's one-hundred-dollar bill in front of Simon's face.

Earlier today, Simon would have bet he'd never see that cash again.

The group surrounded Simon in their velvet coats, top hats, Victorian dresses and shawls, bringing him unsteadily to his feet.

"You're lucky David spotted you as our choir was making a last pass through town. Otherwise…" The doctor gave him a serious look. "Well, it's Christmas. We'd best not talk about what might have been. Do you know someone who can drive you to the hospital? You should get an X-ray."

"I'm going to be fine. I don't have time for that." With a firm handshake, Simon pressed the bill into the other man's hand. "Donate this to someone in need, will you?"

The doctor searched Simon's gaze before looking down at the bill and then holding it up for the rest of the choir to see.

There were cheerful calls of "Merry Christmas."

Convinced he'd done the right thing, Simon no longer felt cold. This feeling of well-being had to be what kept Emma warm in her tuxedo shirt. Maybe there was hope for Simon yet.

"Can we give you a lift somewhere?" the doctor asked.

"My car's right there." Simon pointed at Emma's Town Car.

"Are you sure you want to drive? You've got quite a bump there."

"I think I've suffered worse injuries." Simon paused. "But thanks for asking."

"MERRY CHRISTMAS." SIMON pushed open the door and stepped inside, nodding to Emma and her mother. His overcoat was missing and he had a bad case of Santa-hat hair that was endearing.

Not that Emma cared. She wrapped the afghan tighter about her shoulders. "What are you doing here?" Whatever he was after, Emma wasn't in a giving mood. Giving in to Simon meant getting hurt.

"I couldn't leave town without apologizing. I—"

"I won't accept." Emma cut him off and turned away.

"Emma," her mother admonished. "Your manners."

"It's all right, Mrs. Roberts. Emma and I understand each other." Simon looked at Emma in a way that made her want to forget what a butt head he was and remember how tenderly he'd kissed her. But that was what had gotten her into trouble in the first place.

"Oh, yes. You forgot your briefcase." Emma took a step toward the hall.

"Did I?" He reached for Emma's hand, his eyes so intent upon her that she stopped. "I've harbored lots of dreams for all the wrong reasons, Em. And now I have just one Christmas wish."

Simon gently tugged her closer. "I've got a lot to make right in Reno. Come with me. Tonight. I know it's Christmas, but that's the best time to make amends." His voice dropped. "Say yes. Give me a chance to prove I'm more than the heartless suit who manipulated you into driving him to Vegas on Christmas Eve."

Emma could barely fill her lungs with air. "What about your meeting? Your hot prospect for success?"

"I e-mailed them my regrets. There are more important people to be with on Christmas." Simon's smile was hopeful. "Besides, I'm pretty happy with the prospect in front of me."

Emma didn't dare hope, and yet... "Why should I say yes?"

"Because there's something between us and if I go to Vegas I know I'll lose it. I'll lose you, Emma."

Momma gasped and sank against the wall, whispering, "I've never heard anything so romantic. If you don't say yes, I just might."

Emma laughed, finally letting herself believe that the man she'd caught glimpses of throughout the night really did exist. "It's not a proposal, Momma. That won't come until later...when he's proved himself." To both himself and Emma. "Yes, Simon Castle, I'll go with you to Reno, if only to make sure you know how to give properly."

Simon's kiss was far too brief. They had too much to do.

EPILOGUE

"I NEVER KNEW MAKING these beds was so difficult," Simon admitted, tucking the sheets tight around the corner of the king-size bed and all its special padding, wishing he could crawl into it with Emma and not get out for days. "Do you think I should get rid of them?"

"Nope. There are standards to be upheld at Castle Hotels," Emma said, picking up the large goose-down comforter and heaving it into the middle of the mattress. "You do want repeat business, after all."

"I think next year I'll hire more staff and offer those bonuses in advance of Christmas." Not first thing Christmas morning like this year. Simon had been lucky to get some of the staff to come in.

"We're done with our side of the floor," Mrs. Roberts said, sticking her head into the room. Her smile wasn't as bright as it had been the night before.

"This is the last room on our side." Emma smoothed out the comforter and began plumping up pillows.

Owen and Doc appeared behind her, looking as worn out as Simon felt. Many of the Santa Express workers had driven up to Reno after midnight when their deliveries were done. Simon checked his watch. Between the regular staff and Simon's volunteers, they'd managed to clean all the rooms by noon.

Owen arched his back. "I'd say Christmas dinner—"

"And the beer," Doc was quick to add, although his grin was frayed around the edges.

"—are on you, Castle."

There was a whir in the hallway and Marlene appeared in her wheelchair. "The presidential suite is ready for your guests, Mr. Castle."

"Thank you. Can you escort these gentlemen and Mrs. Roberts to the suite?" Simon looked at Doc, Owen and Mrs. Roberts in turn. "I hope you don't mind sharing the presidential suite. It's the best in the house. We'll have dinner brought up in less than an hour."

"I knew you were a good man the moment I laid eyes on you," Mrs. Roberts said when she was done hugging Simon.

"You turned out all right," Owen allowed as he shook Simon's hand.

"Oh, I almost forgot," Marlene said. "The rat is gone."

"Owen, you didn't…" Emma gave her brother a suspicious look. He'd mentioned something about doing away with the rodent when Emma had explained why it was there.

"I'm too tired to shoot the rat." Owen frowned.

"Don't worry. I called the union rep and told them about the changes." Simon turned his attention to his secretary—the woman he'd been with longer than any other.

"Marlene, did you get in touch with Frank, Richard and Carrie?" He'd instructed Marlene to give his overworked driver, hotel manager and assistant the next two weeks off, as well as notify them of their Christmas bonus. As soon as things were under control here, he'd let Marlene start her two weeks. He'd also called Wallace's mom this morning and promised her a job if she still wanted to work for him.

"I did, sir."

"Please, call me Simon." He met Marlene's gaze squarely, aware of Emma's hand on his shoulder. They'd talked about this on the drive back to Reno. "I was wondering if you wanted to move into my rooms here at the hotel. I'm going to need a bit more privacy now." He glanced back at Emma with a smile. "Everything here is wheelchair friendly, you know, and the staff would be at your command."

Marlene looked flustered. She'd weathered so much with Simon that he could understand her being unwilling to trust him.

"She may want her space, Simon," Emma said softly beside him, trying to give Marlene an out.

"If she does, I'll just have to arrange for her to move. She deserves a better place to live." He'd had Emma drive them by Marlene's place on the way into town. He couldn't imagine a woman in a wheelchair feeling safe in that neighborhood. "Just so we're clear, Marlene, I'm reducing your hours, not increasing them. Although I am giving you a promotion to vice president of operations with a generous raise because I can't get along without you."

"Yes." Marlene released a breath, eyes bright. "Yes, sir…Simon." She put out her hand to shake his, but he leaned closer and hugged her instead. When he straightened, Marlene handed him something. "Your BlackBerry."

"Not on Christmas, Marlene." Simon didn't even glance at the screen. He only had eyes for Emma.

When Marlene had led the others to the elevators, Simon locked the room he and Emma had cleaned. She leaned against the wall across from him, her expression so warm Simon couldn't imagine he'd ever be cold again.

"Thank you," he said.

"For what?"

"For somehow seeing something that no one else—not even me—could see. I'm not sure I'll be able to live up to your expectations." He'd known this amazing woman less than a day, yet he was scared he'd make a mistake and ruin everything.

Emma closed the distance between them, a mischievous shine to her eyes. "Simon, let's make a New Year's resolution to fall in love…and to love each other until there's no Christmas spirit left in this world."

"No Christmas spirit left in the world?" He laughed, opening his arms for her. "That won't happen in our lifetime."

"Exactly."

Dear Reader,

What fun it was to write this book. An expectant mom on a luxurious train, speeding through the snow toward a family Christmas in a cozy Virginia City home. A good man, intent on claiming the woman he still loves—and the child he didn't know about. I loved telling this story.

Of course, I had all the answers. Rachel Ford and Andrew Durham don't even understand the truth about their past as they embark on the Santa Superchief. They can't see a future.

During a night filled with Christmas carols and labor pain—and visitors who remind Andrew and Rachel how fragile family is—they begin to see visions of what could be, if they reach out to each other and dare to believe in the future they want.

Because believing, at Christmas, makes dreams come true.

I'd love to hear what you think. You can reach me at anna@annaadams.net.

Best wishes,

Anna

ALL THE CHRISTMASES TO COME

Anna Adams

First, to the girls on the third floor of Hawkes—
Sarah's other family: Cresta, Julia, Margalena,
Riley, Erin, Laura, Meredith, Nicole and Ali.
While we've been far away, she's had love and
a home with you. How can I ever thank you?

And to Brenda and Melinda—thanks for letting
me spend this Christmas with you. I loved
brainstorming, chatting, writing—and especially
getting to read your stories first. Working
with you has been a holiday!

CHAPTER ONE

DEEP IN RESEARCHING contract law for a legal textbook he was writing, Andrew Durham only realized he wasn't alone when the door to his home office slammed into the bookshelves behind it.

"Andrew, get your ass out of that chair. Rachel's having your baby, and she moved out of her apartment today. Find her or you're going to regret this moment for the rest of your life."

With all the grace of someone who'd been hit over the head with a plank, Andrew spun his chair to face his sister. Temper radiated from Delia's eyebrows to her pink-tipped nails.

"What?" After *Rachel...your baby* he'd lost the thread. "That can't be right. Rachel?"

Having *their* baby?

Delia rushed at him. "Get up. Do something. You two took months to decide you were wrong for each other. You don't have months now." She yanked his arm so hard he fell off the chair. His teeth rattled when he hit the floor, but the bump to his butt cleared his head.

"That's why she left." Last Christmas he'd

proposed—over tinsel and evergreen and Bing Crosby crooning her favorite holiday songs. He'd set the scene after they'd put his daughter, Addie, to bed. He'd balanced on one knee, feeling idiotic but hopeful. Only to watch Rachel back away from the green velvet box that held his grandmother's ring— which he'd saved for the perfect woman.

The perfect woman had asked him how he felt about having another child—their own. Shocked because he'd never kept his feelings secret, he'd explained again that he couldn't start over with all that new-father stuff. He'd met Addie's mother at a conference. Neither of them had mistaken a weekend for a relationship. Nine months later, as unprepared for parenthood as he, she'd literally dumped Addie on his doorstep.

Savage, protective love for his daughter had bowled him over. He'd learned to be a dad despite no god-given paternal instincts. And had abandoned a promising law career to write legal texts from home.

Last Christmas Addie had been five years old. He'd finally begun to breathe again. Starting over with car seats and diapers and vaccines and sleepless nights… Worrying that a simple cold would advance to pneumonia because he didn't know what to do next?

Not even Rachel could convince him that sharing the work and worry as well as the good parts would make it all better and easier.

Enduring an uneasy truce, they'd tried to make things right for a few months, but Rachel wanted what she wanted, and he wouldn't even pretend to be the man to give it to her. They'd loved Addie too much to continue the tension and escalating arguments. Rachel had packed her things and left. At the time, her sudden departure had stunned him. Now he got it. Her pregnancy—with his child—had made escape urgent.

"How'd you find out, Delia?"

"You broke up with her. I didn't. She was my friend, and I stopped by her place to give her a Christmas present. Her apartment's empty, and her car's gone. The landlord said she shipped the car and she's taking some train home to Virginia City." Delia reached to help him up.

"It's called the Santa Superchief. She rode it every holiday with her parents when she was a child." Andrew stood by himself, leaning toward the window over his desk. His office faced the backyard. Addie and her friend Joey came running from the side of the house, peppering each other with the Wiffle balls he used to practice his golf swing.

Christmas in San Diego wasn't exactly snowsuit-and-mitten time. Virginia City would be a lot colder. Would Addie's coat even fit?

"Will you make lunch for the kids?" He started for the door. "And I don't mean order pizza, Delia. We can't wait for that."

"Now is not the time to make fun of my cooking. Where are you going?"

"To find warmer clothes for my daughter." He turned back and yanked his middle desk drawer open, digging inside. "I have Mrs. Ford's phone number somewhere. Rachel's probably planning to stay with her mother."

"The landlord said she's gone for good, you damn idiot."

"Remember not to swear in front of Addie." He hated sounding like a tight ass. Maybe Rachel had thought he was one. She'd left him, left their home without saying a word about a baby.

Delia pushed him toward the door. "I'll find the number. Why'd she go now? The landlord said she'd be lucky to get over the state line before she delivered."

"I guess she was desperate." He couldn't meet his own sister's eyes. "Or maybe it was because the Santa train was a tradition in her family." They'd planned to take Addie as soon as she was old enough to enjoy the two-day trip.

"You should call for a reservation." Delia sounded calmer, her way of trying to comfort him. "Do they let you reserve seats on a train?"

"The best seats on this one go early. I'd be lucky to get Addie and me on it at all."

"You have to try. Forget about calling Rachel's mother. She'll tell Rachel you're coming, and your baby could disappear."

"I thought you were still Rachel's friend."

"I am." Delia's frustration tightened her voice.

"Then what are you saying? She'd never try to hide the baby from me now that I know."

Delia pushed her hands down the skirt of her

dress. "She *has* run away. She left you in May, and she had to have known she was pregnant."

After he'd insisted for months he didn't want another child. "You know how we argued. She believed I wouldn't want the baby—I kept saying I didn't want to start over with more children."

Delia made a *come on* face, but suddenly clenched her fist. "Why didn't I think of this before? Call Rachel. You must still have her cell-phone number?"

"She changed it." After she'd asked him to stop calling. He nodded toward the yard again. "Will you call the kids in?"

"Sure."

He phoned the train line. They still had a couple of coach seats. They'd sold out the compartments months ago. He made two reservations.

Then he grabbed jeans and sweaters for Addie and himself and shoved it all into one large zippered push-bag. He couldn't find Addie's winter coat so he snatched up a pink sweater and a white sweatshirt. She'd fit into the holiday landscape like a plump, pink snow-girl.

Downstairs, Addie and Joey were choking down black-crusted grilled-cheese sandwiches and tomato soup under Delia's fierce prompting. As he came into the kitchen, Addie shoved her bowl away, streaking the counter with red soup.

"What's wrong, Daddy? Aunt Delia's being scary."

"I'm sorry, honey." Delia wiped Addie's chin and then tugged her close. "You have a surprise. Daddy's been getting your things ready."

"Joey, I'm sorry we have to send you home." Andrew interrupted Delia to keep her from saying anything that might raise Addie's hopes about Rachel. The mother of his unborn child might ask him to jump off the train the second she saw them, and Addie'd already mourned her for months. She didn't need any more disappointment.

Delia nodded. "Maybe this little one should stay with me."

He hesitated and faced a truth he'd rather avoid. He didn't want to hurt his daughter, but he'd use her if Rachel gave him no other choice. Rachel had decided he didn't love her, but she'd have a hard time turning her back on Addie twice. He needed time to convince her he'd been trying to protect her, not reject her. Besides, Christmas Eve was only two days away. "I don't want to be away from Addie at Christmas no matter what happens."

"Oh. Yeah." Delia reached for the little boy. "If you're ready, Joey, I'll walk you home."

"Sure. Mom's making cookies." He poked at the burned edge of his sandwich. "She gives them away to the people she works with, but I just beg till she lets me have a couple."

Andrew patted the boy's shoulder. "Excellent plan. Merry Christmas, son. Addie, are you ready? You can finish your sandwich in the car."

She and Joey exchanged a look, and she grabbed a coloring book and crayons from the dresser behind the table. "Let's go."

"Andrew, I have that phone number." Delia passed

him a scrunched-up sheet of paper. "I wonder if you should make it all fair and call?"

He glanced at his watch. Playing fair would be foolish. Besides, the train left in an hour. "Thanks, but we should go. If traffic's bad…" He couldn't miss that train. If he had to race it to each station, he would.

Delia caught him in a quick hug. "I'm so angry with you for—" She stopped. "But I'm so afraid you're going to lose your chance with this one."

"Me, too, and this time it's all my fault. Come on, Addie." He grabbed at his daughter's hand, and she ran to catch up.

"Daddy, what's wrong?" Her uncertain blue eyes melted his heart. "I think you're mad."

"No, bunny." He drew her to his side, smoothing her pale brown hair. "It's like Aunt Delia said. We're leaving for a Christmas surprise, and I don't want to be late."

"Will I like it?"

He tried never to lie to her. "I hope you'll love it, baby, but sometimes you can't be sure until the surprise works out." She'd have a lot to deal with—a new brother or a sister. She already loved Rachel like the only mother she'd ever had.

Why hadn't it been this easy to see another child in their lives last Christmas? A little boy—another girl maybe—who nuzzled her bottle and sucked her thumb with Addie's contentment. He didn't think Addie'd suffered a lot, stuck with him as a single dad, but he was starting to feel helpless again.

How could he make Rachel understand? He'd been

foolish, but now that he knew about the baby, he wanted it as much as he wanted Addie. It was Christmas. He could use a miracle that made Rachel believe.

CHAPTER TWO

"LAST CALL FOR the Santa Superchief. All aboard—
and kiddies, look sharp—we never know if a jolly
old elf will hitch a ride."

The conductor's patter hadn't changed in all these
years. Rachel Ford eyed the gray-haired man in his
ornate blue uniform. Was he the same guy?

Watching him over her shoulder, she kept moving.
If she stopped, she might need the assistance of a crane.
Thirty-eight weeks pregnant, she moved with the lithe-
ness of a beached whale. She pulled her bag, counting
down cars. Perspiration gathered beneath her bangs.

In front of her, a man and woman pulled their
luggage while a girl of maybe three danced on tiptoe
between them. In a red coat too warm for San
Diego, she peered into the train windows to catch
Santa lurking.

Rachel slid her free hand across her belly, far too
heavy with child to feel so hollow. She'd meant to be
on the train early, but she'd had a lot of goodbyes to say.

She'd even driven past Andrew's house one last
time, angry with herself, still pining for him and
Addie. He hadn't loved her. He'd made up that

ridiculous story to get rid of her. What kind of a man—a good father—expected a woman to believe he doubted his ability to be a good father twice?

But why would he lie to her after he'd asked her to marry him? It never added up. Only leaving had made sense.

Addie and Joey hadn't seen her, too engrossed in strafing each other with Wiffle balls. On the verge of giving birth to Addie's baby sister, she'd turned the rental car around and driven to the rail station.

Struggling down the red carpet lined with oversize faux peppermint canes, she tried to soak up some of the happiness around her. She reached her car at last and started climbing the steps, but a conductor grabbed her bag.

"Let me get that for you," said the woman.

"It's heavy," Rachel said, as the handle left her fingers.

"All the more reason. Let me see your ticket." She needed only a swift glance. "Ahh, compartment A. Good—you'll have your own restroom."

Rachel laughed, having paid dearly for that privilege. It already felt like money well-spent. "You've been this pregnant?"

"Twice." The woman held out her hand. "Call me Maggie—and promise you won't go into labor on my train."

Rachel crossed her heart. "If I have anything to say about it." She was heading home to her own mother, who loved her unconditionally—although she insisted Rachel was wrong to hide Andrew's child from him.

Maggie wrestled the bag up the last metal step. A few feet down a narrow, wood-paneled corridor, she opened a compartment door. "Here's your home for the next two days."

Rachel took in plush burgundy velvet and more of the strangely luminous paneling inlaid with pale carved flowers. "Wow—this is more luxurious than my apartment."

"Mine, too," said Maggie. "Now, you're probably wondering about dinner arrangements."

"My first concern."

In the warmth of Maggie's good humor, Rachel found her lost sense of anticipation. Her doctor had argued against moving, but had finally faxed Rachel's records to her doctor in Virginia City with the disgruntled hope that she wouldn't have the baby before she or the records arrived.

The train's outer doors clanged shut, and she jumped. The engine powered up and the train rocked once. Rachel leaned down, desperate for a last glimpse of San Diego. She'd made the right decision, so why did she feel afraid? Guilty, even.

"We won't be moving for a few minutes yet." Maggie peered through the window. "Are you looking for someone? Anybody joining you?"

She shook her head. Her hair brushed her face, and the tickling sensation dragged her back to the real world. Andrew couldn't have been clearer about not wanting children with her.

"I'm moving home, but I've lived here for about seven years, and I'm going to miss the city." The city… Be honest. She ached for the man she still loved—and his daughter—who might have been hers, too, if Andrew hadn't been so afraid of the future. Without him and Addie, staying had become pointless.

No matter how hard she'd tried not to think of them, her life and theirs remained entwined. She rubbed her stomach again. The baby stretched, no doubt wondering where all the space had gone.

As if she sensed Rachel's unspoken heartbreak, Maggie squeezed her arm. "Can I get you anything?"

"No." Rachel turned away, sniffing hard. "Thanks, though."

"The dining car is two down. Turn left out of your door." Maggie crossed the small space and pointed at an ivory-colored button with a glowing red dot in the middle. "This calls me any time. Whatever you need." As Rachel lifted her eyebrows, Maggie grinned. "You've heard that old saw about bartenders being good listeners? They have nothing on train conductors."

"Anything to keep me out of labor?" Rachel asked.

"Well, yeah." Maggie opened the door. "You unpack and I'll come back when dinner's served. You sure I can't bring some herbal tea? Maybe a pack of crackers?"

"I'm way past morning sickness." She leaned against the door as Maggie went into the hall. "I'm not normally such a weakling."

"I'm not normally so understanding and helpful." Maggie went to the next compartment and pressed her finger to her lips. "Don't tell your neighbors."

Grinning, Rachel shut her own door. Her smile faded as she faced herself in the gilded mirror.

"HEY," ANDREW SHOUTED at the conductor who was gripping the train's last open door.

"You're almost too late," the other man said, but he came down the stairs already reaching to help with the bag. He glanced at Andrew's tickets. "Come aboard here. They've shut the doors up ahead. You're just a few cars on, but you can reach it through the corridor." He yanked their bag up the stairs, freeing Andrew to lift Addie. "Have you heard who's traveling with us this trip, miss?"

"Who?" Addie's gaze was almost too serious. "My daddy says this is a Christmas surprise. Are those real peppermint sticks back there?"

"Not those." The conductor eased the door shut behind Andrew. "But someone you're going to like will bring you treats later. I'll put your things away for you, sir. Later, at bedtime, you can get any belongings you need."

"Thanks."

Andrew set Addie down and turned her in front of him just as the train jerked forward and kept rolling.

"We're going, Daddy."

What if Rachel hadn't made it? How comfortable could a train be for a woman so late in pregnancy? He measured all the moments he'd lost, the days and nights his child had been growing inside her.

He'd had a right to know, but he rubbed his mouth

and tried not to feel angry. It wouldn't get him anywhere. Right now, he had to find Rachel.

Addie scuffed her sneaker toe on the plush carpet. "Daddy, this is nice. I thought the train would be all metal like in the movies."

The walls were paneled in wood more expensive than any surface in their house. No wonder even the coach seats had cost so much. "Hold my hand." He steadied her as they entered a new car, but Addie tumbled against an older man's shoulder, and Andrew eased her back, preparing an apology. The man's warm smile startled Andrew.

"Merry Christmas, little girl," he said, clearly more in the grip of the season than Andrew felt.

"Thank you, sir. Same to you."

"What a polite girl. You must be excited about this trip?"

Addie frowned. "Well, I wanna know about the surprise." She swung around to Andrew. "Who's coming, Daddy? Someone I know?"

The man and his wife laughed, but a palpable longing made them serious. "They're that young for so short a time," the man said.

Andrew understood the man's regret. The past six years spun past his memory, the happiness of Addie's unrestrained joy in any colorful toy that caught her fancy, frightening illnesses that worsened with terrifying swiftness in childhood, the first time he'd had to leave her with a babysitter. Doing it all alone, he'd been grateful to survive—continually surprised to find Addie thriving. Maybe he should have managed to live a little more—and appreciate.

How had he fallen into the same situation with another child? He'd been careful with Rachel. So careful he'd driven her away. He obviously had more to regret than the couple gazing with nostalgia on his little girl.

"Merry Christmas," Andrew said and led Addie through another car to their seats.

She scrambled on her knees across burgundy velvet to claim the window. "I like this train." She pounded the fat, luxuriant upholstery. Carolers entered the car from the other end and she sang along in their homage to Rudolph. She hung over the back of the seat until the singers left, and Andrew managed to pull her down beside him. "We're going faster and faster."

And time was speeding past, too. "Are you hungry?" The dining car might be a good place to search for a pregnant woman.

"Remember Aunt Delia gave me that yummy sandwich." She rolled her eyes. "I'm starving."

"Aunt Delia tries." He craned his neck for a conductor. "Wonder when they start serving dinner?"

"Where are we sleeping?" Addie kicked her legs up and down. "Does this turn into a bed?"

"No, but it reclines."

"Huh?"

He showed her. "You think you'll be able to sleep here tonight?"

She hated change and loved her own little bed. "Are you going to make me wear my jammies in front of all these people?" She skewered the young couple across from them with a resentful look.

"No." He hadn't thought this out. He could end up ruining Christmas for his daughter, as well as losing her younger sibling. "We'll just brush our teeth. They'll have blankets." Even airlines still offered blankets.

"Sounds strange." She returned to her window. "I usually sleep in a bed, and I have all my toys. Can I get my baby out of the suitcase?"

"Sure."

"Good, because she doesn't like being in the dark too long." She sat finally and turned to the window.

Andrew took her hand between his. She smiled at him, but her eyes looked wet. "This will be fun, Addie."

"Okay, Daddy, but you'll stay awake?" She sandwiched his hand between hers, barely covering his palm. Then she leaned against him. "I don't know anyone else here."

"I'll take care of you. You'll always be safe with me." He hugged her until she squirmed away.

Addie had been his first concern for six years and now he was risking her peace of mind. He had no choice. If things worked out, Addie would have a sister or brother and her beloved Rachel back, and that was a future worth risking.

CHAPTER THREE

"I CAN BRING YOU A TRAY," Maggie said.

Her offer tempted Rachel. The seat hugged her body, and she felt all warm and cozy. But her doctor had cautioned her to get up and walk often during the trip. "Thanks, but I've got a thing for Santa."

Maggie held the door. "He's started his rounds so you have a shot if you've been good this year."

"Pretty good." She hadn't intended to be bad. Her birth control had gone awry and she'd lied by omission. Of course, Addie niggled at her conscience. Rachel and Andrew had made their own choices—but that meant Addie would never know she had a little sister.

Rachel balanced against a cool, wide window in the hall. "It's getting colder already."

"We're starting into the mountains." Maggie glanced back as they reached the next car door. "That your first baby?"

"Yeah." She'd considered Addie her first for a long while. You only had to watch Addie for a second with other children or with the dolls she loved and nurtured to know she'd be the best big sister in the world.

"Here we are." Maggie opened the dining car door.

Again, the walls glowed, their warmth reflected in crystal and gleaming silver. Rachel eased into a place set with bone china. It should have been fun, a break from her normal life. This year, the holiday train was simply a way home. Kind of a waste, when she spied the happy families around her. "Thanks, Maggie," she said.

"While you're eating a good meal for that baby, I'll make your bed. It's a little early, but you could probably use a few extra hours' rest."

Maggie turned away, and Rachel peered at her own face again, this time in the mercifully blurry window. Grief could make a woman look haggard, and she was mourning Andrew and Addie as if she'd left them today, not seven months ago. She'd secretly hoped Andrew would come after her and be delighted with the baby.

Fool.

The door at the other end of the car opened and a little girl skipped through, her light brown hair swinging in a ponytail. Rachel's breath caught. She looked like… Her grief must be stronger than even she guessed.

"Addie."

She'd wanted to see her, been tempted to climb out of her car and hug the daylights out of her, but was she hallucinating? Beaming, Addie hopped to a table, the small, happy spirit of what this Christmas should have been.

"Wait, sweetie. The waiter will seat us."

That voice. It had whispered love words in her ear and broken her heart.

Andrew and Addie. She wasn't hallucinating.

Andrew was thinner, his face drawn. He caught Addie before she could climb into a chair at the empty table she'd appropriated.

Rachel only realized she was trying to stand when her stomach hit the lip of her table. Addie and Andrew were real. Not spirits. Not what should have been. They'd come.

To find her?

As if the tide of Rachel's hope swept into Addie, she turned. Rachel's whole body clenched at Addie's joy.

"Rachel!" She ran, slipping this way and that, until she fell into Rachel's arms. Her hug was as tight as a noose, but then she hopped backward.

"What's wrong with you?"

Rachel nearly choked on a laugh. She couldn't make herself look up at Andrew so she focused on his daughter's wide eyes.

"I'm—" Would Addie understand? Would Andrew want her to know? "I gained some—"

"Rachel's having a baby," Andrew said.

Rachel read nothing but bleakness in his dark gaze. He'd given up hope. He had to know the baby was his.

"Are you angry?" She forgot Addie for a moment.

"Yeah," he said, "and shocked."

"How can you have a baby, Rachel? You don't have a daddy for it."

"The same way I have you," Andrew said.

"Except she does have a daddy. I'm the daddy for Rachel's baby."

"How? Don't daddies live with their babies?"

"I hope so."

"Not always." Rachel tried again to stand, but Andrew touched her shoulder.

"Please."

His hoarse voice cut straight to the bone. He'd blurted out all the things she wouldn't have dared tell Addie.

He had lied to her last Christmas. He obviously wanted their child.

But her plan hadn't included him. He'd turned his back on her and the family she'd wanted—more than she'd wanted him.

"I can't do this." She gripped the table ledge, creasing the rough tablecloth. "Maybe we can talk later, but right now—" She looked down at her belly, at the baby that would be here before she learned how to handle Andrew.

"Later is too late." His gaze followed hers. "We aren't going to reason with each other. You're carrying my child."

"I don't get it," Addie said. "Are you and Daddy married, Rachel?"

"You know daddies and mommies aren't always married." Andrew's desperate expression admitted this was more complicated than he'd expected.

"Daddy and I are friends." Friends—the last thing she'd ever wanted to call Andrew.

"But I'm going to have a brother."

"Actually, you're having a sister," Rachel said.

"You know?" Normally, the man in control, Andrew sounded as if he couldn't get enough air.

She empathized, reaching for her water glass as the world spun. "Yes."

"Daddy, Rachel and my sister need to come home with us."

"I agree."

"No," Rachel said again.

"I'm asking you to—"

"I know what you're asking." Marriage. In front of Addie? "You didn't want me or—" She stopped. Some things, Addie didn't need to know. She touched her stomach and avoided the pain in Andrew's eyes. She'd hurt him. That much was clear. "It's too late. I don't want you this way."

"No." Andrew lifted Addie into a seat across from Rachel and then took the chair beside her. "It's just in time."

"I have to live with my sister." Addie leaned across the table to take Rachel's hand.

Rachel closed her fingers around Addie's. "Don't worry. You'll always get to see your sister." How, when Addie lived in San Diego, and Rachel planned to stay near her mother in Virginia City?

"I'm the big sister. I have to take care of the new baby." She looked to her father to back her up. "Right, Daddy?"

"Absolutely right." He didn't touch Rachel, but she felt tension in his knees against hers, in his mouth, too tight to ever smile again.

She felt his need for their baby, who was never supposed to be his. "How did you find out?"

"Your landlord told Delia and she told me."

"I should have asked him not to say anything."

"Thank God he sang like a canary."

"That's not funny. I didn't want you to know. In fact, you made it clear you didn't want to know."

"I was wrong. You can see I love Addie more than anything."

More than he'd ever loved the mother of his new child. That was all she needed to know. A woman wanted to be somewhere in her husband's priorities. She wasn't jealous of Addie, but she wanted Andrew to love her as much as his little girl. She deserved that much. "I'm not in trouble," she said. "I want a family, not resignation from a man who finds himself with a familiar problem."

"Neither—" He also stopped, aware of what he shouldn't say in front of his daughter. "No one around here is a problem." Addie straightened, opening her mouth slightly. Andrew turned to see what had snagged her attention, but then leaned toward Rachel. Daring to take cover behind Santa's entrance. "Every argument I made looks foolish now, and I'd take it all back. I want you and the baby. *I* want our family as much as you do."

"Words are easy." She took advantage of Addie's fascination with the man in red, too. "I never believed you—it was too ridiculous." He straightened with wounded eyes, heartrendingly like Addie. "You'd never have tried to see me again if I weren't pregnant."

"Because I didn't want to hurt you," he said. "You wanted a life I didn't think I could give you. The baby changes everything."

"You can be a good father without marrying—"

"Daddy, he's here. Turn around. He's got candy in his pockets."

Rachel fought her own body's awkwardness, trying to stand as Andrew turned to Santa. She finally found her feet, intent on getting out of there even if she had to wrestle Santa for wiggle room.

"Wait." Andrew grabbed her arm. "I'm asking you to marry me."

"I noticed," she said, as her way out narrowed even more. "You don't want to be caught in a custody fight."

"I have rights." He didn't even try to pretend she mattered.

"Nice." She let bitterness into her tone. "Don't threaten me."

"What?" As if he didn't understand.

"You aren't taking my child and you'd better believe I'll never walk away." Without volition, her glance slid toward Addie, whose mother had done just that.

Andrew let her go and she felt chilled—because of his coldness. "You know me better than that," he said.

"You made up a crazy story to get rid of me."

"I asked you to marry me. How can that mean I didn't want you?"

"How could you not be a good father the second time around? You're great with Addie."

"I must be better than I thought if you can't see how scared I am that I'm screwing her up." He lowered his voice, as Addie glanced back, but she was only checking to see if they'd noticed Santa. "I'm sorry, Rachel. I was wrong. I even brought Addie and told her about the baby. That must show you I'm serious."

"Only if you're trying to convince me you'd use one of your children to blackmail the mother of another."

As soon as Santa made room, she eased past him—and he plugged the hole between Andrew and the aisle as he handed Addie a candy cane.

CHAPTER FOUR

THE DOCTOR HAD TOLD HER to walk the aisles. A few hours later, Rachel followed his prescription—just to keep her circulation active.

She also searched each face in the coach section, but she'd never admit she was looking for Addie and Andrew. It was too late to trust his change of heart. He harbored no secret love for her. He wanted his child, exactly as he wanted Addie.

In the fourth compartment behind hers, she found them. She grasped a seat back, watching Addie twist for comfort, a frown lining the soft skin between her closed eyes. She rolled toward Andrew, her hair standing on end as she lifted her head.

"I can't sleep, Da—" She saw Rachel. "There you are." She dove over the edge of her seat. Andrew looked up, too startled to stop her. Addie reemerged, brandishing a jewel-toned candy cane. "Santa gave me this for you, Rachel."

"Thank you." She had to go closer, to take the candy. "Did you ask for an extra?"

"Yes, because you like candy canes."

"I'll sure keep this one." She held it with both hands, close to her heart.

"You have to eat it before it 'spires."

"What are you doing here, Rachel?"

Not much of a welcome in Andrew's abruptness.

"Rachel?" he said again.

"I don't know."

He leaned toward her.

She clutched the candy cane even closer. And she latched on to the one excuse Andrew wouldn't question. "Addie," she said. "I wondered if Addie was sleeping well."

"How did you know where we were?"

She'd hoped to see them. If they'd been in a compartment, she'd have wandered—searched—the length of the train and gone back to her own bed. "You couldn't have bought your tickets as early as I did."

"I'm very tired, Rachel, and I can't sleep." Addie gave her father a stern look. "I need a bed."

"I have one." And she must be out of her mind, subjecting herself to the grief of saying goodbye to Addie again. Because she'd have to. "There are two in my compartment. Like bunk beds. Could you sleep on a top bunk, Addie?"

"Can I, Daddy?" Addie was dangling off the end of her seat again. She rose with a well-loved doll, one with brown matted hair and painted brown eyes, half kissed off her face.

"I recognize her." She'd given the doll to Addie last Christmas.

"This is Rachel." Addie held her up with pride, like any mother. "Rachel, meet Rachel. You can kiss her," Addie said.

Rachel kissed her namesake because otherwise she would have had to swallow a lump the size of Mount Everest and find words. The doll hadn't shared her name before she'd left Andrew and Addie.

"Are you sure about sharing your room with Addie?" Andrew asked. "I don't want you tiring yourself, and my girl is a Chatty Cathy at bedtime."

"Specially in a strange bed." Addie had clearly heard about her failing before.

Andrew ruffled her hair. "Have you been standing on your head? Your hair's starting to look like your dolly's."

"Can I go?" She started clambering over him and he grabbed at her as her hands and feet dug into him.

"Wait," he said. "We have to talk."

"We'll talk in the morning." Why dither? She had a chance to spend unexpected time with Addie, and those minutes were growing shorter as the train rushed toward Virginia City. "Day after tomorrow, you're going back to San Diego. I'd like to share the compartment with her."

He knew this was her last goodbye. His face went blank. His usual defense when emotion threatened. For a second, she wondered...

Not for long.

"Let's get your things, Addie. Have you brushed your teeth?"

Her enthusiastic nod should have rattled the teeth right out of her head. Rachel took Addie's hands and helped her the rest of the way over her father.

"Kiss Daddy good night, and we'll put your Rachel to bed."

Addie wrapped an arm around her father's neck. He kissed her, but he never looked away from Rachel. He had a right to be confused. She couldn't explain her own behavior because she couldn't forget days and nights filled with wondering what they were doing, how much Addie had grown, whether Andrew thought of her once in a while, too.

The baby kicked suddenly as if reminding her she had more serious problems now.

"Meet me for breakfast," Andrew said.

"What time, Daddy?"

He turned his watch over and grimaced. "It's almost three in the morning. Let's say around ten."

"Will they still be serving breakfast at ten?" Rachel asked, not trying to evade him. "I wouldn't want Addie to miss eating."

"I'll probably be awake and I'll come get you if they're going to stop earlier."

Letting awkward seconds pass, Rachel nodded and turned Addie toward her own compartment. Maggie was in the hall.

"Would you mind lowering the other bed?" Rachel asked. "I'm having company."

"Sure." She smiled at Addie with the wistfulness of a mom who missed her own children and then made up the other bunk as if she'd been dying to work in the middle of the night. Rachel thanked her, and Addie echoed her, sounding sleepier by the second.

"I'll probably stay awake," the little girl said after Maggie shut their compartment door.

"Probably." Rachel helped her into bed and gave the other Rachel's slightly dirty face another swift kiss. She tucked Addie's blanket up to her chin. "Sleep well, sweetie."

"I can't." Her eyes were already closing. "You'll be here in the morning?"

"Absolutely." She wished she could promise to be there all the mornings of Addie and Andrew's lives. She cradled her big belly in her own arms. She couldn't promise anyone what the future held.

She'd never understood how leaving could hurt so much when leaving had been the only answer. Familiar loneliness bore down on her again, at higher speeds than the train was going.

A MAN WITH ANY SELF-RESPECT wouldn't show up half an hour before he was due to meet a woman, but Andrew couldn't afford self-respect. How could he explain how much he'd missed Rachel, how he'd refused to let himself think of her because the smallest memories of her—always a little wind-blown, always laughing—had made him want to crawl to her?

Talk about a jackass. He still loved the woman whose love he'd killed. Lurking outside the dining car, he kept glancing at his watch. His situation was too dire for a trick, too important to trust mere honesty to save him. Rachel seemed to believe only their unborn child had brought him to this train.

"Daddy, Rachel's room is better than our chairs."

Thank God. Addie was dragging Rachel toward him. Rachel, who rocked from side to side with the movement of the train and her unaccustomed girth.

"Did you sleep well?" He took her hand. He could pretend he wanted to steady her, but he needed the touch of her skin.

"I'm fine," she said.

"Won't you let me help you?"

Her steady gaze was answer enough.

"Help me, Daddy. Hold me up so I can see what's on that table. I'm starving."

He lifted Addie so she could see the buffet of fruit and bagels and croissants. She stretched. "I don't see eggs."

"Maybe you can ask for them." Rachel's love-rich voice shortened Andrew's breath.

He studied her face, which was thinner, more delicately honed by impending motherhood. Her smile for Addie revealed her weakness. She might despise him, but her feelings for his daughter had only deepened.

Their turn came to be seated. Addie hovered over her chair. "Can I go look at the food, Daddy?"

He could use a moment with Rachel. "Don't touch anything."

"I'll put my hands behind my back."

Rachel laughed. That had been their answer to Addie's compulsion to touch every object she came near. Since birth, his tactile daughter had been fascinated with textures, which often caused trouble in bakeries or clothing stores they visited after a bakery.

"Should you let her go that far away by herself?"

"I'd reach her if she needed me."

Rachel faced him. "I know that about you."

"But you don't think I'd do the same for you."

"You want to help. You want your child now that it's real and not a nebulous possibility."

"I was wrong, Rachel." He cut to the chase. "I still get terrified every time Addie has the sniffles, and I'd rather be vaccinated myself than see her go through it. I don't find diaper changing cute and car seats are an enigma wrapped in a mystery, but I'll do it all again. I want to do it all again. With you and this child." He reached for her, but she turned away.

Her skin flushed.

He gripped the table to keep from slamming his fist onto it. "You don't want me to touch you. Your first instinct is to keep my child away from me."

"I know I can't do that." She turned to make sure Addie was out of earshot. Still she lowered her voice. "Now that you know, I won't oppose visitation. I want Addie to know her sister."

Her troubled gaze searched his face. At last, he saw a hint of doubt. He waited, afraid to ask if she was thinking of giving him a second chance—if she could still want a family with him.

"I haven't changed. I want a husband who adores me *and* cherishes our child."

"What if that's me?" he asked.

She considered, but then she spurned him with a shake of her head. "If you loved me, you'd say so. You wouldn't ask if I thought you could."

CHAPTER FIVE

"ARE YOU MAD AT DADDY?"

"No, honey." Rachel tried to settle Addie and her doll in bed that night, but Addie wriggled to a sitting position, baby Rachel clutched in an over-affectionate hug.

"Why wouldn't he let me come see you all day?"

"You're here now." And Rachel had to wonder if Andrew had deliberately kept Addie with him to leave her alone with traitorous thoughts.

"Because I made too much noise for the man in the seat across from Daddy. He kept staring at me, looking mean until Daddy said I could sleep here again."

He'd dropped her off and said good night, questions in his eyes, rejection in the stern set of his shoulders.

"I'm glad we get another sleepover." Letting Addie go after this would be fresh torture. No woman should have to give up an almost-daughter twice. She should hate Andrew for that alone.

"You like my daddy?"

Sort of. Not often. "Sure I like him." Rachel forced a smile that felt more like rictus. "Now you and little Rachel get some sleep. Do you want me to read you a story?"

"And sing me a song. I like Christmas songs right now."

"We'll try some more Rudolph."

It took the exploits of Rudolph, Frosty and the mean Mr. Grinch before Addie nodded off with a bit of baby Rachel's hair in her mouth. Rachel considered pulling it out, but decided against possibly waking her roomie.

A knock at the door startled her. She snatched it open, not altogether stunned to find Andrew on the other side. He glanced over her shoulder. "Is Addie awake?"

"She just fell asleep."

When he looked at her with widened eyes, she remembered Addie had been playing with her hair while she sang.

"You had to wrestle her into her bunk?" he asked.

She tilted her head, trying not to smile, pretending he only irritated her. Without Addie as their buffer, she was more aware of him. The spice that scented his skin, his still unfaded tan from taking Addie to their community pool. Those crinkly lines beside his eyes had seduced her more than once.

She pulled back. No more seduction.

"Wait." Andrew caught her wrist.

She wanted to resent his touch. Instead, she imagined him sliding his hands down her back, pulling her into the heat of his body.

And she grew weak. Take advantage of a man's guilt just to appease loneliness that had stalked her with memories of him? Not a chance.

"Good night, Andrew."

"Come out here. Talk to me."

She shook her head. "We've said everything."

"Let's talk about the future."

With one hand on her stomach, she reached for the door handle. "I know my future."

His mouth opened. She almost felt the breath easing between his slightly parted lips.

His pain should have pleased her. She'd wanted him to hurt as she did. She'd thought she wanted to hurt him.

"I'm sorry." For what? "I mean I don't want you to feel bad, but think how bad we'll both feel if we get married and then you find the woman you want to share your life with."

"You are that woman." But he'd told her too many times that he didn't want the children—the family—she yearned for.

"I'm smarter than you," she said, "about this anyway. You kept saying you couldn't be with me because I wanted children and Addie was enough for you."

He pulled the door shut, in case Addie should hear.

"What you meant was, you didn't want those things with me. You love family. You're going to find the woman who makes you want more."

"We have a family." He pulled her close, actually smiling as her belly bumped him. "You and I were raising Addie. Believe me when I tell you I was an ass, and I pushed you away when I should have been on my knees, begging you to stay."

"Make me believe you." He looked blank, and she shook her head, shrugging at the same time.

"That's the problem. You can't, and I can't stop be-lieving all you want is this baby."

The baby seemed to be lulled by train travel. After a relatively quiet day and a half, she stretched—or something that made Rachel's stomach tighten as if she'd stumbled into a python—and then the protest kicks started scrambling her organs.

It was like carrying a goalie who was practicing for a big game. She supported her stomach with both hands. Andrew looked down.

"What?"

"Hard kicks." Focused on her body, she managed a grin. "Trying to find more room to stretch, I guess."

"Are you sure you're all right?"

"I have about two more weeks." The baby settled back down. "Maybe I should have waited, but I've gone through this whole thing alone. I was even afraid to tell my mother at first."

"She must love me."

"More than me, I'd say." Her ears still rang with the constant admonitions. "From the moment I told her, she said you had a right to know."

"You should have listened."

His voice was low and husky. She had to be using up his store of restraint, but he'd left her no choices.

"I thought this baby was going to be mine alone." She inhaled, so aware of Addie, asleep in her compart-ment. "This may be the worst time to discuss what you want, but I'd just as soon have it out of the way."

"I want my child."

Not the woman carrying his baby. Just his child.

"That goes without saying." Paranoia gripped her. "But you'll have to deal with a mother this time."

"Rachel, do I have to tell you you're hurting me? Do you know how many times, in the middle of the night, I wonder how Addie's managed to survive? If you think doing it alone makes it easier, you have a rude shock coming."

"The past nine months have been filled with rude shocks."

"All nothing compared to what comes next."

Andrew's parents had divorced when he was two. His mother had tried to be a good parent, but she still seemed perpetually bewildered by the turn her life had taken. His father had "graduated" from most of the rehab clinics on the California coast. Andrew had hardly seen him since Addie's birth because he didn't trust the man, and he didn't want his daughter picking up any bad habits.

"I don't know how much nurturing we learn from our parents." Her mother was equipped with lioness instincts. "But Addie is strong and happy. I hope our child is as healthy and well-adjusted. Especially now."

Down the corridor, the door opened and Santa weaved toward them. He held out his hand to Rachel. She'd grown used to strangers being affectionate with a mom-to-be so she shook his hand.

"Your little girl made quite a bargain for that extra candy cane."

"Did she?"

"I love kids like her. She told me not to bother bringing her minioven because you might believe in me if I gave you the candy." He laughed with Santa-gusto. "She reminded me what Christmas is supposed to be. That's why I take this job."

"Does your family mind spending Christmas on the train?" Surely he didn't leave them home over the holiday.

"My wife left me several years ago," he said, sobering. "The kids are all grown. I get back a little Christmas every year on this train." He looked past them. "Maggie, girl, I have stockings for your two."

Maggie, who'd appeared out of nowhere, went with Santa after a careful glance at Rachel.

Andrew came close enough for her to feel his heat in the cooling space. "Why do you hope especially now that the baby will be well-adjusted?"

"She'll be living part-time with you and part-time with me." She'd rather her daughter—and Addie—had a conventional, Mom-and-Dad family.

"We have to talk about you living in Virginia City," Andrew said.

And so it started. But she recognized the bravado behind his arrogance, so she tried to be gentle. "That decision's made. I want to live near my mother."

The baby stretched again. She caught her breath and flexed one hand against her compartment door. Outside flashed a landscape of time-honed mountain and flying snow.

"What? Rachel, what's wrong?" Andrew looked her up and down as he would a firework that might go off without warning.

"This kid must be stretching from head to toe."

Andrew's anxiety was contagious. "But I'm not going to explode." She touched his shoulder. Pressing her palm against his hard muscle felt strange and yet painfully familiar. "The baby's fine."

He moved and her hand hung in midair until she flattened it on her stomach, as if she didn't feel rejected.

Andrew fiddled with the drape that half covered the window. "You don't believe I could want you back?" Anger seeped into his eyes and curled his fingers. "Even though I never wanted you to leave?"

"I don't come to your mind first. You're here because of this baby."

Turning from the window, he faced her again. "I thought I wasn't right for you. I've had luck with Addie. I wouldn't have tempted fate again, but if you could have settled for me and my daughter I never would have let you leave."

"It wouldn't have been settling."

She was lying and they both knew she'd wanted her own babies that badly. She looked away first, feigning interest in the frozen night. Though every inch of the train exemplified luxury, a hint of must drifted off the curtains. "Pregnancy plays up your sense of—" Again, her stomach tightened, but this time, pain radiated from the small of her back. "Oh, God."

"Rachel?" He caught the fist she tried to press into the base of her spine. "Are you—"

"I'm wondering. It hurts." It really hurt—a cramp in her back and then something more than tightness across her stomach. A contraction. "It might be one of that false kind."

"False kind?" He held on as if he could save her with his strength.

"You know—Braxton-something."

After a moment, he smiled—probably despite himself. "You know less than I do. Braxton-Hicks, Rachel. You didn't read a book?"

"Several, but I can't remember everything when I'm about to give birth on a train." She grinned, a little queasy. "You know they'll charge me extra for leaving with a new passenger."

"You make it worse when you try to joke. So do me a favor and don't until we know you're safe." He maneuvered her toward her door. "Let me get you inside and then find a doctor."

"No." She pulled his hand off the doorknob as he tried to open it. "Addie."

"Addie will have to adapt," he said.

"Find the doctor first. Let her sleep a little longer."

He wanted to argue. She saw it in the vein that had risen at his temple. Instead, he let her go, and she could have sworn he said something under his breath as he turned away.

"Wait."

He stopped. "I need to get you help."

She hated being beholden to him of all people. "There's a button near the bed with a red light. If you press it, the conductor will come. But don't wake Addie."

"If I do, I'll tell her I came to say good night."

"Okay." The threat of another—whatever it was— persuaded her. "But try not to wake her."

"Sure." How could he make that one word imply she'd lost her mind?

He slipped inside and a second later came out again. A few minutes passed like several hours with Andrew watching her.

Maggie returned, surprise arching her eyebrows. She realized right away what was going on. "Rachel, you promised."

"We could be wrong. Neither of us is very experienced."

Maggie nudged Andrew with a smile. "You and I may have plenty of time to discuss that, considering your little girl. For now, I happen to know we have a doctor two cars down. He'll be so excited when I put him to work."

She made her way down the train, leaving calm behind her.

"He'll check you out and tell me to get off your back and let you sleep," Andrew said.

As a new pain started, Rachel tried to keep a straight face—and prayed Andrew was right.

CHAPTER SIX

"WE MIGHT AS WELL WAKE that little girl of yours," said the man who'd introduced himself as Dr. Tinsley. "She may be learning a lot about life tonight." He checked Rachel's pulse. "I can't tell where we are without an exam, but this young woman looks like most others I've seen who are about to deliver a baby."

"Don't say that," Rachel said.

"I've heard women stop being rational in labor."

"Andrew, you may think saying that in a dry tone makes it less insulting. It's not."

"We can stand in the hall and count contractions half the night, or I can carry Addie out here and let Dr. Tinsley find out what's going on with you. But only one of those options is sane."

Dr. Tinsley folded his arms. "My wife will come looking for me if I stay for contraction counting, and she doesn't like having her Christmas interrupted."

Another pain gripped Rachel. "I'm not afraid of any mere woman. Aliens," she said, rubbing her taut belly, "now they scare me."

"You're not carrying an alien. You're just afraid. What's your name again?"

Andrew actually groaned. The doctor looked at him, light from the fixture above his head glinting in his sliver hair. "I'm bad with names, but great at delivering babies. I'll give you a list of satisfied clients."

"Sorry." Andrew took the situation into his own hands and opened the door. "Addie, time to wake up a little, sweetie."

Rachel held on to the doorjamb. In a moment, Andrew returned, his daughter lolling in his arms. "I'll wait right here," he whispered.

And it mattered. Now that the moment presented itself, she didn't want to deliver alone. "I'm supposed to be tough," she said. "Women on this very ground delivered their babies and then skinned a rabbit if they were lucky enough to find one."

Andrew paled. "Skinned a rabbit?" He tucked Addie's head beneath his chin. "Are you okay?" He turned to Dr. Tinsley. "What's happening to her?"

"You're both overreacting." He nodded at Addie, still asleep. "You're having another baby, not a national emergency. Come along before your daughter wakes up, and then we're all in trouble."

Her mouth was so dry her tongue no longer fit. Rachel drank in the sight of Addie, her soft face even more delicate against Andrew's sweater. "Whether I wanted to share the birth of our child with you or not, we're in it together now."

He dared to look relieved.

"Now changes nothing," she said. "When this train reaches Virginia City, I'm putting—" She lowered her harsh whisper because she didn't want

Addie to hear or think she didn't still long to live with her. "I'm putting you on a plane to San Diego."

THE SECONDS TRUDGED like centuries as Andrew rocked Addie with the motion of the train. At last Rachel's compartment door opened and Dr. Tinsley looked a touch more serious.

"She is in labor," he said. "Why don't we take your daughter to my wife? We're on this train to take her mind off the fact that our grandchildren are in Paris for Christmas. She'd welcome your little—"

Please God, let him be better at his job than he was at remembering names. "Addie," Andrew said, "and don't take this badly, but I don't know you or your wife. I'm a little reluctant to hand my daughter over to—"

"I've never had to try so hard to do anyone a favor." Dr. Tinsley wrapped his stethoscope around his neck with enough annoyance to make himself wince. "I have to tell the conductor what's going on, and I'll ask her to move my wife as close to this car as she can."

"Thanks. It's not as if I don't feel like an idiot." He pressed his chin to Addie's head. "But she's my daughter."

Tinsley's face softened. "Come with me. The sooner we get back, the sooner you can join your wife. She's going to want your company soon."

"Soon?" Andrew turned down the hall, unable to avoid looking back at Rachel's closed door. He ought to tell the doctor how things really stood, but they'd already given the man enough trouble.

"She's only had a few contractions, but she's dilating quickly. Let's find the conductor and my wife."

After they explained to Mrs. Tinsley, she looked at Andrew as if he were Santa bearing the gift of a child she could care for. Maggie moved the doctor's wife and Addie into the seats closest to Rachel's compartment. With Addie settled, complaining in her sleep, Andrew returned to Rachel. Tinsley and Maggie were discussing what they'd need.

Andrew knocked on the door, breathing hard.

"Come in."

His hands were sweating. He rubbed his palms together and opened the door.

"You're back." Perspiration beading on her forehead, Rachel rose from her slump on the seat. She caught his hands, and the fear in her grip dissipated his. He pulled her close.

"Shouldn't we stop this thing and get you to the nearest hospital?" He breathed her scent off the top of her head. He'd missed her so much that even now, holding her almost made him forget....

"Dr. Tinsley says it's probably quicker to get to Virginia City. There's not much between here and there." She wrapped her arms around Andrew's waist. "I *am* okay, and he doesn't mind giving up his last night on the train to help me. I trust him even if he is a little bossy." Linking her hands behind his nape, she pulled herself close again.

He leaned over her, realizing she was having another contraction. "Funny how you trust that guy right away."

"I kind of have to."

"Are you positive? You're comfortable with him, Rachel?"

"I've forgotten what comfortable feels like."

"Another one already? Maybe you should sit down?"

"Dr. Tinsley said it was going to happen fast. I'm not sure I'm ready to be a mom. You don't think I caused this, leaving so late in my pregnancy?"

"Maybe seeing me caused it." He hugged her. It took this to make them talk as they had before, like friends, lovers, about-to-be parents. "Babies come when they're ready. We'll be ready, too. I learned to be ready for Addie."

"She's going to make the best big sister." Rachel pulled away, but when she looked at him, he couldn't read her feelings. "When you all visit the new baby."

He let it go. "Why don't you sit down? Try to relax."

Another knock at the door preceded Maggie and Dr. Tinsley. The other woman planted her hands on her hips.

"So I really can't trust you." Maggie eased Rachel to one side. "Let me open your bed. Do you want some ice chips? The doctor tells me that's all you can have. Nothing else to drink or eat."

"I'm fine."

"You all step outside so I have room to work, and we'll be all set."

"I'm just going to have another word with my wife," Dr. Tinsley said. "She didn't plan on a working Christmas."

Andrew watched him hurry along the thick carpet.

"She won't mind. She all but thanked me for letting her watch Addie. Have you noticed how many people are on this train because they miss their families?"

"It was always like that. There were always older people traveling without children, but I never noticed it before."

"I guess it's one way to celebrate Christmas with children around." He might never be sure he was the best father Addie could have, but he sure counted on every Christmas with her. He dreaded the day she claimed her independence, even though a healthy childhood would train her to do that.

Rachel held the door, her fingers trembling against the heavily lacquered wood.

"Try not to be afraid," he said. "I'll be with you."

She stared hard, but he didn't want her to read his unsettled mind. At last, she relented. "It hurts already, and I have a feeling it'll get worse before it's better."

"If I could do it for you, I would."

She tried to hide a smile. She had the right to laugh.

"I'm not trying to be smarmy. I let you down, and I wish I could make it up." Words stuck in his throat. "You can believe in me."

"I have to now."

Her tart humor seduced him. She braced herself in the doorway and endured another contraction with her eyes slitted and her body hunched.

He wanted to twist the train like the toy it resembled. Something. He had to do something. Helplessness made him turn away. Being afraid now felt sensible.

"You don't have to have a plan for every

contingency." Her voice came through gritted teeth. "Neither of us expected this."

"The baby?"

She straightened with tears starting in her eyes. He'd never seen Rachel cry because of pain. Once, when she'd come upon a guy hitting his dog in the park, she'd boiled over with rage and she hadn't even noticed she was crying. She'd all but demanded the guy hand his dog over to her as she'd love it instead of trying to beat it into submission.

"I know you didn't get pregnant on purpose. I thought you might have meant going into labor on the train." Where had that doctor gone?

"I jumped to conclusions." Rachel grabbed her stomach. "I think the baby has decided to break out the hard way."

"Any way at all looks hard to me."

Rachel's mouth opened slightly. Her moist lips caused him an untimely jolt of desire. He tried to hide it, but she laughed and he wanted more than anything to hold her.

Behind her, the door opened and Maggie ushered them in. God, for an ambulance.

"Do you want to change clothes?" Maggie asked Rachel.

Andrew cursed himself for not thinking of it.

"I have a nightshirt," Rachel said.

"Put it on, then. I have a list of things to collect for Dr. Tinsley."

Andrew left the small compartment on Maggie's heels.

"Andrew," Rachel said, her voice tight with pain. "Don't go."

He froze. All these months without her and now she wanted him to help her change?

She coughed, but he saw the fear she was trying to conceal. "I don't want to be alone."

"Okay."

"Keep your back turned, though. I don't want you to see me this way."

"You've never understood the first thing about me." As if he wouldn't find her body, swollen from carrying his child, attractive.

"I believe you now, about being afraid. It doesn't change our situation, but I believe it could make you do crazy things." A sudden sound he didn't recognize nevertheless punctuated her declaration cum warning. "Oh, God. My water just broke."

He had to help her.

"No." A zipper opened and more rustling mingled with Rachel's soft groan. He tensed, but she must have noticed his involuntary movement. "Don't, Andrew."

"I can't let you suffer."

"It'll be worth it in a few hours. I won't have any dignity left, but maybe I won't care once I hold my baby."

He turned then, in time to see the well-worn, blue-striped, white nightshirt drift over her swollen belly, her slender thighs, her cold-looking knees. His throat locked. If she believed he'd been terrified of starting over, he had a chance to convince her he'd been an idiot and knew better now. "*Our* baby."

"Take on your half of what I'm feeling now, and I'll be impressed."

She eased onto the bed, her face as pale as the sheet beneath her.

"Let me get that damn doctor back here."

CHAPTER SEVEN

"AM I GOING TO DIE?" Only half joking, Rachel grabbed Dr. Tinsley's arm. With the grin of a man who'd heard it all before, he removed her clawlike grip and patted her shoulder.

"You may wish you would, but no. In about an hour or so, you're going to give birth. What a way to start Christmas Eve, huh?"

She tried to agree. Over his shoulder, she saw Andrew, ashen-faced, also trying to smile. No matter how glad she was to have him with her in this torture chamber, telling him so would have made her too vulnerable. "Don't you dare faint," she said, when what she meant was "Don't leave me. I'm scared."

He flexed his hands, and only then did she realize what an iron grasp he'd taken on her small sink. "I'm fine," he said. "Until you start screaming again."

Offering the doctor even a veiled apology was easier than letting Andrew know how much she needed him. "I guess I was counting on that epidural."

"I can't believe your regular physician advised you to take this trip," Dr. Tinsley said.

She was in the mood to blame someone else, but honesty prevailed. "He argued."

"A sometimes pointless exercise with heavily pregnant mothers."

"Like you, he was a touch patronizing, and he couldn't understand how much I needed to be with my own mom."

She inhaled. *Breathe through the pain.* Ridiculous concept. But it took concentration and maybe stopped women from going for the throat of any male within reach.

Dr. Tinsley grinned and rolled down his sleeves. "Won't be long now. Let me check with Maggie on a few things." He clasped Andrew's shoulder as he passed. "And I'll look in on your little girl, too." He shot Rachel one more look. "Try to focus on the reward of holding your baby."

"Thanks," Andrew said.

She hated him for a moment. He lowered himself to the side of her bed. "I was right, you know," he said, his irony a clear attempt to comfort her. "Watching you in labor is the most horrific thing I've ever seen. When does all the beautiful stuff start?"

She laughed as much as she was able. "Weakling. You should try it from this side."

"I'd rather." He stood and strode two steps that took him to the window. "I hate having no control."

Which explained why he'd been so afraid of having another child. A lifetime, out of control, stretched ahead of her.

"What if I'm bad at being a mom?" She

clenched the sheet in her hands. "What if this kid grows up to steal lunch money from her class-mates and starts knocking over banks instead of going to college?"

"Nothing like high hopes, Rachel." He came back. His thighs brushed her leg and she tried to move away from him. He noticed with a pointed look, but said nothing. "I'll help you," he said. Saying yes would be so easy. "And Addie will be a great big sister. She'll whip this child into shape if you and I screw up."

"I can't afford to believe you want to stick around."

Frustration rippled across his face. "Even if you never want to see me again, we are about to start raising a child together."

Another pain, impossible to ignore, ended the con-versation. She reached for his hand, unwilling to need him, unable to deny herself the comfort of his touch.

"Any human would do right now," she said.

"I know." His nod might have hidden laughter or anger. She couldn't tell which.

SOON, RACHEL HURT TOO MUCH to snap at Andrew anymore. He missed it. He hadn't been around for Addie's birth, but Rachel's labor looked like a slow march to death.

The more she suffered, the quieter she grew. With her bottom teeth putting a dent into her upper lip, she was pale and wide-eyed and too damn strong for any woman's good.

"Scream again, Rachel. Swear and hate me."

She lifted tired eyes that only made him want to

protect her more. "I'm doing all that in silence, believe me." Another pain erased her shaky smile. "I think something's different."

"What?"

"I don't know. It feels different. You'd better get the doctor."

"I don't want to leave you—"

"Go." She put some hatred into the word. He grabbed the compartment door, trying not to see his own shaking hand.

The older man had gone for a break and a tall glass of ice water Andrew envied as he found him with his wife and Addie. Andrew wiped his own dry mouth and laid his hand on Addie's small shoulder. "She says something's different."

The doctor didn't move, but Addie wrapped her arms around Andrew's waist. "I wanna see Rachel."

"In a little while, honey." Andrew hugged her and handed her back to the doctor's wife—all the while trying not to snatch Rachel's only port in this Christmas-train storm from his comfortable seat.

The doctor set his glass on the table between his seat and the one his wife was sharing with Addie. "I guess she might be ready to push."

Andrew felt the world tilt. What he knew about childbirth, they'd already surpassed, but pushing, he got. "Are you coming?" He must have asked it in a harsh tone. Three heads swerved his way. He tried to smile. "Now?" he asked.

"Let's go together." The doctor actually took his arm as if he needed assistance. "You know, women have been doing this for some time. Be careful or you'll scare your daughter."

"Our child is coming into the world on a train. Rachel's had no medication, and she looks like she's dying. Who knows how sanitary this place is?"

"Let's not borrow trouble."

"I won't let anything happen to her or the baby." What he meant was "Please don't let anything happen to the woman I love and the baby we've made together."

The doctor stopped. "They'll be fine. An ambulance is meeting us in Virginia City, and we'll be there in just a few hours."

"Not soon enough." He was the one who'd been too late. He could only pray Rachel would let him back into her life so that he could handle some more diapers and car seats and those damn inoculations.

"I WAS JUST LUCKY DR. TINSLEY was on the train, Maggie." After hours in pain, the lack of it left her exhausted, able only to stare with wonder and unbelievable, unending love at her own daughter, suckling at her breast.

"He rides this train every year." Maggie fluffed another pillow and eased it beneath the baby and Rachel's bent arm. "Your little sweet-pie isn't the first he's delivered."

"Kind of a Christmas tradition, then?"

Maggie smiled, but then tucked her hand around the baby's head. "I'd say she's one of a kind, wouldn't you?"

Rachel could only nod, too full of awe to answer. She felt small beside this much love. "Grace was worth it."

"Even having her father along?"

Honesty overtook Rachel. "I couldn't have done it without him. He was brave for me, and he let me be cranky when I had to be."

"That's all a man can do when his baby's coming." Maggie scooted the pillow to a more secure position. "Unless you're lucky enough to marry an OB. That'd be the smart thing."

Rachel laughed. The baby jumped and then settled again, finding comfort that astounded her mother. "Who knew I'd be comforting to anyone?" She didn't need an answer. Her ready bond with her daughter, a connection that deepened and warmed with each passing second, answered every question.

"Now that you're both clean and tidy, can I let Andrew and Addie in?" Maggie took the door handle. "The second I open this, they'll fall inside anyway so you might as well say yes."

"Yes." Rachel didn't know what came next— other than letting Andrew see his daughter. That part frightened her—sharing her baby with a long-distance father, but Addie… She couldn't wait to show off the baby to Addie—and vice versa.

Maggie opened the door to an empty hallway.

Rachel stared. Maggie lifted both eyebrows. "That's odd. I thought they'd be figuring ways to get the thing off its hinges."

"It's heartbreaking." She tried not to mind, but her

hormones must be freaking. She wanted to cry. Trust Andrew to put distance between them now.

Maggie stepped into the hall, but then came back. She looked so uncertain, Rachel felt concerned.

"You asked Santa why he rides this train, but you never asked me," Maggie said.

"I thought it was your job."

"I have two children." Maggie turned the doorknob and it squeaked. "Two boys. They're with my mother right now, getting ready for Santa, trimming the tree, wrapping presents they've made for me."

Tears burned the back of Rachel's eyes.

"I have to take this trip. It's the best pay I get all year, and the bad decisions I've made—with their father—mean my boys need the extra money. I'll drive back to California all night and arrive with the morning, but my boys will have to wait to open their presents until I get there. They're always awake first."

"Is it that much money?"

The other woman nodded, staring at the floor. "It's my penance, and maybe I'm put on this train to remind women like you to keep your family safe. And together."

She was gone before Rachel could move to hug her or offer the slightest comfort.

"RACHEL WON'T CARE IF WE DON'T have flowers, baby."

"We're opposed to," his daughter said, *opposed* meaning *supposed* in Addie-speak.

"But there are no flowers in the dining car and

none in the bar." Where they'd looked at him as if he were a serial killer for bringing in his child.

"Let's ask Miss Maggie." In the narrow aisle between seats, Addie yanked on his arm, and, at the same time, rammed a guy's elbow into the sleeping young woman at his side.

"Sorry," Andrew said, as the man looked up, affronted. Then he saw the small bouquet at the woman's hip. "Can I buy those?"

"Dad," Addie said as if he'd struck the mother lode of good ideas.

"Do you know what time it is?" the man asked. The woman covered her flowers, protecting them.

Andrew glanced at his watch as he dug out his wallet with his other hand. "Six fifty-three. Can I buy your—" They must be newlyweds. Shiny rings, shinier faces. And she was acting as if those flowers had been hewn from gold. "Bouquet?"

"No," the girl said.

Andrew had already fished a fifty from his wallet. The new husband eyed it with reluctant avarice. "That's a lot of money for some used posies."

"Brad." The wife moved the flowers to her other side, protecting them from her groom as well as Andrew.

"They're for my new sister's mommy," Addie said.

"Your sister's—" The bride stared at Andrew.

"My—" He wanted with all his heart to say *wife*. His stomach lurched, but he steeled himself and resorted to another tack. "My daughter believes we shouldn't show up empty-handed." He agreed, but he wanted to give Rachel a marriage license and a ring of her own. "I have another twenty-five in my wallet."

"No." The girl held out her flowers, reluctance in her extended wrist and her young eyes. Hadn't these kids possessed parents? They both looked too young for SATs, much less a wedding march. "You take these. Your wife must be the one who had the baby tonight."

Addie's accusatory stance made him want to confess all his sins. He held back and plucked a pink rose from the bouquet, which he handed back to the girl.

"Thank you," he said. "We had the baby." He turned Addie toward Rachel's compartment at last. "Let's hurry, little girl."

"You didn't tell her the truth. She thinks you and Rachel are married."

"Don't fight me now, Addie." She resisted moving so he scooped her into his arms. "Hold your feet in so you don't kick anyone in the head."

"Why don't you and Rachel get married?"

"You know I asked Rachel."

"You must have done something she didn't like. I want Rachel to be my mommy."

"I know." He meant to die trying, but he couldn't let Addie think they stood a chance. If Rachel hadn't given in, faced with a lifetime of single parenting, she might never find the will to trust him with her future.

He found Rachel's door, drumming on it harder than he'd intended. Some sound came from inside. Hardly a welcome.

"Let me down, Daddy."

With his pulse beating in his throat, he set Addie on the floor and restored her hard-won booty. The bunch of flowers looked bigger in her hand.

"Did she tell us to come in?" Addie asked.

"What else would she say?" That was his story, and he'd stick to it. Whatever she'd said hadn't sounded enthusiastic.

He opened the door. Addie rushed in, all but heaving the flowers at Rachel's head. "Lemme see, Rachel, lemme see!"

Rachel scooted backward so Addie could pile onto the bed beside her. Andrew tried to draw Addie back to keep her from hurting Rachel.

But the baby. She was even more gorgeous.

"She's Addie all over again." His own voice, cut by love and dread for all he might lose, hardly seemed to belong to him.

"Flowers?" Rachel held the baby for Addie to ooh over.

"Addie made me arm wrestle some guy for them." He wanted to grab them all in his arms and shut out the past and the future that loomed like an open wound of need without Rachel and his new baby in it.

"I thought you were staying away." Tears in her voice drew him at last from staring at the soft-faced infant she was cradling.

"I won't be able to, Rachel." He touched their baby's hand, only to have his index finger taken in a grip she'd need to fend off Addie's ready affection.

"Can I hold her?" His little girl was already reaching.

"Sit beside me, and you can help." Rachel, all soft and tired and young-looking in a clean pink nightshirt, eyed him over the children's heads. Then she had to pay attention to Addie. "Careful now. We can't hug too hard or we'll hurt her."

"I can't stay away from either of you. You're my family," Andrew said. "All of you."

CHAPTER EIGHT

IF ONLY HE'D SAID *WIFE* or *lover* or even *girlfriend,* for pity's sake. Family implied she was only the mother of his child—not an inconsequential position in any man's life, but not the only spot Rachel wanted to hold.

She wanted him to be blindly in love with her—as she'd been with him.

Alone with the girls while Andrew scouted for breakfast for her and Addie, Rachel looked from one sleeping child to the other. She couldn't love either of them more. Addie was as much hers as the new baby—as Grace. She'd always thought of the baby as Grace, despite it being Andrew's mother's name.

Maybe she'd wanted something of him in her life for always. He'd never abandon Grace.

The compartment door opened, and Andrew brought bagels and chocolate milk, the weakness she and Addie had often shared. Rachel had to smile so she averted her face.

"You'd better wake her." Addie was nestled in the arm she wasn't using to hold the baby. "I'm afraid I'll drop Grace."

Silence met her use of the baby's name. She'd

avoided saying it since he'd first come back to the compartment. She'd give anything to take it back now.

"Grace?"

"I hear something in your voice." Still, she refused to look at him. "I like the name. That's all it means. Don't take it too seriously."

"You named the baby after my mother."

"If you don't like it—"

"Cut it out, Rachel. You know I'm glad."

"You sound angry."

"Because you're pretending we don't matter to each other. We don't have any more time to pretend. We have two girls who love us—who need a mother and father, and that's what you and I are to both of them."

She pressed her face to Addie's silky hair.

"It's not enough, Andrew. We aren't like those other families out there. I have to be an example to the girls, and an intelligent woman who values herself doesn't marry a man who only feels responsible toward her."

AN AMBULANCE MET THEM at the train depot and rocketed up the snow-laden hills to the hospital. By the time they'd had a few tests and been given a clean bill of health, Rachel's mother burst into the exam room from which Andrew and Addie had been evicted.

"Baby," Elizabeth Ford said, clearly mistaking Rachel for Grace. She wrapped her own daughter in her arms and then abruptly released her to scoop Grace out of her hospital-supplied bassinet. "She's perfect, Rachel. Absolutely, positively perfect. Good lord, how much she looks like Addie."

"Did you see her on your way in?"

"Sleeping with her daddy on those hard chairs out there." She looked up. "This sweet little morsel's daddy, too."

"Mom, don't start."

"You started this, you and that young man. You don't have sense to do the right thing. When I was a girl, we had a saying. You play, you pay."

"That was never a compassionate attitude, Mom."

"I agree, but maybe you should pay attention to its essential meaning."

"You're worried for me." Rachel slid off the examining table and began to dress. "You don't want me to be a single parent, and you're even a little afraid I might not be able to take care of my daughter on my own, because it was hard for you to care for me after Daddy died."

"Oh, a mind reader."

"But I've known from the start that I would be her only parent. I'm ready."

"You're full of—"

"Be careful. What if the baby retains a subliminal memory of the first words she hears you speak?"

Elizabeth laughed. "I'm a nice woman with delicate sensibilities, but I know you're fooling yourself. And so is Andrew. You loved each other. You didn't even leave him because you thought he didn't love you."

"That's exactly why I left. If he'd loved me, he'd have wanted children as much as I did."

With one hand, she helped Rachel back into her

pink shirtsleeve. "He looks as exhausted as you. I guess neither of you slept?"

"We dozed after breakfast. Mom, he has to pick up presents for Addie. He left everything except her clothes in San Diego."

"We'll look after her while he shops."

"Thanks. I wanted to volunteer, but I couldn't without asking you because you'd have to help." Her mother's flash of triumph made her frown. "On my first day as a mother, hours after I've given birth."

"We'd better get out of here before the stores close." Elizabeth fished a thick blanket out of her suitcase-sized purse. "I brought this in case you needed it. What are we calling this dumpling?"

"Grace."

"Grace. Lovely. That's—"

"Andrew's mother's name, but it goes with Elizabeth…."

"You can name the next one after me. If Andrew's mother gets a baby, I should, too."

Rachel swathed Grace in the pale green blanket. "I didn't realize you knew so much about Andrew."

"I believed he was going to be my son-in-law. Grace and I have e-mailed a time or two."

No doubt to express mutual disapproval over their wayward children. Rachel had a bit more empathy for their feelings as she looked at Grace and imagined her own child in a similar pickle twenty-eight years from now.

She signed out and they started for the waiting room. Andrew rose, his smile broad for Elizabeth.

"This is your fault, too," she said, close to his ear.

"What's your fault, Daddy? Is Rachel's mommy mad at you?"

"I'm mad at Daddy and Rachel," Elizabeth said, kneeling beside Addie, "but not at you and your brand new sister. Will you come home with Rachel and Grace and me while your father goes out for a while?"

"I don't—know." She pushed a hand into her hair and glanced sideways at her father.

"We have to make cookies for Santa, and we need help trimming the tree," Rachel said. "And you can help me look after Grace."

"I need to pick up some things for your baby sister." Andrew helped Addie into her sweatshirt.

"I should help you. I know more what she needs 'cause we're almost the same age now."

Andrew smiled. "I think Rachel needs you more. She doesn't feel too well, and Santa likes a lot of cookies. She might need you to bring her Grace's diapers. And Elizabeth can't do the whole tree on her own. Who'll hand her the ornaments and help her string the lights?"

"I am good at all that." Addie reluctantly took Elizabeth's hand. "Oka-a-y. If you need me, I'd better stay with you and Rachel and Grace."

"We do need you." Elizabeth tucked Addie's hand against her side. "Do you think we should bake chocolate chip or peanut butter or oatmeal?"

"Choplate chip."

"How lucky am I? Santa likes my favorite kind." Elizabeth led Addie toward the doors.

"Let me take Grace," Andrew said to Rachel. "You look tired."

"According to my mother, you do, too." Nevertheless, she let him take the baby. She both hated and loved the sight of her daughter in Andrew's arms. Temptation whispered she could see them like this, like a family, any time.

It was a temporary dream, like Christmas itself.

THEY DISTRACTED ADDIE with the tree and cookies until Andrew came back with diapers and infant clothing and a red velvet coat Addie insisted on putting on the moment he pulled it out of the shopping bag.

"What about Gracie?" she demanded, fastening her wide black buttons.

"I got one for her, too." Andrew took out another red velvet garment, a snowsuit that looked small enough to fit Addie's doll.

"Is she that tiny?" Rachel asked.

"Yes, but she'll grow fast."

All but bounding from the discomfort of Rachel's guilty, wary silence, Elizabeth claimed she had the rest of the house to decorate. Soon after, Andrew went out to get more wood for the fireplace.

By the light of the Christmas tree and the flickering fire, Rachel nursed Grace and tried to imprint the sight of Addie, one elbow on her bent knee, one knee on the rug in front of the tree, peering into the stacks of presents.

"Are there any for me?" she asked.

"My mom says yes, and I have something for

you." A silver tea set her mother had given her when she was Addie's age. She'd planned to give it to Addie anyway, and now she had the chance.

"Oh, don't tell me when it's under the tree. Last year, I went downstairs while you and Daddy were asleep and I peeled back the wrapping paper on some of the presents."

"Addie."

"Shhh." The little girl put one finger to her lips. "He'll be back any second. Don't tell him. I couldn't help it, but I'm growed up now."

Longing like hunger filled Rachel. She could see this moment replayed year after year, Christmas after Christmas. One day Addie would persuade Grace that Santa was coming, though she'd ceased to believe, herself.

Andrew came back, bringing cold and pine scent and another armload of firewood. Something in her eyes made him look at her twice.

"What?" he asked.

She couldn't find words without confessing her deepest want. He and Addie would make her whole.

Faint jingling bells wafted from the kitchen. Bolting upright as if she were on a spring, Addie swung to face them.

"Santa." Awe dropped her voice and glowed in her eyes.

Rachel envied her. If only a grown woman could believe so simply in what she wanted.

"Sleigh bells," Addie said. "I hear sleigh bells. It *must* be Santa."

"Addie, honey, come help me hang these?"

Rachel almost cried as her mother flourished the sleigh bells from the hall, bursting Addie's bubble. The little girl's face crumpled, but suddenly, she grinned.

"I'll bet Santa will hear those, and he'll know where to stop." She grabbed her father's sleeve. "Daddy, will Santa bring something for Grace? You think he knows about her?"

"Santa knows everything," Andrew said.

"I hope so, but I'd better make something for her, just in case. Grandma Elizabeth, do you have some crayons and some blank paper?"

Yet another silence played background to the crackling fire as Elizabeth's mouth straightened in a thin line. She swallowed several times before she spoke. "If I don't, we'll just go buy some for you and Grace."

She held out her hand to Addie, but then waited as the little girl skipped into the kitchen. "She called me Grandma," she said. "Grandma, Rachel."

"I heard."

"But did you listen? Do you know what it can mean?"

She left, and Rachel stole a look at Andrew, who had turned from stacking the wood to stare at Grace. His tender expression nearly undid Rachel.

She pushed to her feet more aware of every ache. "I need to change her diaper." She barely got the words out and then stumbled from the room, careful only to shelter Grace.

The telephone rang before she could make the stairs. She answered it in the hall.

"Rachel? This is Donna Roberts."

Donna Roberts and her family ran a program called the Santa Express that provided gifts and meals for families who might have gone without otherwise. She was always looking for volunteers. "Mrs. Roberts, how are you?"

"Not as fine as you if what I hear is more than gossip. Did you really have a baby on the Santa Superchief?"

"I did, but we're both well."

"I'm so glad. You know your mother has been excited about the coming birth. Excellent Christmas present for her."

"For all of us," Rachel said, and that much was true. She might regret Andrew and their relationship, but she'd never regret the infant they'd made. "Do you want to speak to Mom?"

"If she's not busy."

"Mother." Rachel set down the phone, glad it had stopped her from running away. "Mrs. Roberts."

"Thanks, honey." The kitchen phone clattered as her mother apparently dropped it and then kicked it across the linoleum to Addie's delighted giggles. "You can hang up now. I've got it."

Rachel turned back to the living room. Andrew was still sitting on his haunches, staring at the flames.

"I'm not a coward," Rachel said.

"No." He brushed his hands down his thighs and she remembered similar moments, pushing him to the rug, chasing the stroke of his hands with hers, wanting him urgently because they'd been circumspect all day with Addie as an audience. "I have been," he said. "An idiot and a coward." He looked up. "But I'm not now. I want you and my daughters. I want our family and I will not give up."

"Rachel?" her mother called, and Andrew stood. "Andrew," her mother went on, "that was my friend, Donna. She runs a—"

"Can I go, Daddy?" Addie asked, unable to wait for Elizabeth's explanation.

"Go where?" Andrew asked.

"I'm trying to tell you. My friend runs a charity called the Santa Express. Her family delivers Christmas gifts and meals tonight and then breakfasts in the morning for folks who can't get out. I've been helping since Rachel moved away. Apparently, she and her family have to be out of town tomorrow so she wanted to make sure I still planned to show up for my deliveries."

"And Grandma Elizabeth says I can go, too." Addie flung an arm around her father's waist. "Just like in *Little Women.*"

Little Women? Rachel turned to Andrew. He stared between her and her mother, his face flushed.

"I thought all little girls were supposed to read that."

"Daddy read it to me," Addie said. "I liked Jo best, but Beth made me and Daddy cry."

Rachel couldn't look away from him. Her mother, on the other hand, grabbed Addie and left the room.

"It made you cry, too?" Rachel asked.

"Beth had a hard life." He turned toward the kitchen. "If Addie's helping your mother in the morning, I'd better get her into bed. Don't make fun of me for trying to do the right thing."

"I can't picture you doing the voices, but I'd like to hear it. Do you need some help wrapping her gifts?"

"I had them do it at the stores." He headed for the kitchen.

Dumbfounded, she stared at sleeping Grace, peaceful and trusting in her arms. How could a man who'd been afraid of having more children cry over Beth March and talk about it?

"Andrew?"

He came back, but he didn't look as if he wanted to see her.

"I don't actually believe in stereotypes, but crying with your little girl is pretty brave."

"You never believed me, did you?"

"I thought it was one of the lamest excuses any guy ever invented."

"Nope. It was the truth. Then."

CHAPTER NINE

THE REST OF THE HOUSE was silent when Grace's newborn cries dragged Rachel out of sleep. Grimacing as she slid out of bed, she scooped the baby from the bassinet her mother had cleaned and set up in her room.

Gripping the banister with one hand, she eased down the stairs, anxious to keep the baby from waking anyone else. Her mother had never left the Christmas tree lights on when Rachel had been a child, but she'd left them on tonight for Addie.

Rachel settled into the armchair that had seen her through homework and phone marathons and daydreams of spending Christmases here with her parents and her own husband and children. Grace nursed hungrily while Rachel watched the tree's lights blinking.

"Can't sleep?"

"Mom, did we wake you?"

"I guess I'm as attuned to my baby as you are to yours."

Rachel grinned, but then licked her lips. "Will you get me a glass of water? I'm so thirsty."

Her mother went into the kitchen and returned with a glass of water she set at Rachel's elbow. "It's nursing. You need more fluids."

She nodded, sipping. "Will I do this one day? Bring water to my little girl as she's feeding her own infant?"

"If you're lucky."

Rachel hugged Grace closer. She already missed having the baby move inside her, but this was so much better, overwhelming, unconditional love that just was. Not like with Andrew, which was all tests and doubt. Shouldn't love between a man and a woman be this easy, too?

"Mom, I don't know how to believe in Andrew."

"You just do it."

"This is no Christmas movie where I see that he's a good dad to both his daughters, so I can jump in and hope he'll be a good husband, too. I want my girls—and in my heart, that means Addie, too—to believe they deserve a man who'll love them, not because it's right, but because he can't help himself."

"I'm not taking up for Andrew. I blame you both. You overcomplicated your lives, but what if he feels everything you need him to? He's come this far."

Rachel cradled the back of Grace's head. "I left him six months ago. He stopped calling. He never came. He can help himself."

"You ask too much. You say it's no Christmas movie, but you want the big romantic ending when what you really need is a beginning. Picture Andrew—"

"With someone else? I have."

"No, baby, alone. Imagine him alone. What if you are his one true love? A woman might excite him sexually one day. He might make friends at the playground with other mothers, but say he loves only you. Imagine him alone every Christmas Eve of his life. You love him. You want him to be happy. Do you want to be the reason for his loneliness?"

"The movies you watch are sad."

"You may be making one of those for Andrew and for your girls. Think about that."

ANDREW HESITATED AT THE TOP of the stairs. He could go down now and argue with both women and wake Gracie or he could let Rachel rest and offer her his love in the first light of Christmas morning.

Her mother was wrong. He wanted to tell her—make them both see they had a cockeyed view of the future.

But tomorrow would be better, when Addie and Elizabeth were delivering Christmas meals and he'd have Rachel and Gracie to himself. Her mother had applied as much pressure as he had. Rachel could use a break.

He went back to his room. In a little while Rachel and Elizabeth came upstairs. With whispered goodnights, they returned to their beds, too. He resisted a compulsion to see his new daughter safely into her bassinet. He'd never had to share Addie. That would take getting used to.

Night crept by, second by second. From the open door of the room next to his, Addie's soft snoring kept Andrew company until dark blue light crept into the snow-heavy sky.

He was just drifting off when his door swung open and Addie leaped onto his bed. "It's time." Her whisper probably raised the roof. "Santa came—we gotta wake up Gracie and Rachel!"

He persuaded her to let Rachel and the baby sleep, as they'd been up during the night. And on second thought, Addie decided it would be more like *Little Women* if she didn't open any of her presents until she and her "Grandma Elizabeth" delivered their breakfasts.

Elizabeth came to the door. Andrew signaled to her that he'd help Addie dress. Soon, the woman and the little girl left hand in hand.

As soon as Grace began to whimper, he hurried to the kitchen and poured a glass of orange juice, which he ran upstairs to Rachel's room.

"I'm up, Mom. Did Grace cry?"

"Not yet," Andrew said. He put the juice on her nightstand as she sat up, covering herself with her blankets.

Andrew went to the bassinet, loving Grace's absorbed stare.

"Morning, sweet one," he said. "Ready to eat?" He glanced at Rachel. "Not making a bottle seems strange."

"I'm already getting a little sore. The nurse at the hospital said I would, though." She stopped as if she wished she hadn't said that. "What are you doing in here?"

"We have to talk. You know we do."

"I thought you'd eventually say so." Her anxious eyes followed Grace's waving hand. "She must be hungry again."

He passed her their baby. "I heard you and your mother last night."

"What?"

"She was right about one thing."

Rachel must have forgotten she was feeling modest around him, because she lifted Grace to her breast with no shyness. "I know you'll learn to care about someone else."

"No." He handed her the juice. "You need more fluids."

Rachel laughed, her eyes wide. "I keep forgetting you're like this."

"Like what?" Pathetically, he wanted her to say something nice about him.

"Easy to be with. Funny."

"You always said laughing was foreplay."

She turned to Grace, blushing, and he enjoyed the slightest revenge for her amusement at his reading material.

"We might not have had you, little girl, if I didn't get your father's jokes." She stopped, but only for a second, and her gaze accused him. "You eavesdropped."

"And I wanted to argue."

"But you held back. You always hold back."

"Usually when I think I'm wrong, but this time, I knew I was right, and I wanted to talk to you alone."

He brushed her hair behind her ear. She shivered, and he forgot to breathe. His touch still affected her. "I don't want you to come to me because you're afraid I'll learn to love someone else or I'll be alone."

She looked up, but he knelt beside her. Grace complained and he realized he was leaning on Rachel's thigh.

"I loved you without learning how," he said. "I just love you. Because you took me on with Addie, because you called me first when you had good news, because you fought so hard to stay with me when I got scared." He rubbed his head. "I'm saying this badly. Remember all those bedtime stories? We'd both be yawning wide enough to break our jaws by the time Addie fell asleep, but then we fell into bed with each other, and we made love with urgency. We never stopped needing each other. That's not something you learn."

"But it doesn't promise a future either."

He shook his head. "I don't want you to choose me because you're afraid of losing me. I want you to come home because you love me. I need you to be my wife and want our girls—because Addie's as much yours as Grace is mine."

"I know we both want our family."

He rose and caught the nape of her neck. She opened her mouth to protest. He kissed her with need he'd suppressed for nearly a year. Only when the baby caught him a swift kick in the sternum did he lean back, rubbing his chest.

His voice was so thick he could barely speak. "She's protective."

"What are you doing?"

"Telling you the truth. I love you. I want you. I need you. And by the way, I love our daughters, too."

"How do I believe you, Andrew?"

Hope surged, almost as strong as Gracie's left foot. "You just do, the way Addie believes in Santa, despite Joey's best efforts to persuade her he's fake."

"That's it, Andrew. You persuaded me you were fake, but I started thinking you might not be when I was in labor."

He kissed her again. "I'm not fake, now. I'm cured." He rubbed his chest again, drinking Grace in as if he had to make memories of her. "You just wait until that first doctor's appointment. You're going to be scared, too. They poke at them and..."

"Don't tell me." She pulled him close, kissing his chin, brushing his cheek with her eyelashes. "Maybe it *would* be easier with you along."

"You take any excuse that eases your pride over the hump. I know you love me."

"You do?" Her eyes asked him how.

"I trust you."

"Daddy?" Addie called from downstairs.

"Did you hear that front door open?" he asked, wishing they'd had a few more minutes to themselves.

Addie took the stairs as fast as she could, but she skidded to a halt in Rachel's open door. "You're coming home with us," she said.

Rachel laughed, and she put her arm around Andrew's shoulder. Feeling pride in her possession, he brought her hand to his lips. Again, she shivered.

"I believe in choosing what we both want, rather than choosing you because I'm afraid of being alone. I can do it for you all." Rachel looked at him, her eyes honest and open and hopeful. "I believe I can."

"I believe, too, in you and me." He held out his other hand for Addie. "Come see Grace."

She climbed onto his bent knees, her little feet hardly pressing into his thighs. "Doesn't that hurt, Rachel?"

"No. You'll do it one day when you have a baby."

"Yuck." Addie curled her lip and jumped down. "I have to go tell Grandma."

"Tell her what?" Rachel asked.

"That we're going to be together all the Christmases from now on."

She bounded from the room.

Andrew resisted a moment's fear and searched the face of the woman he'd loved and almost lost. "Are you sure you're okay with that?"

Rachel quirked her index finger beneath his chin. "Kiss me again and we'll start the future." She pressed her forehead against his. "But hurry. Those two downstairs are soul mates. One of them will drag the other back any second."

* * * * *